TRYING LIBERTY

Trying Liberty

The Quiet Revolution on Long Island

NOVEL BY
A. CHARITY HIGGINS JOHNSON

Trying Liberty: The Quiet Revolution on Long Island is a work of fiction. Names, characters, places and incidents are the products of the author's imagination or are used fictitiously. Any resemblance to actual events, locales, or persons, living or dead, is entirely coincidental.

Copyright © 2025 by A. Charity Higgins Johnson
All rights reserved. No part of this book may be used or reproduced in any form, electronic or mechanical, including photocopying, recording, or scanning into any information storage and retrieval system, without written permission from the author except in the case of brief quotation embodied in critical articles and reviews.

BOOK DESIGN | The Troy Book Makers

BACK COVER IMAGE | Original photo, Quaker home interior

FAMILY TREE | Designed by A. Charity Higgins Johnson

INTERIOR MAP | Simplified version of "New York, Queens, Kings, Richmond counties." Burr, David, 1829 New York, Atlas map, New York. From: Dave Rumsey Historical Map collection https://www.davidrumsey.com/luna/servlet/s/941w90

MANUMISSION DOCUMENT | Manumission of Rachel by Phebe Dodge, from Archives, Friends Historical Library, Swarthmore College, Swarthmore, PA. Photo by A. Charity Higgins Johnson

Printed in the United States of America

The Troy Book Makers • Troy, New York • thetroybookmakers.com

To order additional copies of this title, contact your favorite local bookstore or visit www.shoptbmbooks.com

Library of Congress Control Number: 2024924020
ISBN: 978-1-61468-941-6

For my husband and family.
And for my mother, Ann Higgins,
a true Friend, and who helped me
understand Quaker ways.

TABLE OF CONTENTS

Preface ix

Family Trees xi

Map xii

Rachel's manumission xiv

PART 1 | DISTURBING THE PEACE 3

PART 2 | RUPTURE 113

PART 3 | UNKNOWN TERRITORY 257

Epilogue 309

Appendix –Historical facts 310

Bibliography 312

PREFACE

Papers inspired this story. Specifically, slave manumission papers of the 1770s, some signed by my ancestors. These Long Island Quakers had kept the documents safe for freed slaves.

All manuscripts have the names of the free slaves, their 'owners' and two witnesses. Working through extensive family trees and spreadsheets, I got the impression that it was a handful of Quakers (or Friends) who spearheaded the movement. Whoever it was, the leaders had secured slave manumissions at the start of the Revolutionary War, before the nation was formed.

But one manumission was distinctive, that of Rachel, freed by Phebe (Willets Mott) Dodge. In Rachel's manumission, Phebe Dodge specified the moral problem of holding a slave. For several reasons, I believe she, her children and the Willis family were likely the leaders at the time. (A well-known leader, Elias Hicks, saw his ministry bloom well after this time).

In 1771 about 17% of the population of Long Island were blacks from Africa, nearly all were slaves. The story starts in 1775, right after the Quakers of New York made the decision to free their slaves. To free a slave and to treat them as equals was a continuation of the Quaker way of life, often snubbing accepted practices and laws of their contemporaries.

1776 was the beginning of Long Island's extended entanglement with the British. The army waged war on Brooklyn (part of Long Island). And then it installed the army on the island. The conditions for a newly freed slave went from difficult to gloomy.

Despite the war and the deprivations under the British, preserved records show that between 1775-1798 there were 173 slave manumissions. More impressive is that the bulk of the manumissions, nearly 55% of them, occurred between 1776-1777. By 1783 virtually all Long Island Quakers had freed their slaves.

Still, once manumitted, the freed slave had the difficult job of adjusting to a new state. He or she would have to adjust to a radically different lifestyle, one with heavy demands, obstacles, and struggles. I cannot underscore enough the complexity of the problem they faced by not having a footing in the Colony. The society they were supposed to enter offered them only a void, not a place: they could not own a business nor own property.

The appendix has a brief list of documented facts. The bibliography is extensive. What is in this book that cannot be verified is a work of fiction, based on speculation or imagination.

TRYING LIBERTY

Phebe Willets (1699-1782), her spouses & children

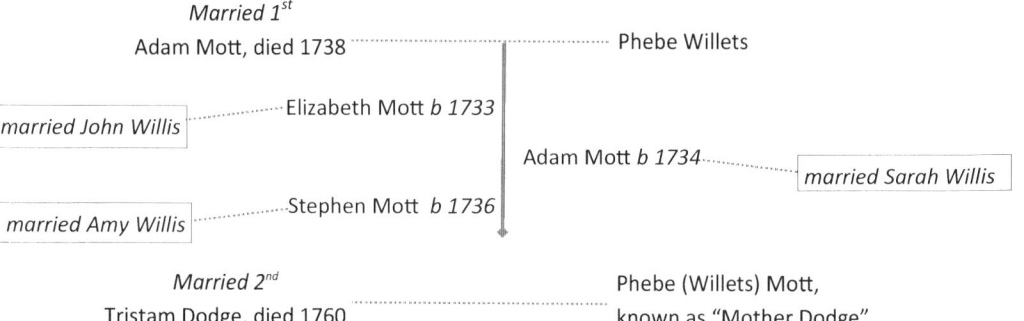

Mother Dodge's kin by marriage: Samuel & Mary Willis & their children

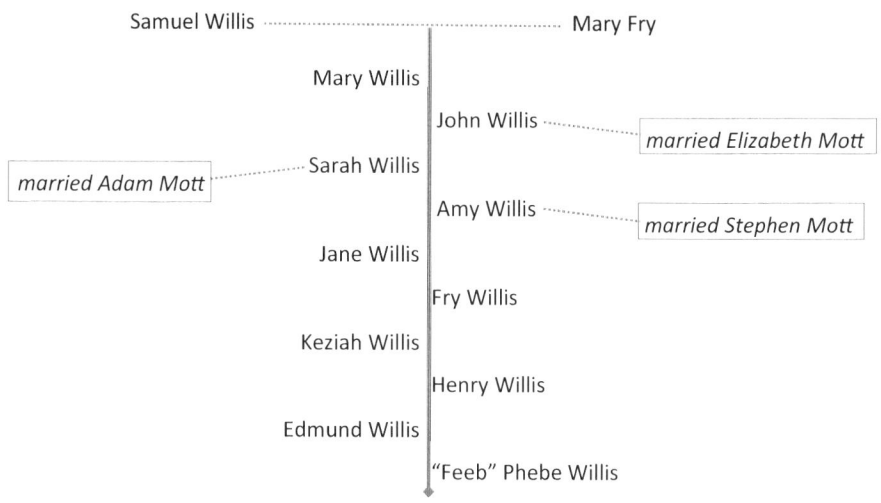

Rachel of Cow Neck & her (fictional) family

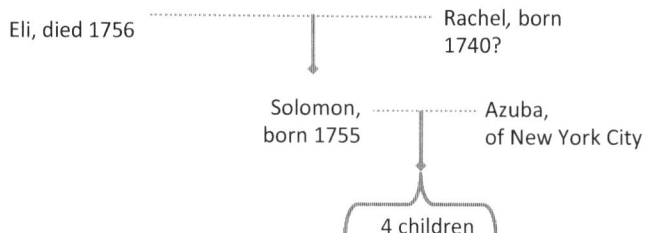

xi

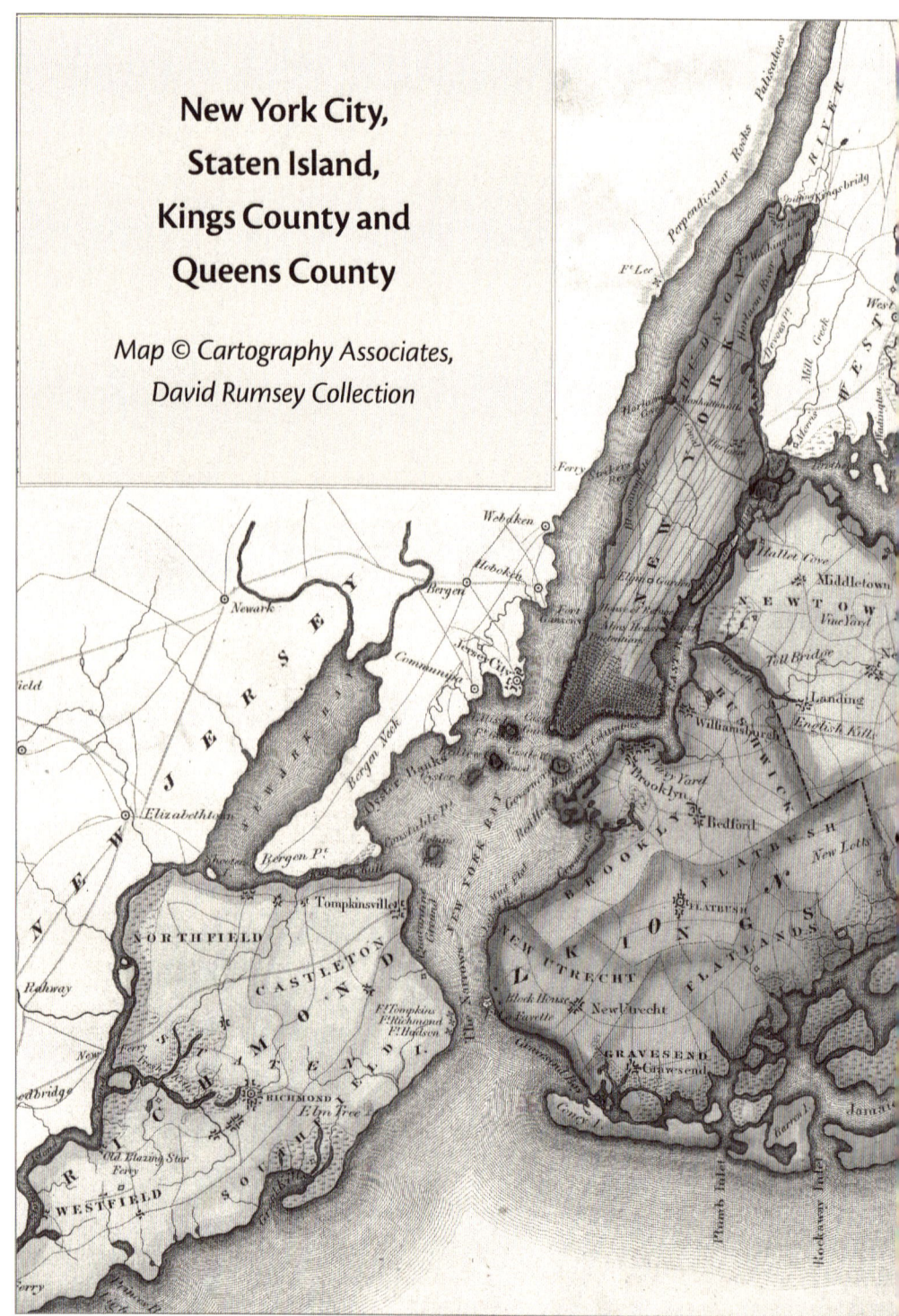

New York City, Staten Island, Kings County and Queens County

Map © Cartography Associates, David Rumsey Collection

Rachel's Manumission Record
(Friends Historical Library, Swarthmore, PA. Photo, author.)

INTRODUCTION

"43 YEARS AGO I WAS FREED. It's been almost as many years since the war. Nowadays when I hear folks talk, I believe they forgot how things were then. The folks who say the colonies took the British easy are fools, it ain't true. Folks then were mostly afraid to take sides. The war stirred everything up. It was scary. And afterwards nothing was ever the same.

Two things were hard-won: my freedom and this new nation. We, freed slaves, did not walk out to freedom. When I was small, I learned how to sew a sampler. Phebe's daughter and me both used a model, that's how we learned. But as a freed woman I made a new life without a pattern, and without an example. I was walking blind, and it was hard.

I know today not everyone is free, and not everyone is equal. The struggle for a righteous society goes on. We always live on the brink of independence; it is a sharp edge, sometimes it is raw. Independence is not set and certain. But I would never go backwards."

Her withered hand held the page open as she considered. She turned the pages back to the front page. She added: *Rachel, business owner. Philadelphia, 1819. Former slave; manumitted, March 15, 1776.* Shutting the diary she placed it inside the hinged box, a gift, which had served as a portable desk for her for more than 40 years. It was her final diary entry.

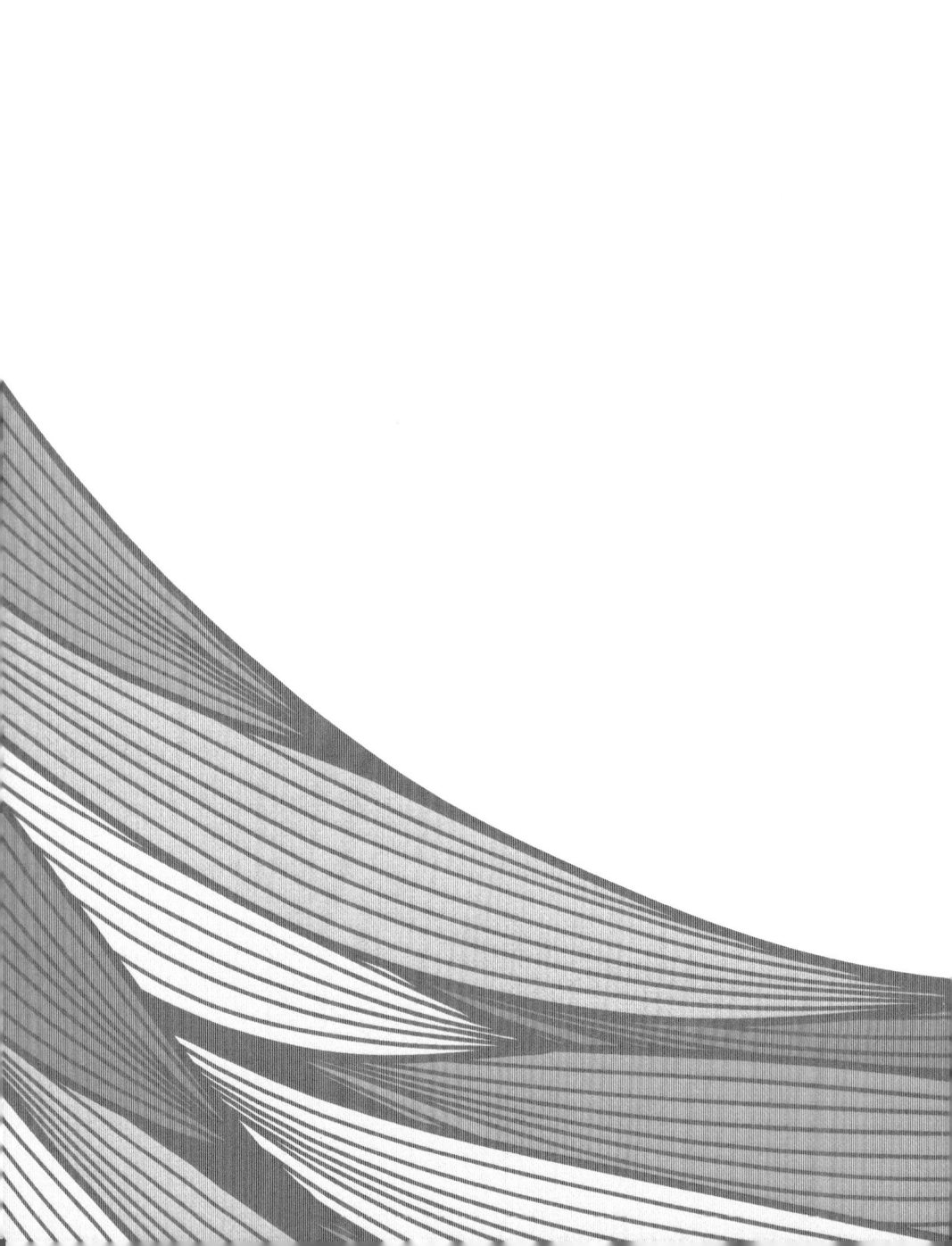

Part One
DISTURBING THE PEACE

CHAPTER 1

Westbury, Long Island, New York Colony, March 1775

Squirt was waiting with friends Amos and Big Jack in the wet, oozing partially frozen mud in the road not far from the Quaker Meeting House. The longer he stood, the colder he felt, as the thawed ice permeated his cracked boots. He was certain their long wait outside would be worthwhile: it always had been.

The trio was waiting on the path outside of one of many tiny Meeting Houses on Long Island where Quakers held Sunday services (if you could call them services). The Quaker faith had no priest nor minister, they did have elders, a clerk, and a few preachers. In winter Quakers gathered to worship in their homes, then with the onset of warmer weather, they gathered in large groups in a reopened Meeting House.

All winter long the trio would speculate on when the Meeting House would reopen. It was a game: they would choose a date, but change it on a whim, or a sign, or a dream one of them had. It made no difference: it was a fixture for the trio, a reliable topic for speculation and betting. The trio had been together a long time—though they had not known each other in childhood. Years ago—he could not remember how many years—the three of them roved on their own. They knew one another, and from time to time helped each other. Over time they called on one another for aid more often. Then a few years ago, they had formed a small band. They were not related by blood, bond nor land. What bound them to one another was something indefinable and loose, but it was there. They had dubbed themselves The Wanderers.

They had roamed the width and breadth of Long Island, and as far as the City of New York, some thirty miles away. But eventually (and fortuitously) at about the same time they had each become tired of roaming. Their decision on what location would be the site of their abode turned out to be easy as each of them had the same place in mind. They liked Cow Neck, a "neck" of Long Island that jutted north into Long Island Sound. Cow Neck, in addition to its natural beauty, had a fair number of Quaker farms. They believed they could find no better neighbors than these Quakers.

The cold thawing mud crept up further, nearly covering the tops of Squirt's boots. Squirt was not bothered by much of anything (at least that is what he told people). But this morning, after his first steps on the early spring road, upon feeling the icy fingers of water curl around his toes, he finally admitted to himself that he needed newer boots. Since then, he had been half occupied by the thought of replacement boots. Leaky boots would not keep him from showing up on Sunday morning to greet the Quakers as they began dispersing from worship meeting.

In the British Colonies, Quakers were considered odd. They were a docile group of worshippers and never violent. Quakers would not swear allegiance to anyone, including a monarch or ruler. Now that the tie between the colonies and England was near its breaking point, he heard people grumbling about the Quaker refusal to swear allegiance to the Crown.

Squirt had a soft spot for the Quakers and felt they were unfairly judged. The Quakers had shown them only kindness and generosity. The Wanderers had all agreed that though Quakers were ridiculed, they were probably New York's best-kept secret. That the Quakers were mocked unfairly gave the trio a sense of bondedness with them: they too had long felt the sting of being outsiders.

Although the trio was excluded from proper society, the Quakers never treated them so, but rather, the opposite. Yes, if no one else viewed them as equals, the Quakers did. This was the reason the trio had formed this regular Sunday habit: they stationed themselves outside the Quaker Meeting House. Though they never spoke about it (except in the most general way, "We gotta laydown early, tomorrow's Sunday!"), they had an unspoken understanding that they would be there to greet the dispersing Quakers.

After each meeting, a number of Long Island's finest humans would pass them, and rather than being shunned, the trio would be hailed and greeted with the same respect given to any man or woman in Quaker society. These brief conversations on Sunday had an uplifting effect on them. The kindness and consideration passed between the trio and the Quakers had a grounding effect on the trio.

These Sunday greetings gave Squirt a sense of meaning, and he felt he was as important as these men and women. They paid no attention to his looks, or how he was dressed or what he smelt like. Their backgrounds and their stations were of no importance. No. Each quiet Sunday, they were treated as property-owning men. And this made each of them stand a bit straighter, feel a bit better, and treat each other more kindly. They lived in the glow of Quaker friendship all week long.

Naturally, when the meeting houses were closed each winter, it was their least favorite day of the year. Which made this day, when the Meeting House was reopened, a special day for the trio. Just seeing familiar faces again would make the week ahead better.

Being here today was especially dear to Squirt. When the Wanderers were together, typically one of the other two men—and not Squirt—was usually noticed and spoken to, or bullied, depending on who they encountered. The other two men attracted attention: Amos had red hair like fire, and Big Jack was a hulk of a man, reminding Squirt of an ox. Additionally, Amos was dull in about every way, while clever Big Jack had a hot temper that would explode without warning. Squirt was often overlooked; he was accurately perceived as normal. His physical deformity was his eyes, which had always been bad. He had lost his parents as a child and lost his way when his last family member died when he was just 13.

For some reason, the Quakers had singled him out as the spokesman of the trio. He wondered if it was because he had learned manners as a youth before he was orphaned. Whatever the reason, Squirt was the one who was usually entrusted with gifts given to the trio. If Quakers had anything to spare, food from their farm, or clothing, such as a spare jacket, they might press it into Squirt's hands, as if he were the leader of the gang.

A gang they were not. They were but three rovers, not wishing to be tied down to a piece of land, or a woman. Their mutual acceptance of one another gave them the luxury to come and go as they wished, free and untethered. If there was a leader, the other two bestowed that position on Big Jack. He was shrewd, gregarious, and easily recognizable by his size.

A young Quaker boy came running towards them, a bundle in his hands.

"Morning Squirt, Amos, Jack," Daniel Mott greeted them, "From Grandmother Dodge."

The bundle was so large, the boy's arms could barely reach about it. Amos' eyes widened at its size. Squirt gave a little shake of his head, catching the boy's eye, he subtly indicated that today Big Jack, and not himself, should accept the bundle.

The boy was quick to take his meaning, and he turned to press it into Big Jack's arms, "Grandma Dodge said take it. The winter was a long one."

The boy turned and was off to his playmates. The men fell on the bundle: inside they found two large loaves of bread, jam, and some other food stuff—possibly dried meat—and even butter. Sheer joy.

Squirt smiled, "We're fixed!" They got tired of the winter's fare of a few fish, maybe a squirrel or rabbit, some root vegetables, and stolen goods.

Big Jack was peering into the bundle, "There's more inside." He wrapped it up carefully. "We'll look at the rest later."

Amos spat and cleared his throat, rubbing his hands together. "I can't hardly wait!"

Big Jack put the bundle under his left arm and the three men straightened their coats, it was time to greet the Quakers by name. As the small gathering of Quakers left the building for home, the three men reveled in the calling out of their names, the friendly smiles, and handshakes. Squirt watched the people exit the small Meeting House, looking for Grandmother Dodge, but did not see her. When he saw her son and daughter-in-law, he made his way to them to speak to them.

Stephen Mott reassured him that his mother was healthy but had decided to remain home one more week. Squirt could believe the hard cold benches of the rough-hewn Meeting House would be unwelcome to an elderly woman. This Meeting was a summer meeting house. Squirt asked Stephen to pass on their appreciation to his mother.

The Mott and the Willis families were good folk, but Phebe Dodge was an exceptional person. She always kept an eye on them. If winter was hard, they felt it. Somehow, she sensed their need and made sure a blanket came their way. She was not above them, she thought of them as flesh and bone. Squirt warmed at that thought.

Squirt's spirit felt happy by the rare warmth of a friend who thought of them even when she did not see them. Perhaps it was more than happiness he felt—maybe it was love, a good kind of love? Though he could not thank Grandmother Dodge today, she would surely know the gratefulness he felt.

CHAPTER 2

The New York Yearly Meeting banned members from owning slaves in 1774

. . . .

Home of Phebe Dodge, Cow Neck, New York, Late March 1775

SEVERAL HOURS AFTER THE QUAKER MEETING, Elizabeth Willis entered her mother Phebe Dodge's house on Cow Neck. She normally spent First Day, the Quaker's name for Sunday, helping her mother. She helped her mother instead of Rachel who had the day off. Helping her mother gave them a chance to visit.

Elizabeth was middle-aged and resembled her late father, Adam. It took but one look at her daughter's face for Mother Dodge to know something was bothering her.

The women fell to work on the chores and their conversation was trivial, it was a typical Sunday in every way. Her mother waited for her daughter to talk about what was on her mind. Eventually she grew tired of waiting and asked, "Liz, dear, thee has something heavy on thy mind."

"Yes, mother, I do. My husband, I—" Elizabeth paused, took a deep breath. She sat down on the nearest bench. "It's not about me and he. I-I-I need to speak to another Friend. I don't know who I can trust to talk to about this. I want to talk to thee, only not as thy daughter but as a Friend."

Outsiders called them "Quakers" but those in the "Society of Friends" were, to one another, simply, "Friends."

"Speak thy mind fully," her mother urged.

"Does thee recall my friend Rebecca Smith who married out of Meeting?" Marrying someone who was not a Friend meant you were disowned from the Society of Friends.

Phebe pondered, "Rebecca Smith. Was she the pretty girl with the darkest black hair I ever saw—she met her husband in Philadelphia?"

"Aye. She is extremely troubled. Which leads me to fear, we are also going to be troubled soon." Elizabeth pulled a thick letter from her pocket.

"She sent this last week. I was very much in mind not to say anything but—" She stopped. Then she whispered, "What she writes makes me afraid!

"Let me read part of her letter, so thee can understand." Elizabeth began reading the letter aloud. "She wrote, 'We in Philadelphia are suffering, not as they are in Boston…'" Elizabeth scanned down to another place, then continued reading. "'…my husband Robert was in Richmond with his cousin. There was being held a convention in the same city. His cousin was pressed to be the recording secretary, and he joined his cousin at the convention. Robert was struck by the speech-making, but especially by a man called Patrick Henry – he spoke forcefully and powerfully.'"

Elizabeth skimmed ahead, silently. "She's upset because Robert joined the American cause. He explained he could not get Henry's words out of his mind, and after hearing Henry's speech, he is convinced of the American cause."

Elizabeth continued reading the letter. "'Thee might understand my sentiments if I read a portion of Henry's powerful speech. Henry exhorts all Americans to fight for liberty.'" With her mother's consent, she read most of Henry's impassioned speech.

When she finished reading, she put the letter aside, "Mother, I'm worried that this Rebellion will be at a great cost to the Friends. It is hard to be Friendlike to both the British and the American rebels.

"I fear we will receive retribution from the English Parliament, that the Friends will be disciplined with the same severity as American rebels. England sees us as one whole, not as separate groups.

"And my deepest worry is that our way of worship, nay, our way of life will once again be forbidden. My blood runs cold at the thought. I've not been sleeping.

"To the Crown, the colonies are a trial. To enforce its control, will the Crown act? Will it make prohibitions which hinder, or even stop our way of life? As English subjects, we are in liege to and must pay homage to the Church of England. It's possible the King could again forbid us to worship as we do. We would face punishment when we do not conform."

Phebe saw her daughter's point. English power was not exerted solely by taxes and laws, but also through the Church of England. But, even for an old woman like her, it had been decades since she had felt the reach of the Church of England.

"I've been a free Friend all my life and shudder when I think of worshipping in the English way! If the King invokes this order, and we refuse to obey, will we be persecuted?" Elizabeth continued along those same lines until she was talked out.

"Liz, I know the unease of the times breeds fear, but I credit the King understands well that he needs the Friends in the Colonies! England is far away, and this matter is still a troublesome fancy." Her mother tried put to rest her fears.

The English Crown owed much to the Friends on Long Island. But the strength, the value of the Friends influence did not belong to the past. In cities throughout the colonies, the Friends were used in responsible positions and were useful to English governance. The Friends as a body were dependable, peace-loving, and amiable colonists. They had been proven and surely Parliament was aware of the strength and the stability that the Friends infused into towns and cities in America. Someone once said that their influence in America far exceeded their number.

Elizabeth was skeptical, "How can thee be certain the King will not make the Friends subject to the Church of England?"

"Years ago, Britain made an agreement with us: they would not demand we be called up to war as long as we paid Parliament a fee." Phebe knew she had evaded the question; she had nothing more to offer than a story from the past. Elizabeth countered that this was a new King, and a new Parliament and that times had changed.

Phebe changed tack, "Truly. Still, since the agreement, the throne has come to trust us."

Elizabeth was unconvinced, "I hope both Americans and British would agree we can remain neutral." The daughter would not disagree with her mother.

Although Elizabeth had aired her mind, Phebe sensed an unspoken edginess in her daughter. "Elizabeth, what is it that is truly bothering thee?"

Elizabeth's throat tightened; the bitterness of fear tasted like iron. To her the specter was real: the Friends were vulnerable and would be placed squarely between the fiercely warring factions.

"My head is filled with questions. I have sought calm but have not found it. Peace escapes me. Nothing is as it should be! I am continually burdened. I am tired and confused," Elizabeth cried to her mother plaintively.

Phebe pondered. Giving guidance was quite simple, but receiving it was difficult. She replied gently. "Thee is looking for peace all about thee—circumstances will never give peace. No. Thee must be instructed by the Divine One."

Her mother was right. As an adult Elizabeth knew that simple platitudes were unhelpful. The doubts and the questions that stalked her would not be swiftly gone. She was worrying about her worries and forgetting to give thanks for the day's gifts. She knew what she had to do.

She was glad she had said something. Her mother's presence lent a stability that she needed now that so much was coming loose. To have spoken openly about the conflict with another Friend was calming. Speaking her fears put light on them and now that her frame of mind was restored, she could think clearly.

Elizabeth, now well-soothed, went to work on her mending. Phebe mulled over the changes about them. Was it affecting the Friends and their practice? The Friends reviled conflict. But living in unity was not always possible, and when disagreements surfaced the Friends set about to seek unity. To get that, they had silent prayer asking for Divine help to give them shared clarity and direction, doing so was slow but satisfactory. Lately, however, Phebe noticed the atmosphere at Meeting had felt charged: differences were popping up regularly. Was it because of the tension they were all living with? Changing times were challenging times. Minor conflicts with British officers and soldiers were occurring more often. Everyone was struggling under the strains caused by the tension dividing Americans from the British authorities.

Phebe was distracted from her ruminations by a sound from the corner of her property, a rustling. Rachel, her slave, was returning from her day away. Her mind wandered to Rachel and her family, her friends and something else—what? Something niggled at her, and she could not bring it forward. She had been awakened by something in the letter from Elizabeth's friend. What was it? It was something concerning Rachel. She asked Elizabeth to re-read the sentence in her friend's letter where she quoted Henry.

Laying down her work, Elizabeth picked up out the letter, found the place and read, "Is life so dear, or peace so sweet, to be purchased at the price of chains and slavery—"

Phebe interrupted her reading, "Such powerful phrases! I wonder if some rebel Americans are more awake to injustice than we are."

Elizabeth shook her head, confused. The Friends would not take a side. Seeing her confusion, Phebe explained, "It's the word 'slavery.' It reminded me of the Resolution of last year. We have been forgetful: we ought to have liberated our slaves by now." She stood up, "Few of us have freed our slaves."

Phebe moved to the window to watch her slave Rachel making her way to her little house.

Elizabeth recognized the moral incongruity of Friends having slaves. Her own shame at being a slaveholder was rekindled. How was it that they had got caught up in it? After all, as Friends, they were familiar with the effects of injustice—though these effects were subtler for them. Friends were free, Friends could hold property, and more. Negro slaves had none of the advantages Friends enjoyed.

"Mother, I have gotten hardened, dull. Till now I even forgot about the Resolution!"

Phebe agreed, "Aye, slavery should be a red stain on fresh snow."

Owning a slave had been discouraged in the Society of Friends for many years. But it was not till last year that slavery was banned by the Quakers of New York. For as long as she could remember there had been slaves in the colonies, sometimes they had been Indian, some were white, but most of them were negro.

Every time a slave was purchased, slave traders profited from it, just as they might a bolt of fabric. They lined their pockets every time they sold a slave. It was legal and profitable to abuse and debase another human in the name of slavery. Phebe wished the law would make slavery illegal, putting an end to the commerce of men, women, and children.

But there was no excuse for her own tardiness. It was clearly against the nature of God to imprison another person like this. How had the Friends slipped into the rut of slaveholding? Most Friends she knew held at least one slave, including herself. Was it the easy acceptance of slavery all about them that formed their thinking?

"Thee has tried to free Rachel. Does she yet resist?"

"Aye. Rachel has refused her freedom. Mayhap she is afraid of it?" Phebe wondered aloud.

Manumitting Rachel should have been easy, but she would not agree to it. Nevertheless, every year Phebe offered to free her.

Elizabeth shrugged, "Yet, who are we to withhold freedom?" She noticed the sun was setting quickly. After gathering her belongings, she secured her bonnet over her cap and set out for home.

When Phebe's second husband Tristam had left Rachel to her in his will, she had promptly offered Rachel her liberty. But Rachel had turned her down and since then had been mulish if Phebe spoke about her liberation.

Then last year at the Annual Meeting of Friends in New York colony, they had come together in unity over slavery. They had committed their agreement in writing saying slavery was against their conscience. Any unanimous agreement which was put to paper and upheld by all the Meetings in the colony was called a "Resolution." Now all New York Friends were to set free their slaves.

After the Resolution, Phebe explained to Rachel that her liberty was *required*, but Rachel remained obstinate. Then again, a few months ago on New Years Day, Phebe begged Rachel to accept her liberty. But once more she was rebuffed; Rachel's stubbornness kept her a slave. This was cause for speculation: Was there something that the slaves knew about liberty that was unknown to her? Was there a difficulty she could not discern?

Even though Rachel had resisted her repeated requests, now that spring was here, Phebe was determined that Rachel would gain liberty.

They would have to do so carefully—once freed, no one should be allowed to claim her as a slave.

* * *

Home of Elizabeth and John Willis, Hempstead, NY, March 1775

Although Elizabeth was calmer after seeing her mother, as she neared her house, she could feel a headache coming on. There was nothing to do about the situation but to follow her mother's good advice. But she needed to be left alone.

As Elizabeth crossed her lot towards the house she met "Little Phebe," her 14-year-old daughter, coming out of the milk barn. Little Phebe informed her mother that both her brother and her father were gone on errands. The news pleased Elizabeth; she could take a bit of time alone now. Who knew when her next chance would come? These were troublesome times, she needed to becalm herself.

"I'm taking to my room. I must not be disturbed," she warned her daughter.

She turned toward her house, and Little Phebe, solicitous of her mother, latched the barn door. She would return to the house where she would keep the fire for her mother, making sure no one disturbed her.

* * *

Home of Henry and Leticia Smith, Hempstead, NY, March 1775

Leticia Smith stared down the road. She was bored, restless and itching for news. She had been remarried for three years now and her home with Henry in Hempstead was far removed from her previous home. The constraints of distance since her remarriage made it impossible to keep her old friendships alive.

The Smith home was at a crossroads, and close to the "plains" of Hempstead on superior farmland with plenty of neighbors. At first, she loved her large home. Once she had settled into her new home and adjusted her husband to her own liking, she turned her attention to her new neighbors. She was surrounded by Quakers, a peaceful people who irked her. She was convinced it was their fault that she felt unsettled and restless: they were eerily tranquil. They were dull clods: they had to be, they wore plain dress and hardly seemed to gossip.

Leticia and Henry went to their church. In fact, they went to church regularly not only to stave off gossip and criticism, but to see and to be seen by others. And, of course, to catch up on gossip. But, unfortunately, none of her friends from church lived near her.

Leticia had come from a life of poverty. Luckily her first husband had some money, and she gained comfort. But upon his death, his children were his heirs (he had been married before). Although he had willed her some goods, it was not enough for her widowhood.

When Henry had courted her, she had almost dismissed him. But then she found out he had more land and more money than her first husband. Unearthing this information made Henry a suitable husband: she would finally have her heart's desire. Indeed once she remarried, she found she was well off. With wealth, came an elevation of status, and this new status was exhilarating.

The Quakers' moderate speaking and plain dress annoyed her more than was reasonable. Their habits reminded her of their indifference to status. The Quaker disregard for her wealth smarted; to her it was a personal slight.

To make it worse they had these irritating standards: they did not use titles when addressing people, and would not bow or curtsy to anyone, no matter who they encountered. That they did not recognize her status in society exasperated her.

She shook her head in anger, what a waste, what a let-down—to be surrounded by the equality-minded Quakers.

Now she had begun to worry about their wealth. When she and Henry were first wed, he had been generous. But within a year he had fallen under the spell of gaming. She was now having doubts about their marriage. In the past six months alone, his gambling habits were quickly emptying the coffer, and their indebtedness was swiftly growing. Henry promised to stop. Her nagging had not changed him. Now she was panicking—where would this lead them?

These days her first waking thought was the spectre of ruin. Because she spent her waking hours in the grip of fear, it was taking its toll. She could not sleep, and the continual fatigue and worry sapped her strength. She dragged around the house, and it was hard to finish tasks.

"Thank God," she thought, "we have slaves, or we'd be ruined!"

Their slaves tended the inside of the house. They also kept the fields, the barns, their contents, and their animals. She rarely gave them a thought: they had been here when she married, they were to her like the animals on the property, only they got sick more often.

Leticia was shaken when last month debt forced Henry to sell some land to pay back his creditors. He blustered he was "well rid of the land." But since the sale, they were not better off. Every week Henry said something about the need to tighten their belts, by which she believed he meant that she ought to spend less. When he started talking that way, she found a reason to leave the room immediately. He wanted her to be thrifty! Just the thought of that made her shiver.

To distract her from her gnawing worries, she had taken to prying into her neighbors' business. Though the Quakers rubbed her the wrong way, at the same time their oddness held a certain fascination for her.

The Quakers' "plain" habits meant they had simple ways. While Leticia got caught up on the latest modes of dress on her occasional visit to the City of New York, her Quaker neighbors ignored styles. Quakers never gambled, so would never feel the consequence of losing money.

That her Quaker neighbors could live happily in their simplicity stirred her to jealousy. The Quaker contentedness, paired with their dismissive attitude towards wealth and status, both bewildered and fascinated her. With the passage of time their unruffled exterior made her itch to find their vulnerability. But they were closely knit, and it was impossible to get inside their circle. As a nonQuaker, she was an outsider. That fact spurred her to burrow her way into her neighbors' lives by snooping on them. Besides, when she was bored, snooping on Quakers broke up the tedium of daily life.

It was dusk when Leticia stepped outdoors to shake out a rug, she took that moment to crane her neck towards the Willis house. Their houses were close enough to see people coming and going. (Another house she spied on was Jemima and Elias Hicks. Jemima had just had a baby, and her life looked boring.) Leticia saw Elizabeth approaching her door. Elizabeth's face was a blotchy red from crying. Leticia had never seen Elizabeth upset. What had happened? This was the moment to pop by her house with an excuse.

Little Phebe answered Leticia's knock, but she blocked her way into the house, telling her Elizabeth could not see her now. But she was not easily put off and crowded the girl and managed to peer around her neck.

"Oh, dear! Phebe, I had something to return to her," she said, quickly adding, "And a favor to ask her." Quakers were pliable; this would work.

"Nay. Mother is not well," the girl said. As she said it, Leticia knew she was hiding something. What would loosen her tongue? She tried a different approach.

"Ah, dear, poor soul!" Leticia declared pityingly. "But, oh, I so need her help...." She let her voice trail off. "I need to speak to her, but if you believe she's better off left alone… Um, I'm very troubled—and I value her opinion."

She turned one shoulder and made as if she was leaving. Phebe shifted from one foot to the other and said, hastily, "Perhaps I could help."

Leticia struggled to mask her face from the triumph she felt. If she did it right, she would get a tidbit of gossip.

"Oh, I am so worried about things," she stated intentionally vague, "I wondered if your mother was concerned as well. But…" She let her voice trail off in worry, as if Little Phebe could know what was on her mind.

"Oh, she is! She is badly upset." the girl responded. She had taken her bait. Leticia smiled encouragingly. "Her friend in Philadelphia gave her unwelcome news— there will be war. Something about the Continental Congress." She stopped, realizing she had said too much. Hastily she added in a lowered her voice, "Umm...that is, I believe the colonies are anxious to be done with King George."

Leticia waved her hand airily, "Oh, yes. These rumors… New York is beholden to England and host many English citizens." She sensed the girl's guard had come up. She needed to be particularly cautious in choosing her words, "Surely, our colonial assembly will be loyal."

Little Phebe shook her head, "The rumor is that the colonial assembly is going to be disbanded."

The young lass had a startling amount of information! She had not gotten wind of any of this. How did the shy and mouse-like Quakers get so much news? It was to their credit.

Leticia kept on playing the game, teasing information from the girl while hiding her ignorance, "Oh…well… yes. Still, Long Islanders will not have to choose, at least not the Quakers. After all, you have a friendly agreement with the Crown?"

A shadow passed over her face. "Yes, um—" she paused.

Leticia persisted, "Mayhap the Parliament has become suspicious and doubts the loyalties of the Quakers?"

She saw she had gone too far. Now it was too late for the girl's face was set, unreadable. Leticia tried to re-engage, "Surely someone is telling the King how peaceful Quakers are."

The girl shrugged; her expression blank. "I cannot tell thee; I do not know."

As she said it, she turned and glanced over her shoulder at a closed door behind her. Leticia knew Elizabeth was behind that door, she thought she heard movement inside the room.

Though Leticia would not get any more from the girl, for the time she was satisfied. Why Elizabeth had come home upset was now clear: the Quakers feared disfavor from England should conflict erupt. Leticia felt buoyed by her trivial achievement.

"Phebe, good lass, thank you! You have stayed my fears. Please give my best to your ma. Tell her I can share my salts with her if she would like." To maintain her reputation, she added in a pious tone, "She'll be in my prayers."

* * *

Cow Neck, NY, March 1775

Rachel was tired but content after a morning filled with church and friends, then lunch with her son Solomon and his family. Today she had returned to Cow Neck early and spent some time in her own house before crossing the yard to Mother Dodge's. Most Sundays ended with the two of them eating together, sharing news.

Rachel had always lived on Tristam Dodge's land. It is where her parents had lived. After Tristam's first wife died, Tristam married Phebe Mott, the widow of Adam Mott the Younger. Then when Tristam died, as was custom and law, his son received the land and the house.

Tristam had written his will so Phebe could remain in the house. Tristam's son Joseph lived in his father's house only briefly, for Joseph's uncle had willed him a large plot. Within eight months Joseph Dodge had moved to the larger plot, leaving the care of Tristam's homestead to Mother Dodge and her children.

Rachel recalled her initial shock when, after Master Tristam's death, Mother Dodge offered her her freedom. Mother Dodge had explained to Rachel that she felt "burdened in her conscience" at owning another human being.

But Rachel refused her freedom: she was happy with her lot. Besides, where else would she go? Moreover, she had heard of the terrible struggles, nay, the severe deprivations that faced freed slaves. How could someone like her, born and raised a slave know about life as a freed negro? Freedom was but a word: no one had schooled her in it. Mother Dodge meant well. But she had no knowledge of what she would face as a freed slave woman—that was what scared her. The cost of freedom was too steep to pay, and she had turned down Phebe's offer.

But Mother Dodge did not give up. Again, on New Year's Day, the first one after Tristam's death, Mother Dodge offered Rachel her freedom. She said it was "a new beginning for the new year." Again, Rachel refused her offer. Mother Dodge did not hide her deep disappointment. But she did not give up. Every New Year's Day Mother Dodge made the offer, and each time Rachel turned it down.

Mother Dodge insisted on building a small house on the lot for Rachel. Phebe told her that though she was not in fact free, Phebe wanted her to have a sense of independence. Rachel prized the snug little home, making it her own and sleeping there most of the time. She only stayed in the Dodge house when the weather drove her to it.

Despite her widowhood and old age, Phebe was still independent and could give Rachel every Sunday off. Stephen and Amy Mott lived close by, and both her sons worked on the farm each week. A hired hand came in for some of the daily outdoor chores. The two women easily managed the indoors and the kitchen gardens.

Phebe showed no signs of slowing down. She was a formidable but genial woman. Her hair was pure white but still curly and thick for her age.

Rachel could not picture living anywhere but Cow Neck, even though lately they had been bothered by the increasing number of whaleboats. She usually paid no attention to the long-standing conflict with Britain. But now the conflict was spoken of everywhere she went.

The people of Cow Neck got mighty angry when their trade across the Long Island Sound was interfered with. These boats regularly crossed from the North Shore of Long Island to the New York mainland and the New England colonies. A whaleboat was an open rowboat, about 30 feet long, manned with eight or more oars. Goods could be traded, but it was now illegal to sell anything between any colony without the King's levy being paid.

The whaleboaters in the Sound were of two kinds. If they were British whaleboats they were to patrol for untaxed commerce between Connecticut, or New England islands, and Long Island. But other whaleboats were launched by fervent New England (usually Connecticut) "rebels" to Long Island. These secretly transported untaxed goods to New York or other points. They also used Long Island to conveniently bypass British soldiers in New York City. Circular letters would make their way from New England to American rebels on Long Island, then from Long Island to New York City.

Rachel entered the house to help Mother Dodge get their supper.

"Mother," Rachel began, as she leaned over the table working. "Have you heard about the offer from the British lord?"

"No, Rachel, I haven't. What is it?"

Rachel, not wishing to read Mother Dodge's face, kept her back turned, "A lord somebody – they say he lives in the south— has promised to free any negro slave if they will fight for the British, instead of the Americans."

Phebe did not respond. What was on Rachel's mind that she would bring this up? Rachel was in many ways still a mystery to Phebe. She eyed her friend: though no longer young, Rachel was as strong as she had been when Phebe had first married Tristam.

Rachel looked up and caught Mother Dodge staring at her, lost in thought. Mother Dodge turned to the fireplace, responding, "No, I've not heard that. But how can he make an offer when there is no fighting?"

"No. That's right." said Rachel and she decided it best to leave the topic alone.

The Quakers chose to ignore the riots, shooting, and the skirmishes in Boston, and elsewhere throughout New England. They also turned a blind eye to the shortages, the rising taxes, and the increasing trouble for mariners. Why should they be exempt from the troubles? Though sensitive to the plight of people, she had never heard Quakers address the awful and abundant abuses by the British overlords and their soldiers. What a contradiction. The Quakers' blind spots perplexed her, and she was occasionally frustrated by them. Then she felt a pang of guilt at condemning the Quakers. They were, after all, those who loved her and trusted her.

After supper as Rachel was clearing the table, Mother Dodge surprised her by reopening the topic. "If this rumor has any truth, perhaps this lord believes there is a possibility there will be real fighting. If the rumor is true, then he's got to believe the British regulars might be overcome by the American rebel militia unless they have help."

Rachel was speechless. Mother Dodge rarely spoke of military news. But before she could think of a reply, Mother Dodge changed the subject, "Thy church, are they all slaves, no freedmen?"

Rachel nodded. Rachel's "church" was simply a gathering where they would sing, pray and someone would give a simple "word from the Lord." These were spontaneous sermons, devised from what the congregants learned from a relative, friend or sometimes the families they lived with. Everyone who attended was a slave. They met outside in good weather, and in bad weather, they found a lean-to to shelter in, or they did not meet. Rachel knew Europe sent ministers to the colonies or they studied in special schools in the colonies. But she knew of no negro, freed or slave, who had been schooled for the ministry.

"What do the members of thy church think of this offer?"

"Mostly they believe it to be good for us." Rachel knew what the next question would be.

"And how does thee feel about it?"

"I am greatly troubled," She stopped. Mother Dodge's expression of encouragement prompted her to continue, "I feel scared. War is a terrible thing. And I am afraid for my son, for he supports England."

Mother Dodge was listening intently, Rachel continued, "I fear this King—who is acting generous now—may change his mind if he wins." She glanced at Phebe, noting her expression was somber.

"And if the King changes his mind, what would we, the negroes, do then? After the war we would have no homes. We won't even have our old masters or mistresses!" She paused, "I think he wants us because he wants more money from the colonies."

To Phebe, Rachels' opinion of the King's motives sounded more pragmatic than cynical—after all, the slaves were valuable commodities to him. She had no more questions, and the evening passed like any other. After Rachel had left for the night, Phebe reflected on both conversations: the one with her daughter and with Rachel.

She never thought freedom should be exclusive to one group. According to the Friends' belief that God had created everyone, it followed that freedom and equality was for all—Africans, Orientals, Europeans, and men and women. While it was not universally practiced, many Friends wrote against and preached against slavery. Her friends

John Woolman, and Anthony Benezet of Philadelphia were powerful figures in this activity.

Now rising tensions between the colonies and England were making freeing the slaves more complicated. It was hard to picture the land about her engulfed in a war—it was too horrific to think about. But at the same time, she understood, deep down, the American's thirst to be free from the monarchy. The European tradition of classes and titles was still in some form alive here in the colonies—mostly in the cities. And so, she appreciated why the Americans were in this struggle: the independence they craved was like air and light to the soul. More than that, freedom was the way people felt they were admitted to humanity.

Thinking of war unnerved her. If she was nervous about the future of the colony, what about Rachel? Her future would be fraught with difficulty. Phebe groaned aloud at the thought of what could happen to her beloved friend Rachel.

After she had gone to bed, sleep eluded her, as visions of the chains of slavery haunted her. She had seen plenty of the world, including slave markets. In an exercise of compassion, she had once accompanied another Friend onto the unspeakably inhumane pits that were called slave ships. Uneasy, she lay awake for hours past midnight, unable to sleep.

CHAPTER 3

Cow Neck, New York, Late March 1775

MARY FRY WILLIS was ready early to be fetched to Cow Neck for her weekly call on Phebe. Her son-in-law, Phebe's son, Adam, lived near her in Westbury, and he drove her there once a week. While the two women kept busy, Adam helped his brother Stephen Mott with chores. Even though Stephen was at his mother's farm several times a week, certain jobs needed an extra hand.

When she was younger, Phebe had been a traveling preacher and was well-regarded by the Friends. All three of Phebe's children had wed three of Mary's. Mary's son John married Elizabeth Mott, Amy married Stephen Mott, and Sarah had married Adam Mott. Intertwined by family and common affairs, their bond was reinforced.

Their long-time friendship had revealed to Mary what a spirited and complex person Phebe was. Although she was a Weighty Friend, Phebe was approachable, and people felt at ease with her. Mary had never felt smaller after being with her. Phebe was also unconventional, and her interests were broad ranging.

In the case of a premature rush to judgement by others, she spoke out with the simple caution, "We need to understand first of all, the Spirit of the law, so it is not overshadowed by the letter of the law." She would remind Friends that their disciplines, their guide to Christian living, were but "a guide to facilitate our way, and not to hem us in, nor constrict our thoughts." Outspoken though she was, she was liked and frequently heeded, probably because people knew she spoke from a place of love.

Phebe also made friends with those who were not Quakers (a practice often frowned upon). But the Meeting turned a blind eye to her habit, for such friendships had often turned to benefit the cause of the Friends. Phebe confided in Mary that she sometimes felt 'confined' by the biases of Friends and her association with non-Quakers provided stimulus, a type of 'fresh air' for her thoughts.

As the wagon rounded the corner, the house came into view. Phebe emerged from the house and though she was past 75 years of age, called girlishly out to Mary. Once inside, the matrons set to work. After their preliminary back and forth, Mary, seeing that Phebe was distracted, asked her what was on her mind. Phebe hesitated then responded, "It's Rachel."

Mary waited. In the silence which followed, she finished a piece of mending, then picked up the next piece from the mending pile. "Tell me about Rachel." she coaxed.

Phebe's felt her throat tighten at her sense of frustration, "This morning I determined I must finally free Rachel, but I cannot if she will not allow it. Why is she resisting so?"

"Thee ought to think hard on it. Clearly, she has different thoughts on this from thee and, mayhap there are things thee does not know about. Maybe her situation is fraught with diverse trials—ones thee might never have thought about."

Phebe was brought up short. "Aye! Thee is right. I have spoken too much and listened too little."

Phebe picked up a piece from the mending pile. She turned the conversation to Mary's large family. Only a few of her children were still unmarried. Jane had recently announced her intention to wed. Their youngest was 19-year-old "Feeb," so nicknamed to distinguish the Phebes in the family. It was Feeb who troubled her mother, for she was fair of face and knew it.

Mary told her about Jane's intended husband, her grandchildren, and her difficulties with Feeb. Phebe took a turn sharing her family news and after a lull, she switched topics, "Has thee heard anything from the New York Friends about the Manumission Society in New York City?"

Mary bit off a thread and cocked her head. "No, I never heard of it. Why?"

"Only that Willet Seaman and I have been exchanging letters this year and I was wondering if thee knew of it."

"What does manumission mean?"

"I think it's from Latin, it just means to free a slave. Willet is one of the chief members of the New York Manumission Society. Does thee remember Willet?"

Mary did recollect the former Friend, Willet Seaman. His marriage to a non-Quaker had put him "out of meeting," yet they both deemed him a Friend in heart, if not officially.

"Aye, I do."

"He is part of this Manumission Society in New York, and has been ever since it began as a small group with James Coggeshall, William Shotwell from New Jersey, and the Embree family. But now several prominent families are joined. It's made up of all sorts of people. I'm somewhat counted in, as I exchange letters and such."

"I am glad to hear about this! But tell me, does thee suppose the society can continue long? Manumission is ambitious in…" She paused, groping for the right word, "in such a climate now." Mary was referring to the American-British conflict: the folks in New York City were affected by it.

"Willet says the troubles in New York hurt the activities of the Manumission Society and now interest in manumission was flagging. He was mightily discouraged. All attention is on the conflict and division. Willet said plainly there is no question that we will be at war. The question is when." Phebe's voice trailed off.

Mary was shocked into silence. After a minute she asked, "In the case of war, what does he say the British would do with the negro slaves?"

"He believes they would likely force them to fight, to strengthen the British hand."

Mary's mind reeled at the possibilities. "Phebe, if there is a war, if the British win, imagine how punishing they will be to the rebels in New York."

Phebe shook her head, "If that happens, I doubt they will ask which side people took but will punish all equally. Even Friends. Anyone who does not take up arms or swear allegiance shall be treated as a rebel American."

Uncharacteristically, Mary continued her unfettered speculation, "If, somehow, the rebels win the war, what will happen then?"

The question produced a new thought for Phebe, "I suppose these colonies would have to set up some government or just stay as we are, separate colonies." She paused and wondered aloud, "But could we survive as separate colonies?" Then, thinking about England, France, and Spain. "I reckon not."

Mary picked up the thread, staggered by the concept, "It's hard to picture a nation out of these colonies, it would be nigh impossible. But up till now, I never thought of what it would take to be separate from England. Truly, I can scarcely think of this colony as being anything but a colony of England."

Phebe sat back and dreamed aloud. "If we ever separate, then it is my fantastic hope and prayer that the colonies would be the kind of society where peace and equality might flourish. Like no society in Europe—nor anywhere in the civilized world."

The colonies had long since received Quakers who found Europe unwelcoming. Not only them, but the colonies had been a refuge for others: Mennonites, Moravians, Huguenots, and others enjoyed relative peace in the colonies.

Mary could not imagine this envisioned future. There had been much talk of conflict and war, but she had never thought about her life afterwards.

"The possibility that New York might not be a mere colony but part of something bigger, makes me think differently. Would it be good or wise to form a nation with slaves and slave-owners?" Mary's question was rhetorical; they both knew the answer.

Mary got up to stir the fire, and as she stood, she spied a letter from James Titus on a nearby table. "What has James written?"

James was a Friend who lived in New York City who also had a farm on Long Island. He cultivated a rich circle of friends and acquaintances from assorted and divergent backgrounds and beliefs. His correspondence was a treat because he presented a window to a broader world, expanding Phebe's understanding and her views of the world beyond Long Island.

"I've not yet read his letter." Phebe responded, "It only just arrived, and I wait to read them. I relish them so."

* * *

After Mary departed Phebe settled into her rocking chair with her shawl around her shoulders, mulling over their conversation. Mary had asked good questions: Did Rachel have other reasons not to be freed? She turned over the possibilities in her mind till the sudden squawk of a jay awakened her from her nap.

Phebe had assumed Rachel chose to remain enslaved because freedom was like a distant country, too foreign to dream of. But was it something else? Could it be because (outside of Rachel's known and comfortable sphere) society was threatening? This was not without merit: outside of Rachel's enclave here, Phebe knew there were dangers for Rachel, terrible dangers that would never exist for Phebe.

At its most basic level, there was no "society" for Rachel. Looking at her life from this vantage, Phebe understood why she was anchored to this location, it was home. Moreover, Rachel was tied to her mistress with invisible cords of trust and love. Her head ached thinking of Rachel's situation.

To clear her head, she retrieved the unread letter from James Titus. Their correspondence had begun after a lengthy exchange at a Yearly Meeting. In letters they shared their private doubts and fears about the British and American conflict. They speculated about a successful outcome for the Americans, both believed it seemed unlikely.

In her last letter, she touched on slavery. Today she opened his letter hoping to be bolstered by his words. She was not disappointed: James had written passionately about the injustice of slavery. James' letters were animated, filled with pointed expressions. His rigorous thinking was conveyed succinctly. His language did not mask the vigor of his passion but bolstered it.

He wrote: "I repeat to thee what I have repeated to every human in my hearing: when I was impressed with a sense of urgency to free my slaves, I did so. And, if I could, I would free all slaves! I believe that until all people in New York Colony are free, then no one is free."

Phebe reread that sentence several times. She would memorize it as it was the exact phrase she needed. One short utterance spoke to the spirit of the times, and at the same time broadened the scope, looking ahead to what might be. It was a phrase that would resonate when she spoke about the plight of slaves. But it was more than a phrase to persuade, this gift of words was something she could repeat to herself when her own courage failed.

Always ready in her pocket was a stubby pencil and a scrap of paper. She pulled them out now and she copied his phrase on the paper: *Until all people in New York Colony are free, then no one is free.*

* * *

The next morning the rain which had come in the night had ceased. The sky was clearing, and a north wind was blowing, bringing in cooler weather. There was something about the hue of the sky, an aching beauty and its luminousness that gave Phebe the heart to do what she must: to convince Rachel to be freed. Phebe felt something else, a sorrow anticipated: there would come a day when Rachel and she would no longer work side by side.

Rachel entered the house then with water and fresh milk. Once they finished breakfast, they tackled the daily chores. As they were folding linens, Phebe noticed when Rachel moved, her movements were stiff.

"Rachel, thee *does* know I am grateful for thy help." Phebe began.

"Yes, Mother."

"Thee knows I don't pay much mind to birthdays, but what, pray, is thy age?"

Rachel straightened up over the bed sheet she had been tucking in and smoothed it out. "I don't quite know."

"Can thee guess thy age?" Under her mobcap Rachel's hair had some grey, but her unlined skin made it difficult to approximate her age.

Rachel contemplated, "My son has his own children. That is, they're no longer babes." She paused, "I reckon I must be two score and five."

"Thee is 45!" Phebe could not conceal her shock. When Tristam died, Rachel had seemed but a child. Where had the time gone?

Rachel's father had died in an accident. Rachel's mother had been Tristam's slave. She had died a few years after Phebe wed Tristam. The Dodge plot on Cow Neck was all Rachel had ever known; it was comfortable, and she was secure here.

"Has thee considered—" Phebe stuttered, not sure what words to use, "that this may be a good time to live with thy son?" Phebe broached the topic with caution. She was ignorant of the strength of the tie between Rachel and Solomon's wife Azuba.

The abruptness of the subject brought Rachel up short. Rachel stared at her in silence, shaken by the sudden request: Mother Dodge was asking her to move.

Only a few months ago, Mother Dodge had given her the yearly New Year's Day offer to be freed and now she was repeating herself. What was behind this suggestion? Rachel felt unsteady. She had never doubted her mistress's satisfaction in her work. She believed she was safe with her and trusted her completely. Although Rachel was not a Quaker; she was a good Christian. What was amiss? Why the abrupt question? What had happened? Had she misused Mother Dodge? Was she taking liberties? Or did she need younger help?

Rachel's eyes filled with tears. Though shaken to her core, out of habit she continued working, trying not to show that she was trembling. She worked steadily with unseeing eyes, as she recalled the period after Master Dodge's death. At dawn on the day Tristam's will was to be read, she had gathered her belongings in one bundle for she was sure her new mistress would give her bad news. It was widely known that Phebe Willets Dodge was against slave-keeping and indeed within their first year of marriage, Master Dodge had released all his slaves except for her.

But that day Mother Dodge surprised her. After the reading of the will, she came directly to Rachel and gently told her to unpack. She would stay and could care for her own mother who at the time was sick and close to death.

As Rachel nursed her mother throughout her illness, Mother Dodge did most of her work. As her mother's needs increased, Phebe made sure Rachel had the time and energy for her own mother.

Then after her mother's burial, Rachel's uncertainty returned: was she at the end of her time on the Dodge farm? Would she be released? What about her son, her only family, who was still young. Would they be separated?

When they finally spoke of it, Mother Dodge asked for her opinion and subtly suggested Solomon would be happier if they remained on the Dodge property until he was grown. Rachel agreed, but in truth, she herself was not ready to move from the only home she had ever had.

Moreover, she had grown close to Phebe's children, and was more like an elder sister. She empathized with them in their pain and joy. They were her kin, and even after Phebe's children were wed and had families, she still counted them as her family.

Then years later, after her son was married, Rachel remained on Cow Neck. She stayed for her safety: this was when there was a surge in "blackbirding" – a practice of making money by finding freed slaves, seizing them, and selling them as "escaped" slaves. The blackbirded slaves were re-enslaved but under a new master, in a different colony. The thought of being blackbirded filled her nightmares.

And then the years drifted on, Rachel was at ease with Phebe. She had come to think the two women not only needed each other, but also gave one another a sense of home.

"Pray, why do you ask? Is it because I do not work well now, or because you want me finally freed?" Rachel asked bluntly, knowing that her mistress would not be offended.

"Thee has caught me. Aye, tis true, I believe it better if thee is a freed woman, better now than later. I-I can no longer hold a slave." Phebe admitted.

Rachel could not believe what she was hearing. Her blood ran cold, she was confused and angry. She had an odd off-kilter sensation, as if she were dizzy, followed by a sudden feeling of humiliation.

She felt well and truly demeaned. She had never been shamed by Mother Dodge. But right now, for the first time in her life, she felt she was indeed a slave, and so, a mere object in the hand of another human being. Rachel's heart was pounding, and her thoughts were tumbling. Rachel glanced at Phebe; her mistress was watching Rachel's face closely, but she remained silent.

Rachel felt dampness at the corner of her nose: she must be crying. Her throat was tight, she was unable to speak, but her feelings were speaking for her, and they spoke in tears. She felt betrayed, her world was wrecked, there were no words.

Mother Dodge had just told her straightforwardly what her wish was. But, why? And, why now? There could be only one reason, and it had to do with Mother Dodge's Quakerliness. All these years she had been her slave, but now she had to leave because it suited her mistress' Quaker principles.

Rachel finally squeaked out a question, "And now thee needs for me to move out? How have I wronged you?"

Mother Dodge's face fell. She turned fully towards her, saying "No! Rachel, thee must know this: thee pleases me very much! All the time! And thee is a good and loving companion." Mother Dodge said tenderly, putting her hand on her arm with warmth. After a long moment she asked, "It's not as simple as it sounds. Perhaps thee would listen to my story—then, mayhap, thee shall understand?"

Rachel nodded.

"I am old. My body is refusing to do what it used to. For many years—since before thee was born, I have had a powerful sense that having anyone as a slave is wrong. Thee knows, it's my wish that my speech and my life as a Christian would be in harmony.

"I have a sense that if thee does not allow me to release thee, then I will die restless. Thee can understand why I wish to free thee, but never without *thy* consent."

Rachel wiped her tears and sat down to her mending. She had to think this over; the approaching death of her mistress was a subject they avoided. Finished folding, Phebe sat down nearby and fussed with things in her sewing basket, passing the time. Silence reigned for a quarter of an hour, till Phebe spoke.

"Though I must free thee, I know full well thee has thy own life. It's not for me to direct it. I must do what is right for thee, not just for me."

Rachel lifted her head and cocked it as she scrutinized Mother Dodge. For the first time, she saw herself from Mother Dodge's viewpoint: her own slave was stopping her from carrying out what she believed her moral duty was.

And now, for the first time, she saw she had some kind of power over Mother Dodge, and not the other way around.

Rachel's brow furrowed in thought, "Nay, it's my own fear about an unknown future. That is why I want things to be as they always have been."

To be free? How could she? What would she do if she were free? Her mind could not let in those thoughts: they were scary, scarier than anything. Yet, Mother Dodge was right. Times had changed and Rachel could not cling to the past. And Phebe was old and would soon die. The troubles and turbulence in the colony brought new challenges. Also, she speculated, might there be new possibilities for a freed slave?

But she had no schooling and no real learning. Her world revolved around the old woman across from her. Phebe was the one person she would trust with her life; she had always looked to her for wisdom. But maybe if she leaned on Mother Dodge, then maybe, little-by-little, she would help make her an independent woman.

Rachel was impatient with indecisiveness in anyone, but especially in herself. She felt done with dithering. She had to decide. She took a deep breath, "If you say so, then that's what shall be. But," she added quickly, "don't be thinking it's as easy as waving your hand and letting me go. I'll be reminding you that I am not as young as I once was. You cannot just suddenly send me off."

The corners of Phebe's mouth curved up; this is what she wanted to hear from her. But Rachel had not finished speaking her mind. "There is my side of the problem too." She was a bit awed by her own boldness. Even as questions, ideas and possibilities tumbled about in her head, she was certain Mother Dodge would help her think them through.

"Aye! Do tell me: I wish to hear all of thy dilemma. All of it, Rachel, don't spare me any truth." Phebe arose and put a hand on Rachel's arm, to encourage. "We still have time for thee to tell me thy concerns. And that way we will be set for the problems ahead. Heaven will move what it needs to if we are in agreement with Him."

Phebe's assurance of complete and undivided support touched Rachel deeply. As she absorbed what they had just pledged to one another, she had a sense of giddiness.

Strangely, now that she had opened her mouth and consented to freedom, a deep desire to be freed was awakened. All these years, her entire life, she dared not hope, no, she had fought back hope. In the past, there had been too many dangers and too few avenues of protection for a freed slave. But things would be different with Mother Dodge's help. Aye, now she could almost taste her freedom. As the initial giddiness ebbed, a sense of strength and determination budded inside Rachel.

"Mother Dodge, it's well said that when the Lord's got your attention, you are a force and cannot be stopped."

"Now is the right time: the winds of change are blowing across the colonies and at the same time, my time on earth is drawing to an end. With thy consent, we will, with God's help, get this done."

As Phebe declared this, her desire for the slave's manumission intensified to a near palpable level. Slavery was so very deeply entrenched in the colonies. The heinous inequity was acceptable to most people—few people thought of it. She believed the universal freeing of slaves in the colonies would be more disruptive than fighting the King of England.

In the past Phebe had asked freed slaves for advice. They said the same thing: that every freed slave had to organize his own world. Some remained as paid servants, the few who struck out on their own were daring outsiders—having lost their old community. That was the exact difficulty of righting moral offenses: when you attempt to right a wrong, there are always problems.

Phebe added, "Thee is as close as a sister or niece. But we must tread carefully when freeing thee. That is why first we shall lay our plans."

Rachel trusted Mother Dodge. She would have to lean on her guidance as she inched her way into a frightening new way of living. She had a new sense of dignity. No, it was not new, it was already there, well-rooted. But now it was flowering.

* * *

Early the next morning, Phebe headed outside to start mapping out the gardens for spring planting. This kitchen garden was her favorite one to work in: from it she had a clear view of Mott's Point and the Sound beyond. Near the garden was an outcropping with a boulder which was her favorite spot to drink in the morning sun, especially true in spring.

Today, the surface of the boulder was still slippery, and she took care when she mounted the outcropping. From her view atop the boulder, she looked at the waters of the Sound. The number of boats coming to Cow Neck had increased in the past year: confirming the rumor that rebel colonists on Long Island were in frequent communication with those in Connecticut and Massachusetts.

As Phebe gazed across the waters of the Sound, she allowed her mind to wander. During the chilly winter months she had missed this view, missed the fresh breeze, and missed the warm sun on her face. When a strong gust of wind blew in off the Sound, she pushed her bonnet back off her head. The whipping wind in her hair freed her cooped-up soul.

The waves looked calm, but the breeze was steady. The apparent calm of the Sound was, she knew, a deception; the waters below her were so choppy that to sail a small bark in it today would demand a strong hand and steady nerves. The perception of a calm sea was seen only from her point on solid ground and above the shore.

Perhaps that was the difference, as it is with so many things: Like being a negro slave. Rachel was born, just as she was, flesh and blood, but the difference was something Phebe could never know. Phebe could only *look* at being a slave, she could never be in Rachel's skin. She would never feel nor perceive the world as a slave would. The powerless slave was born into a capricious world. Although she was full of empathy for slaves, it was insufficient. Her grasp of Rachel's situation was incomplete and inaccurate because it was devised out of her own perception of the world, from her own fancy.

In like manner, from high ground, the choppy surface of the Sound appeared to be ripples on a pond and looking at it yielded no hint, nor gave any sense of the real dangers she would know were she in it. For Phebe to cast herself in a slave's role was a fool's errand—she could never replicate Rachel's life in her mind.

But Rachel was just as much a God-created human as Phebe. That there was no difference between them made the yawning gap between her position in society and Rachel's feel wider.

She spied a whaleboat coming across the Sound, a reminder of the brewing war. She wondered if war would prompt King George to shutter Friends' worship. The British had shot unarmed people in Boston, after all. It was possible. The thought came to her that any persecution of the Friends would pale compared to the cruelty that would befall slaves under the British hand.

In that case, without plans, the Friends could not help the slaves. It would be too late. They ought to lay plans now so freed slaves would not wish for the cover and protection of their former owners in case of war.

She nestled into a curve formed in the boulder. Seated, she thought about what steps had to be taken so freed slaves could enter society. Then she caught herself: what *society* was she imagining they would join? Slaves were non-persons—they could hold no property because they were property.

The Resolution to manumit all the slaves in New York was noble, godly, and inspired. But was it enough? No. It was the stark truth.

There were but a handful of talented slaves for whom freedom would improve their circumstances. But the rest of the slaves would be worse off, freeing them with no skills nor property would be an unkindness. Their situations might even worsen if a full-blown war interrupted their new freedom.

Last year, she had spent much time jotting down the reasons slaves ought to be trained. With no training, freed slaves could be put in harm's way. As late as last year she had petitioned the Friends to give the slaves training, but little interest was shown, and nothing had happened. Should she persist, should she try again?

She reckoned there must be well over 150 slaves held by the Friends in the surrounding area and these all were to be freed. And here was another obstacle: how would the Meeting free so many slaves in a brief time?

No matter how large a tree was, any felled tree could fit in a fireplace, once it was chopped into pieces. Phebe was inspired: If the Meetings on Long Island saw 50 slaves each year to freedom, then by 1778, there would be 150 slaves freed. She would get her relatives, especially the Willis family, to assist her. But that was not enough, she had to cast a wide net.

She pulled herself up and stretched. She was old, but she felt she had at least three more years: her health was good, and she was strong. She would recruit help.

"I reckon I know what to do about Rachel," she announced to the chipmunk who had just peeped over the boulder at her, "I will free her, but first prepare her. By this time next year, she shall be ready once she is freed." She breathed in some fresh morning air and only then realized she had not even started planning her garden.

* * *

Dodge Home, Cow Neck, NY, Spring 1775

Phebe was up early the next day. In the cold light of early morning, she was tidying up before Rachel appeared in the doorway. Her mind went to Rachel's decision and felt a thrill of excitement that her long-awaited dream would be a reality.

Then she thought of the promise she made to herself to see the Meeting's slaves freed within the next three years. It would be a long and hard fight, met with strong resistance. Laziness would keep people from freeing their slaves.

But there was more to do than simple manumission: Friends needed to prepare both their slaves, and themselves. Once the slaves were manumitted, their lives would be greatly altered for the consequence of the act would be felt through every aspect of life. It was a sobering thought. People were already on edge, and many were panicking at the bad blood between the colonies and England.

Long Island Friends were farmers, and a freed slave would mean the family would have to shoulder more of the work. In most cases, freeing a slave would heighten worry about money. Either way, there would be a burden added, physical or financial, or both.

If she led the Friends to free the slaves, she would face opposition, both secret and public. She expected accusations, difficult questions, and rejections. Some Friends would resist even as they gave lip service. (These Friends would need special coaxing.) A few would stoneheartedly ignore the guidance of the New York Meeting.

Some might ostracize her, and her family could become targets of this anger. For that she felt a stab of sadness and guilt. But the question that nagged her now was how to motivate enough slave owning Friends. She had to broaden her reach.

Suddenly tired, she sat down in her chair, leaned her head back and closed her eyes. Reopening them, she pulled the scrap of paper from her apron pocket. She stared down at James Titus' quote from his letter: *Until all people in New York Colony are free, then no one is free.*

The words rekindled in her a fire. It was possible that she, and her family, would suffer consequences for their efforts. But pain was not a sign that something was wrong, no, sometimes it was a sign of a bent thing pulled to right.

She heard Adam pulling up to her door. Mary would be entering any moment. She smoothed her hair, her cap, and her apron. Today she would seek Mary's wisdom.

Phebe took her seat near the fire, and Mary settled in the cane chair nearby. Once settled and busy, they exchanged news. When their conversation lagged, Phebe asked Mary's counsel. "Thee knows I am set to free Rachel. But I need thy advice."

Phebe rehearsed how little the Long Island Friends had done to free their slaves, then added, "I feel strongly we must act on it quickly. If war comes soon (and I believe it shall) it might be too late then."

Mary agreed. Phebe kept speaking, "Ten years ago the Yearly Meeting disallowed the buying and selling of slaves. But…" she trailed off.

Phebe looked squarely at Mary, "I fear when I free Rachel, my one act will be swallowed up. It will be a solitary act and the force of it will go unfelt and unnoticed. But what a picture of God's goodness it would be if we all freed our slaves." By now Phebe had stopped her work and leaned towards her friend as if to underscore the urgency.

"I fear we shall run out of time. I am an old lady. What else can we do to speed up this work? It is such a big task."

"Thee has thy sons and daughters to help, and our family." Mary offered.

"Aye; but I must cast a wider net than our two families!"

"I reckon thee wants help from a Public Friend but one young, well-spoken and full of energy." And Mary offered up some possible people, but Phebe shook her head at each suggestion.

"Nay," Phebe explained, "The person must be a soul filled with enthusiasm. Someone who can stir up our fellow Friends."

Mary looked into the fire for a long minute, thinking. "Thee could ask Jemima Seaman's husband—I mean, Jemima Hicks. Elias is a right talker and bursting with energy. He is good at rousing people."

Elias and Jemima Hicks were related to Phebe, and Elias was a close relative of Mary's husband Samuel.

"Yes. I've heard him speak." She thought about Elias. He was young: she judged him more than ten years younger than her children.

"And they still live in Jericho?" Phebe checked. Jericho was one of the many villages stretching from west to east in the middle of the County. Mary and Samuel Willis, her daughter and husband John, as well as Adam and wife Amy Mott lived nearby in Westbury. That area of Hempstead was almost entirely populated by Friends.

"Aye," said Mary, "Elias does carpentry. He works Jemima's parents' farm too, but he wants to preach," she said. "He likes roaming about; he's always popping by someone's house. And people are drawn to him."

She paused. "Come to think of it, he's waiting to be recognized as a Public Friend. I hear he's gotten impatient at the slowness of it all."

"Why is it taking so long?"

Mary shrugged, "I don't know. I heard of no reason."

"Foot-dragging." Phebe responded from experience.

When Elias was a Public Friend, what he would say in Meeting would be taken with gravity and accordingly, his word would have influence. He was ideal for the cause of manumitting slaves because he had what they lacked: youth, with its vigor and freedom of movement.

"I think we ought ask him. I would speak with him, but he will pay more heed to thee."

"But I cannot do so soon. Next First Day I address a committee meeting."

Mary stood to stir the fire, "Jemima will be at the quilting bee, and I reckon Elias will drive her there, then thee can speak with him."

Phebe's daughter Elizabeth was hosting a quilting bee for a mother who was certain to be having twins. Phebe saw her opportunity: Elizabeth's house was large, and she and Elias could speak in private.

"Yes! I need only take him aside for a few minutes!" Phebe envisioned welcoming the energetic Elias to the effort.

Mary looked at Phebe's small table, strewn with letters. She spied a book underneath the pile, and slid it out. Picking it up she read the title aloud, "*Considerations on the Keeping of Negroes.* All of Philadelphia is reading this and I wish to read it when thee is finished. I can give thee the book of poetry by Phillis Wheatley."

"Take it home with thee today. I am eager to read Wheatley's book; I have heard much about it."

"Oh, yes! She writes beautifully. I only wish there were more freed slaves who wrote."

The sounds outdoors indicated that Adam was approaching to fetch her home. Mary bundled up her mending. Phebe placed the loaned book in a protective bag before handing it off to Mary.

CHAPTER 4

Cow Neck, New York, Late March 1775

As welcome as spring is, it brings with it more work. For that reason, Phebe and Rachel agreed that it was odd for Martin Schenck to be out visiting his neighbors. Especially since Martin was not known to be social. They deduced he must be meeting people about the conflict with Britain.

Spring also ensured an abundance of domestic tasks demanding that Phebe and Rachel work side by side. They shared those long hours in conversation. Phebe took advantage of their time together to talk about Rachel's situation after manumission.

At first Rachel was adamant about her desire to remain at the farm as Phebe's paid help, but Phebe challenged that notion: Tristam's son was the legal heir to the property. Women were not allowed to own property even Phebe was a long-term guest. When Phebe died, there would be no place for Rachel here.

But Rachel balked at change and suggested she work for Stephen Mott. Phebe suspected Rachel's real reason was her belief that the only work fit for her was to be domestic help. She pointed out the hardship it would be for Rachel to continue working as she aged. Rachel was already feeling the strain of heavy work and she admitted it.

Phebe challenged Rachel to do something new, something different. This idea was hard to absorb and Rachel was too scared to turn away from the only work she had ever known.

Rachel shook her head, obstinate, "Nay. This is what I do, and I do it well." She was suddenly proud of her work.

Phebe felt she understood Rachel's path of reasoning. Loyalty borne out of habit was a fiercely strong thing. But it was problematic when it disguised itself as a virtue. Loyalty itself held no virtue, it was a barnacle living on a vessel.

Rachel had only to try something, something she was good at, but one which would change the course of her life. Naturally, she would be scared, radical change was not done all the time. But Phebe sensed Rachel's anguish and stopped pressing her. She would leave her alone and give her time to warm to the idea of change.

After this conversation, Rachel spent all her waking hours considering her choices, sometimes with fear, other times with hope. Several days passed before Rachel finally gave in, admitting to Phebe that though she was terrified, she was willing to try something different. Phebe reassured her of her and her family's unconditional support.

"If I am not to be paid to work for thee, what then is it that thee has in mind for me to do?"

Rachel was adept at fancy needlework, something Phebe had no need for. But she had learned from a friend in the past year the number of skilled fancy needleworkers had become scarce. Although there was little use for her skill in Queens County, New York City was full of potential patrons. Phebe explained the situation and suggested that she take in needlework for money. She could at least try it.

To Rachel the idea of exchanging needlework for money was hard to conceive of. "Nay," she balked, "I've not got the skills to be paid."

"But thee has the skill. Thy skill has never been proven outside of Cow Neck. Thee is but timid about thy ability. Why not try, if only to find out? If, in the end, thee cannot do it well enough, or if the business fails, then I promise thee can still work here, but only for payment."

Rachel was still skeptical and apprehensive, but now open. Phebe helped her plan. Rachel would test her skill and work on the farm until she was comfortable with the business. Rachel finally consented to this plan, but insisted she would stop working for Phebe only when she could support herself on her handiwork.

"If the fine women of New York demand fancy needlework, why should they not pay a former slave for the handiwork they crave?" Phebe reasoned.

She wasted no time in sending a few samples of Rachel's handiwork to women in the City of New York. The rapidity of events flustered Rachel: agreeing to the idea was easy because there was no possibility of failure and humiliation. The thought of her handiwork being handled by the wealthy women of New York made her shiver inside.

But what if it came to be? She, a negro slave, would be making her fine handiwork for the ladies of New York! Not only that, but they would pay her for it. She could not grasp it.

Rachel's nascent business gave Phebe the need to call on her neighbors, including Mrs. Schenck, Martin's wife. The mistress was covered by a large apron, her sleeves were rolled up and her arms covered in flour. In Phebe's brief visit, Martin's wife managed to complain at length about Martin's frequent absences from home.

"That rascal! He believes he can just go to the taverns with the same men every night and no one will suspect anything."

She shook her head in disgust or disappointment.

"See," she explained, "he got to be sympathetic to rebels. After all, our family is in Massachusetts colony. They have it bad there, what with the British fist falling on them." She paused and let out a long breath. "I just wish *something* would happen," Mrs. Schenck vented.

She wished for war. That her friend and neighbor had such a strong bloodthirst tilted Phebe's world. She was used to hearing of strife and divisions in the non-Quaker world and had seen all sorts of methods by which people clamored atop one another in their lust for power.

But this was different: Now English citizens wished to fight their own. It was true that the British had cruelly and unjustly punished the colonies of New England. But was answering barbaric behavior with barbarism going to help anything? A sense of unease and dread swelled in her. Bloodthirst opened the door to bloodshed, which led to sorrow. Phebe was deeply chilled.

When Phebe got home, she found her eldest son Adam on her porch. Adam lived in Hempstead and was deeply involved in the functions of the Meeting.

Still bothered by her neighbor's state of mind, she asked Adam how widespread the warlike spirit was on the island. He would have knowledge as he regularly attended the Hempstead Town Meetings.

Adam was noncommittal. "All I know is the people up here, Cow Neck and Madnans Neck, and all these other little communities, are becoming trouble for Hempstead."

"How is that?"

"They always bring up the problem of the British, and taxes, and what their laws have become. They are overly suspicious: they insist we are being watched closely by the British."

Phebe knew not all the boats in the Sound were manned by rebel Americans. She was also sure she had met British officers roving Cow Neck.

"Thee doesn't think so?" Her intonation made it clear she was doubtful.

"Well, perhaps." Adam conceded, "But I disagree when they claim the British are planning to box us in here on Long Island."

"Thee does not think there could be some truth in that?" His mother was surprised. "Is it not possible? Surrounded entirely by water, Long Island would be easy to take by the sea."

"Not likely. I have not seen soldiers encamping near us, I wouldn't fret about it. Besides, the British would have to use more than just one ship. Also, why pursue Long Island? The City of New York is the jewel—they will target New York before chasing a bunch of farmers."

Phebe shook her head, "The faith thee has in thy fellowman is good and right. But thy position is simple or blind." Seeing her son's pained look, she explained, "Consider the British army. They will do as they are commanded. And when they do, the fair people of New York shall flee ahead of their might. I have seen the British exercise their power over and against the Friends and its memory still makes me shudder."

* * *

Rachel's son Solomon was furious. The day before his mother had told him of Phebe's plans—nay—the plans the Quakers had for all slaves of New York. His outrage towards Phebe and her kind had intensified, taking over every other thought, worry or care he had.

The night after seeing his mother had been a sleepless one, and the next day, he had been irritable with his family, and short with Azuba. He knew then he had to get away; to clear his head he took a walk. On his walk, he saw that shielding Azuba from his mother's plans was no good; she would eventually find out. He would have tell her. The thought was hateful to him, for it would open her old wounds by stirring up painful memories of her years in New York City. He hated to have her relive any of it. But it could not be helped.

When he returned, he led her to the side of the house, to a small grove of pine trees, and told her everything his mother had said. She wept; the tears were tears of terror and bitterness. No matter how he tried, he could not comfort Azuba.

While he could not change Azuba's past, he could at least have it out with Mother Dodge. The next day, soon after dawn, he slipped away from his home in Flushing and headed northeast to Cow Neck. Phebe opened the door to find Solomon on her porch—he rarely visited her. Solomon's complexion was mottled; clearly, he was angry.

At first, he refused to sit. He was his own man. He was not obliged to her. When he relented it was for two reasons. Phebe was his second mother, but he also held her in high regard, both for her wisdom and her kindness.

"Solomon, what is thy trouble?" He started at her question, "I know thee well enough to know only trouble would bring thee here now." She straightened her shawl and leaned forward to listen.

"My ma tells me you're fixing to free all the slaves in New York." His voice held a challenge.

"Aye, but not the province. If God provides the strength and the will, then at least in Queens County." Reading his face, she added, "It doesn't set well with thee?"

He shook his head; his tongue was too thick to speak.

Seeing his hesitation, Phebe spoke words of explanation, but only to fill the silence until he was ready to speak, "Solomon, I reckon slavery is wrong. Once the wheel of slavery got rolling, we got caught up in it. But now this great wheel must be reversed. It shall be some kind of quiet revolution, but it must go back.

"It's only fitting. Just as the American rebels lay claim to fairness, this is no different from what thee should require." She paused and peered at him. "Thee does want this, doesn't thee?"

Though her comments dampened some of the heat and intensity of his feelings, they were not extinguished nor satisfied. He aired his grievances. "Aye! I'm as human as you. But we see it different," Solomon said.

Phebe stayed silent and waited. He swallowed—how to explain to this woman who never had it different?

"Let me ask you this one thing: have you been treated worse, because you are a woman and not a man at any time (not by Quakers)?"

They both knew the answer to this question. She had a sudden flood of memories. As a traveling preacher, she had felt the difficulty of being a woman, she was barred or prohibited from any number of things men were allowed. Though she had not let opinions or slights prevent her movements, it was only her dead determination, her keen insight and her wit that got her through. What pained her the most was when she discovered how often and how regularly men ignored a woman's point of view. Not for its value, but because the comments came from a female mouth.

Solomon had made his point.

"Thee does not wish for slaves to remain slaves, does thee?" she asked bluntly. Solomon flinched inwardly. Her pointedness hurt but he accepted it from her.

"No. But, Mother Dodge, take my children, they are children of two freed slaves. They know little: they have never been schooled, they cannot read or write. Why? Because I only just finished teaching Azuba.

"I wanted to start them, but they are digging in their heels, refusing to learn. Now, they tell me they are too old to learn and they complain to me. Do you know why? Azuba told me they do not want to be different from their playmates."

Phebe sensed he was heading for a bigger topic. "What should we do then?"

He shook his head. "I don't know. I'm not certain." He shrugged, "Think of my children; then look at yours when they were little ones. Yours (and most Quaker children) got learning, most all have skills, and some were apprenticed.

"But mine? What will they do in a few years? Be hands like me and Azuba? And their children, my grandchildren, will be hands. When I look ahead to the day my grandchildren are adults, I feel sick—they won't read, they won't write or cipher. They'll be raising a family and still working as hands for whoever pays them—till they can't work no more."

Phebe straightened up. Solomon's worry was akin to hers. But he was thinking of his children's welfare while she was thinking of those slaves who could be independent now. The two of them, the elderly widow and the negro man, were grappling with the same challenge: how to improve the lot of the negro in the colony.

"Thee is right! My thinking is lacking!"

Solomon took his opportunity, "The white man made our situation. Does not the white man have to change it?

"Fair enough is your dream to free us, but what then? What becomes of us after you leave us? We have no one to turn to—families, neighbors and even towns—as you do. The most we have is a group of slaves or new freed people. Most of us cannot read, cipher, or write.

"The whites don't need our skills, just our backs. None of us runs a real business—we are not allowed to. We will never run a business. And land? The negro is not allowed to own land.

"Maybe there is a blacksmith here or there, one who owes his learning to a kind master, but what happens when he has to cipher his accounts? Hardly anyone has learned ciphering.

"These laws block the negro from the possibility of feeding ourselves. We are trapped—Azuba and I are freed, but not like you are. We are not at liberty as you are." Solomon, for the first time, pointed his finger at Mother Dodge. She represented all of the weight, burdens and restrictions levied on his back.

"What you are dreaming is only a dream. We want freedom, yes. But we wish for schooling, apprenticeships, and our own land to farm. We love our families, but we have nothing for them: not learning, not land, nothing. Kept out of schooling and kept from owning any land, then we must keep to ourselves. We will survive but we will not flourish. You have no sense of the depth of our problem! Worse when slaves were torn from our wives, our families and sold off, it shredded us. Yet now we are expected to build a society!?

"Did you know that last month a neighbor died, leaving her little child alone—the mother's master didn't want the child. We took her in—that baby is an orphan, he was too young to work, too young to be sold, and had no one left in the world.

"You want us to be freed, but can you see our fix? Although we may find a freedom from our current hell, when freed, will we find another kind of hell?"

Phebe was trying to absorb his world; but even as she did, she knew she lived untouched by his reality. He was right, she had never given thought to the binding harshness of the law and its punishing effects on the negroes. Where she lived was a separate world, separate in every aspect. His word picture had drawn back the curtain, giving her a glimpse of his world.

She knew slaves should be prepared for freedom but now she was alarmed by her narrow understanding and her raw ignorance. She was blind: her high view of freeing slaves for conscience's sake was all very well, but the hard truth was it was not as simple nor easy as she had fancied it.

He looked up when she reached forward, grabbing his hand in her age-softened ones.

"I-I-I," she stuttered, unable to find words to express to him her lack, her deficiency. "Telling me all such—it's as if thee is describing the world, and its colors, its sounds, its laughter to someone deaf and blind." she moaned to him. She was obviously saddened and frustrated.

"I am somewhat enlightened—though I have more to learn. But thee has cleared my understanding like never before. And I know I am ignorant."

Solomon believed her words were heartfelt, sincere.

"Solomon, please consider calling on me regularly so we can speak openly like we are now?"

Solomon shook his head, "Nay. I have much work."

Phebe tried to hide her disappointment: Solomon was a leader of sorts and had influence in the negro community. But he was his own man. She would not press him, she had too much respect for him. "If I need more insight, may I ask for thy opinion?"

Solomon was torn. He did not make many promises because he did not like to feel beholden to anyone. But Mother Dodge was singular and he held her in high esteem.

"I will plainly tell you the truth if you can hear it. But, if I feel or sense your opinion is opposing plain truth, then I shan't return."

Phebe agreed, "That is fair."

Though her familiarity with the law was scant, her young grandsons had more freedom of choice than an adult negro. Solomon had barely touched on the complexities and the dilemmas that put the negroes in a corner, legally.

As she saw it, the British American Colony was a society established to protect itself, not to promote the well-being of the colonists—no matter their race. But even if all Long Island or New York Colony freed their slaves, families would still be shorn apart in other colonies.

Phebe took a good look at Solomon's grave face. She saw the intensity of his distress and the hurt in the back of his eyes, and it punctured her. There was nothing she could do or say that could turn back time, to undo the wrongs to this portion of God's own family. She wanted to weep. Yet at the same time, she had too much anger, dismay, and frustration to cry.

Phebe asked in a lowered voice, "Is there anything I can do or say to help thee, thy family, thy friends?"

Solomon looked at the ground. He covered his face with his large hands. Bending over, he sobbed silently. His heaving lungs pulsed under Phebe's comforting hand resting on his back. Moments later her own tears came, soundlessly rolling down the rivulets of her wrinkled cheeks.

CHAPTER 5

Home of Stephen Mott and Amy Willis Mott, Cow Neck, New York, April 1775

STEPHEN MOTT TOOK A BREAK from his labor in the field, standing and stretching his back, he looked across the field checking on his daughters. Twelve-year-old Daniel was working alongside him while the eldest daughter, Phebe Anna (who was called Anna) was tending the little ones. At 9, she was advanced enough to play with older children, but she still cherished playing games with young Mary, Jane, and Abigail, who ranged from 7 to 2 years old.

From where he was, Stephen could not tell what the girls were sitting on, but they were facing Anna. They leaned forward attentively as Anna spoke, all the while weaving her fingers in the air, telling artful stories from her own—somewhat odd—little mind. Anna was quick-witted, but she also had a whimsical air and an artless charm. She was never cross and was always kind and generous. He felt the child didn't have a flaw, but her playful spirit frequently vexed Amy, particularly when Anna neglected her chores.

Today Anna's chore was to clear out the garden but true to form she had her sisters spellbound. Stephen did not have the heart to pull her away from the little ones. Anna's face, when the sun's rays were on it like this, lit up her dancing blue eyes like the heavens. When he saw those eyes, all force of will and any thought of admonishing her vanished like smoke. No, today he did not have the heart to pull her away to do chores.

He told himself that her stories were harmless, thinking, "I'll leave her be for now. She can have a moment in the spring sun with her sisters at her feet. Soon enough she will be a woman, with grown up cares." He turned back to his labor.

Stephen's wife Amy had seized this first dry and warm day of the spring to undertake the many spring-cleaning jobs in the house. She bustled about the main room, removing winter's grime and grit, sweeping and scrubbing. In mid-scrub, she suddenly recollected that the quilting bee would come in two days' time, thereby shortening her work week. At that instant she realized she needed her daughters' help, especially since a cousin and a niece who usually lent a hand, were both absent all week. She wiped her hands on her apron, stepped out the door, and called for the girls but heard no response.

She panned the fields looking for her husband. Stephen, a tall man with a broad smile was nearly always jovial. He had an enviable sense of humor, and everyone seemed to like him. It helped that he was generous with his time, easily lending a hand to help anyone out. And though he and Amy had the largest family, Stephen was primarily responsible for the care of his mother's farm. Of Mother Dodge's three children, they lived the closest to her, but Amy felt that in keeping with his nature he would have done it anyway.

After calling several times, she gave up. She could just see the top of Stephen's hat, but he was not responding. She would have to fetch the girls herself. Anxious to finish her work, she fumed inwardly at the interruption as she started off towards the place she believed the girls were working.

"Mama!" cried Mary, the first to see her mother approaching, "Anna is telling us what happens when Jack Frost leaves, how he goes up into the sky and sends down to us all the butterflies."

Mary's beaming face dampened the flame of Amy's irritation, tempering her response. "Thee, Anna, must stop storytelling. Girls, I need thy help. I have much to do and too little time! Come!" She beckoned them.

Anna popped up from her crouch, eager, "Oh, Mama! Thee needs me? Abby, Mary, Jane, we have the best mama!"

She rubbed her hands on her apron, delightfully cheerful. She was not the tidiest child: her hands were muddy and streaked with grass, and Amy noted, red from cold. Grabbing Anna by the shoulders, Amy turned her round. Sure enough, the back of Anna's dress was wet and mud-streaked from the frosty earth where she had been sitting, oblivious to the cold and damp. She wondered where this child had come from, she was so strange.

"Phebe Anna, Mary, and Jane go to the chicken coop. Father put the new boards in place, it needs sweeping and a fresh bed of straw. Take care to get the corners, get all the cobwebs. Abby, here, come." She took the littlest one by the hand.

The three small girls trailed behind her on her return to the yard. While other families kept their chickens indoors for the winter, Amy could not stand the smell. The coop was but a lean-to, used for shelter in the cold.

As she and Abby trudged back to the house, her pique with Anna vanished. She mused on what to do with the child. She was outgrowing childhood. Perhaps it was now time to have Anna come along with her to Elizabeth's for the quilting bee. Aye, Anna should learn to live, to work, and to act like an adult; maybe that would cure her of her outlandish childhood fantasies.

She already had Jemmy, an aunt, coming on the day of the quilting bee to oversee the tasks to be done and to keep an eye on the youngest children. Anna was not needed at home.

Amy took a short detour to the side field, not far from the chicken coop. She could hear the girls inside it; Anna was orchestrating the clean-up. In the side field, Old Banjo Billy was clearing the wet earth.

Banjo Billy and his wife Jinny were trusted slaves. Neither Banjo Billy nor Jinny made a secret of their support for the American rebel cause. Banjo Billy always asked Amy for news about the rebel conflict and somehow always wheedled his way to get Amy to pass along to him what little news she had gleaned. He would first cheer her up with his singing and his jokes till she turned pliable, and willing to divulge the little news she had.

She had a keen sense of empathy for the couple. Now that the "Boston troubles" had traveled throughout all the colonies, would their lives be worse? What would Banjo Billy and Jinny do if the colonies became independent? Guilt crept over her. She was a settled Quaker in her homeland, but for those two, Banjo Billy and Jinny, their future was uncertain.

The couple had come to them by a circuitous route: they were on the land when the owner died. Their owner had no will and the family lived quite a distance away. The couple pleaded with Stephen to allow them to stay and "help out." Stephen eventually agreed to one year, but it had extended itself to several years.

She knew Mother Dodge was on the verge of freeing Rachel in accordance with the New York Yearly Meeting's Resolution. She and Stephen had unfinished business regarding the future of their own slaves. But there was always unfinished business with a large farm and a growing family.

CHAPTER 6

Home of Sarah Willis Mott and Adam Mott, Hempstead, New York, April 1775

BEFORE BREAKFAST SARAH MOTT suddenly remembered she made promises she could not keep. She shook her head, wondering how she could be so scatterbrained. She would need Adam's help.

When Adam entered the house after the morning chores, she approached him, "Oh, husband, I'm in a fix!" she began, "I forgot. I promised to fetch my mother and sisters to Elizabeth's house."

Adam picked up their little son Samuel, "Aye. But thee also promised Elizabeth thee would arrive early. I will fetch thy mother and sisters so thee can leave soon."

Grateful and relieved, Sarah replied, "No need to fetch them home later. Father will when he returns from the City."

Adam raised his eyebrows in question. "Thy father is still making trips to the City?" Samuel Willis was elderly.

"He wanted to. He is exasperated by Feeb's mood these days."

Adam was confused, "Feeb?" He had no idea why Samuel's own daughter would be exasperating.

"She has been difficult ever since that man Francis moved away."

"Why?"

"Oh, Adam!" Sarah saw Adam was lost. "Feeb was smitten, and Francis hurt her. Has thee not seen Feeb's tear-stained face?"

Adam shook his head. In the few minutes he had him, the baby had gotten restless, and Adam gladly relinquished him to his wife's outstretched arms. The baby settled contentedly on his mother's hip, one thumb in his mouth.

"At home she weeps so! Did thee not know that Francis and Feeb were ready to petition the Meeting to be wed? But then suddenly, without a word of explanation, Francis moved to Philadelphia to work in his father's business!"

"Isn't she too young? Feeb must be only 14!"

Amy laughed, "No, husband, thee has lost count! She's a woman already. She'll be 20 next year!"

"How has she gotten to be so old?"

Ignoring this, she continued, "He abandoned Feeb with a mere 'farewell.' And she has not heard from him since. It's been two months—she mopes about all the time. She is an adult by years, but she acts like a child."

"I see why thy father would take off for the City." Her father Samuel was a spry 71-year-old, but a young daughter's long face would be hard to endure.

"My poor Mother: she is at her wit's end! She escapes from Feeb's moods by calling on others as often as she can."

Though he had plenty of chores, Adam was happy to help Elizabeth's family.

"Sarah, thee thinks only of others. Allow me to fetch them." He saw the worry in her eyes, "We shall leave early. As thee said, thy father can fetch them home. Do not worry; we will get the spring work done in suitable time." He smiled at her fondly and gave her a peck on the cheek. Upon seeing this, their baby, still planted on Sarah's hip, let out a hoot of glee and clapped his hands.

* * *

Mary Fry Willis watched Feeb fuss with her new bonnet. It bothered Mary that her daughter's bonnet was less than plain, it was borderline fancy. But Feeb had shown considerable skill in its making, and she did not have the heart to deny her this one pleasure.

Francis' disregard for her daughter had annoyed her but she had since made peace with the fact. Admittedly, she could not put herself in Feeb's shoes, for she had never been thrust away in that manner. Francis' rejection of Feeb cast a shadow over the Willis home. But now she felt the gloom had over-stayed its time; Feeb continually moped about and would frequently break out crying. Though the entire family had been shocked and saddened at the break-up of the couple, they had grown weary of Feeb's fragile emotions.

Keziah, ready in her cloak, stepped outside. As Adam helped her into the conveyance, she informed her brother-in-law that there would be three passengers. Inside the house Mary called out to Feeb. Within minutes the two silently slipped out of the house.

"Oh! I came early, I was certain of a wait." Adam's voice registered his shock at their promptness.

"Not today. These days, we leave the house whenever we can." His mother-in-law sounded vexed.

Adam's sister would still be scurrying around, and they ought not arrive too early. What could fill the extra minutes? The women were waiting to start out and they could not tarry here. They set out, Adam pondering his next move.

As they approached the Prior farm, he had an idea. He brought the wagon to a stop. As he alit, he explained, "I need to ask Edmond Prior a question about something I borrowed. I won't be long." He walked out of sight around the corner of the Prior barn towards the house.

"Mother, why does he have to stop now?" Keziah complained. Feeb heaved a loud sigh, signaling her unhappiness.

Mary shushed her daughters, "Keziah, Adam is losing a goodly amount of time from his work to fetch us there. Let's be grateful."

The women sat in the cold dawn listening to the early morning sounds. When Adam finally returned, he was still conversing with his companion: a fair-complexioned man whose hatless black hair shone in the morning sunlight.

Keziah whispered to Feeb, "Edmond has gotten to be handsome!" She giggled quietly so their mother could not hear.

Feeb was insulted that her sister was ignoring her posture of grief. After all, there was a hole inside her now after Francis had treated her so shabbily. Still, out of habit, Feeb obliged her sister. She studied Edmond as he conversed with Adam. The Priors had always been their neighbor. Though they lived near one another, they rarely saw each other except from afar. She studied him: he was exceedingly fine-looking, and his face had kind lines to it. His voice was melodious, low-toned, and steady.

The men finished their business. Edmond drew near the wagon and greeted the occupants. Adam had no need to introduce his mother, but refreshed Edmond's memory of his sisters-in-law, "Thee recollects my wife's sisters, Keziah and Feeb." The young women greeted him in turn.

Adam climbed back to his perch, they bid Edmond farewell and once again started off for Elizabeth's. But Edmond remained where he was as they left, smiling, and waving to them.

His eyes lingered on the prettiest Willis girl. He wondered, "Might she? No, she was a good Quaker girl." He may have heard she was close to being wed anyway.

But then before they had rounded the final bend, Feeb turned around, smiled, and waved at him once again. Edmond remained rooted where he was long after they had rounded the bend and had disappeared out of sight.

* * *

Mary's husband Samuel remarked to his 23-year-old son Edmund how strangely quiet the house was without the womenfolk. Edmund agreed but his thoughts fixed on his fiancé Abigail, wondering what she would be doing now.

Samuel Willis had spent two days in New York, returning in time for a late lunch. Nearly ten years older than his wife Mary, he still made regular trips across the East River to conduct business. His blue eyes were yet undimmed, but his white hair was thinning. After the shared lunch, Edmund returned to the barn, while Samuel headed toward his chair to read, certain he would fall asleep before he had read two paragraphs.

After Samuel's nap it was nearly time to fetch the women from Elizabeth's. It was a fine day to travel. Samuel was a bit early, and the women were not yet finished. He joined his son John and Adam Mott who were deep in conversation outside the house. As he neared them, he overheard John say that Mother Dodge was "fixing to free her slave."

"Huh, what's that?" Samuel asked.

"Aye, Father," John expanded, "I said Mother Dodge has in mind we shall all set free our slaves too."

Samuel stroked his chin, "Thy mother mentioned something about that. But…that's what we were set to do anyway. Yesterday I was in New York, and I heard tell that an abolition society has been formed by some Philadelphia Friends."

"I must confess. We have not done anything—Elizabeth and I have not even talked about freeing ours!" John Willis felt a bit of shame at being tardy.

Their conversation was cut short by the arrival of the women. When Feeb walked by her father, she greeted him cheerily. Samuel wondered what had happened when he was away. He had raised a few daughters, and there was a reason for such a sudden shift in her mood.

He turned back towards John Willis and Adam Mott, asking quietly, "Adam, what happened this morning? My daughter's cheerful." He looked over at Feeb who was beaming.

Adam had noticed. "I cannot tell. I only know when I picked them up, she was sour, and Keziah said she was weepy at home. That's when we started out. But by the time we arrived at Elizabeth's, she was like this—happy. I thought it strange."

Samuel pursed his lips in thought. He asked Adam, "Did thee stop anywhere before Elizabeth's?"

"Yes," he scratched his chin, "I stopped briefly at Edmond Prior's."

Samuel shuddered; he suspected this was the cause of Feeb's sudden change in mood. He clung to faint hope that he was wrong: Edmond Prior was a fine man, but he was no Friend. He foresaw a bumpy road ahead if Feeb set her cap for him.

CHAPTER 7

Cow Neck, New York, April 1775

Phebe Dodge had returned from the quilting party. Once inside, she collapsed in her chair. She leaned her head back as discouragement washed over her. She had been certain that Elias Hicks would be willing to devote himself to freeing the slaves in Queens County. But she was wrong.

Elias was anxious to be a Weighty Friend. But he turned down her request to be at the forefront in the manumission effort. When asked why he refused, he said he wished to be "mostly a traveling Friend" and he had to "establish" his presence as a Public Friend.

How had she misjudged him? Was he making strategic moves? Should she remind him that Public Friends take public actions? Phebe shook her head. No. She should not force a promise from him. Force was an enemy of love.

Elias had missed a childhood in Hempstead. Born a Friend, he had lived his formative years in Rockaway with relatives after his mother died when he was young. Later, after his father's remarriage, Elias was again on the family farm in Jericho in Hempstead. He was a puzzle. Perhaps Elias was unsure of his place in the Friends Meeting? Was that such a foolish thought? Maybe not.

Phebe removed her cloak and hung it on its peg. She moved to the extra window that Tristam had put in after their marriage. She gazed out the window with unseeing eyes, ruminating. She felt too old for this battle: should she give it up? She wished to let the young, energetic members take it up.

Then she remembered her recent visit from Solomon. She had been at a loss for words then, like she was groping in the dark. It was unknown territory. Solomon's frankness had made her feel miserable.

Now she had mixed feelings over Solomon's visit: she should see his openness as a blessing. He had spoken the plain truth to her. And yet, part of her wished he had not spoken his mind. Now she knew discouraging things she had never thought about. In truth, she was still absorbing his perspective, and still digesting her feelings.

When Rachel came inside to put on the water, she was aware of the worry on Mother's face.

"Not a good day, Mother Dodge?"

Phebe shook her head but remained mute. Rachel gently helped Phebe change into her other dress. Touched by her friend's ministering, Phebe reflected on how good Rachel was to her. She watched as Rachel moved about humming cheerily.

"I need a lie-down before supper," Phebe started towards her bed, but she'd not gotten far before Rachel said, "Willet Seaman stopped by here."

"Was there a message?" Phebe asked.

"Something about a society in New York City. He started to talk about it, but said never mind, he will write you. He said it is having problems now because of the British troubles."

That the Manumission Society of New York was having difficulties was not surprising.

Rachel continued humming as she worked, she felt happy. Only a few days ago when Mother Dodge had asked her to open up, and she had bared her soul: all her worries, from the silly, trivial and the ominous, big ones. In a way, since her confession to Mother Dodge, she had somehow felt her actual manumission had already taken place. Apart from the signing of the document and the change in arrangements, it had taken place in her heart.

Phebe was sitting up in her bed. Her tiny room opened to the great room where Rachel busied herself with the evening's shared supper. It occurred to Phebe that maybe Elias' delay was for the better, for now. There was much to think about and more planning that needed to be done.

Solomon had shaken her world. Although their exchange left her rattled, and his words had been painful, it was the jolt she needed. Solomon's talk had flung open a window in her mind, and as fresh air flows in, new thoughts came to her. Before Solomon's visit she cherished a perceived ideal of liberty, rooted in the Friends' principles.

She believed some people had a need, or a greed for power over people. And one display of this power was slavery. She had noted in her reading that usually histories were about the victors, and not the conquered, never the underlings or slaves. Civilizations serve the powerful. Societies are built for and around the powerful. In New York, the free white man is at the center of all power.

In New York, as in all colonies, the center was held in place by the British laws. Property and ownership laws were key to both keeping and increasing wealth. The circle was closed by the fact that only free white men were eligible to hold positions of authority. But those in authority were also the only ones with power to create laws about property, leadership, and ownership. These eligibility restrictions meant that power was well-guarded. There was no threat to power dissipating from the circle. Moreover, this power would not fade: successive generations were heirs to the same laws.

As long as this circle of power remained closed, the negroes would never gain true equality. The thought ate at her, for this trial was not limited to negroes but extended to most people—to white women, indentured servants, even to anyone on the edges of society. A thorny issue.

Her thoughts drifted to the personal: she had picked up an undercurrent in Solomon's speech, he did not state it, and perhaps did not realize it existed. He wished to be respected. Both the laws and the attitudes towards negroes would have to be reversed before he got that. As it was now, negroes had no authority, little influence on their destiny, and were given no respect.

The feeling of being respected was a product of freely exercising one's God-given talents. The slaves needed not just freedom. They had to be able to choose what they would do, and to be given the opportunity to prove themselves. People flourish when they can make their own choices, but the colony had to give them the means and the space to do so.

Both Rachel and Solomon had schooled her in their situations, thoughts and wishes. She felt utterly challeneged. Manumission was noble, but in practice it would be more complex than she had believed. To start with, the particulars of each slave's situation ought to be accounted for.

Taken together, slaves had one common experience—that of being enslaved. Apart from that, generalizing their situations and their desires was flawed. While they ought to be freed, this fact was not consent nor permission for carelessness, hastiness, nor callous manumission by their "owners." Their present "owners" ought to avoid the trap of believing they had authority in ascertaining their former slaves' future.

Rachel had just returned from hanging out the clothes. Still humming, she neatened the baskets near the door.

"Rachel," Phebe needed another mind to help her think about this.

"Elias shan't help me now." She paused but Rachel made no comment, so she continued, "I recently learned three stories, and three opinions about manumission—thine, Solomon's and Azuba's—and all three stories are very different."

"But your Meeting will help?" Rachel said quickly. Phebe sensed the fear in Rachel's question.

Phebe's response was slow and deliberate, "Our meeting, like any group of people, is useful because they can get a lot done. But taken together, it has no understanding of the degrees of differences between people. The Resolution was a general intent for all of New York. But in practice, we do not have special insight into the desires and needs of each slave who will be freed, whatever our good intentions may be."

Rachel did not respond but smiled agreeably. Phebe shook her head; Rachel did not comprehend the weight of her question. She rephrased her question. "If thee was the mistress, or master, how would thee instruct thy friends to free their slaves?"

"A slave doesn't have much choice, but to be free if they are told to." Rachel said wryly.

Glancing at Mother Dodge's expression, she saw her attempt to cheer up Mother Dodge had failed.

Phebe persisted, "But we Friends want freed slaves to be happy in their freedom."

Rachel moved to the kettle-pot over the fire, stirring the contents. She responded thoughtfully, "Then they should follow what you did: Have them first set down with the slave and ask questions, and lots of them."

As Phebe rested, she felt her resolve return. Rachel's simple advice was absolutely right. She still wished for help. Maybe Elias was but delaying his help, and he would someday assist her. She would have to draw on a wider circle for help: her large family, as well as dozens of friends.

Long ago in her youth, Friends were thought dangerous or foolish. But that had changed in her lifetime. But what of negroes? Life had worsened for them. Why? Because they were stamped with an invisible brand. Once they were on the ship bound for the Americas, they ceased to be human, and were from then on, an object, a commodity for trade in a market. The mark? the cast of their skin. The thought sickened her.

CHAPTER 8

Flushing, New York, Easter, 1775

Easter Sunday fell in mid-April. Rachel took the Sunday meal with Solomon and his wife Azuba. It rained, but it passed before the meal was over. Azuba would not hear of Rachel helping with the chores but put the older children to work while the younger ones dashed outside where they splashed one another with puddles from the rain. Solomon wiped the dampness off a bench for her and Rachel eased herself on to it.

Rachel gazed out over the field sloping down to the water's edge. The field shimmered with a brilliance found only in the new-born green of spring. Puffy clouds floated as great ships on the horizon, passing on soundlessly. Once they passed, the sky gave up a golden sunset but shot through with pink rays. She said something about it to Solomon, who was leaning against the door jam, broodily picking his teeth. Her words stirred him from his reverie.

He responded mechanically to his mother's questions. She had taken out her handiwork and begun to work on it as she chatted. But soon it was impossible to ignore his mood. She paused and addressed him, impatience in her voice, "Solomon, the rain has stopped, and it's turned into a beautiful afternoon, yet here you are brooding."

Solomon looked his mother all over: neat and tidy. Was that a trait she had picked up in a lifetime of working for and living with Quakers?

Solomon took a deep breath and said, "Ma, why do you pay no mind to the times and dangers all about us." His tone was sharp.

"What do you mean?"

Solomon shook his head as to himself; a gesture Rachel recognized as one of disgust at her ignorance or her misunderstanding him.

"Speak your mind, son. Don't leave me to puzzle it out."

"Ma, I'm going to take the offer, the one the lords have made for us."

His mother's head whipped up, "What offer is that?" Though she knew, she had to hear him say it before she would believe it.

Instead of answering her question, Solomon turned and asked her directly, "What do you think of the rebellion?"

Rachel looked down at her handiwork. She had not really thought about it enough to respond, and she believed Solomon knew that of her. Naturally, every white person on the island talked about it, but her own circle hardly mentioned it. Her friends were negro slaves of a certain age and had not the privilege of choice, and most had formed no opinions because they had no voice in situations of this kind.

White women were disallowed some legal privileges, but they had choices aplenty. More than any negro slave woman. She had never had the power to choose. What happened, happened. Her world was planned by others and run by others.

That is, until lately. She was starting to believe that her state as a slave was about to change. But she had not given it much thought. Maybe she had learned to be satisfied with decisions other people made for her. Or, perhaps unlike Azuba, she had been gifted with more and had found contentment in that. Solomon was hinting that she was of a lazy mind.

From childhood she had accepted whatever her overseers told her, as her mother had. After all, it *was* easier—if her overseers were wrong, it was not her fault. In this respect, her adulthood had a childish hue to it. But Rachel had been blessed: she had had kind masters. Still, she had little experience in thinking about her direction. It had always been set, there was no reason to pay heed.

But since the conversation and her decision with Mother Dodge, she was about to enter an entirely new life. She would be in charge, be responsible. She was both excited and deeply terrified at the thought that she would soon be her own master.

She heard Solomon cough. He had asked her a question and he was still awaiting her answer.

"I'm not sure how thinking about it would change much, Solomon."

Solomon wheeled around, his tongue loosened, "It is something I have given much thought to. Did you know that Lord Dunmore of Virginia Colony said any negro who will fight with the British will be freed and be full British subjects after the British win the war?"

Rachel started; her son spoke as if the war was already going on. "And this pledge to slaves is something you, my son, believe?" she asked, fearing she knew his answer.

"Aye," Solomon's chin raised, "I'd rather be a freed man under the orderly conduct of good British rule than a negro under the rebels. The only thing the colonists do well is fight one another."

"What do you mean fight one another?"

Solomon laughed, "Ma, you're kept from the news! Connecticut is fighting with Pennsylvania over a piece of land. New York and New England cannot agree on the border."

Rachel shrugged, "Oh, yes. But do you take the English as more peaceful? I remember the wars with the French and the Indians, with the Spanish, and everyone who they could not remove or buy out." Solomon looked unmoved.

"And" she continued, "what about the people who fled Ireland and Scotland? They fled their homes because of the harm of British rule."

"But the British have the best regulars in the world. And what have the rebel militias got but a few stump-jumpers and some addle-headed city boys? Besides," he added, "this is the best offer."

He was unable to shield his eagerness as he continued, "Some mornings I lie abed, and think of that day that I will be my own man, and the only niggering corn will be for us, and no one else."

Rachel flinched inwardly, though everyone called it 'niggering' corn, still, she hated the word. It expressed the habit of mind that slavery and negroes were one and the same. It dawned on her that this was a belief that was probably truer than she wanted it to be.

Solomon added, "Think of that, Ma! You can be proud of me; I will be my own man!" He touched his chest for emphasis.

He wanted her to say how it pleased her, and how proud she was of him, yet she was filled with sadness and the words stuck in her throat. Something told her that the British had not a chance of winning, but every rebel American would die first. This nation was their own child, and they had claimed it by fighting. They may be poor, few and untrained, but they were tied to this land. The British throne must have made some foolish demands; they would have been wiser to make peace with the American colonies.

"Who is this Dunmore?"

"He's governor of Virginia Colony and a Lord!"

"How sure is this? Maybe this is a half-formed thought, idle chatter overheard by house slaves and a rumor that you heard?" Deep down she feared for her son.

He shook his head, "No. I hear he's going to put it on paper. A promise. But, of course, I must flee to Virginia first." He laughed bitterly, never having pictured himself escaping to the south.

His mother pushed on, urgent, "But, Solomon, think: you know full well that the British come and go as they will. Because what is this place–these colonies—to them?" her voice was rising, animated,

"Naught but a mistress, one they can take and live with or not, as they wish. You may be right about the British lord. But I believe you're wrong about the American rebels, the rebel passion is strong.

"What you miss— what you do not see, is their strength, their passion. Have you forgotten that these men were trained by the British, and armed by the British for so long? If it comes to a war, the rebels will protect their own. And they will keep it up even after the King's attention wanders, or when his parliament complains about the costs of the war. Boston was a lesson: the rebels are mule-headed."

Solomon shook his head, disagreeing, "No, the British will crush the Americans like a bug. No one will be left but women, children, and slaves. Perhaps then we slaves will be counted as traitors like the rest?"

Solomon had a point. She never allowed herself to think the British would count a slave as a traitor. That a black woman might be counted a traitor? Was it possible?

Solomon looked directly at her, "Ma, Mother Dodge is set to free you next year. You told me the plans you've made: about the house being yours, your freedom to take work or refuse it, and the freedom to go where you want. Look around you! Open your eyes! If the British win a war, you *will* be a traitor.

"But if it happens that Americans win the war, they will look to re-enslave you. On Long Island, we negroes are so many! Maybe a quarter of all the people? Do you think the American rebels, if they win, would let us stay free?" he shook his head.

Rachel sensed something else was troubling her son. "This is not only about the war, but something else. What is it?"

Solomon shook his head. He exhaled loudly, "To the Americans, we are blockheads, helpless and weak negroes. We, or at least I, want to be a New Yorker, but in every way. But will I be one? Nay, never.

"I met a man at the docks last week. He told me in Britain negroes live as others do. In the colonies, how lucky are we if we must live always looking over a shoulder waiting for some rogue venturer to swoop down, grab us and declare that we are their property?"

It was true: it happened regularly in the City of New York, and even sometimes in the countryside.

"I will do everything I can to make sure my family are freed people. And the best chance for my family to have a life of freedom and peace is if the British win and make this place more like Britain."

Solomon's expression darkened, "This country was born in violence, guns, and chains. And American sea trade? It's not just rum and tobacco, but our own people, bought and sold, as if store goods! No," His voice had a tremor. "Worse! Abused! Our masters treat their animals better than they treat us. They don't trust us and never have, and they never will!" Solomon spat to punctuate his disgust.

Rachel felt she had taken a punch in the stomach; her breath was rapid and shallow. Her son's explosive anger took her by surprise, and her first impulse was to slap his face. She was deeply hurt by his words because he had obliquely attacked the families who had treated her so well. Although his judgement of white people was mostly accurate, his statement put the Mott, Dodge, Willis families, and all the people who had helped her and loved her, on the same list, branding them as the same.

There were scoundrels, bad masters, and blackbirders: the worst kind of people. The Quakers had been fair and loving to her and to her family. When Solomon was a youth, they often treated him better than their own boys. Besides, no one was immune from the pressures of their own kind; sometimes you had to mend your ways, which was what Mother Dodge was doing now.

But Solomon's rage was red-hot, and she had to hold her tongue, to check herself from lashing out at him. Rachel's late mother had had strong views about their own people—a belief handed down to her from her grandmother. She had said they were a "cursed" people, which is how they ended up as slaves in another land. The story was fanciful nonsense.

She tried to put herself in Solomon's situation: he was married to a fine wife. But Azuba had grown up in the poisoned ground of the City of New York. Azuba's viewpoint was formed in that place, not the surroundings Cow Neck offered. She saw things differently from Rachel and Solomon, and she was outspoken about it. Azuba made it clear she had no use for anyone but their own people. She despised Indians, calling them sneaky, cutthroat thieves and liars, and she had no use for the English or the Dutch either.

The City was a place apart from the rest of the Colony. To Rachel, it was a foreign country compared to the kind, generous folk in Queens County, and Quakers in particular. Sadly, Azuba and her mother had been treated with beastly cruelty by their masters in New York. Azuba's life was a truer representation of the life of a slave than Rachel's.

In the wake of her impatience and ire, a wave of sympathy washed over her. She understood the cause of Solomon's opinion. At that moment she knew there was no use in reasoning with Solomon. She did not agree with him, but now she saw why he felt he needed to act.

"Son, what will this mean for your family?"

"Ma, I thought it through. If Britain wins the war, we will all be better."

"And if the Americans win?"

Solomon shrugged, "In that case, Britain has all that land in the north in Canada that they need settled."

She had heard of Canada. It was far away, and it was cold. She would probably never see the family in that case. That troubled her.

"You are right. You must think of your family. Solomon, what will happen to your family if you do not return?" She asked, doubt and sadness mixed together.

"I did not ask your permission." He had not answered her question. "We do not need your help, only your prayers."

"You always have my prayers. We are bound together even if we are not of the same mind on this."

"How will you fare while I am away?"

"I will be taken care of. My situation is different. You are a man—I am a woman, and I will always be a widow woman, whether slave or free. Even when I am freed, I will still be without the rights that a man would enjoy. Either way, I accept that people, whether they be cruel or merely hard-hearted, will still treat me as a slave, but I won't allow their foolishness to ruin my happiness."

Solomon must have been satisfied with her answer for he was silent. Their conversation was over, and Rachel had done little handiwork. Since she would do no further handiwork, she stowed it.

"I worry that King George shall not be kind towards any colonials, no matter their color or allegiance. And so, we shall all be his enemies." She felt but did not say that the British would not hesitate to break a promise if it suited. After all, what kind of standing did a white commoner have?

Solomon shook his head, "Ma, who do you heed about this, if not your own flesh and blood?" He looked away, then turned back, "Are you listening to that madman Banjo Billy?" he asked, referring to Stephen Mott's slave, "He opposes the British, and yet he's all about the Mott household. Probably has infected your homestead too."

Rachel shook her head. She knew Banjo Billy and Jinny's opinions: they made no secret of them.

"Can you even be certain you will be freed?" Solomon frowned at her.

But when Rachel started to explain her conversation with Mother Dodge, Solomon cut her off. "What if things worsen so fast that you remain a slave? Have you any idea how terrible things are? The colonial leaders argue and bicker. They will never get along. It's not possible for them.

"What if it all breaks down and all their promises come apart? In that case, no slave will have his freedom. Don't you think that the greater portion of work will be on the backs of slaves?"

He pushed on, Rachel catching disdain in his voice. "You have this dream that they will see us as equals. But look at us! Not one of us has schooling, or a trade, or owns a business! We do not own land yet work on the land. Why, from the start we were carrying the whole society on our backs! There was nothing shared, only taken!"

For the second time Solomon spat on the ground in disgust. Rachel stood up, rattled at his vehemence, "Solomon! We cannot return to the past! Our forbearers were in Africa, but we have been with the Europeans for generations, we are no longer African."

Solomon's voice rose. "What we are makes no matter here! I am sick of being taken from!" He held up a hand, "And do not say they shall school us to make us like them. It's far, far too late for those measures."

His voice was so loud that the children stopped their games, and Azuba came to the door of the home. Rachel stood up to leave.

The sun was setting when she reached her doorstep. She loved her tiny home. As many months of the year as were warm enough, she slept in it. It was humble, clean, and tidy—and hers. After a quick bite of cold dinner, she readied for bed.

Her mind went back to the debate with Solomon. She searched in the conversation for one comforting thought but found none. Her sole consolation was that at least Solomon had entrusted her with his thoughts. In truth, they were both right, but they were at odds on what to do about it.

CHAPTER 9

Cow Neck, New York, April 1775

ADAM AND STEPHEN were at their mother's to put in the spring planting. They looked forward to this task as it gave them time to visit.

"Perhaps now that I've brought along another hand, we shall have the work halved," Adam waved his hand in the direction of his son "Little Adam," who was making good use of his young muscle at the other end of the plot.

Stephen saw no one nearby and believed it safe to speak to his brother openly. Though his nephew Adam would turn 13 this year, he preferred not to speak of war around him.

"What's thy news?" asked Stephen. Adam lived in the heart of the island and was a reliable source of news.

Before responding Adam stood erect and stretched out his back and arms, in doing so, he looked around. If he was sharing news, he did not wish for anyone to overhear.

Not seeing a soul, cautious Adam resumed working and in lowered tones he spoke to Stephen, "The 2nd Provincial Congress sent 'round a demand that delegates from every town in the Colony be sent to the City of New York. But the Friends in Hempstead Town dug in and refused, of course. To our minds sending a delegate would show support of war and conflict."

The Friends' position was one of peace. And since Hempstead property owners was largely made up of Friends, the Town's position in these cases mirrored the Friends' principles.

Stephen added what he knew, "And Jamaica Town came out not to send delegates to the provincial convention. Was it not on the Fourth-Day, last?"

"Aye. But," Adam grunted as he turned a patch of sod at the end of the harrow, "that is not the end of the story.

"After it turned down the demand for delegates, the Town passed a resolution against it, reasoning that the demand was illegal. They claimed it would make the town ripe for mobs and for riots."

Stephen raised his eyebrows in surprise. That the Town of Hempstead would pass a resolution against the Provincial Congress was bold.

"After that the Town sent messengers—Thomas Hicks and Joseph French—to the Provincial Congress to tell them that there would be no delegates coming from Hempstead."

"Why?"

"I understand they were sent there 'as a statement of the Friends' disagreement with war.' But when they arrived, neither man was given a chance to state the position of peace. They were instead received as 'official delegates' from Hempstead."

"No!" Stephen cried. It was like a boyhood prank. He saw the ironic humor in it, but he stifled his laugh.

"Aye, Friend Hicks insisted Hempstead was not attending. Both men protested vigorously but the Provincial Congress closed their ears to their protests. And now their names are recorded as delegates to the Congress from Hempstead."

Stephen shook his head; the story was so incredible he forgot to work.

"Congress claimed since Hicks and French had been sent from Hempstead, they represented Hempstead. Not only that, but the secretary wrote it out in bold hand. Decisions made in Provincial Congress hold true not only for Hempstead, but for all of Queens County."

Despite the gravity of the matter, Stephen could not contain himself. He let out a chuckle, "I can just see Thomas' face! He must have been furious!"

Adam grinned at Stephen, till now he had not seen the humor in the event. But leave it to Stephen to see the twist in the situation even as he absorbed the gravity of it.

"He was outraged. And especially because now Hempstead is the laughingstock of Congress."

"Ah, Adam, but we Friends are used to ridicule," Stephen objected.

"That's the sum of my news. But they are not done with their meetings. After what happened in Massachusetts colony in the 4th month, the Congress is resolved to continue, so I hear." Adam looked down at the newly broken sod, shaking his head, "We should have gotten Mother's garden started weeks ago."

"Thee says that every year." If Stephen could keep Adam talking, his brother would not complain about the work.

Little Adam had neared the two adults. The trio worked along in silence. When the sun started to burn, Adam sent his son along to fetch a drink for them. When the boy was gone, he seized the moment for his brother's advice.

"How are we to endure this? Both the Provincial Congress and the British are calling us from home and hearth, forcing us to ally with a side. And, we are," he lowered his voice, "always watched, always judged by our neighbors."

Stephen shook his head, "Thee worries too much. Of the two of us, I have the larger family. But, with God's help, it shall be well."

After a brief pause, he added, "Mother asked us, you, me, Elizabeth, to help her in urging all families to free their slaves. She is fixed on the idea that all the slaves held by Friends in Queens County be soon freed."

Unsurprised, Adam asked, "Tell me if it be true: Mother is finally going to free Rachel."

"Yes, tis true! Only this time Mother is working with Rachel to give her the dignity of work first. It will take some time."

"How long?"

"I think she said next spring." He added, "She's not satisfied with simply freeing slaves, says it's not enough. She quotes the proverb, 'make not small plans, they stir not up the fancy.'"

Adam chuckled to himself, that was in character, their mother always dreamt big.

Stephen continued, "Freedom is a start, but only a start. She is studying the problems that slavery made and covered over, those that fix the negro forever in a position lower than any of us.

"Think on it, how can they support themselves apart from being servants and laborers? The force and the habit of people in the colony would say that that is their proper position. I agree with Mother: they should have a trade or skill, and even be schooled."

Adam's brow furrowed. He thought about schooling negroes and wondered how many freed men in Queens County could not read and write.

"But not only that. She's also concerned for their happiness—how can they be happy if they are separated from family? It's not enough to be contrite about holding slaves." He struck the ground with his hoe accentuating his point. "We cannot undo the past. But she holds that if we listen closely to the slaves and find out what they wish to do, it opens the possibility of giving them a place in society. If we remain British colonies, perchance they will be better off." He addressed Adam's unasked question, "But if we become independent, we ought to be prepared. In that case, who knows what the new governor will wish to do?"

His brother jumped in, "Surely in a new independent province, slavery would not be legal?"

Stephen shrugged, "Who can know what is to come? No matter, Mother said we should give all we have to repairing what is, as she says, 'the irreparable harm caused by the act of enslavement, which debases the human soul.'"

Little Adam was nowhere in sight. Adam asked in a whisper, "What is thy feeling on the colonies?" This was Quaker-talk for the American rebellion.

Stephen continued working steadily, "Thee knows up here on Cow Neck, most support it. If thee is asking whether the rebels shall succeed, I think not. But I reckon New York is a natural spot for a conflict—the port is as pleasing as it is practical to the British."

He added, "Right now, I am a listener, that is all." Adam understood that to mean his brother would not report his neighbors to the British officials.

Adam feared the future. He detested the strange goings-on. Had the world come down with a disease? Everything felt out of control. He gave voice to his feelings of helplessness, "We were living a quiet and peaceable life. Until certain men decided to reverse it all. Now it's mayhem!"

His brother responded with a thoughtful, "Hmm. Does thee presume that the Friends are without responsibility in this chaos?"

Adam was bewildered. He asked, "What's that? I don't get thy meaning."

"What I mean, is that we Friends have, at least in part, contributed to this."

Adam shook his head, still mystified.

His brother elaborated, "Look at how we have always lived. We refuse to use titles when we address those who demand it. We treat our slaves—though they are slaves—like our equals. Not only that, but our women are free to travel and to preach.

"We are justified in disregarding these conventions because we understand that there is no race nor sex in the eyes of God. But, in

England, the same men who we Friends will not bow to, are granted special privileges and the highest status from the King.

"Now judge thee: what do our actions say to our neighbors when we will not doff a hat, nor bow to the lords?"

Adam's eyes widened as he recognized the truth of what was said, "Thee has given a good amount of consideration to this."

"Yes. I have given thought to the roots and sources of our time. We Friends complain yet. I wonder if we ourselves have helped to make these strange times."

Adam was thoughtful. Stephen had spoken truthfully about Friends and their behavior, but was his interpretation right? Had his own people sown the seeds of equality, which was now widely spoken of all about?

The Friends had always declared society ought to be level. Had the behaviors and principles of the Friends unintentionally stoked the fire of this conflict?

* * *

Spring's arrival multiplied the volume and pace of work on Phebe's lot. And although she did not work in the fields as she once had, she did a fair share of the work. She and Rachel did most of the clean-up outside and around the house and outbuildings. They also took up the spring-cleaning indoors.

This year's labor felt different, less tedious. With Rachel's eventual manumission in view, their time working side-by-side was ideal, because as they worked, they discussed plans for Rachel's business. Out of their conversations they recognized Rachel had a need to learn the basics of business. This prompted Phebe to find a Friend in Meeting to give Rachel guidance.

Learning about business fueled Rachel's curiosity. She asked Phebe to help her improve her other skills. Every evening Rachel eagerly applied her mind to improving her reading and writing. She was an apt student and always eager to show anyone what she had learned in Phebe's lessons.

In quiet moments Rachel would read aloud to Phebe, continuing long after Phebe fell asleep. Rachel was determined and dedicated to the new venture. When the chores were done for the day, if she was not studying, Rachel did needlework. She strove with the vigor that comes with ownership.

When Mary arrived for her weekly call, the women took their usual places. Phebe noted that Mary's hands fairly flew across her mending. Her friend's pace of work suggested Mary was carrying an unspoken burden.

"Mary, what is thy news?"

"Thee does know about the goings-on in Massachusetts?" Phebe had heard only some whispered conversations at the Meeting House. She shook her head.

Mary fairly burst out, "Phebe! The talk is that war has started."

Phebe stopped her work, looking up in shock.

"A week ago, the British regulars, angered by colonists in Massachusetts who were storing up munitions, marched on several villages. But the Americans found out and sent men out to the towns round about to warn people." Phebe listened, transfixed. "They roused enough militia to face the British."

"With guns?" Phebe asked.

"Aye, guns!" Mary continued, "That old fox, I mean, General Gage was already moving against the rebels, first out to a village called Lexington, and then on to Concord."

"To what purpose?" asked Phebe.

Mary shrugged, guessing, "To shut down the American cause. I suppose taking guns and munitions is all part of that."

If true, and Phebe had a sense of the American's attachment to his gun, she thought it a foolish move by the British. It would only provoke the American "rebels."

Mary finished her story, "Now all the colonies are alarmed. People in New York are saying it's going to spill out all over Long Island."

Their conversation turned to the freeing of slaves: when it would be best to free a slave: before the start of the war, or after? They agreed that before was better. They talked over ideas on how to prepare a slave ahead of time. When Phebe showed her Rachel's needlework, Mary was astonished by the skill.

"Does thee not fear that her own people will feel she is too fine for them?" Mary asked.

"I never thought of that! I hope not."

Mary asked Phebe about progress in the business.

"I've been working to get her handiwork passed around New York. Some has been sent to a friend of mine in New York City."

"Would Rachel wish to move there? She could."

Phebe shook her head. "I asked her. She insisted on remaining here for now." She felt pleasure, she felt it a tribute.

"…It was so bad that most of thy neighbors stormed out—but not till they made their opinions known, in yelling and in cursing!"

With a start Phebe realized her mind had drifted. Mary had not noticed but was still talking,

"Where was this?"

"At the latest Hempstead Town meeting. They never did finish what they began. Now they're going to hold another meeting, and I fear it will be worse than the last. These two groups: those of Hempstead Plains, and those from Cow Neck and nearby villages are split over the war.

"I must warn thee, that" she lowered her voice to a whisper, "many of thy own neighbors here on Cow Neck support the rebel cause. They boasted of it at the Town meeting."

Phebe knew of her neighbors' sympathies. She had witnessed the frequent visits between Martin Schenck and Thomas Dodge, and in the past week, there had been animated talking in the doorway at

Thomas' house. Phebe carefully folded the mended clothes, turned, and picked up her knitting. She felt sure her neighbors, the Schencks, and others had been at the Hempstead Town meeting voicing their views. She knew of the false rumor that the Friends had secretly sided with the British.

Mary said, "And I asked her about him, but she said no—she doesn't have any desire to marry him."

Once again Phebe had been daydreaming. Mary was on a new subject, and she had no idea who Mary was speaking about.

Mary continued, "Everyone—or nearly everyone in Meeting has advised me to tell her who to marry. As thee knows, I do not set up marriages for my children. Am I wrong?"

"So, no one has caught her eye yet?" Phebe was relieved that she did not need to admit to her absentmindedness: she was sure Mary was talking about Feeb.

"As I said, Francis had her eye, but now he's gone to Philadelphia, and he'll not be back. Thomas Butler fancies her, but she's cool towards him." Mary paused.

"Still," she leaned towards her friend, "I do fear Edmond Prior has got her attention now." Mary's eyes were large with apprehension, "It scares me, because he is not a Friend."

CHAPTER 10

May and June 1775

THE CAVE SUITED the three Wanderers. There were not many caves on the north-side of the island which were unused. And this cave was the best on the island, or so they boasted to one another. Big Jack, Amos, and Squirt considered this cave their "home." It was home if only because they were at rest here, a rest not found elsewhere. Years ago, when Big Jack was in a cheerful mood (thanks to a full stomach and plenty of spirits) he had dubbed it the "Lords Meeting House."

No one could remember exactly how and when the Wanderers drifted together. Amos and Squirt had known one another before they knew Big Jack. The two men had come together because they were not acceptable to society. Once Big Jack appeared, he was readily accepted for he too was an outsider. Over time they had formed an equitable, if tiny, society. And this gave each man a sense of comfort, one they carried as they went their separate ways, sometimes for months at a time.

The sun had been up for a while. Squirt had long since risen and had gotten a fire started: he liked fires. Big Jack was nowhere to be seen. Big Jack might be with a lady (Big Jack insisted all his women were ladies) or he might be off on one of his long streaks away. Big

Jack was prone to leaving when he had the "mulligrubs." When he was down, it was better for everyone if he stayed away. When Big Jack returned from being away, his mood was sunny, and he would praise the other two for nearly anything, and loudly bless God.

Squirt heard Amos coming towards him. Amos was usually up first, and always acquired the morning's food. He often returned with eggs. Since it was June, it was still too early for much fruit. But there would be some early flowering food to scavenge, and, of course, tender dandelion greens (if he had the patience). Perhaps he might get some strawberries today. Whose strawberry patch was the finest in Cow Neck? Squirt felt sure he would bring back stolen dried venison, but that would be better than an empty stomach.

Amos sauntered in and squatted on a log.

"Morning," he greeted Squirt, offering him dried venison. They ate in silence. After Amos had finished, he stood and stretched. He suddenly broke off stretching as if something had occurred to him.

"Squirt," he said. Amos turned and disappeared into the well of the cave, when he returned, he was holding a package. "Quaker Lady Phebe, she seen me yesterday, seeing it was Sunday. Give me this."

With his good eye Squirt looked at Amos. Amos did not pay attention to his clothes or hair, and he had odd tics. Amos was also afraid of a lot of things. And he, like Big Jack, did not like people telling him what to do. He would withdraw, a turtle in a shell, when he came across new people. But he trusted most Quakers.

Squirt indicated that Amos should open the package. Amos produced three simple light undyed tunics, and three vests, of leather.

"Lookie here!" Amos crowed, then coughed.

"'Tis almost like she knew we needed them," Squirt marveled. His blouse was torn and even he could see it was stained.

Amos crowed, "Ha! Quaker Lady, her type looks after everyone." His shoulders slumped with a suddenness signifying his change of mood.

Amos turned his sad eyes on his friend, "Squirt. What are we going to do once she keels over? I ask ye?"

Squirt was alarmed, "She is dying, is she!?"

Amos' head snapped up, "Course not! But she will soon, seeing she outlived her two husbands, ye know."

Squirt felt both relief and impatience: relieved Phebe was still well, but aware that he had to put up with Amos' superstitions. Amos believed she would remarry a third husband and then die. Amos' superstitions were tightly held and always wrong.

Squirt objected, "Quaker Lady's about 75. She is not fixing to marry anybody."

Amos shook his head defensively and quoted a superstitious proverb, "A widow twice would be a widow thrice."

"She has been widowed for a long time now. She is not going to marry again!"

Amos shrugged and tossed one of the shirts to Squirt. He coughed and wheezed from the exertion. To 'cure' himself, Amos took tobacco.

They heard Big Jack's whistle from afar. Big Jack entered the cave. In his youth he had been large and raw-boned. In his prime women had praised his good looks and he always bested men in fights. The echoes of those days stayed alive in his mind and though his form was no longer the same, he kept faith that he was still the handsome vigorous man of 18. Indeed, there was some charm in the man.

He was marked by age, and personal neglect. His eyes used to be engaging, but now he looked wild-eyed. His unruly hair was long and unkempt, and his wide mouth was now gap-toothed. Although his mind was sharp, he was growing duller. He walked with a slight limp. He would have terrible fits of rage, but he could not recollect having them. But he could read, and sign his name, which was more than the other two could.

Big Jack had spent a night out. Squirt noticed he had a sack full of plunder. He secretly hoped he would share it. If not, Squirt knew he would still get by. Squirt never squabbled over possessions: they all rot, go missing or break anyway.

Big Jack placed his sack on the floor of the cave and grabbed what was left of the venison. He did not talk or look up till he had finished all the meat. He left the cave to relieve himself. When he returned, he sat down, signaling that he was ready to engage with the other two.

For no apparent reason Amos blurted out, "Strawberry season's coming."

Big Jack nodded, then belched. He turned his attention to his sack. From it he pulled a few good scraps of pilfered goods, some from ships, some from farms, and some were "found."

Despite his size, Big Jack was light-fingered and swift. People were easily distracted by his bulk and his gregarious charm. Before they knew it, Big Jack pocketed an article when they were not paying attention, but it was always something they would not notice till he was long gone.

Amos and Squirt praised Big Jack over the items he had carried back. Typically, then, feeling suddenly generous, he would pivot, asking the other two what they fancied from his haul. He reserved the right to keep what he wanted but he was always generous. After dividing Big Jack's plunder, the trio enjoyed companionable conversation for a spell when Amos suddenly recalled the package from Mother Dodge.

"Look," he said. "Quaker Lady Dodge gave this to me yesterday saying to share with ye."

Big Jack stood up, took the tunic and vest, and started to blubber. Then he wailed, tears streaming down his face. The other men, used to Big Jack's ups and downs, simply waited.

When Big Jack spoke it was nearly incomprehensible because of his sobs, "don't deserve… kind… never did nothing but good… a mercy…"

Big Jack's tears slowed, and the sobbing ceased. He stood in place, stroking the new clothes, as a mother would a newborn.

Squirt said, "Quaker Lady, she is always on our side, right, boys?"

The others agreed. Squirt added, "She made them let us stay here." The memory of the Quaker widow standing up to the townspeople warmed their hearts. "I heard tell—and I believe this—she stood up to her last husband." They smiled at the thought.

Amos added, "We are like her sons."

His comment set Big Jack off on a crying spell once again. Again, the other two had to wait till Big Jack calmed down. While they waited Amos dug around for some dry tobacco and Squirt examined Big Jack's new-found booty more closely.

When Big Jack's sobbing abated, Amos changed the topic, "Any news?" Amos was eager for the latest gossip, for there was always plenty.

Big Jack slapped his head. "Aye! There's this new government set up—what do they call it? 2nd Continental Congress—second cause the first quit." He paused to think, "And just last week a fella from Virginny—I remember him from the Indian wars, called Washington, is the head of the Army.

"And there was a big battle with the British outside of Boston." He paused, and muttered, "I forgot where."

His voice trailed off as he sat thinking, startling the other two when he leapt up, getting their attention, "You know what this means?"

"What?" enquired Squirt.

"We can be free! If we get out from under the British pigs." Big Jack always called the British "pigs."

"And, we can join the army!" Big Jack beamed. "We're young enough, and healthy. They need all the men they can get, and we will get paid money from the Colonial Assembly."

"Paid in what?" asked Amos, who asserted money was "of the devil." He did not use money of any kind, not British, not French, not even Spanish. He preferred bartering.

"I don't know." Big Jack scowled. He did not want his good news soured by questions.

Amos stroked his chin. "Talk about the 'terms'—what'll I get?"

Squirt listened but kept to himself. He knew he was not well enough to be in the militia, nor were the other two. Through the years Big Jack had forgotten he was not well in the head and had tried to join in with regular society. Then something would happen, and he would end up back with the other two. Squirt had stopped reminding the other two of their conditions for they paid him no mind.

Today Big Jack talked a blue streak; he had a large vocabulary and could speak persuasively. He worked hard at convincing Amos that service in the United Colonies was for them. He painted a vivid and detailed picture of the life they would live as gentleman officers. And, then after the war, he detailed the glory the Long Islanders would ascribe to them for their having given their all.

Big Jack and Amos agreed the Continental Army would be lucky to have them. Squirt wondered how long this fascination with the military would last. Not one of them was suitable for the army.

* * *

Elias Hicks' wife Jemima closed her grandmother's cupboard. It had been in the house that her parents, Jonathan and Elizabeth Seaman, had given them. When her father was ailing, her parents had moved to a smaller one nearby.

Jemima heard Rachel was starting a business and was also being schooled; Rachel would be truly freed when she was finally manumitted. Jemima was captivated by the perfection and the logic of Rachel's situation. It was obvious to Jemima unless they went beyond simply manumitting their slaves, it could be an unfruitful exercise. In a way, it seemed morally wrong if they stopped at simply freeing their slaves.

Though their own slave Ben was not yet freed, she had started thinking about how to equip him. Soon Elias would be a weighty Friend. He would then be obliged to pay attention to this matter. But Jemima was patient and believed everything flowered in its own time. Elias would be awakened.

* * *

Gideon Seaman was troubled as he left the committee meeting. Initially, he had been responsible for the slow approval of Elias Hicks as a Public Friend. Gideon learned Elias had preached to a small group of independent people in Pennsylvania, broken from the United Brethren. Gideon objected to that and had presented it to the committee as a questionable action, wondering if Elias was inappropriately associating with non-Quakers.

When the committee asked Elias about it, he defended himself, "I did nothing wrong. The Spirit bade me."

Indeed, Elias had done nothing wrong. His answer satisfied the committee. Gideon's doubts about Elias' fitness as a Public Friend lingered.

But his fellow committee members disagreed, giving reasons for their support of Elias. They painted a picture of Elias, showing him in a different light. Elias had not heedlessly broken principles but had reached out in love to the United Brethren. Their words were fruitful, and today, finally, the committee had reached unity over Elias, and he was now a Public Friend.

As Gideon rode on, new doubts about Elias' fitness as a Public Friend assailed him. This was peculiar—he had never had this experience before. In the past whenever unity was reached in a committee, he remained at peace.

Now he wondered if he had been moved in the flesh to placate his fellow committee members. Or, was it guidance of the Spirit? Gideon could not put his doubts into words. Since he could not pinpoint his doubts, he questioned the purity of his own heart. Did he dislike Elias? Even if he did, his feelings should not hinder a public ministry—a public ministry was a gift of God.

Gideon chided himself: what was going on with him? Today when Jonathan Shumway insisted that Gideon deliver the news to Elias, it had, for some reason, angered him. Since Elias' wife was his kin, Gideon's feelings towards Elias were especially vexing. He was still brooding over this puzzle as he swung in at the gate at the Hicks house.

"Ben! Is Elias at home?" Gideon hailed Elias' slave in the garden. Before Ben could respond Elias emerged from the shed, shielding his eyes from the sun.

"Hoy, Gideon." Elias greeted Gideon with a smile.

After asking after Jemima and the children, he went directly to the purpose of his visit. "Elias, I've come to give thee news: The committee has got thy letter of certification ready."

Elias fairly jumped with happiness. He clapped Ben on the shoulder. "Hear that, Ben? I am now a Public Friend!"

Ben's eyebrows went up as he smiled.

"I can now preach! I can travel and preach!" Elias was nearly prancing with delight, he turned once and stopped, seeing Gideon's expression. "What is it? Thee looks like thee needs to tell me sad news."

"No, that is all. But I would add, perhaps thee should give Mother Dodge some special thanks."

When Elias cocked his head in question, Gideon explained, "She gave the committee a strong validation of thy fitness for this sacred task."

He did not add that the committee had a surprise visit from Mother Dodge. She had appeared unannounced at the start of a committee meeting. They heard her out, for though she was no longer a traveling minister, she still had a weighty presence. Perhaps it was her influence that had given him confidence in Elias.

"Elias, my advice is to call on Mother Dodge to thank her. And do so soon."

CHAPTER 11

Cow Neck, New York, Early June 1775

EARLY IN JUNE Phebe was weeding her kitchen garden. All her life she had battled the weeds, continually uprooting the bad from the earth to allow the good to flourish. Despite her joy at the thought of freeing Rachel, she was just starting to comprehend the traps laid for her.

Lost in her thoughts, she did not hear the gate squeak on its leather hinges. When she heard footfall on the path, she turned and found Elias Hicks striding toward her. "I have come to thank thee, Mother Dodge," he said, grinning.

Phebe, knowing what he was thanking her for, waved aside his thanks, asking him instead if he had freed his slave yet.

"I confess, I have not." He was embarrassed at it. First Jemima and now Phebe was asking about Ben.

"Surely as thee is traveling and preaching now, thee ought to." She paused, adding, "Thee cannot preach in good conscience until thine own house is in order." He acknowledged this and set out to leave.

Seeing he was set to go she added, "Every person thee will meet is formed in the image of God. Consider that and place thyself in that slave's shoes, or that Indian's shoes, or the pauper's shoes."

* * *

A few weeks later Phebe sought the counsel of both Samuel and Mary Willis. She wanted to hear from Samuel for he was practical, level-headed, and had sound thoughts about perplexing situations.

"I need advice. We will not advance the resolution to free slaves on Long Island as long as war is on our doorstep. These skirmishes between the colonies and Britain are continually pulling our attention away from it. The Friends' energy and attention on the slavery problem has waned. What can we do?" Phebe was out of ideas.

Samuel and Mary confessed their own reach was limited. Mary spotted dark clouds, and rushed outside to take in the wash before the rain.

Samuel was quiet for a moment while his wife was out. He turned to Phebe. "Might thee ask for the formation of a Special Committee for manumitting slaves?"

Samuel's suggestion was obvious, perfect, and simple. Phebe smiled, "Aye, this is what we should do!" She had been in such a rush to free slaves, she had not thought of requesting one.

There was a process to form a Special Committee: it had to be put to the next Monthly Meeting. Even though the process took time, Phebe saw the continuing benefit of a committee. Such a committee would outlive her, for once it was established, a special Committee for the Manumission of Slaves would not be abolished until they achieved the goal.

*   *   *

A Tavern, Cow Neck, August 1775

The late August sun was setting as Stephen left his mother's house. He was heading home but first he would drop off a basket of herbs from Amy with the innkeeper Francis. But when Stephen stopped at the back of the tavern there was no sign of Francis, nor of anyone else. The yard was strangely still, leading Stephen to think no there was no one in the tavern. He was about to leave when he heard voices from inside the inn. To keep his promise to Amy, he approached the back door of the inn. Francis was just inside the back of the tavern, wiping his hands.

"Ah!" Francis said loudly, startled by Stephen's entrance.

"Thee was not about outside, so I came in." Stephen surveyed the room. The tavern room was empty, but there was a candle flickering on a table. Tables were shoved together against the walls, and benches were piled upside down on top of them, awaiting the floor cleaning.

"Oh, yah. Oh, no." Francis stumbled. His mother had been Dutch, and his command of English tended to break down when he was nervous. "Now everyone's gone home, and I am fixing to clean this inn on the morrow." Clearing his throat, he looked uncomfortable. "Will take the whole day."

Stephen raised his eyebrows, "Is that a fact?" He recognized this as a lie to cover up the real reason the inn was shut to regular customers.

A man brushed by him, with another man following the first. The two men hurried to the opposite wall and disappeared through a closed door but left the door ajar. Stephen could see into the room: several men sat around a table, speaking in hushed tones. Francis glanced over at the open door and rubbed his chest nervously. Francis took Stephen's elbow. Steering him back to the outside door.

"Stephen, ye know me," he cocked his head to the side, in a pleading gesture, "Always an eye to improving things for the good people of Cow Neck."

His comment brought Stephen to a standstill. Francis wanted him to leave. Stephen nodded his head towards the room filled with men, and simply asked, "Rebels?"

Francis did not respond but gazed over Stephen's shoulder into the growing dusk. When he finally turned his gaze back to him, he gave a slight nod of his head but stayed silent. Francis tucked the basket from Stephen under his arm, turned to go, giving him a backward wave of farewell.

On his way home Stephen ruminated about the conversations he heard or had been part of in Cow Neck, the ones he had not given much attention to. What had he just seen? Inside the tavern he had picked out almost all his Cow Neck neighbors, including some relatives of his late stepfather, Tristam.

They were just a group of farmers. Surely this meeting was about the war, and he was not included because he was a Friend. What were the rebel "Americans" (as they fashioned themselves) on Cow Neck cooking up?

This gathering reminded him of the last town meeting down in Hempstead. His brother had pressed him to join him there and, for once, Stephen had.

Once there, Stephen was surprised at how many Friends were involved in the Hempstead meeting. During the meeting, many Friends freely voiced their fears and their objections to the Rebellion. At some point someone pulled out a pledge of loyalty to King George, which many people signed. They pressured Stephen to sign it too. But he balked: Friends never swore loyalty to men. Still, they all pressed him, explaining that they were not vowing, but instead, giving their "word" to the King. Stephen refused, maintaining that giving a pledge of loyalty and swearing loyalty through a vow were equivalent.

He suspected those who signed the pledge were afraid of losing land and farms when the Rebellion failed. They feared they would be labeled a rebel. And as rebels they would surely lose all ownership of their land to the conquering British.

When he recounted the town meeting to Amy she scoffed at the pledge of loyalty. Amy was a realist. She pointed out the uselessness of signing a pledge to the King. The pledges of some farming Quakers in the colony carry no weight in England. "In the end we will all be counted as rebel Americans. No one will look at those pledges," Amy astutely determined.

Stephen was so lost in his thoughts, without even noticing, he was nearly home. After passing under the large oak tree, he smiled at seeing his nine-year-old daughter Anna playing with a neighbor's daughter Becca. Anna was five years younger than her friend. Becca Doughty was a kind, sweet girl and Anna almost worshipped her.

The girls were giggling in high-pitched girl tones. Anna had plenty of work helping around the home, so he was delighted to see Becca here. His daughter's life needed more sweetening. He hoped she would grow up to be like her namesake.

* * *

Inside Francis' tavern on Cow Neck, Martin Schenck, the Onderdonks, Joseph Dodge and several other men, continued their weekly meeting. The talk always involved the Continental Congress and the British, naturally, but today their talk was about the dunces in the Town of Hempstead. The men of Hempstead continued to ignore the dark storm clouds approaching, ones which would soon rain down the British wrath on all of Long Island.

They had every reason to be concerned: Their private lives were affected. The British on Long Island expected them to treat them with the same respect and deference as if this were England. Naturally, from the beginning it had been that way, but as the rift between the colonies and England widened, the attitude of the British superiors had grown increasingly arrogant. To most of the colonists, the British attitude was repugnant. But it was the Dutch, the grandchildren of the earliest European settlers of Long Island, who were especially angered by the English attitude and behaviors.

The thing that unified them all and frustrated them the most was their inability to have direct control over their livelihoods. They were supervised, cowed, or harassed by the English as they made a living. Cow Neck, on Long Island's North Shore, long known as an advantageous place to live, had become the worst place to make a living, and all because of British interference. The British put all kinds of obstacles in place. They especially targeted colonists whom they believed harbored anti-British sentiments. The locals had always sent boats to nearby eastern New York, places such as Rye, New Rochelle, or Mamaroneck. But now they were frequently either searched or seized even though there were few official limitations within the colony of New York.

In the past, Cow Neck had traded freely with other colonies. But now trading activity was fraught, for the British were routinely seizing boats to Rhode Island, Connecticut, Massachusetts, and even to the small islands. Moreover, the British had also imposed new, tougher sanctions in other nearby colonies.

The problems with the British were reason enough to vent their anger, but now they knew the rest of Hempstead was shutting them out. It was not a flight of fancy: they were routinely ignored in Hempstead Town Meetings by the Quakers who dominated the meeting. The men had pled for assistance in combating the British, but to no avail: Quakers would not fight. Additionally, the Town had also turned down direct pleas for help from the residents of Cow Neck.

The men were now fed up. They sat and drank and vented their frustrations till finally one of the elder Onderdonks raised his voice, "It's time we act!"

The room fell silent. He stood up, one hand resting on the table for he was a bit wobbly. He began listing the events of the past four months.

"Number one," he held up one finger, "Remember back in May the Town of Hempstead voted to not have anything to do with Congress. And remember, instead, they sent two men to the Provincial Congress to tell them that. It was just our good luck that Congress turned the tables on them. The messengers (who were mere delivery boys) were instead, taken as official 'representatives.' But that was, as I said, luck. I think we all know that was in jest, but we seen that Hempstead won't be obliging to its own Congress!

"Let me ask ye, is that any way to run a town? No. Hempstead showed itself to be a pack of cowards then. That's them's true colors." He stopped, rubbed his impressive belly, and belched.

Holding up a second finger, "Number two. Talk about America's 2nd Continental Congress. What did they do when the British army showed its true face with the battles at Lexington and all that?

"Did Congress pull back? Did it dither? Nay, when the Brits struck the Colony, Congress pushed forward. And now they're pulling all colonies together for a real war. Each 'n every village is gonna help to make a real American army. And, besides that, towns are getting up militias all over the place.

"Everywhere but here. No, not us. Hempstead got no militia! And I ask ye, why? We're blocked by those stubborn idiots: Quaker farmers. I'll tell ye why they're stubborn: because they're afraid! And what do we do? We sit here just drinking and stewing because of them." He paused.

His listeners were losing interest, they each worried over this day and night, and Onderdonk was saying nothing new.

Onderdonk held up his third finger, "Number three: Las' month, mind ye, Congress sent the Olive Branch Petition to the King. And it came within a hair's breadth of us, the Provinces, giving him total loyalty." He made no attempt to keep the sneer out of his voice as he said the last part.

"Lucky for us, Congress also had on hand that other thing—about arms." He turned to the man at his side, "What do they call it?"

The fellow looked up, "'Declaration of the Causes 'nd Necessity of Taking Up of our Arms?'"

"Aye. And I have it here. I can read it to you if you forgot it," he offered. But the men groaned and waved for him to go on speaking. They had heard this before.

"Finally," he held up his fourth finger, "Number four: This is the final nail, men. This month the King called the colonists "traitors," refused to read the petition, and said that we are in rebellion. He told the Parliament to put down the rebellion once and for all!" He growled out the final few words.

His audience sensed he was winding up his speech and one by one gave him their full attention. "It's clear. We now know his opinion about us, his so-called 'subjects.' I mean to say, and I'll say it here and anywhere else, that King would have us all dead! We must act now! Why do we tarry?" He sat down.

"I'll tell you why," piped up Sands, "It's the Town that's stopping us." The sleepiness and nonaction of the Town of Hempstead wore on all of them.

"Aye, he's right!" added one of the younger Onderdonks, "I say it's time we finish with the plain people. The Quakers run the Hempstead Town Meeting with an iron hand. Can we just break them?"

"But how? Have ye any notion on how?" Martin Schenck was impatient. He pushed his long brown hair straight back.

A young Dutch fellow leaned forward, stood up, and said loudly. "We to break them!"

Martin shook his head, not understanding the Dutchman's English. But his cousin understood and yelled out, "Aye! Pieter is right!"

Martin shrugged to indicate that he did not understand their Dutch compatriot. His cousin elucidated, "Why can't we just break from them? Break from the Town?"

Sands looked at Martin from the corner of his eye, what he said had sparked something in Sands. "That's it!"

"Explain what you mean," growled Martin. He was bored: the

meetings had become tiresome—he wanted action, not complaining.

Pieter had seated himself. Sands rose to be more easily heard, "Listen! The Town blocks our votes and drags its feet. They don't care for action. They play their childish games, and live in a dream, whereas we are men and we're begging them for action.

In truth, what are they to us? They are but an anchor and they shall drown us! If we wish to be taken as men supporting the American cause, well, maybe we should act like it!"

Martin was weary, "Sands, tell me what action we should take."

Sands was looking down. When he looked up again at the group his eyes were gleaming, "Just what he said!" he indicated the Dutchman. "We can break from Hempstead: it's simple.

"We've been looking at it the wrong way 'round, it's been in front of our noses the whole time. Isn't it true the colonies wish to run themselves by separating from our overlords? We men of the north must do more than talk and plead. We can separate from our overlords in Hempstead! Aye, if we want to lead, first we *make* ourselves separate and independent of Hempstead!"

The men all began arguing for or against the idea, while Martin sat and stroked his chin, pondering the proposition. Martin was not just a crusader. He was also a practical thinker. He saw Sands' proposal contained not only the seeds of idealism, but also financial benefits to Cow Neck.

Sands might have found a way out of their predicament: self-government on this part of the island would free them from Hempstead, which would allow them to act speedily and to associate independently with the Provincial Assembly, no, now it was called Provincial Congress. Then when at last New York was fully independent from Britain, their independence would be rewarded.

Martin weighed in, stopping the chatter, "In my opinion, Sands is right. If we do this, men, we will have it the way we want it." He spoke with such authority and volume, that he shut down objections, waving away questions and doubts with a flick of his hand.

"As I see it, we will get what we want, action. And we will be ready to respond to the Provincial Congress at the same time. Let's first put it to a vote. After that, if we agree, we will get into the details."

At the end of the evening Martin returned home to tell his wife that Cow Neck had seceded and was now called "North Hempstead."

"What's that mean?" she scowled.

"We are no longer bowing to the will of Hempstead."

His wife shook her head, muttering under her breath that the men had not judged the size and trivial value of their little piece of land.

Martin ignored her comments, "We've set a date to make the announcement to the Hempstead officials—September 23. We have much to write up, and to organize."

Once they applied to the Provincial Colony, they would be a new Town: North Hempstead. With that was done, Cow Neck and neighboring parts in the north would be free to send delegates to the Provincial Congress. Martin was proud of their decision. His wife was unimpressed. She snorted and reminded him the fence needed fixing in the morning.

After snuffing out the candle for the night Martin told his wife, "Now when whaleboaters come ashore, they can come to North Hempstead and find safe and certain harbor."

His wife wondered aloud if she would survive when the British army took Cow Neck. But Martin did not hear her comment, he was already snoring.

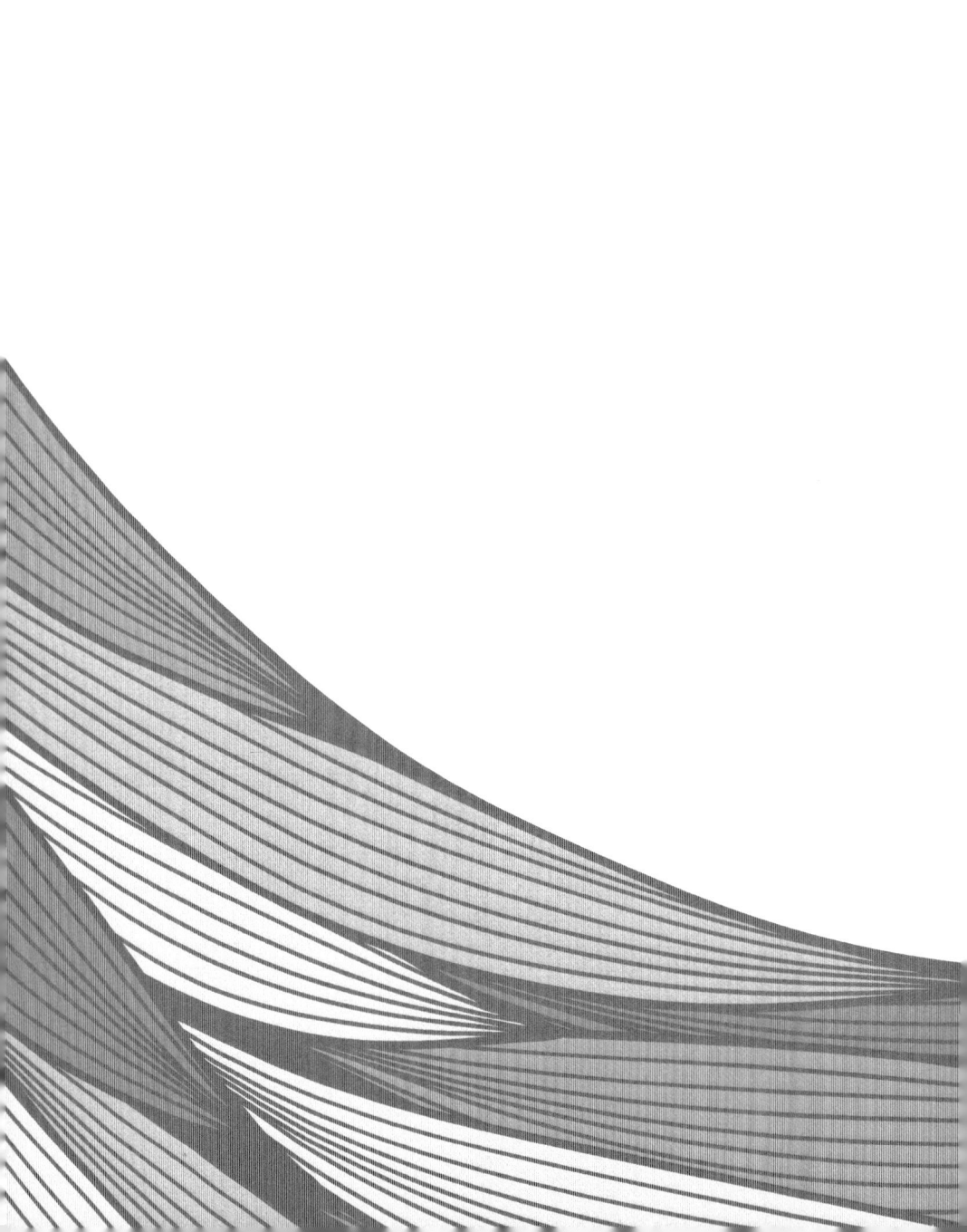

Part 2
RUPTURE

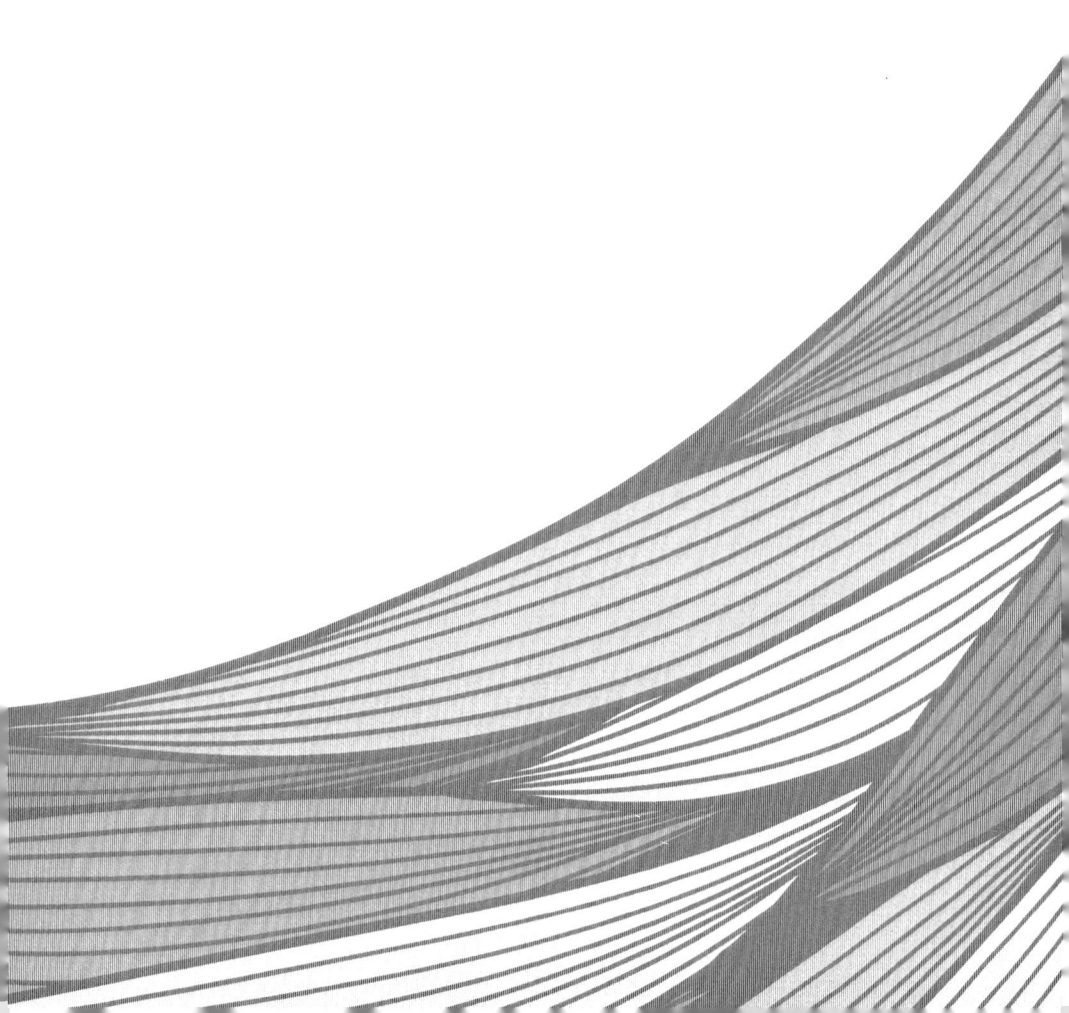

CHAPTER 12

January and February 1776

SINCE NORTH HEMPSTEAD'S assertion of itself as a separate political entity from the Town of Hempstead, the schism between the towns had widened.

A few people in Queens County held that the separation was temporary, a kind of a fever, which would pass, and the Town of Hempstead would once again include North Hempstead. But days passed. News of ongoing skirmishes and disputes kindled doubt over a quick reconciliation. The rupture between the towns remained in place.

The division and rising tensions from vocal supporters of those loyal to Britain as well as the "American rebels" weighed heavily on the Friends. No matter what changes rippled through the towns of Queens County, the Friends could not overcome the distrust aimed at them from the opposing camps. And by the end of 1775, they sensed a new level of antipathy for their pacifism. The normal criticism they received became harsher, laced with name-calling. The children would come home in tears, telling of how they were called "King-lovers" or "Royalists."

Across the Island everyone seemed to have a prediction about the outcome of the conflict with England. Friends, while not referring to it, privately held their own opinions. Phebe was surprised: she had foreseen a bit of this but had not believed that Friends would be so distracted by the rising conflict.

As 1775 drew to a close, news and rumors of war swelled. Even Friends started to pay more attention to the near-continual stream of information. Perhaps instinctively, they knew that their farms, their livelihoods were at stake.

Phebe and others on the special committee for Manumission stewed over the growing inattention towards the freeing and training of slaves.

In late December, Phebe took up residence with Adam and Sarah. She saw their house as an ideal location in Hempstead. From there, she easily made calls on Friends about manumission, insisting the idea of training slaves as a critical feature of manumission. By the end of her stay, when Sarah asked if Phebe was satisfied with the response from Friends, she answered candidly, "I hardly can measure it for the rumor of war has consumed us."

One Sunday Rachel returned to Cow Neck from visiting friends after church. It was late afternoon, so late it was nearly dark. The sky had that look about it. It would soon snow.

Rachel stopped at her home to store some belongings but did not bother removing her cloak as she spent each winter night in the main house. Mother Dodge should be back from Hempstead and Rachel was eager to catch up with her. As she was setting out for the main house, giant snowflakes brushed her cheeks and blew against her eyelashes. She could make out no light inside. Was Mother Dodge home?

"Strange," thought Rachel.

Upon entering Phebe's house, Rachel was shocked to see Mother Dodge collapsed in her chair still dressed in her outer clothes. A weak fire was burning but the house was still chilly. Only one candle was lit.

"Dear one," said Phebe in a feeble voice. From her chair she waved her hand at Rachel in welcome.

Rachel had never seen Mother Dodge in this state. She bustled about lighting candles against the coming night, built up the fire, and starting the kettle. Finally, she helped Mother Dodge out of her outer clothes.

"Are you sick?" Rachel squinted to see Phebe's pale drawn face. Phebe did not respond, but settled deeper in her chair, drawing around her the knitted shawl for warmth. Phebe started coughing. Rachel waited.

When she stopped coughing, Phebe explained, "Stephen fetched me from Adam's. But I wouldn't let Stephen come in because he would fuss over me. He ought to be home with Amy; she's awful sick. And too, the snow…" Phebe stopped speaking, paused, then sneezed violently.

Stephen had left them fresh bread and cheese. But Phebe turned down food, taking only hot water into which Rachel had boiled dried herbs. Mother Dodge complained she could not warm up, no matter how bundled up she was. Her face was flushed, but despite the fire she could not stop shivering. No matter what they did, Phebe was still miserable.

Rachel pressed Mother Dodge to nurse her illness in her bed. She consented but needed Rachel's help to change into her bedclothes. When Mother Dodge was finally settled. Rachel checked the clock, but it was still early evening.

Rachel ate supper in the silent house. After supper she busied herself with Mother Dodge's bags, and other chores. When she next checked on Mother Dodge, she found her in a deep sleep. Rachel felt her forehead, as she suspected and dreaded, Mother Dodge had a fever.

Rachel's stomach lurched. Mother Dodge could not be sick; she could not die. No. Rachel felt she had to do something. Her heart was thundering in her ears. Mrs. Schenck could help her. She had lived through all kinds of calamities with her family and would surely know what to do. Putting on her cloak, she raced next door through the deepening snow. Mrs. Schenck, alarmed, promised she would be over shortly.

When the neighbor arrived, she took her time examining Phebe. "What did she take for supper?"

Rachel shrugged, "No food since I've been back. She had a small nip of herbed water."

"Did she drink it?"

Rachel confessed Phebe had not drunk it. The woman took a small bottle from her basket and shoved it in Rachel's hands, "If—um—when she wakes up, get her to take this, it will ease her." Rachel felt sure it was rum.

Mrs. Schenck shook her head over Phebe's illness, "I cannot tell you what it be. Give it some time, and if we're lucky, it won't kill her. You stay here with her till we can get you some help. Try to have her drink from that bottle, but don't be surprised if she sleeps."

At the expression on Rachel's face, her neighbor's expression softened, and she patted her arm, "Don't worry. When the snow clears tomorrow, I'll have Martin fetch Amy."

"No. I was going to fetch her, but we cannot. Amy is sick herself."

"I'll send him to fetch Elizabeth instead. And I'll be back in the morning." Once again, she gave Rachel a reassuring pat on her arm and left.

Rather than sleeping in the loft, Rachel dragged a pallet close to Phebe's bed to tend her through the night. The morning dawned bright, dry, and cold. A layer of fresh snow was on the ground. But Phebe was worse. Late in the morning, as promised, Mrs. Schenck arrived with herbs and potions. She left Rachel with a mountain of advice and directions.

Elizabeth showed up in the afternoon. By then Phebe was worse: her forehead felt hotter, and when she coughed, it was a choking sound. Elizabeth and Rachel spelled one another caring for Mother Dodge. That first day blurred into several days.

Phebe slept, refusing food and drink. When she talked, it was strange, broken; she was not in her right mind. This worried the women, and they worked hard at getting Phebe to drink something, even rum. At one point, Elizabeth turned to Rachel and shook her head slowly, her eyes had a hollow look.

"Rachel, Rachel." Elizabeth began, choking as she spoke, almost in tears, "We must not let Mother die." Then she added something Rachel never forgot, "For thee has not yet begun to live."

Before the week was over, they were spelled by Sarah. In that time Amy Mott was almost back to health but took extra care, remaining home till she was completely better. Mary Willis was still out of town but her daughters Keziah and Feeb spelled Sarah and Elizabeth now and then. Rachel was able to get her rest with the extra hands, but she still refused to spend the night in the loft. No matter who was there, she slept on the ground floor.

After two weeks, Mother Dodge's health had but little improved. She was barely eating, and still slept all day. The length and strength of her illness alarmed her family to the point that they called in a doctor.

The doctor was not encouraging. "Lung fever." he said grimly.

"Thee is certain?" Elizabeth cried.

The doctor's certainty was on his pale face. Rachel's heart raced. She asked the doctor, "Will she mend?"

He looked at her sadly, and replied simply, "Lung fever kills the aged."

Elizabeth sat down with her face in her hands. The doctor left, charging into the bitter wind, and Rachel went back to tending Phebe. While Elizabeth was sobbing, Rachel was seized by fear. Unbidden thoughts tumbled through her mind. Without Phebe, her plans would die out, and she would be forever a slave.

When Elizabeth's sobs tapered off, she shooed Rachel out to her home for a break, with the assurance she would get her if she needed help. Reluctantly Rachel returned to her small house. The wind had ceased and the warm afternoon sun had melted the snow, leaving small patches in the yard between her house and Mother Dodge's. Rachel had spent little time inside her own house since before Christmas. She tidied it up and made a fire to warm her afternoon. She saw her handiwork, it lay untouched. She picked it up, sat down and methodically went to work. As she worked, her thoughts moved between the past and the future.

When she was little, Master Tristam Dodge had wanted to take her to a small island in the Sound. But he could not find the island. Master was confused and upset that he could not find the island, "It's been there all my life. And now, suddenly after the storms of this year, it's not. Without the island, I do not know where I am—and yet somehow, I must get us back home!"

The words he uttered back then had new meaning for her today. Like the island that gave Master Dodge a sense of place, Mother Dodge was that island for her: steady and always there. Without Mother Dodge she feared she would be lost, perpetually lost.

Wasn't it Mother Dodge who had built a fire of hope in Rachel's breast? With Mother Dodge gone, would the fire die out? Or would it burn? Would she be helpless?

She looked down at her handiwork. With fresh eyes she examined the work in her hands: what she had done so far was beautiful. But what about next week, or tomorrow? Would she have the heart to pick it up again? Was there any point in doing it if she lost Phebe? She doubted she would have her own business, even if she were freed. Without her own business, she would never have her own money, her own life. No wonder she had no heart to work.

Tears of bitterness and anger streamed down her face, covering her cheeks and neck, landing on her hands. She was angry that Mother Dodge would draw her big pictures, and then leave her. The tears came strong and hard. No, nothing in her anger was Mother Dodge's fault: it was because she was born a negro slave.

The night was closing in. She looked out her small window. In summer it afforded a view of the garden and the trees but with the overcast sky, all was dark. A perfect picture of how she felt: all was darkness, a veil shrouded her future. She had stopped weeping, now she was wrung out.

Yet, even as she sat looking out into the darkness of the late winter dusk, she determined that if Mother Dodge lived to free her, she would support herself with her own hands. She had faith that somehow she would be a freed woman.

As she stared out the window, a calm settled within her and she felt rebuilt. Phebe Dodge had faith in me, she reminded herself. Her conviction was rock solid, and she would not fail, no matter what fears she had. Rachel reckoned she'd caught the faith of Mother Dodge.

* * *

Mary and Samuel Willis had spent New Year's in New York City with an elderly relative. But the City was unpleasant with its undercurrent of conflict. And the discomfort drove Mary and Samuel to change their plans at the last minute. They left the City on New Year's Day.

Sarah Willis Mott welcomed her parents when they returned on the third week of the 1st month. They were barely out of their outer clothes when she told them of Phebe's illness. Mary's jaw dropped, and she turned to don her outer clothes all over again, but Samuel put a restraining hand on her arm.

"Mother, thee cannot go tend to her now! Not so soon after thy return," Sarah chastised.

"She is right. We ought to rest." Samuel sat down, addressing his wife.

Mary's daughter and Samuel were speaking sensibly. Despite her wish to see Phebe, Mary knew she was not being sensible. She was drained.

"Tell me everything," she prompted Sarah.

"Mother Dodge has lung fever. But we are taking turns tending to her. Mother, don't fret. Keziah and Feeb have been tending her as well."

Despite their fatigue, her parents seemed energized. Sarah asked them about the time in the City.

Samuel leaned forward, "After we left the City, we stopped by Newtown to visit cousin Samuel."

Samuel Nottingham told them he was worried sick about the coming fight with the British. He was convinced a fight was going to happen nearby. For safety, he had already sent his wife and children away to his wife's relatives, up the North River.

"He has also emptied his farm of all but the bare necessities and was about to take his milk cow to join his family. When he started to wonder out loud about his slave's future, thy mother brightly suggested he free her. Here is the end of the situation," Samuel was beaming. "We drew up her manumission and witnessed it. No one can question Hagar's right to be free.

"He worried about his farm if a battle comes. And though we could do nothing about that, we offered to fetch back Hagar's manumission record. It will be kept in the Meeting House. If she is challenged about being freed, she can find it."

Her father took a paper from his pouch, and carefully unrolled it on the reading table: "*Samuel Nottingham Newtown Flushing frees his female slave 'Hagor.' 19th January 1776 Signed Samuel Nottingham*" followed by the signatures of Mary Willis and Samuel Willis.

Her mother added, "This spring when Cousin returns to check on his land, he will buy his neighbor's slave, and free him too."

"Does Uncle Samuel truly believe his area will be in the middle of a fight?" Sarah asked.

"Aye, he has no doubt. He says the whole of Brooklyn, even Flushing, is easy prey for a battle. Unless the British take the City first. He shares the opinion of everyone else I have heard: that it's the prize. For folks down in Newtown, there's no safety but in leaving."

Sarah considered the news from Brooklyn, Flushing, and Newtown, "Perhaps we should consider another place to hold Yearly Meeting, then?"

The New York Yearly Meeting was held in Flushing. It was quiet and pastoral compared to New York City, yet conveniently near the City.

Samuel considered, "A building of that sort would be tempting to any army that invades there."

Mary glanced at him, startled that he believed in the possibility of armed fighting in Flushing. She felt a wave of fear, her husband was often right. She shivered, though they did not live in Flushing, they were still close enough for an army to be on their doorstep quickly.

* * *

Phebe's lung fever hung on through the frigid January. There were several times her attendants were certain she was on the brink of death.

Little by little Phebe's illness lost its strength. She had improved but the fatigue and the cough still stayed with her. By the end of the month, Rachel had given up all hope of ever sleeping through a night again or of seeing her mistress hale. And even when Phebe had shaken her fever, was taking more tea, and her cough had lessened, Rachel still dared not hope.

One morning, early, she heard Phebe call her. "Rachel, bring tea, and sit by me."

Rachel braced for a coughing fit, but none came. After a few minutes, Phebe started talking business, "Now that I'm alert, I have in my mind a list of people who must call on me."

A surprised Rachel chided her. "You have been ill a long time. You need to regain your strength first."

"What month and day is it?"

"First month, thirty-first day." Rachel did not hear herself, but she was speaking as the Quakers do, substituting the word "first" for January.

Phebe shook her head in wonder at how long she had been sick, "I dreamt I was dying."

Rachel sucked in her breath—was that a sign? As if reading her thoughts, Phebe shook her head, "Rachel, if it is a sign, it's but a signpost to myself of what I am lacking before I die. Before thee is free, I have one more thing to do."

Rachel could not think of what was missing. Mother Dodge was giving her everything—a new business, and she could already read and write better than most whites she knew.

"Thee can do a fair job of making sums. But thee needs more lessons. Only these are lessons on how to account for thy money. We shall begin ciphering lessons as soon as I can sit up in bed."

Rachel stared at her, disbelieving. Mother Dodge, still sick and scarcely able to breathe, was once again speaking about how to help her live as a freed woman.

Phebe added, "We must do this. For all these years of loyalty and loving friendship—it's a gesture. A token of my gratitude. After all, thee's had no voice and little choice." She gave a small chuckle at her own joke, but it ended in a bout of coughing.

Though Rachel understood Mother Dodge's sense of guilt, she was schooled in a lifetime of slavery, had no ready way to think thoughts of advancement. Even after these months of preparation, words like freedom and equality were ideals, not reality; they were words without form or shape. The landscape of the moon was more easily pictured in her mind's eye than these ideals. She was silent for she had no words. She blinked away tears, thanking God for Mother Dodge.

Throughout the weeks of tending Mother Dodge, Rachel had stayed busy not only with the household chores, but also with her handiwork. The demand for her work had increased since the New Year, thanks to Mother Dodge's connections, mainly through Willet

Seaman's friends in New York City. Each introduction led to a commission and each commission led to a new introduction. Rachel had a stream of commissions and returning customers.

Rachel's business had burgeoned swiftly and once her ciphering lessons began, she was a ready student. And it was not long before she no longer needed help with ciphering.

To speed Phebe's recovery, Rachel paid close attention to the advice of neighbors. By the end of the first week of the 2nd month, Phebe had enough strength to sit in her chair. Her mind was clear, even though her body was not back to strength.

Now that Phebe's health was coming back, her brain was as busy as ever with plans for the slaves of Hempstead. Knowing she had narrowly escaped death, she sensed an urgency to redeem every moment. Samuel and Mary Willis and most of their adult children were asked to call on Phebe. For two days before their visit, she devoted herself to writing and re-writing a multi-page document.

A February thaw preceded the day of their gathering, and the day dawned bright and clear. Rachel swept the floor, helped Phebe get comfortable, admitted the family, and then moved to her loft to work on her accounts. From there she heard the murmur of their voices as they spoke about manumission.

After the family had left Rachel put her books away, and returned, finding Mother Dodge looking pleased, her face was pink with color. Although she still coughed, she looked well. Rachel passed the table and noted a document laid out on it. It read: *Committee on Manumission and Life in Society*. She looked up to see Mother Dodge smiling.

Phebe explained it contained her designs and ideas for training slaves. Today the family had reviewed it and then advised her on it. "They were a great help! Oh, did I mention to thee the next meeting of the special committee will be here next week? And that document," she stabbed a finger towards it, "will be our guiding star, our map, so we don't wander. I shall ask thee to display some of thy work to the committee. I did not ask before, but I assume thee shall be willing?"

Rachel smiled to herself; Mother Dodge was well.

* * *

The week following when the committee on manumission gathered at Phebe's house, Rachel was ready to be a living representative for soon-to-be freed slaves.

At a certain point in the meeting when Phebe was speaking, she paused and looked over at Rachel. This was Rachel's signal. Phebe had just finished asserting that training need not be lengthy, that many slaves were already skilled (though not formally taught) having gotten trained through observing family members. At her signal Rachel stood up and spoke to Phebe, "Mother Dodge, this piece is near done."

The committee members had believed Rachel was mending. Mother Dodge and Rachel spread the coat on the table before the committee.

"See what Rachel can do." Mother Dodge directed the committee as they crowded around the table to examine the coat.

Mary Townsend fingered it, and said, awed, "Why, this is a greatcoat for a man!"

It was an elaborately embroidered great coat. Rachel had even embroidered the collar. It was nearly done. Now she was working on sprays of silk thread flowers on the cuffs. Quakers, though "plain," could appreciate the skill it took for the laborers of the "fancy-dress." The entire committee recognized Rachel's talent, and Phebe beamed with pride.

"Well done!" Mary complemented Rachel. "Rachel, how did thee do this?"

Rachel looked at Mother Dodge, who smiled encouragingly, prompting Rachel to tell them all about her fancy-work business. They questioned her on it at such length that Jacob Underhill invited her to sit with them as she responded.

Impressed, Jacob addressed Rachel, "I am shocked. Thee, a middle-aged woman, born into slavery, has done something remarkable. Thy skill and the artfulness is astonishing!" He waved at the greatcoat. Rachel's complexion changed hue—she blushed with embarrassment.

Silas Titus added, "Rachel, I am pleased for thee—and for me. For what blesses the soul of one in our village blesses all." The committee murmured in agreement.

After the committee returned to their seats, Phebe invited Rachel to outline how many commissions she was working on, and how much money she had earned so far. The committee members' eyes were round with surprise and a bit of awe.

Phebe seized her moment. "Rachel is a wonder to me. For years, I could not work out why I had a slave. But I now see the hand of Providence.

"It's no secret that she long refused manumission but has finally agreed to it. For now, she feels safer here with me, but she is stepping out boldly to be part of society. Her example is, I pray, an inspiration to this committee."

Mary Townsend, energized at seeing Rachel's fine work, squeaked with excitement, "This is a well-taught lesson. We ought help slaves with their occupations."

Silas agreed, "I say we take this at a moderate speed and not move too swiftly nor too slowly."

Jacob believed Rachel's previously untapped talents were the key to her livelihood. He asked detailed questions about the duration of her activity and her training.

Phebe maintained that the marriage of Rachel's native skill and her patience had made Rachel's learning period brief. "Might it help us all to change the committee's name to the Committee on Manumission and Life in Society?"

"Aye! It is more true to fact."

Silas asked, "We must urge Friends to have talks with their slaves about what they should (or could) do after manumission."

There was common agreement on this. Jacob, intrigued by the brevity of time in Rachel's case, volunteered to organize a list of ideas of skills, occupations, and trades. He thought the list would help the Friends when they questioned their slaves.

After the meeting, Phebe was spent, but she had a wide smile on her face. "Thee heard them speak, Rachel. What does thee think?"

Mother Dodge had asked for Rachel for an honest assessment, and it pleased her. The Quakers, she believed, would, in the end, do their best for every slave.

CHAPTER 13

Cow Neck, New York, March 1776

ANOTHER NEW SPRING was close. Word was that James Titus freed his slave on the 7th day. Rachel's manumission paper was yet to be written up and witnessed. That Rachel had been operating as if she were freed was of little consequence. Phebe was aware of how critical this record was to proving Rachel was freed (though manumission alone was not a guarantee of her safety).

She had already formulated the manumission in her mind, writing pieces of it here and there. Now she was going to put it together. She sent word to her sons to be at her house the following day. The statement would be finished, signed, and witnessed then.

The morning dawned fresh. After breakfast the sky was cloudless. "I don't believe in omens, but this type of weather! It inspires me," she declared to Rachel as they worked on the morning chores.

Phebe sat down to craft Rachel's final manumission statement. All her life she had read recorded minutes. As an adult she had come to appreciate their value: they were helpful when there were contradictory or confusing recollections, and they clarified the reasons behind actions. Without such a statement, Phebe's reason for freeing Rachel would remain unknown, and unclear. And in such a case, one had to imply or attribute a reason for the act. Since there was no law demanding Rachel's freedom, Phebe felt it her duty to lay out her reasons for doing so. Rachel's manumission would inspire and enflame its readers in the years to come.

Manumission statements were simple, powerful legal tools in the province. But hers would not be just a legal instrument. Phebe believed that everything she wrote was a world of intentionality. Her thinking should be plain to each reader, and therefore she had thought much about it. She desired the burden of slavery to weigh heavy on the heart of each reader.

For some time, she had been scribbling down fragments to include in the statement. Today she opened the box where she kept these papers and poured them all out on the tabletop. Sorting through the disparate pieces, she read them through slowly, thoughtfully. Her statement must easily understood. She was methodical and deliberate in her choices.

The statement could not be long, it had to fit on one page. How would she summarize her reason to free Rachel? She picked up one scribble—it looked promising, but it was aimed at Friends. She set it to her left. She wanted to reach beyond the Friends, and form a statement that would be easily understood by any Christian. She found a scribble that looked promising; one which could help men and women of faith see how precious humans were. She continued sorting the small bits of paper.

Once she had the wording, she had to pull it together. She sketched out everything she wanted to say on the back of one of the papers. She moved to her cupboard, pulled out a large piece of rag paper and copied it there.

She read her finished document critically. It captured the essence of her belief; it was brief and legal. But her handwriting! It had turned spidery, it was the handwriting of an elderly woman. Her sons would be here tomorrow to copy it in ink and to witness it as well. Her spine tingled with excitement at the thought of the finished statement. Caught up by the urge to show it to Rachel, she went out to look for her, finding her around the corner, gathering eggs.

"Rachel, when thee comes in the house I have something for thee to read!" Phebe could not keep the excitement out of her voice.

When Rachel entered, Phebe practically ran to the table. "It won't be witnessed till tomorrow, but I can read it now! Or does thee want to?" She extended it to Rachel. Rachel shook her head, fearing she would weep, she asked Mother Dodge to read it aloud instead. Phebe read:

15 third month, 1776

Know all men by these Presents that I, Phebe Dodge, of Cow Neck in the Township of Hempstead and Queens County in the province of new York, have for some years been under a Concern of mind on account of holding Negroes as Slaves at our Disposition.

I being possessed of a Negro woman named Rachel and am fully satisfied it to be my duty as also a Christian act to set her at Liberty. Therefore have and do hereby Manumit and Sett free from Bondage the said Negro woman Rachel and for myself my Heirs Executors and Administrators do forever release unto the said Negro woman Rachel all my right and claim whatsoever as to her Person or any Estate she may hereafter acquire and do further hereby declare that the said Negro woman be fully freely and clearly Sett at Liberty without any interruption from me or any person Claiming or to claim from or under me.

In witness whereof I have hereunto Set my hand and fixed my seal the Fifteenth Day of the third month one thousand seven hundred and seventy six.

Phebe Dodge

in the presence of

When Phebe finished reading, Rachel took the proffered paper to read it herself. After all the conversations, after all the work she and Mother Dodge had put into this for her freedom, all those days and nights of her own solitary dreams of this time, here was the moment. A handful of words on a piece of paper would unlock, nay, push open a long-sealed door.

What would her mother have thought? She would be happy and proud. What would Solomon say? She did not understand his thinking. How happy her friends would be! Or would they? They were as human as she: would they smile at her at the same time hide the envy in their hearts? Her heart raced at this thought, a trickle of cold sweat started at the back of her neck. Would she lose her friends over this?

Rachel was still staring at the paper in silence. Phebe's smile faded when she saw fear and not joy in Rachel's reaction. Something was amiss: Rachel had been eager for this—why the sudden check? She could not piece together the cause for Rachel's sudden reticence.

As Rachel re-read the statement, mouthing the words as she did, Phebe understood then whatever was happening within Rachel were feelings and worries she could not share, and could never share. When Rachel remained silent, Phebe spoke in measured tones, choosing her words carefully, "Rachel, I do believe everybody can understand this."

Rachel nodded. Phebe added, "We cannot know what will happen to either of us. But I vow I'll stick with thee."

Rachel had no words. There were too many emotions. They were all bunched together, stuck in her throat. Phebe moved towards her and put her arms around her as if she were her own daughter. Rachel buried her head in Phebe's shoulder and cried, long, loud wails.

Rachel could not understand what was happening to her, why were her feelings such a muddle? She was happy, she was sad, and she was afraid.

"It's good thee weeps now." Phebe comforted. She stayed with Rachel like that until she was cried out and needed to pull away to blow her nose and to wipe her eyes on her apron.

Phebe sat down and took up mending, "I chose those words, and no others because I wish for those who read it to read the love in it."

Rachel sat down near her and took up her own work. She knew what Grandmother meant. Looking up from her busy hands, Rachel added, "Aye. And love provides for free choice."

CHAPTER 14

Flushing, New York, April 1776

The manumission of Levineah, of Hagor, of Josiah, of Rachel and of other slaves served as a spur, stimulating the Friends to action. The Committee on Manumission was kept busy.

This year spring was gentle with plentiful pleasant weather. Rachel was cheery as she put on a newly turned bonnet before setting out for a morning with her friends at church. Normally she went from church service to Solomon's house. But she had received word from Solomon not to come this Sunday. It was not her nature to be meddlesome, so she did not ask him why, even though she wondered.

She made it widely known to friends that she would be alone, hoping she would be invited to a friend's home. She was not disappointed: Sister Clara invited her to dinner. Her husband Jasper Black had been born a freed black. He had used his own money to buy Clara's freedom.

Clara was an excellent cook, she had been a cook for someone in New York. This Sunday Clara again showed off her cooking skill and there was nothing left of the rabbit stew and pan-biscuits she served up.

Clara and Rachel had finished the cleanup while Jasper sat on the stoop smoking. The two women brought the bench out to the porch.

From their perch they chatted as the sun set. The spring was aglow with new grass and the wind was soft and sweetly pungent. It seemed all nature was singing with happiness, creating in Rachel a sense of rightness. Early spring's fresh winds swept in with fresh hopes. This year she was particularly grateful: with her plans were well in place and Mother Dodge's health restored.

Since the March, Rachel had barely kept up with the demand for her handiwork. She was proud of how she kept her accounts. Now that she had learned ciphering, she had asked Stephen, Amy or Adam to look over her account book once a week, and for two straight weeks she had made no ciphering mistakes. That she could see to her own money was something she had never dreamed she could do. Shortly she would scarcely need help with her books.

Now her manumission was final. She had been a freed woman for two months. The thought was staggering. She still worked a bit for Mother Dodge, but for payment or barter. Rachel saw the wisdom in this: working for money meant she could turn down work. To have the freedom to refuse work was a revelation. Mother Dodge had written up a work agreement, giving Rachel only five days of light work. In addition, she had lifted some of Rachel's tasks so they were now done by family members. This gave her time each day for her own work or her business. Saturday and Sunday were completely free.

Rachel rarely mentioned her manumission or her business to her friends. She knew she was blessed to be in her position and did not wish to stir up envy. But she correctly suspected that everyone in her church knew of it.

Rachel had hoped she could speak with Clara and Jasper about being freed. Their conversation had flowed freely and she was hopeful. But once they joined Jasper outside, Clara was subdued. She paid close attention to the work in her hands, kept her head down and said little. Jasper smoked and gazed off as Rachel chatted. But she sensed a strain;

Clara did not respond to her remarks. Rachel talked less, waiting but silence grew longer. Before the sun had fully set, Jasper turned to look at her.

"Jasper, you look like you going to bite my head off," Rachel said lightly.

"You talk like that anymore and I will," he glowered. "You don't understand things."

He meant she did not understand slavery and she was insulted. She shook her head. Jasper suddenly came to life, standing up. His eyes bored into hers. He snapped, "Let me tell you something."

Rachel put her work in her lap and looked up at him. Clara didn't move. Jasper walked in a circle as he spoke.

"I bought my wife, and my children, from slavery. It was my own money—hard-earned. And I thought I knew the sly tricks, but I didn't, and I don't, I still fall into many a white man's trap."

When he stopped, he looked directly at Rachel and held up a warning finger to prevent her from speaking. He continued his story.

"I worked hard all my life, raising this and that thing, and selling them. I saved a lot, but I got tired of farming all by myself and then the selling it. Besides, who buys from the negro? They only buy what can't be boughten from his kin or kind.

"Let me tell you about the time I needed money. I needed to get more money in an easy like way; I was selling clams at the time. I heard of a buyer of clams up river in Newburgh who used to live here. I saved up some money and hired me a boat, and two other men. We hauled clams up the North River to sell them to him. When we got to Newburgh, I went out to find him. When I was gone looking for the buyer, a man of that place—a white man—come, took my men and my boat! All of it!

"I looked everywhere for hours and finally found the boat. But when I went to drag in my boat—one Joseph Van Alen claimed my boat! And like that, he took it. He dare take my boat. I was steaming mad! I went round knocking on doors and found some selectmen of that town for help. You know what happened? They, the Newburgh selectmen, took a meeting about it." He paused and looked at Rachel with a sharp eye.

"What do ye guess they did? Brought me justice?" He turned his head and spat, "Nay. They jailed me, a freeman, for stealing my own boat!" He shook his head, "My word that I was a freeman was no good—not good enough. Why? Because I am a negro."

He glared at her challengingly.

Rachel asked uneasily, "What happened after you were in jail?"

"I was young then. I escaped; I ran away. The path from Newburgh to New York is long, but it's an Indian trail and easy enough to make out."

Jasper was pacing. By the time he finished his story, his face had darkened with outrage.

"Think on that! I was but a stranger, but I was working. I live honest. It's not easy because I live in hard service to the world.

"Now I say to you: I was robbed more than once. In Newburgh I was a captive in a jail and nearly sold as a slave, though I was born a free man." Jasper fairly shouted the word free.

"Why? Because the Van Alen man was a white man, but I, Jasper Black, am a negro: that is why it was all right. That's when I learned my lesson. Ye know what my lesson was?" Rachel shook her head dumbly.

"To the white man, everything good is too good for the black dog."

CHAPTER 15

Cow Neck, New York, April 1776

ONE DAY ELIAS HICKS appeared at Phebe's house with a sack in his hand. He asked to see Rachel. Mystified, Phebe told him she was in her little house. When she invited him to leave the sack in the house, he turned down her offer. A few minutes later he returned to bid her good day. She noted his sack was empty. He did not mention it and she did not ask.

Before the day was over Rachel mentioned that Elias had made her a small desk of sorts. It pleased her for it was a portable one with a hinged lid where she could keep her ciphering book and her pencils. Elias, a fair carpenter, had made it easily. Phebe tried to coax Rachel as to the reason for this gift, but Rachel would not say. Phebe had to be comfortable with that. Elias and Rachel had a secret; something had happened for them to connect. She believed their new bond was to their mutual benefit.

Rachel would never tell Phebe the reason. She would never tell her of the day when she was left alone in the house over a month ago. Nor of the moment the door was flung wide open by a British soldier. Nor of her mounting fear as he looked about for others, and seeing no one, smiled a sick smile. She would not tell how he grabbed her at the waist, and had put his face up to hers, leering.

She could not put into words, even for herself, what happened next. It was as if she had crossed some previously concealed barrier. Had this happened before her manumission, she would have cringed, pulled away, tried to run. But now, somehow as if being her own person, making her own money, had changed her. She took charge and moved closer to him, not instinctively, but against instinct. When she pulled in close to him, his leering face changed, he grew excited. She then realized he was open to her lead.

Then she was the spider, weaving her web. She stepped to one side and then stepped back, to be closer to the iron kettle on legs. And he had stepped with her, leaning into her. She leaned and swayed with him. Then in a swift movement she dipped, grabbed the handle of the kettle, and swung it round to his head.

Her next memory was of Elias at the wide-open door, and then he appeared at her side. She was babbling incoherently. Elias took the lead and together they moved the unconscious soldier out to a stand of trees.

Later Elias sat Rachel down and advised her to keep this a secret, to speak to no one. He reminded her of a world outside the door that did not believe she was valued as a human. She was still numb, but she comprehended well his message. The secret would die with Elias and Rachel. She made the decision not to tell Phebe—there was no reason to involve her nor worry her.

When the soldier (who had come from the City to see the country), was later seen, he was wandering aimlessly, babbling like a madman. The soldier never recovered his faculties.

* * *

Cow Neck, May 1776

On a warm May afternoon, Elias Hicks appeared on Mother Dodge's doorstep. He had been away for some time preaching on his first trip as a traveling Friend. She had not seen him since the day he had given Rachel something from his sack.

Elias said this spring his eyes had been "greatly opened to the hardship, nay, the abuses, the negro slaves endured." He was shocked to his core at how normal, how common it was for negroes to be treated as animals, or worse. At the least, they were overlooked, as if not part of humanity. When they were freed, some meandered, aimlessly, without purpose. There were only a few places where freed blacks lived side-by-side with whites in harmony, but in those situations both the whites and blacks were impoverished.

She was relieved to learn about his recent enlightenment, and asked him, "In all thy travels, has thee ever met or even heard of a wealthy negro?" she asked.

Elias sat bolt upright. "No. No such person exists."

Phebe asked, "Is there any sound reason why?"

It was a rhetorical exercise, they both knew, meant to open his eyes to what did not exist, but should.

Elias suggested that if Friends refuse to free their slaves, then the Meeting should not have unity with them. He asked Phebe to agree with him. But to his surprise she declined, at least, she said, "for now." She reminded him kindly that the best persuasion was a gentle persuasion; it was the way the Friends operated.

* * *

As Rachel was sharing the evening's meal with Mother Dodge. She imparted news she had learned at church: the British—who had withdrawn from Boston to Halifax—were now encamped on Staten Island as well as New Jersey.

"It's now said that both the British and Hessian soldiers are trickling into the colonies. Just when we had believed we were rid of them,"

Rachel said, realizing that there was something foolish about believing the British would give up easily and withdraw entirely.

Phebe shook her head, dismayed. The near complete British withdrawal from Boston had been met with jubilation. But most had understood it for what it was. When the British had quit Massachusetts, they made use of their leave to sort out their campaign.

Spring was waning. Although Cow Neck was out of the direct path of traffic that went west and east across the middle of the island, life on the North Shore had its drawbacks: it was pitched close to near Madnan's Neck, a vulnerable location exposed to invaders. As it was, Cow Neck had seen a jump in the boat traffic, as had the rest of the North shore. The increased traffic was due to the so-called "London importers" (who had no overseas connection but trafficked across the Sound) and policing of the British patrols as they conducted their near continual scouting of the Sound.

On Cow Neck, Phebe's livestock and food stores tempted marauding gangs, whaleboat men, and stray British regulars. Despite the work in their own homes, Adam and Stephen and John Willis stopped in more often, sometimes with the flimsiest of excuses. Elizabeth did not disguise her worry over her mother's safety, and pressed her to move in with them. But Phebe resisted moving.

CHAPTER 16

Long Island, New York, Late May 1776

Before rising on Sunday Rachel's first thought was, "It's my first May as a freed woman." Getting ready for the day, she savored this thought. She had finally begun to believe this was her year, and she had even started calling it not 1776, but "Year One." As she prepared for church she reveled in the promises ahead of her, in the promise of spring and its rich beauty. Although she had seen Mays as glorious as this one, spring had never seemed so wonderful to her as it did this year.

True, she missed her son, it was the sole cloud in her sky: Solomon was in the British army. In April when she had celebrated Easter with Azuba and her grandchildren, she gingerly asked after Solomon. But Azuba merely shrugged. She had had no word from him but was not worried. Azuba read but little, so Rachel did not expect they exchanged letters. When Rachel pressed her, Azuba finally declared she knew he was well for he had managed to get money to her.

Though the year had begun poorly for the whites, Quakers and non-Quakers, Loyalist and American rebels, 1776 had been a good year for Rachel. She was pleased that her handiwork business was thriving. It was growing so fast she worried about keeping up with the demand. She had not stopped working for Mother Dodge entirely. Working for her brought her pleasure, but she did not need the money.

That she was liberated and not dependent made her feel like there an irrepressible spring within. Just to know she was free to make her own decisions had made her a different person. Now opened before her was a new world of choices: she could easily move to Flushing, or New Jersey, or Rhode Island where she had family. Though she never gave it serious thought, the fact that she could move gave her pleasure.

Today, for the first time in months, Rachel had nothing to do after the church service. She usually stopped in to see Azuba and her children but today they were in New Jersey seeing after her mother. Rachel lingered long after church before finally turning towards home, a couple of fellow congregants walking with her. At the fork in the path, she parted from her friends, taking a shortcut leading to Shelter Rock Road. She meandered homeward deep in thought.

The days were noticeably longer now but there would be no moon tonight. Taking her time, she wandered away from the path, in search of the season's marsh marigolds, dandelion greens and scurvy grass. She took note of their locations so she could return with a basket the following day.

"Apart from church, I shall spend the entire day alone," she mused. She wondered if she should have remained, there were a few fellow congregants who had stayed on to sing. She reminded herself of what she had to be grateful for.

Her heart fluttered a bit picturing what her life could have been like. She had heard stories that kept her up at night: stories of brutality, pain, deep suffering, and a sense of desperate melancholy from which some slaves never recovered. Some slaves chose to kill themselves, their hopelessness was that deep.

Rachel wandered further afield, paying no attention to where she was, lost in thought. She awakened from her reverie only when she came to a crossroads.

She looked about, muddled, "Where is Shelter Rock Road?" She began to wonder if she was lost until she recognized an ancient, gnarled oak tree. She was shocked at how far she had strayed for the tree she recognized was near Middle Country Road. Now the sun was setting and night would soon fall, she had to get home quickly. It would not be safe.

She turned back, starting for Cow Neck as she did, she heard the sound of approaching hoof beats around the corner. The rider came into view, his clothes were rough, travel-worn, and dust-covered. He approached Rachel, once near her, he reined up.

The stranger's face was hidden by the brim of his battered hat, so she could not see him. As he jumped from his mount he said, "What have we got here? A runaway!"

She remained silent and continued walking towards home (a strategy which had kept her out of trouble in the past), but the stranger grabbed Rachel's arm roughly.

"No sir," she answered belatedly, bowing her head. Suddenly afraid, she leaned into the thought of what she had once been, taking cover in a convenient lie, "No runaway, sir. But the slave of Phebe Dodge of Cow Neck."

He held her tighter, "Ah… Cow Neck, up north. I see what you done: a neat trick, to be telling me you're from so far away, and so late in the day."

He was no Quaker, and Rachel was sure he was not a Christian. She knew men like this: his mind was made up. She also knew what he was about to force on her—his own will.

"No, sir. That is, sir, she is a Quaker, and a good one. She released me for the day, it's my day off, it is Sunday." She appealed to the stranger's respect for Quakers if he had any.

"Ah! A Quaker woman! All the better for me: they're a beef-witted lot and not about to squab with me. Ye'll do—ye look a strong one!" He chortled, a harsh laugh. He kept an iron grip on her arm, all the while mocking negroes and Quakers.

The stranger paused his jabbering long enough to fuss with the horse. He removed the rope, the only tack on the horse, and hit his rump with a loud thwack. The horse galloped off wildly. He must be a thief who had stolen the horse but was now done with it.

The whole time he had kept a firm grip on Rachel. Then he began walking, his hand still on her arm. She tried to break his grip by going limp as a corpse. But he was not fazed, he kept a grip on her the whole time as her feet dragged in the dust behind.

He was strong, so strong he managed to drag her around a corner of the road and off into the bushes, at least a hundred yards. She changed tack and struggled, hoping to tire him. When he relaxed his grip, she hoped to break free. But he was an ox of a man. And no matter how hard she struggled, he successfully dragged her along. Then he stopped, spun her around suddenly, and deftly pinned her arms behind her.

There before her, hidden in the overgrowth, was an oxcart, its back open. The cart was crammed full of her people, heads down. Her captor shoved her towards the cart where a stout man stood before the open flap of the cart. The stout man wrapped his beefy fingers around her arm and leveraged her towards the open end of the cart.

Fire burned in her and she resisted, digging her feet into the ground. It was but a momentary resistance for she was no match, and the two men propelled her bodily into the oxcart with the others. The stout man nimbly leaned in, chaining her arms and feet to the floor.

Rachel cried out, "No! Help! You can't do this! Help!"

The first man slapped her hard with the back of his hand and her cheek burned in pain. A fellow captive peered up before he quickly looked back down. Rachel spat at the captor and received another, harder, blow. There was a small gasp from someone in the oxcart. Rachel put her head down and rattled the chains, testing them. The man next to her gave a slight shake of his head as if to say, "It's no use."

Both captors warned their prisoners to remain silent, threatening brutal reprisals. The captives were properly cowed and stayed mute, they did not need a reminder.

The oxcart did not move but stayed hidden in the overgrowth for a long time. Rachel's upper lip was wet. It must be blood. She gingerly felt her lip with her tongue. The lip was split from the captors' boxing.

Dusks at this time of year were lengthy. It came to Rachel the cart probably would not be moved until nightfall. The captors would wait for pitch black and its cover of darkness. They needed the veil of darkness to keep from being stopped.

She was right. The cart started to move once the sun was fully set. But instead of taking to the road, it did the opposite, the cart moved slowly into the deep woods. When the sun was fully set, all warmth had left the air, and a chill crept over her. Darkness drew in. She heard idle chatter and the sound of men drinking from a jug. But the cart remained where it was.

The captives remained silent as their captors passed the time drinking a large quantity of spirits. Then came the sound of snoring, the captors had fallen asleep.

Being chained in one position for so long made Rachel feel her age—her joints were stiff. She felt a growing soreness and throbbing of her jaw and face—injuries from the blows she had received. But the injuries did not compare to the fear that gripped her. What would be her fate?

Her fellow captives had not breathed a word. She took this as a warning. She read the tension in their bodies and the fear in their eyes, and it told her more than words.

Late at night, the cart started to move again. Rachel guessed the two men were nighttime drivers and would have the captives off their hands before dawn. The moonless night provided them with total cover. The cart bumped its way out of the hiding spot and made towards the road. As they jolted across the rutted roads, the noisy cart made it impossible to hear the two strangers speaking to one another. This was Rachel's chance to speak to the other captives, asking them the questions that had bounced around in her head from the start: Who are you? Who are these men? Where are we going? She gathered that most of them were like her, Long Islanders, who had been suddenly snatched.

There was a shared belief that the men were blackbirding: kidnapping negroes to resell them elsewhere as "escaped" slaves. These blackbirders would stamp her as a runaway slave who they had recaptured. She would be sold to an 'owner' in the South.

Rachel's blood chilled. She knew she was facing an empty future: she would never again see her family, Mother Dodge, or her home. Fear seized her and she could breathe only in short gasps, her heart was racing. She was panicking. Then with no warning the young girl next to her broke out in loud tears—startling everyone in the cart. She wailed on and on, inconsolable. The poor girl's loud sobs served to lift Rachel from her own spiral of panic. Restricted by chains Rachel leaned as close as possible to comfort the girl. But her whispers of comfort did not help. The girl kept wailing.

"Are you hurt?" Rachel asked, trying to find a way to help the girl. Everyone was afraid the cart would stop, and they would all be beaten. They were helpless victims of bullies.

"No!" The girl continued to wail, only louder.

"What is wrong?"

The girl replied but, in a whisper, and Rachel did not hear her words. She had to ask her the same question again, several times over, because the girl's wailing did not cease. Rachel struggled to lean towards her, the iron dug into her wrists as she did so, even then she scarcely heard her whispered answer.

Then finally Rachel caught a word, "baby…"

Rachel was stunned. The girl must be in her first few months of pregnancy. She could not imagine her terror. This explained her hysterical bawling.

Not thinking, only wanting to help, she made a promise to the girl, a promise she was sure she could not keep, "I'll make sure you and your baby are all right. We will get back home."

Rachel knew she could not change the girl's circumstances. She had no power to do that, but her promise had the power to comfort the girl. And though the girl continued sobbing, she did so more softly.

Somehow knowing this girl was carrying a baby made Rachel feel braver. None of them knew the others' status: slave, freed slaves, free-born. It did not matter, for here in this trap, there was no difference, they were all and each of them a captive, soon to be a slave.

Now the cart was slowing down to cross a marshy area. She felt she must think, must pay attention to her surroundings. She was not certain but guessed that they must be heading south. It was marshy at the southern end of the island, and so this meant they were not going to the City.

Rachel focused on her surroundings and her eyes adjusted accordingly. Despite the dark, the shapes and forms of the terrain were somewhat recognizable. From the bumpiness and narrowness of the brush, she understood the kidnappers were staying off the larger road, taking paths and passes.

The southerly area was a more well-traveled area making it more likely to be seen by travelers. Why didn't they take them north, then into Hempstead Bay, to spirit them across Long Island Sound? Then she remembered that blackbirders avoided New York, Connecticut and the East River for these areas were closely watched for instances of piracy and kidnapping. If the ultimate destination of the negroes was the southern colonies, then this route down the Island made perfect sense. Their final stop would be in a colony in the South.

This thought jarred her. For the first time since they had snatched her, she began to plot an escape. She was too valuable for them to be sloppy, she would be watched, and there would be no chance for her to break free on her own. No one would think to look for her, since it was Sunday, she had no duties at the homestead. Mother Dodge, and the rest of the family would believe she was visiting Azuba. And Azuba would have no idea she was not at Phebe's. Eventually, Mother Dodge would get her sons to search for her, but probably not today.

There was no escape for her. Whether she was freed or not freed mattered not. She was a kidnapped black woman, at the hands of mercenary men.

Once again, she felt despair overtaking her. Panic overwhelmed her, she gasped for air, her throat was closing, and her heart was racing. The despair closed in, and her world turned inky black.

CHAPTER 17

Cow Neck, New York, Late May 1776

When Phebe arrived home, the house was dark, and the homestead was quiet. "Rachel must have gone to bed early tonight," she mused. She lay down in her clothes, too weary from First Day and the visiting afterwards to stir the fire. After a long nap, she finally got up, readied herself for bed, and turned in.

When she awoke in the morning, there was no fire, and the house was strangely quiet. There was no sign that Rachel had entered the house. Phebe stepped out the door and looked out to the bay. It was breezy and there were a few clouds, but no sign of rain. She looked towards Rachel's little house, but there was nothing to see. Oddly, there was no smoke from her chimney, and no Rachel in her own house. Where could she be?

"Strange. Perhaps she's ill." Phebe said to herself. Of the few times when Rachel had been ill, she had lain in bed but got up late.

Phebe took her time getting her breakfast and taking care of the few morning chores in the house. Phebe had a boy stop in every day for outdoor chores such as milking. This freed Rachel for her own work.

Still uneasy about Rachel's absence, during breakfast Phebe decided she would check on her when the sun was higher. But then she heard Stephen arrive to take care of some tasks he had set for himself. Phebe went out to speak to him.

"I can't find Rachel. Will thee check the house and the garden for her?"

Stephen made several turns around the property, calling her name, as his mother stood in the doorway watching. He finally strode to her little house, knocked and put his head to the door. When there was no response from within, he opened her door and entered the dark house.

Coming out, he shook his head, "Her place is tidy but it's cold and empty."

He had hardly said the words when Phebe was at his side. She stepped into Rachel's house and surveyed the interior.

"Rachel's Sunday dress is missing." She explained when she had returned the previous night, she had not seen her.

"What happened? Where is she?"

"I'm not sure, but thee knows how reliable she is. She wouldn't leave all her belongings here."

"Maybe she's staying with her grandchildren?" Stephen suggested.

Phebe shook her head, "I doubt it: when she does, she tells me or Azuba sends me word." She looked back at the pegs where Rachel hung her clothes. "Something is wrong: her Sunday dress is not on its peg and," she added with a quick look around, "all her fancywork is still here. Something is very wrong."

"We must find her as soon as possible. Perhaps she is hurt, or ill, or worse…" Stephen was thinking of blackbirders but did not want to say it aloud.

Stephen quickly canvassed the neighbors for Rachel. The last house was the Sands home. Like the others, Mrs. Sands offered help. Here, he accepted her offer, dispatching the young Luke Sands for Hempstead to get both his brother Adam and John Willis to Cow Neck without delay.

* * *

When Rachel came to, the young girl was close to her. The girl's hand was under her head to protect it from getting bruised as the oxcart bumped along. Oxcart! The cause of her panic came back to her.

The young stranger whispered, "Are you good?" before removing her hand.

"Yes," responded Rachel, silently thanking the Lord that the world was still filled with kind people to look after strangers.

Rachel righted herself but moaned silently feeling the bonds on her arms as they dug into her. The fear which had driven her panic was now gone, replaced by disgust and anger at the kidnappers. She was filled with rage, *How dare they? I am a freed woman, and these thugs think they can sell me as a slave.*

As her anger swelled, so did her indignation. She would not crumble; she would never again be a slave. She had too briefly tasted freedom! Steely resolve came over her: she would escape.

She wished to scream at the top of her lungs against the injustice. She looked at the other captives: they were silent, they did not cry or even whisper. The young girl was absorbed by her own problem, while the others looked either resigned or despondent. Rachel shook her head—how can her mood, her will, be so opposite!? She would never give up. They could kill her before she gave up her rightful claim as a freed woman.

The cart clunked along clumsily, dipping into ruts, then brushing up against branches bordering the narrow path. Though the oxcart was slow, its progress had been steady. But now it seemed the cart was slowing to a stop.

Rachel thought about escaping. If she were uncuffed from these chains, should she run? No, she would for certain be caught, she dared not think of it. There had to be another way. She had to think. That is what freed people do: they use their wits to fight for their rightful claim.

Within a few minutes the cart had groaned to a stop. The cart wobbled and then heaved as a kidnapper clambered down from his perch. They heard groaning and shuffling. Then the stout man was at the cart, opening the flap.

Though the night was moonless, her eyes could make out shapes in the dark. The man hissed, "You all stay together, men and women. This is a piss stop: do it and do it quick. If you don't do it quick, you're gonna find piss down your leg. After this stop, there'll be no more, and you'll be worse off!"

He snorted at the thought. "No talking or yelling or else yer gonna be too hurt to walk." As if to emphasize his point, he carelessly swung a large club with what looked to be horns all over it. No one doubted him.

While he kept guard, the other man freed them from the hooks on the floor of the oxcart. Though freed from the cart floor, they still had cuffs and chains on their wrists. Clumsily, they clambered out and were then rechained to the side of the cart to prevent them from fleeing. The captors took the women by twos to the bush where they could relieve themselves. There were three women, which meant Rachel was unaccompanied but for the guard who stared hard at her form in the dark night. Once the women were done and rechained, it was the men's turn. Rachel noticed the kidnappers were vigilant, always keeping their eyes on their prizes: a man guarded one group, while the other took the captors to the bushes. Clearly these blackbirders had done this before.

As she waited, Rachel tried to get a sense of their location. She smelled ocean air, but it was different somehow. She recollected that earlier she had believed that they were heading south. If she was right, then that would account for the ocean air.

She thought of the families who would miss her. Azuba would not know for several days, but even then she could not leave her children. Her friends from church would be hindered from searching for her. The Motts and Willis families would search for her. But, she wondered, would they even think of looking to the south? More likely, they would search in New York. She had to do something to help their search. This might be her last chance to signal for help.

As she waited for the men to return to the oxcart, Rachel formulated a plan. It was a feeble plan and might not work, but at least she was doing something. She was still wearing her Sunday dress, and its skirt had a slip pocket. In the pocket was a handkerchief, on which she had embroidered "*R*" and a small bouquet of flowers. She pretended to arrange her skirt. As she arranged it, she let the handkerchief drop discreetly as she turned to climb into the cart. As she settled herself, she breathed a prayer that someone would search here and find it. She was dogged, and refused to give up hope. Doing something was better than nothing. This was her life.

CHAPTER 18

Late May 1776

All but the most essential work ceased as Phebe's family huddled together discussing Rachel's disappearance. In Westbury two other Friends had missing slaves. The parallels to Rachel's situation were too alike to dismiss. The slaves had been alone at the time, and had last been seen early Sunday morning. Adam opined, "If there are three missing, there are likely more." These similarities were not coincidences. Rachel had been kidnapped, Mother Dodge felt she had failed her.

"Rachel had scarcely enjoyed her freedom before being stolen!" Stephen said, his voice shaking with anger, "These kidnappers are bold to kidnap in daytime!"

Adam was thoughtful. "Kidnapping in daytime is risky and I reckon that must be hard to do. They must be blackbirders who do this often. If so, they know better than to travel until it is night." There was collective agreement that it was likely.

Phebe was impatient, "Let's not waste time with reasoning about the how's. We must find her." She took charge of the search, giving directions.

"John, thee start hunting below Plandome Heights then head in a westerly fashion. Though they likely have not gone to New York, still, we ought to check. I want thee there as soon as possible. Get thy friends along the way to help in the search."

She added, "My neighbors on Cow Neck are already searching. But she's likely not here. Sarah and Amy, go back to Hempstead and gather more Friends to help with the search.

"Stephen, in Hempstead take the road east but thee take only a few men from Westbury. Plan to get more help when thee passes through other villages." Stephen knew right away which men he would ask to help.

"Adam, take the road south. But bring with thee thy nephew Samuel—he's got good eyes and a stout heart." She looked at Samuel's father John. "If thee doesn't object. I daresay Adam will benefit having Samuel."

John shook his head, affirming her belief in John's affable nature. She continued, "We must write out a handbill." Phebe dictated the handbill and John wrote it out:

> "REWARD for recovery of freedwoman: Rachel, whose skin is very dark, hair is normal curly, has little grey. About five feet three inches high, about 45 years of age, apparently straight and well made. Having a small scar over her right eye and a scar on the right side of her neck. Also, a small scar on her right elbow, and several small scars between the elbow and wrist of the same arm. Reliable Quaker Friend offers reward."

He paused, "Mother Dodge, what about thy name and the amount?"

"Aye," she waved her hand, "Add that too."

Adam, Stephen, and John Willis copied Rachel's description on separate papers to have their own copy. Elizabeth's family would make more copies of the handbill to post.

Phebe began to pack a small bag. As she did, she continued, "I want to know of all and any signs of her. Spare no energy in this search. We may need to use some coin to do so, be mindful of that.

"I'll not stay here. I will not return until I know where Rachel is—" She waved her hands to still the protests of the family. "I'm going to Elizabeth and John's house; their house is in the center of the island."

CHAPTER 19

Home of Jesse Whitman, Rockaway, Long Island, New York

OLD JESSE WHITMAN could not sleep but he was often restless these nights. It had been windy overnight, and he wondered if it had rained.

Jesse finally arose before dawn and quietly slipped into his garden. He enjoyed the garden almost as much as fishing. He could almost hear the garden calling him, willing him to get started on spring planting. Was it too early? It was his annual question, for Rockaway was to his way of thinking, the warmest part of the Island. He contentedly puttered around, gathering his tools, and cleaning out the dead leaves.

After Jesse was done with his puttering, he paused. It was still too early to wake the Missus, and too early to milk the cows. He realized that he had time to catch a view of the day as the sun rose. He climbed the path which rose above his gardens, to the ridge where he could catch a view to the south.

At first glance clouds hung low over the horizon. He was pleased when he saw the clouds were quickly moving along, giving way to a blue sky.

He sauntered along the rise in the little-used ruts of an old Indian path. As he stepped into the path, his ankle gave a sudden twist and he exclaimed in surprise, hoping he had not wrenched it.

Jesse bent down to examine his foot and ankle for injury, and as he was doing so, he noticed what looked like new wheel marks in the winding pass. Curious, he righted himself to look both this way and then that way, towards the ocean, and from the north. But there was no sign of a cart or wagon.

He went back to study the wheel marks; they begged for a closer look. The ruts were noticeably deeper in this spot, the wagon must have stopped here. He turned his attention to his surroundings and noted the tall marsh grass around him looked flatter here. Perplexed, he wondered what had gone on.

Although he felt compelled to study this further, the cows were lowing, and they wanted milking. This could wait, but they could not. He turned to go back and as he turned, he spied something out of the corner of his eye. It was white, cloth-like, fluttering, caught on a low weed. He bent to retrieve it. Aye, it was cloth, it was a handkerchief. Large enough to be used when needed, but slight enough not to notice if it went missing.

Jesse scratched his head. The fresh wheel marks and the recently dropped handkerchief puzzled him: people did not frequent this area much. Yesterday there had been no passersby, else he'd have heard them. It had been a fine day, the sky had been clear, and he'd spent most of the day in the back of his house puttering around, doing small repairs. Perhaps they had passed when he had napped late in the afternoon?

He looked closely at the handkerchief. At first glance it seemed plain, like the ones that the Friends carried. It had no embroidery, no lace or tatting, and a simple stitch as a border. He turned the handkerchief over. The backside yielded embroidered perfection in the form of an expertly made bouquet of flowers. Intertwined in the flowers was the initial, "*R*."

At first glance he thought the handkerchief's owner was a Friend. But when he looked closer, he changed his mind, for it was an odd mix of plain and fancy. He was a bit of a lapsed Friend himself, sometimes imbibing in strong drink, and every evening he enjoyed his pipe. No one bothered him about this; indeed, his local meeting was filled with lax, easygoing Friends.

He would consider this later. He stuffed the handkerchief in his pocket and started for the barn and the milking. When he finished there, he joined his wife for breakfast. Once inside and at the table, his wife set his dish in front of him. But instead of seating herself, she hesitated, looking down at Jesse.

Sharp-eyed Mother Whitman asked, almost accusingly, "What is that thee has stuffed in thy pocket?"

"I found it in the path up above," he paused, "Did thee hear a cart or wagon yesterday—uh—probably afternoon?"

She shook her head. She did not ask, but he knew her curiosity was whetted. Ignoring her food, she took the handkerchief and sat down to examine it closely while Jesse enjoyed his meal in silence.

When she finished her examination, she opined, "I do not know what to make of it. It is the kind of fabric Friends use, rough enough to admit sympathy against slave labor, but it's cotton. Cotton isn't used by anyone who is connected with the Free Produce Movement."

What his wife knew always amazed Jesse. He had no idea what the Free Produce Movement was, only that it had something to do with slaves.

"The flowers were done with skill and care. But is overly fancy, so this doesn't signify a Friend. Or maybe it does, but one who is young and cheeky. But," she paused a second to organize the thoughts, "Why did she use only one initial? If I had done it, once I went through the trouble of the first letter, I would have added the initial from my other name, too."

She glanced at her husband, "Thee said someone dropped it here yesterday?"

Jesse Whitman considered, "Or last night."

Mother Whitman brightened, "Why, now I remember! I was awakened last night. I thought I was dreaming, there was the sound of voices and then a sound that went: chink, chink, chink. I also heard hooves. I was too tired to get up. I tried to wake thee but thee was dead asleep."

Jesse chewed, considering, then shrugged. It would have to remain a mystery.

CHAPTER 20

Late May 1776

SAMUEL WAS BORED. He repeated the same question to everyone he saw, and he was weary of stopping at every house. Searching for Rachel was no longer exciting. In between stops he had to plod next to Uncle Adam when he longed to sprint ahead.

They crossed over Plainedge and had finally come to the Plains. Samuel had not hidden his boredom from Adam but pestered him to run ahead. Adam was a methodical man. Samuel's youthful zeal and energy was both pleasing and tiring. Finally, when Samuel's complaints had worn him down, he announced a new search method.

"Thee is right, this is too slow. Let's try something different. Let's first go all the way to Rockaway, and then work backwards."

His nephew was puzzled by this new approach until Adam explained his reckoning: if kidnappers were heading for the south, then they were already far ahead of them. If so, it was strategic to go directly to the southernmost edge of Long Island where they might already be. If they did not find them there or any sign of them, they would work backwards from the south, moving northwards. He prayed that someone would have seen kidnappers.

Samuel was overjoyed but masked his jubilation at the new plan with a grown-up sentiment, "If I were a blackbirder, I would get off the Island as quick as I could."

Adam, "Truly said. Now, go ahead. Thee can run as fast and as far as thee likes. That is, until thee reaches the old mill road (the one that's fallen to ruin). Wait there for me."

Samuel sped away while Adam picked up his pace. It was after noon and the sun was high. Adam pulled an apple from his pouch, thinking he should have carried more food.

His shoes were starting to rub him raw. He wondered how long they had been walking. Finally the ruined mill came into sight, and he saw Samuel waiting for him, seated under a tree.

When Samuel spied Adam, he sprang up as if catapulted. "Uncle, uncle!" he cried across the field. Too weary to respond, Adam merely waved at Samuel.

Running out to meet his uncle, Samuel yelled, "I found something!" Despite his fatigue, Adam smiled at the enthusiasm of his nephew.

"What is it?"

"Come and see!" Adam picked up his pace.

"There!" Samuel said triumphantly, pointing at the ground.

"What?"

"There! See the wagon tracks."

Adam stared. Indeed, there were wagon tracks in a little used lane, which was barely more than a path. But the long grass was freshly matted around the tracks.

"That might not signify anything," the older man objected.

"True, but it might!"

"Aye. And it is all we have got." Adam paused to get his bearings, "If they've spirited her away this far south, they'll be going by sea, and from there to other places. Down the coast of these colonies."

Adam and Samuel walked on, following the wagon ruts. When Adam caught a whiff of salt air he judged they should be near Rockaway.

"I believe we're close to the south beach. Run ahead and be the scout."

Delighted, Samuel took off running, keeping his eye on the faint tracks as he sped along.

When Samuel came speeding back, he excitedly puffed out, "Uncle! Up ahead is a Friend working outside."

He escorted his uncle to the place where the path from the Whitman farm met the rise. Just as he had said, there below them was a Friend in plain clothes. The man did not hear them but was concentrating on a small object on the outdoor bench.

The two of them climbed down the path and accosted Jesse Whitman, "Hoa! Friend!"

Jesse was so intent on his project it took him a moment to hear the two of them hailing him. The lad and the man were strangers but recognizable by dress as Friends.

After the pair introduced themselves, Jesse removed his hat and scratched his head, dredging up names from his memory.

"I know of Seamans, Hicks," he continued with a list of names, until from the recesses of his memory he came up with Adam's name, "And I do know Mott."

Adam explained his mother had been Phebe Willets Mott but was now the widow of Tristam Dodge.

At that, Jesse's eyes lit up, "Why yes! Phebe Mott, what a fine Friend: so worthy, so good." He smiled at his memory of a younger Phebe, "Does Phebe still live? How is she?"

Adam assured him his mother was hale. But added that they were in haste, "We are seeking a kidnapped slave."

Adam told him of Rachel's disappearance, but added she was also a freed woman, who earned her own living. "On First Day we reckon she was kidnapped when no one was home. Blackbirded."

Jesse put down the bridle and rubbed his hands together, anticipating adventure, asking cheerfully. "Tell me more, Friend Mott. How can I help thee?"

"Did thee see any wagons, horses or travelers?"

Jesse shook his head. "No. It's been still as the deep woods today."

Adam's shoulders slumped, disappointed. At that moment Mother Whitman emerged from the house. Jesse made the introductions and rehearsed the Hempstead associations. A desperate Adam repeated the purpose of their journey to Rockaway while Mother Whitman listened closely.

"Blackbirders would not be traveling in daytime; it would be too dangerous. Last night I did hear something." She explained the noise, and added, "Wait here." She retrieved the found handkerchief from the house and handed it to Adam, "Jesse found this this morning, on the cow path."

"I forgot all about that!" he said, surprised at his faulty memory, once again, his wife and her active mind had overtaken him.

Adam examined the handkerchief, "Her name is Rachel, which explains the 'R' and she does her own handiwork."

Mother Whitman was triumphant, "I reckon it's hers. She has not got a family name, has she?"

Slaves usually had only Christian names, no last names. Though Jesse had lived with this knowledge his whole life, that fact had never been brought to his attention. Now that she said it, it was a jarring realization. In his middle age it had only just dawned on him that these, his fellow humans, were deprived of the one thing that he held most precious: a family and a family name.

"Why, thee's right." said Adam.

Mother Whitman added, "But thee isn't certain it's hers."

"No. But I believe it is," responded Adam. "Samuel, we need to remove to the water's edge straightway."

"If thee wants to shove off from the water's edge, then thee's got a hopeless situation on thy hands unless thee has got help," Jesse said. When Adam looked at him quizzically, Jesse explained, "Thee needs help in these parts. Folks round here aren't trusting of just anyone. But I can help thee."

"Oh! Would thee?" Adam pleaded with Jesse. A surge of purposeful energy poured through Jesse.

"Aye! But I need help. Does thee have any friends or family on Staten Island?"

"Staten Island!? No, why?" Adam realized even as he asked the kidnappers could possibly use Staten Island as their first stop, if only for rest.

Mother Whitman looked at Jesse in surprise, "Husband, thee doesn't have trustworthy friends on Staten Island?"

Jesse shook his head, "Mother, I know of no Friends on Staten Island who are still alive who can help us."

"Pah!" Mother Whitman replied, "Why a *Friend*? Thee can use anyone, so long as he's trustworthy."

She was right. Jesse walked in circles, stroking his beard as he thought before he halted abruptly, and exclaimed, "I know who can help us and though he be aged, I believe he's still alive. His name is Tunis Egbert and he's from a long line of Moravians. Tunis is Friend-like. And, importantly, he is well-known there by the mariners."

"Jesse is right about Tunis. He is up in years, but he is kind and honest. We have known Tunis and Anne for a long time. If he's alive and able, I am certain he will help." Mother Whitman affirmed, adding, "Thee will find good help from both Tunis and Anne."

Mother Whitman had the last word, she had proven reliable about everything else. Adam trusted her judgement regarding the couple.

CHAPTER 21

Staten Island, New York, Late May 1776

TUNIS EGBERT STEPPED out of his house on Staten Island. His wife Anne did not like the odor of his pipe mingling with the supper, she fussed about it, saying it "confused" her nose. Besides, it was too fine an evening to stay indoors. Outside he could have his pipe while taking in the sunset. He sat down on the bench readying the clay pipe bowl.

Months ago, British soldiers had begun setting up camps on Staten Island. They paused briefly during the winter. When the winter released its icy grip, they were once again at it, setting up more camps, only this time the camps were being filled with an alarming number of troops. He didn't much care for that, not at all.

Normally, strangers did not stick around Staten Island for long. Though the Islanders were used to ships and troops moving through, they always moved on. But recently this had changed, something different was going on—these newly made camps looked like they were going to remain for a long time. Judging from the size of the plots they had already confiscated, he guessed more troops would be arriving. There was a tension in the air now and it was unsettling. These new troops served as a warning, there was trouble afoot.

He mulled over the possible reasons for the British troops: New York was their obvious target. But he fervently hoped that it would not come to that for his daughter was married to a New Yorker.

The Egberts had always lived on Staten Island. A few years prior he had been made the caretaker of the Moravian church, and they had moved to the small house next to it.

Once his pipe was lit and Tunis had taken his first few puffs, he stood and stretched, walking in a circle. He was waiting for his milk cow who should be fetched back to him shortly.

He heard rapid footsteps approaching the church. He stopped to listen and then moved towards the sound of the footsteps coming from the footpath. He peered down the path, approaching him were two men, one about his age, and a younger one, in his 40s, he guessed.

"Hoy!" He accosted them from afar.

"Tunis Egbert?" asked the older man. They were Quakers: he recognized them from their dress.

"Aye, ye know my name, but I'm in doubt of yours." He scratched his head as if he knew them but had momentarily forgotten.

"I am Friend Jesse Whitman." said the elder man. Tunis recognized the family name, the Whitmans were of Rockaway on Long Island. "And this is Adam Mott."

The younger man added, "I am son of Adam Mott, the Younger. Perhaps thee heard of my mother, Phebe Willets Mott."

"Friend Phebe!" For Tunis, the past was as real as the present. "What a powerful figure she cut! How is she?" Tunis smiled, and he took hold of Adam's hand as if he could take in the essence of the mother through the son. Tunis favored Phebe Mott and she was legendary with the Staten Island Moravian church.

"She is well. In truth, she sent us to thee. We have an urgent problem on Long Island and perhaps thee can help?"

Tunis looked to his left and to his right, indicating his unwillingness to speak freely outdoors. He knocked the ashes from his pipe, and gestured towards his house, "Friends, come with me, mayhap my wife has some vittles for us. Or at least we can quench our thirst."

Tunis was delighted the men had come. He despised the troops and their camps, and their presence had stirred something up in him. And now he felt a curious mix of restlessness and anxiety. He wanted to do something. Everyday chores, such fetching his milk cow for the day, fled his mind.

CHAPTER 22

Staten Island, New York, May 1776

TUNIS EGBERT PROVED to be a cheerful helper. He refused to allow the guests from Long Island to help with the hunt. As he explained it, they would be useless or maybe worse. The locals on Staten Island were naturally suspicious of outsiders and it was better to keep their stay brief, Tunis explained. He added that even his own movements were watched by the troops, and he could not be seen to be acting in any way out of the ordinary.

At first Adam was reluctant to leave Staten Island without finding Rachel.

But Jesse Whitman spoke reason to him, "Tunis knows best. I reckon thee must trust him. She is not out of reach of Providence." Sometimes trusting others was the most direct way of trusting God, Adam heard the truth in Jesse's words.

He told Tunis Rachel's story, including the clues Jesse had found in Rockaway. Jesse added he believed the blackbirders had already left or were soon to leave for the south—they would not tarry. Before leaving, Adam handed Tunis the handbill with Rachel's description.

Even before he had finished saying farewell to the men from Long Island, Tunis was already thinking of the best way to search for the woman. Fortunately, his son Abraham lived close by. While there was still light in the sky Tunis set out for Abraham's home.

Abraham's help would be key to finding the woman. Although Tunis knew all the mariners and had many friends amongst them, he needed to broaden the search. With Abraham's help, their reach would expand, so much so they would search all of Staten Island. Although Abraham was not as well-known as his father, he was young and energetic. Given time, perhaps they could retrieve Rachel, or get further information on where she was.

He took Abraham out for an evening walk. As they strolled, he told him about Phebe's request. Abraham was enthusiastic about helping but curious. "Why are you so eager to get her back?" Abraham had never thought much about slavery. Slavery was something all around, it was like the air. Abraham's hesitation made Tunis pause: was his son worried about joining in with the search?

Tunis mulled the question over, "Perhaps age? I'm starting to wonder over enslavement. It is a terrible thing, no doubt. I would not want my wife or my son to be separated from me."

Abraham nodded, "Papa, I will help. I know of more wayfaring men than you. Pirates and thieves come and go all the time, I have heard every kind of story. But make no mistake, I hate blackbirders above all other thieves and pirates! I have had my fill of their wickedness—all for a few coins." Abraham's face twisted in revulsion.

Tunis' relief at hearing his response was almost physical. "Good! Just remember, we must do this in all haste and in quietness."

Abraham smiled and assured his father, "I'll be up and out before the sun rises, when those tars are still in their hammocks."

But his father would not be left out: "I'll meet you here before dawn then."

* * *

Adam and Jesse Whitman had paid extra for a ferry boatman to take them across the Narrows to Gravesend, arriving back home late in the night. When they arrived dead-tired at Whitman's cottage in Rockaway, Samuel was on a pallet in front of the fire. He was awake, and at their entrance he sprang up. He eagerly listened to their news and readied himself to leave for Hempstead to pass on the news to the others. But Adam delayed his nephew's departure till there was some dawn light. Helpfully, Jesse gave him advice on landmarks to look for so he could find his route north to Hempstead. Finally at Adam's word, Samuel raced off in the grey predawn to give his grandmother their news.

* * *

Between Tunis and Abraham, they covered all of Staten Island, but they discovered they were too late. Seamen told them a handful of people, slaves and their captors, had indeed crossed at night from Long Island, and then boarded a waiting sloop. The Egberts were thorough, and separated to search for the sloop, reasoning that if it was still in Staten Island, there was a chance of finding Rachel.

When they met up in the early afternoon, the men had come to the same conclusion: Rachel and her captors were no longer on the Island. They sat in silence for a spell. Abraham spoke. "All is not yet lost. We may overtake them, or we can follow her."

Tunis interpreted their findings aloud, "They are headed for Norfolk or Richmond, I wager. Once there she'll be sold or moved again. Aye, it's Virginia that she's bound for first. We must catch up with her before then, or she'll be stolen off for Georgia and set to work at planting! That won't do!" Tunis shook his head, dismayed. He was unsure of the next move.

Abraham tugged at his beard, then spoke slowly, "Think about it. It was yet night, not yet dawn when the sloop shoved off," Then, standing up abruptly he said, "Let's go down to the wharf. Papa, I know just the man. If he's in port, he'll think it a lark to fetch her back to her rightful owner. The man's no pirate, but he's high-spirited." Abraham urged.

Tunis stood up then, as he did, he checked his pockets making certain that he had a bit of something to help "persuade" the man they were going to meet.

The fog was dense at the wharf. What had been a cloudless morning had turned into a dark, overcast afternoon. Tunis waited under a tree as Abraham walked straight over to an older man giving directions to the hands on a ship. Tunis watched Abraham speak to the man. After listening to Abraham, the man nodded curtly. There followed was a short exchange between the two before the pair walked together towards Tunis.

When he was close Tunis recognized the man as Captain Copes, his gray and white beard and his wild hair made him distinctive.

Copes removed his pipe, coughed a few times, and cleared his throat, "You be looking for the scoundrels heading south?"

"That's right," said Tunis.

"Just so's ye know, I'll be putting out for Virginia at dawn, a regular run." Copes turned and indicated his ship with a nod of his head. "I'll not be promising to return them all. But I can squeeze in one negro on my return run north."

Hope dawned for Tunis. The captain continued speaking, "Those blackbirders could make an honest living if they wanted to."

Copes made it clear he abhorred those who harmed others, and blackbirders were, in his estimation, at the bottom of the list.

"You certain they shoved off to the south? They didn't put about and head in a different direction?" Tunis asked. In truth, he was testing his own idea by making use of Copes' decades of experience.

Copes shook his head, "Not a chance, they're too greedy." Then he cursed, puffed his pipe waiting for another question. When none came, he said, "I've a first mate who knows every slave trader by sight." Copes added, signaling his willingness, "How is it I'll know her?"

"She'd be in the plain clothes of the Quakers," Tunis pulled the handbill describing Rachel from his pocket. He read it aloud and handed it to Copes. Copes eyed the description. Tunis sensed that he was a quick study, and the description was already memorized.

Copes had no more questions. But before parting he gave Tunis advice to pass on to the family searching for Rachel. The family should keep her return trip a secret for as long as possible and should not bring her back home right away.

Further, Copes advised them to send Rachel to New York City upon her return. If not, she would be found and kidnapped again. New York City was big enough to hide her for a spell.

"Tell them they must be patient. And besides, the City is the best place to cover her tracks."

Before setting out from the two men, Copes promised, "If the British ships don't hinder me, I'll be back in a month's time. But," he warned them, "last time we had a rough go."

Tunis smiled to himself: Copes had tangled with blackbirders in the past. He felt pleased they had found the right man for the job.

CHAPTER 23

Summer 1776

MAY TURNED TO JUNE. It had been nearly a month since Tunis Egbert of Staten Island had accepted the challenge to retrieve Rachel. In that time the Willises and the Motts had not ceased their search for her. Phebe was relentless in her pursuit of Rachel and nearly every day she had a new idea, or different avenue to explore. She corresponded with New Yorkers, and people in every major city. She alerted her entire network of Friends, from north to south of her situation, recruiting help.

Stephen, Adam, and John Willis had never worked so hard. The entire family met regularly. They saw the wisdom of Copes' advice and planned for Rachel to stay in New York City for an indeterminate amount of time. The last leg, where they would have her brought across the East River through Kings County, and home to Cow Neck would be planned closer to the time.

Meanwhile the colonies were in chaos. They had temporarily laid aside their disputes but were now quibbling over what to do over the British problem. Within the colony of New York, any unusual activity was suspected. The animosity between the Loyalists and rebel sympathizers increased.

And there were practical difficulties for everyone. Phebe noticed that regular post mail had become sporadic. Rumor was that the British (or British sympathizers) would regularly "lose" a letter if it contained information that was contrary to the King. This ordinarily would not have flustered Phebe. But information about Rachel was sent from Tunis of Staten Island, and post mail was unreliable, so she felt stymied. The only way around the difficulty was to have letters hand-delivered by friends. John Willis suggested she use Joseph Hawxhurst as an intermediary. Joseph and his father had been in business in New York for decades but had a farm in Hempstead. As a prominent Friend who was a routine and regular traveler between Hempstead and New York City, he would be under no suspicion. When asked, Joseph readily agreed to transport her letters to New York, where it would find its way through the Friends' network in the City, then to Tunis on Staten Island.

* * *

Late in June, a mammoth British invasion force sailed into New York Harbor. Adam was working outside as Benjamin Birdsall stopped and told him the news. Birdsall yelled, "Adam, there's "Tories! All 'round New York." Then added, in a panic, "Not only that, but I also just got word there's a swarm of them in Massapequa swamp. Right now, I'm off to check on them."

Adam was more worried about New York and asked, "What's going on in New York Harbor?"

"It's Howe. He come down from Halifax." He lowered his voice conspiratorially, "There's word that Howe's brother, 'Black Dick,' is going to meet him here. If he does, then for sure they'll jam the harbor."

Adam gulped. The news shocked him to his core.

"Yep." Birdsall continued, "Already about 100 ships. Don't reckon they can put many more in the Harbor." Benjamin took off for the swamp. Only later did Birdsall find out how wrong he had been.

CHAPTER 24

Early July 1776

THE CONTINENTAL TROOPS in the City of New York heard the Declaration of Independence read aloud in camp. Not long afterwards American rebels in the newly formed "North Hempstead" celebrated as they heard the same document read on Cow Neck. News travels fast on Cow Neck, and Phebe had the news before Simon Sands flew to their doorstep to tell them.

A few days later Phebe was weeding in the afternoon sun. There was hardly a breeze off the Sound. Phebe was returning to her house from the garden when Joseph Hawxhurst appeared on the road. They moved into the shelter of her house. Joseph eagerly slaked his thirst, but explained he could not stay. Business in New York was pressing. He was on Long Island briefly but had to return to the City.

He pulled a sealed envelope from his jacket pocket. "I stopped by to drop this off with thee before returning."

Phebe's hands trembled as she took it from him. Joseph had been drawn in to the story of Rachel's kidnapping and anxiously waited to hear the news. Despite her eagerness, Phebe slowly and carefully opened the letter. She read it quickly and a smile spread across her face.

"It's from Tunis Egbert." Phebe passed the letter to him. Her eyes were filled with tears, she had no voice.

Written in a bold hand was a simple sentence saying Phebe had a "package" waiting for her, it was now in New York City. She was to wait for further notification of its location.

Joseph was jubilant and in awe that her kidnapping had been made right. He felt some of the same excitement Mother Dodge must be feeling.

"Why did he not tell thee where in New York?"

"To protect Rachel. In case the letter was lost. Right now, Friends in New York are helping her."

News of Rachel's safe return was sent off to the Mott and Willis family. Upon hearing the news, Elizabeth sent off a basket of bread, fruits, and jam to the Whitmans of Rockaway. She included a simple note of thanks from the family. She made no mention of why she sent the gift. The basket was their signal that Rachel was found and was safe.

When they next gathered, the family laid plans for Rachel's eventual return to Cow Neck. Although Rachel was safe with Friends, the harbor full of ships made them nervous. Practically the entire British fleet was on their stoop here in New York Harbor, awaiting orders. The family was on edge, but they strove to be practical: they knew they had to take the "British problem" into account as they planned Rachel's return to Cow Neck.

CHAPTER 25

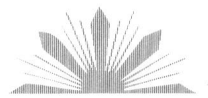

City of New York, July and August 1776

RACHEL WAS STIRRING STEW. She put another log on the fire, it flared up, and her face was aflame with the heat from the steam. She turned to escape the heat but even as she turned, the heat followed her.

She jerked awake. Had she been dreaming? She looked about. She was in a proper bed and the bright morning sunlight was pouring through a window. Was it summer? Rachel's head was throbbing.

A young girl in plain Quaker dress stood over her, her face was marked by kind concern. Wordlessly she held out a cup for Rachel to drink. As Rachel drank, the door to the room was pushed open and a woman swooped in.

"Good morning," said the newcomer, peering closely at Rachel. The newcomer picked up a cloth and dipped it in some sweet oil on the table under the window. She bent over Rachel and carefully rubbed her face gently with the soothing fragrant cloth.

"Rachel, how does thee feel?"

Rachel did not notice that the stranger knew her name. She accepted another drink, and answered, "Better, but…" Her eyes searched the woman's face questioningly.

"Truth! Thee cannot remember what has happened!" The woman's voice was warm. "When the Captain found thee on that miserable slave ship, thee was already ailing." Rachel's surprise prompted the woman to continue, "Aye. Sick with fever. Thee was so sick he wondered if thee'd make it to port alive." She paused, taking Rachel's wrist to dab it with the sweet oil, then moving to the opposite arm.

"Thank God the Captain was somehow able to get thee to Joseph's house but by then thee was like to die." She paused, giving Rachel time to collect this information. "Thee was too sick to stay there and I offered to look after thee. I'm Mary Hawxhurst, Edmund's wife."

Rachel could hardly make sense of what the woman was saying but realized she owed her a debt of gratitude. Who were these people? She gave the woman a wan smile of thanks. But smiling was draining, and she wanted only to sleep. The woman felt her forehead for a moment.

"Thee was ill, well and truly ill. But now thy fever has broke." She paused. "Thee yet has a fever. Not too awful bad, though." Straightening up, she smiled, "This is my niece, Rebecca." She indicated the young girl.

Rachel smiled a weak greeting, but the mention of an aunt and niece stirred something in her. *Family.*

She croaked out her questions, "Where am I?"

"Thee is ashore and safe in New York City. In our home. I'm Mary, my husband is Edmund Hawxhurst."

The City! Rachel's stomach churned: she feared no one on Cow Neck would seek her here. "But, my mis—my friends will never find me!"

"Nay! We sent messages back to Queens County." She placed her cool, light touch on Rachel's arm, "Thee knows Friends do anything for Friends."

Rachel believed this gentle, soft-spoken woman. Mary and her niece set about neatening up the room. Rachel closed her eyes against the sun and against the movement about her.

When they were done, Mary told Rachel, "Today thee must rise from thy bed—if only for a short while."

Rachel thought, no, I haven't got strength. The door was suddenly flung open by a stout woman carrying a basket.

Mary turned to the newcomer, "Polly, thee can take the sheets when we get Rachel up."

She turned back to Rachel and continued, "As thee does, thy strength will rise. Thee hasn't stood on thy feet since they carried thee off the ship last month."

Rachel croaked, still thirsty, "Is it June?"

"No," said Rebecca the niece. She added, "It's 7th month—and a hot one!"

Rachel's shock could not have been greater. "When did I last walk?"

"It must have been when thee came off the ship in 6th month. But thee had a bad fever and wouldn't remember that." Rachel felt stupid that she recalled nothing of this. Mary patted her arm sympathetically.

Polly had remained in the room; a heaping basket of linens at her feet. The niece Rebecca took that moment to slip out of the room. The woman moved closer, planting herself next to Rachel's bed, awaiting the bed linens.

Mary spoke coaxingly, "Rachel, I shall help thee sit up now. We want thee to drink some broth. After that, I will help thee get out of bed. Afterwards thee can return to thy rest." Mary was undeterred by Rachel's limp look.

Washerwoman Polly moved closer to the bed, ready to swipe the bedclothes once Rachel was off the bed.

* * *

When Phebe, the Motts and the Willises learned the gravity of Rachel's illness, they each harbored a private fear that she might die. But they trusted in the wisdom of Rachel's nurse. Mary was worthy of their trust; Rachel was well-tended. And with time Rachel grew stronger, was walking well, and her appetite returned. When Mary pronounced Rachel well, Rachel asked to return to Cow Neck right away.

"No," Mary was gentle, "Now that thy body is healthy, thy mind still needs tending." Rachel did not follow what she meant. Mary added, "Besides, we also must contrive a way to get thee back to thy home."

The attention of the world was on New York. The British blockade of ships filled New York Harbor. Washington and his Continental regulars were bunched up in the City of New York. They anticipated an attack by Howe's troops who were waiting orders, packed aboard the crowd of ships clogging New York Harbor. It would now be difficult, but not impossible, to get Rachel safely across the East River to Long Island.

Clearly the British were ready to take the City. Tension was high: it was sure to be a bloody battle. The City was in continual flux, its many residents were leaving, troops from both sides were coming and going, and meanwhile traders were wandering about, looking to peddle their wares in the chaos of pre-battle anxiety.

Then, in the waning days of July, Rachel had a relapse and her fever returned, but she was not nearly as ill. But Rachel still pled with her hosts to leave. Mary read her Mother Dodge's letter urging them to postpone Rachel's travel. Only upon hearing Phebe's request, did Rachel relent and give in to being nursed again.

At her first chance, Phebe called the family together to break the news of Rachel's relapse. Sarah broke down and gave voice to everyone's worry: Rachel would be lost, stolen, or abandoned in the City once the battle commenced. But Mother Dodge firmly assured them that the Hawxhursts had promised she would be back across the East River as soon as her strength had returned. Despite Phebe's assurances, Amy wept bitterly, deeply hurt at Rachel's hardships.

Adam arrived late. Phebe immediately saw the worry on his face. Apologizing for his tardiness, he explained he had news: the Continentals were dividing their efforts. Soldiers and engineers were hard at work across the East River from New York, building up and reinforcing the Brooklyn forts and redoubts everywhere, especially in Kings County on Long Island.

* * *

Mary and Edmund Hawxhurst had taken care to keep Rachel's presence a secret. Opportunists would view her as an escaped slave. Now Rachel's health was back, and she was feeling strong.

Mary remained reluctant to allow Rachel to travel. She explained, "Thy kidnapping and the fever dealt thee a double blow. Thy illness goes beneath the surface, for the kidnaping put thee off-kilter. Thee must heal from that. Thee must be in a place which allows thy trust in others to be refreshed now that thee is strong."

Mary's keenness caught Rachel off guard: what Mary surmised was the truth. Rachel had never said anything but since her kidnapping, she was afraid of everything and everyone. Every night she had nightmares where she would awaken, terrified and trembling. Sometimes she did not remember the dream, sometimes she did. During the day, though she never left the house, she would jump at the smallest sound. The kidnapping and the horrors of the enslavement had taken a horrible, a brutish toll on her. Though her scars were not seen to the eye, they were just as real.

July became August and by then the Hawxhursts felt like family to Rachel. They had restored her spirits, and, despite the chaos of the City, she was at peace in their home.

CHAPTER 26

Howard's Tavern, Jamaica, NY Tuesday, August 27, 1776

THE MUGGINESS OF THE DAY conspired to produce the familiar repulsive odor inside Howards Tavern. It came from the mix of grubby men, their sweating bodies, their smoke, spit, spilt ale, and spirits. The tavern owner William Howard was working hard, dripping sweat as he worked. He judged it was now about two hours after midnight.

The month's weather had been strange, alternating between hot muggy days, and days when the rain came down in buckets. Travelers from each direction stopped at the inn, shrewdly built at the crossroads of Jamaica Road and Cripplebush Road, and its strategic location yielded brisk business.

Closing the tavern was taking longer than normal tonight. He had given his son the job of putting away the equipment in his regular storage in the cellar. In the meantime, he scurried about in the semi-darkness securing his most precious objects (which included the best liquors) and money in a secret underground storage. He left the ales and the cheap liquor in their normal storage areas as a decoy to would-be vandals. If there was to be a battle (he felt sure it would happen), soldiers from both sides would seek treasure, both solid and liquid, in the tavern.

He silently cursed himself for not doing this earlier, he had been tempting fate all summer. But he had been greedy, wishing to make money as long as he could. That very morning, he had promised his wife to close up, and hide their most valuable goods. She was the voice of wisdom, and he blessed the day he married her. When his wife had first heard that Admiral Howe's fleet of ships hove into view, she badgered him about securing the tavern. Now he was paying for staying open, trembling with apprehension as he tried to get it all stowed. To be fair, innkeepers were always hearing rumors, and he no longer trusted his ability to discern what was true. That was his sole defense for ignoring his wife's counsel to close earlier. He feared the tavern would be ransacked if a militia—any militia—were let loose on it. Tonight to stave off a ruinous loss in case that happened, he worked feverishly.

In late June British General Howe with a few ships had anchored themselves in lower New York Harbor, off Staten Island. He had not wanted to think about closing then. But then less than a week later, he heard there was something like over 100 ships. And yet he still postponed closing.

In July, at the time Congress had spread to every county the "Declaration of Independence" from Britain, there were probably about 200 British vessels in the harbor. Howard's hopes had been raised briefly by the union of the thirteen colonies. Still, all summer the British had relentlessly built their forces in the American waters.

One day two British ships sailed up the North River blasting their guns. On that day, his wife begged him to close the tavern for their safety. But then, to everyone's surprise, there had been a reversal. The British tucked the ships back in the harbor and offered a peace treaty of sorts to the Americans.

Howard snorted at the memory of the British insult: they must think General Washington was a fool if they believed he would consider the British offer of 'mercy towards rebels.' Now as Howard heaved a barrel, it came to him that the display of British force should have awakened him. Grudgingly he acknowledged that the British were practiced in the strategy of war.

Aye, he should have been properly warned by the sheer number of British ships in the harbor alone. Who could blame him for staying open? With so many travelers, what with regular customers, strangers, and militia, business at both his inn and his tavern had never been this busy. He had done well.

The buildup of British troops overflowed from Staten Island to parts of New Jersey. The Long Islanders on this part of the island easily viewed British ships from land. At first it was unnerving, but then oddly, they had gotten used to the sight. He was inured to the sight of British soldiers.

With August even more British warships arrived. Some of the newly arrived vessels carried supplies and soldiers. His wife's brother said there were somewhere around 30,000 soldiers of the enemy. That number was too difficult to think about. The British had the run of Staten Island, and the local folk there were afraid to leave their houses. With all his heart he had hoped to see the British fleet pull anchor and sail off, if only to Boston, or Charleston, Philadelphia, or Norfolk. But the menacing fleet had remained bobbing in the harbor all month long.

Then when the British soldiers had put ashore at Gravesend and a great number of regulars were moved to Long Island. This was his turning point. The British regulars were neighbors now. Regulars were here for war, and war was bad for business. The American militia on Long Island had driven away all horses from the coastal areas, a clear sign they were expecting an attack. The large British presence meant the Americans were not going to pull out. Howard had relented: it was finally time to board up the tavern.

As he worked, he wondered when and if things would return to normal. It was hard to think that life would never be the same.

For the past few weeks, the American militia had been crowded into this little portion of Long Island, swarming all over Brooklyn, Flatbush, Flat Land, and Jamaica. They put up fortifications, patrolled and did what soldiers do when they are waiting. The locals went about their daily lives, and dodged soldiers who were conducting their assignments (though some were avoiding duties).

Then Tom Pritchard had shown up at the inn, breathlessly warning of turbulence ahead. Tom was returning from his daughter's house in New Utrecht, to the south. Though he had stopped for refreshment, Tom ignored his tankard, blurting out there were a huge number of British troops crossing from Staten Island at Denyse's Ferry. He had in fact passed by their camps. There were soldiers as far as his eye could see, "a sea of them!"

The tavern was silent as they listened to Tom's story. After he was fair talked out, they all quizzed Tom. When they had gathered all of Tom's knowledge on the subject, each man speculated about what might happen next.

One customer believed troops would head straight towards American forts up north in Brooklyn, because they defended the City from invasion. Another customer disagreed, reminding them of the weeks of work the Americans had put into their bastions, fortifying their lines. A scruffy regular who had been in the Indian wars, suggested the Brits would attack at the ridge, "the highest point in the area—it's good ground to hold." Someone else scoffed at his idea, he believed the Brits would draw the Americans into a land battle, and then the whole British fleet would sail up from their positions in the Harbor, and simply take the City by surrounding it. Another man objected to that possibility. William listened closely but remained his usual tight-lipped self.

The customers continued their lively debate. But when they leaned toward the taking of the City by water, Tom Pritchard objected vehemently, "Nay. It don't agree with what I seen with my own eyes—I seen too many British soldiers already ashore. There's gonna be a battle right here! I seen them!"

At this Howard's heart dropped. Tom was an eyewitness, and no fool. Howard gathered more details. As he listened, the edge on his anxiety softened when he learned that the British armies who had set down in Gravesend and New Utrecht would be moving soon. He hoped they would march east towards New York, away from the Halfway House.

But then this morning he abandoned this hope. No sooner had he opened when a regular rushed in, breathless, to announce that there were "thousands" of Redcoats at Flatbush. Flatbush! that was near to his tavern, and unexpected. When the customer caught his breath, and had a draught in front of him, he added that the Americans' fortifications at Brooklyn Heights were complete. The next customer had more information: there were American guards at the pass on Jamaica Road as you go towards the Heights of Gowan. Upon hearing this Howard felt slightly better.

Since the British were already ashore at New Utrecht, Howard still hoped for the best. To his way of thinking (as it was most practical) they should head for the Heights of Gowan, by Flatbush Pass, and then directly northwest to Brooklyn. He chose to believe this was what they would do. His tavern was northeast of the Heights of Gowan, not northwest. If they took the northwest route, toward New York, they would miss his place. But even if the British took a longer route, and headed for Brooklyn by Bedford Pass, they would still be far west of his tavern.

Still to be safe, he had decided to close up fully, at least until the Island was settled and quiet. He doubted he would open the next day or even the next week. The days ahead would bring a double measure of trouble and chaos. These thoughts propelled him to keep up his feverish pace of moving, stowing and hiding things, while sweat tunneled down his face.

He was not overly concerned with the safety of his family. The British were drawn to cities, the seats of wealth and trade, like New York. They surely would be heading for New York City, away from his place on the eastern edge of Kings County. East of his place in Queens County, there was nothing valuable at all, only a bunch of farms and a few tradesmen. There were no cities, nothing to draw the British there, either. He held out hope the British would make for Brooklyn Heights, and the Americans would take them out there. As a merchant he had to take extra care around militia.

CHAPTER 27

Howard's Tavern, Jamaica, New York, August 27-28, 1776

WILLIAM WAS JUSTIFIED in closing his tavern. The British had put into motion their grand scheme to take out or at least scare the Americans into submission. They had all the information they needed on the American locations. The well-prepared, disciplined, and well-equipped British foot soldiers had already dispersed across the southern part of Kings County. And they were already on the march.

Their plan was a multi-pronged attack on the American bastions and fortifications. Their starting point was the southernmost point of Kings County, below Brooklyn. One prong would charge up the western coastal road to Brooklyn, attacking the Americans as they went. Then, a couple of detachments were to drive directly through the middle of Kings County, to hit the Americans hard at the Heights of Gowan, and also near the Cortelyou House, by way of Flatbush Road. The British assumed the Americans would be expecting these attacks.

The British could not (nor did want) to hide the size of their forces. Still, they wanted an element of surprise. This took the form of a large detachment marching east, not west. This easternmost prong, headed by General Howe, had already begun his long march north on Kings

Highway. Howe's command veered northeast around New Lots, and then to Jamaica Pass, and from Jamaica Pass westward to Bedford. Howe's detachment numbered 16,000 soldiers and was set to pass close to Howard's Tavern. To take the Americans by surprise Howe's detachment marched by night.

Howe's massive detachment would eventually split outside of Bedford. The detachment was to split, and to attack from two directions, the north and the east side. They believed the Americans would not expect a major attack from the north, and would crumble at the force and the rapidity of the British attack.

Then eventually the several British detachments would merge, forming an enormous army in Brooklyn Heights. Most of the American fortifications were bunched together like 'old ladies huddled' on a jutting stub of land west of Brooklyn Heights. If the Americans remained in Brooklyn Heights, the British were confident they could, in short time, decimate the American army. The British hope was that the Americans would rapidly acknowledge the folly of the rebellion and quickly agree to a peace treaty.

While William Howard was closing his inn, Howe's huge detachment was already on the march. They had moved quietly through Flatlands and around New Lots. But as they proceeded westward to Bedford by way of Jamaica Road, their scouts returned to report there were American rebels guarding Jamaica Pass.

This was a problem: Howe had deliberately set out to avoid encountering American militia on Jamaica Road. Howe's officers queried the spies (three were local farmers) for options. One spy reported there was an Indian path, a shortcut they called Rockaway Footpath. If the army used Rockaway path, they would avoid detection. But Rockaway Footpath was swampy, winding, narrow, and heavily wooded.

Precious time slipped away as Howe was presented with the options and he weighed the merits of Rockaway path. There was no choice but to use the Path. But it would have to be cut back to widen it for the line as they went forward. Howe charged the officers to take Rockaway Path.

The spies attempted to find the entrance to Rockaway Path, but in the darkness they failed: the path entrance was too grown over. They gave up the search, suggesting they find someone who lived near the Path to show them where it lay. The officers directed their attention on the Halfway House tavern at the tiny crossroads.

That night an orderly line of British soldiers came to a halt in front of the tavern. The massive army was ready for a rest. William had just finished securing his secret underground location. Now he was inside the tavern, and his son almost finished in the cellar. He had just turned the key in the final cupboard which held cheap spirits when he heard something odd behind him. He cocked his head to listen better. *What was that sound?* It sounded like someone exhaling.

His spine tingled and his dread mounted. He did not want to see who had entered the tavern, unbidden. He turned, holding up his lantern. Key still in hand, he moved in the direction of the sound, and at the same moment a man stepped into the light cast by his lantern, revealing a fully armed Redcoat.

CHAPTER 28

Jamaica near Rockaway Path, August 28, 1776

"Unlock all doors," the Redcoat demanded. William flung wide the door and stood back. The regular surveyed the interior of the tavern, stepped out again and then a tall officer, whom he took to be in charge, strode into the tavern.

"What's your name?" the officer asked, surveying the room, then signaled the regular, who had already set up a table and chairs, to brush invisible dust from the table. William prized the four chairs, they were hard earned. The rest of the seating was crude benches.

The officer seated himself. Only then did other officers, similarly dressed in splendid regimentals, seat themselves around his table.

"Pour me your best," commanded the first officer.

William scooted to the bar and poured the officers' drinks. Pleased the good spirits were already secreted, he poured them cheap spirits. He wiped sweat from his brow as he worked. As he set up the drinks he fretted. Would they find the secret underground store? Would they ransack his store of alcohol? Farming was hard, but tavern-keeping had its own set of troubles.

To his dismay even more officers streamed in through the door, demanding free drinks. William scurried around, waiting on them.

William learned General Howe was the highest officer seated here and was mystified. Why would Howe, who was in the middle of a significant battle maneuver, be seated, apparently unhurried, idly chatting about the weather? Why would the Redcoats stop at the inn for refreshment? Something was wrong. He noticed Howe watching him closely. Finally, Howe spoke to him.

"You serve nothing but your best to the King's officers!" He winked at Howard knowingly, and he lifted the cup to his lips a second time. William exhaled with relief; he might yet be able to retain the best liquors in the keep.

Still speaking to William, Howe drawled, "The King and the British army command that you be our guide this night."

William was caught off guard, but only for a second. He shook his head, stubbornly, "I'm not healthy," he said. It was worth an attempt even though he believed that Howe was not naïve, and would see through his excuse.

Howe turned his mug about, and then answered, "And who is truly healthy?" Howe's languid gaze turned steely, "You cannot be that much of a fool. You are a British subject of the King, and I commanded you."

William was suddenly shaking. "Aye, sir. I swear this be true. I am nearly blind by night, and after dark can see nothing. To get to my own house," he indicated the attached apartment, "I must go by what I know from daylight and by feel." It was partly true. He could not see long distances, but he had no trouble seeing things close by.

Howe looked thoughtful, then asked, "Have you a son?"

William feared what would happen if he completely resisted, "He's in the cellar, helping me finish for the night. He helps because of my eyes." Part of that was true.

Howe was silent, waiting for more. William finally pointed to the cellar door. Soldiers were dispatched to fetch the 16-year-old, who was dragged protesting from the cellar. His protests halted when he saw his father.

Howe turned to William, "The two of you shall guide us to Rockaway Path."

William hid his surprise. What was going on? The appearance of the British at night was surprising enough, he wondered why they were this far east. Why were they not marching directly to Jamaica Pass? Rockaway Path was mostly unused; it was narrow, rocky, and much overgrown. Then he realized by using Rockaway Path, the soldiers would avoid detection if Americans were guarding Jamaica Pass.

He understood two things: the Redcoats were positioning themselves, and at the same time the Americans were being stalked in their own territory. His bile rose at this realization and a surge of anger moved him to speak rashly.

Belligerently he replied, "We belong to the other side, Sir, and can't serve you."

His son nodded in vigorous solidarity with his father. Howe did not reply at first. He simply continued sipping his drink and took his time before responding to William's outburst.

When he did, he was relaxed and unhurried, "That is all right, your choice: stick to your King and country, or stick to your principles." He shrugged indifferently.

Despite the mass of troops all around them, the summer night was eerily still but for the crickets.

Howe continued in his drawl, "It makes no difference to me. You see," he paused briefly, "If you wish to stay loyal to your fanciful notions then you have boxed me in. You noted earlier that I am in the King's service. Understand that I have my orders.

"This means that this entire island is under the British army, and therefore the very patch of dirt you stand upon is under my authority.

"I have no choice but to force you to obey me. As you will not do it willingly, I shall make you a prisoner. As a prisoner, you will do as I say. And tonight, you shall guide my men over the hill."

William's resistance was not abated. He spat on the ground. "Never! This is my land, not the King's!"

The General shook his head as if dealing with a peevish child. Silencing William with his hand, he asked, "Are you thick-headed? It is not up to you to refuse. If you insist on refusing, I shall have you shot through the head."

The officer turned his head and looked at William's son. William realized he had no choice, if they shot him, Howe would make his son do what he refused to. William quickly mumbled his grudging consent.

William and his son grudgingly led the advance party to Rockaway Path. His son took the lead, easily finding the narrow path which climbed a hill, and then wound down through a valley. William recollected it only when his son led them there. The British were satisfied. They did not have to tarry in the dark, searching for a hidden path intensely overgrown.

The advance party carried tools for the job. They worked in the dark, cutting back the brush, widening it for the lines to march through, coming out near the Pass. The party moved slowly up the path. After an hour, the officer in charge of the party grew impatient with the excruciatingly slow progress and sent back for more help.

When they were nearly at the Pass, the soldiers came upon five dozing American militia, who they took as prisoners of war. Curious, his son asked what would happen to them. He was told there were ships in the Harbor especially for soldier prisoners. William cringed inwardly, wondering what kind of treatment the men would have aboard a prison ship.

The party reached the turn in the Brooklyn and Jamaica Road, but the commanding officer had not forgotten the innkeeper and his son, for their return trip was made under guard. The British were careful: their secrecy was now dependent on the Howards' silence—they could not allow the Howards to alert the countryside to the soldiers' presence. At least not yet.

CHAPTER 29

Hempstead and Flushing, NY, Sunday-Tuesday, August 25-27, 1776

With Henry Smith's money worries and all the war-talk, Henry had had too many sleepless nights. Moreover he did not like that the Quakers were freeing slaves; he could not afford to be without them. If he could not keep his farm nor his lands, he would be ruined. Then, he was certain, Leticia would leave him.

Sunday had begun like any other: he had gone to church with Leticia. After church he lingered, chatting with other men. Naturally, the conversation was about the British. Apparently, there had not been an attack on the north at all, only a small skirmish, little more than a bother in Massapequa swamp. The disturbance in the north was a distraction to pull their attention away from the south shore, around Gravesend. Everyone now knew Gravesend was where the British would invade. Though the City folk believed they would be attacked first, the Long Islanders knew better, the British had been preparing all summer to hit them in Gravesend.

The buildup had come in waves: first by the entrance of 130 ships to the New York harbor, the ships holding thousands of British regulars. Then, more ships arrived in July, and even more in August.

Today Robert Miller told them he had gone to his cousin's on Staten Island and found it was completely covered with soldier's encampments, to the point that farms were overrun by them. The soldiers took what they could when they could get away with it. His cousin was relieved when Robert cut short his visit, confessing that he could scarcely manage to feed his family with the soldiers there.

Henry asked about the ships. Robert said there were all sorts of ships, far too many to count. Robert did not know how many, but guessed there were hundreds. Turnhill added that the British were no longer just aboard ships or at Staten Island, but had come ashore at Gravesend to the south. When he added, "That's no rumor," Henry's blood ran cold with fear.

"How many soldiers? Hundreds?" he asked Turnhill who seemed to have facts.

"No one can say." He clicked his tongue in thought, "At least ten thousand, maybe twenty!"

The men gave a collective gasp. Hearing this news made Henry's head hurt.

As he listened, his hands were clasped behind his back, and he felt someone pass behind him. Whoever it was pressed a small sack into his clasped hands. Henry knew from the feel of the sack that it contained coins. He stealthily slipped the sack into his coat pocket. He hoped, nay, he believed it was winnings from his last bet.

When the men had run out of news, they moved on to speculating about what would happen. Henry would have remained there, but his curiosity drove him to look in the money sack. He stepped behind a tree and withdrew it from his pocket. Upon opening the sack, his day brightened: he had won his last bet.

The news about the British ships and soldiers had rattled him badly, but once he saw the heap of coins in the sack, his nerves were strangely calmed, and his mind was eased. His large gambling debts slipped his mind. These new-found winnings were so large he was stupefied. He could think of nothing else.

He felt good. Why ruin his happiness by telling Leticia that his luck had finally broken? She did not believe in luck, and it would make no difference. Aye, she knew about his gaming, she hated it and nagged him about it all the time.

Just thinking of her and her nagging dimmed this bright day. As his happiness ebbed, the memory of his gambling debts resurfaced. What to do about them? He leaned against the tree to think. Since they had survived badly in debt till now, he could hold off a bit longer, till he won more money. After all, wasn't this new win a sign, a sign that his luck had turned, and that his next win would be the biggest yet? Yes, his mind raced, and his heart skipped a beat at the thought of a new game, one which would add to his winnings. After that, he would stop and would pay off his debts entirely. Leticia would be beaming when he surprised her with that. Cheered, he rejoined the knot of men still exchanging news of the British soldiers.

Later as Henry and Leticia made their way home all he could think of was the money he had stashed in his coat pocket. When he was finally able to count it out in private, he discovered it was a larger amount than he first believed. He felt a surge of relief. The next win would be much bigger, of that he was certain.

But where to gamble? If he played the next game too close to home, word could get back to Leticia. He did not want her haranguing him or worse, stopping him.

For this reason, he had to get out of Hempstead, to leave the area—but where? By nightfall he had settled on a tavern far west of them, in Kings County. This way he would avoid British soldiers, for they were to the southwest in Gravesend. The tavern was well to the north.

On Monday morning he left his house with the dawn. He had waited till bedtime to tell Leticia he was going to Madnan's Neck. It was a lie. Leticia fretted about the soldiers roaming the countryside. She knew both sides were putting up fortifications, and fighting would break out soon. He waved away her concerns and promised he would be well north of any fighting in Madnan's Neck.

Henry felt guilty, he had never told such a bold lie. Hiding the truth was different somehow. He started out going west but instead of turning north towards Madnan's Neck, he turned south once past Jamaica.

At midmorning, the man who ran their farm appeared at Leticia's door to tell her that the British had landed on the North Shore, at Brookhaven, somewhere between Oyster Bay and Setauket.

"The North Shore?! But I heard they were at Gravesend!" She was incredulous. Now she did not know what to believe. The stories about Massapequa Swamp had been discredited but the existence of a huge British fleet in New York harbor was indisputable. The farm steward continued talking about Oyster Bay, to her north.

"And, not only that, but there's shooting!" he added.

"Shooting?"

"Yep. I heard they're shooting all the livestock."

"They're not gettin' ours!" she screamed. None of this made sense to her. Were they surrounded on the north and on the south? Or, was this another trick, to distract?

Henry, already on his journey, knew nothing of the news. He was pleased he had made good time. He was out of Queens County, past Jamaica. The sun was high, and he was thirsty and hungry. He figured he deserved a stop at Howard's Tavern, commonly called "Halfway House" because it was halfway to Brooklyn. Henry was in a convivial mood when he stepped inside.

After lunch and a few short games, he counted his money. When he realized how much those few games had eaten into his funds, he took a break. He sat on a bench and put his head down. Then suddenly he was awakened by a large man with foul-smelling breath. "Ye playing or not?"

Refreshed by his nap, Henry felt buoyant and confident his luck had returned. He sat up, rubbed his face, then he, the giant and a third man placed their bets. The giant won that game. Henry was not shaken but kept playing. The number of willing gamers at the inn made it easy for Henry to keep playing.

Hours passed and the sun was low in the sky before he could accept that his good fortune had not returned. But by then Henry was in no mood to go home. He chose instead to remain in the cheerful tavern, listening, lazing, smoking, talking, and drinking.

It was not till sometime past midnight that Henry finally left Howard's Halfway House. To his surprise and embarrassment, he was stumbling and disoriented.

"Why, I'm too drunk to go home!" he muttered aloud, "I need to find somewhere to sleep this off."

He set out towards a friend's place in Flatbush but had not gotten far at all when he was too tired to continue. He sat down on a nearby log. The air was close and sticky, and he was sweating from the humidity and the effort.

His numbed mind wondered: How could he convince Leticia that his losses tonight were not all that much? No, he was afraid. He couldn't tell her. He wouldn't tell her.

In his drunken state, he easily convinced himself that he would be able to keep this a secret from his wife. Once he had resolved to keep the night's losses a secret, his panic subsided. The moon was dim, and the air was close. He was suddenly drowsy and the log he was seated on was wide enough. He stretched out flat on the log and was soon asleep.

He dreamt there were Redcoats in his house, and he was trying to keep a bag of gold stored under the floorboards a secret while the Redcoats streamed through the door. They kept on coming. There was an endless parade of them. He grew increasingly worried about the hidden gold. With the illogic that happens only in dreams, the endless stream of mounted officers and their horses fit inside his house. His wife stood at the open door smiling graciously as the soldiers entered.

His dream drifted away, and he stirred, half awake. He lay there, aware he was no longer dreaming. He remained still, listening: was that the sound of marching soldiers? He pried his eyes open. He was not at home, but in the woods, lying on a log.

What he saw was so hard to believe that for a moment he wondered if he was still asleep and dreaming. Passing him on the path, was an endless stream of troops and horses. He could not make out if they were American or British troops. Before this Henry had not paid a lot of attention to the conflict, but upon seeing this display of martial might, he grasped the gravity of the war. The sight of soldiers on the move sent him into a panic.

He was suddenly sober. He barely breathed as he listened to the soldiers marching past him. They neither slowed nor paused; the steady stream of men continued flowing like a river. Now fully awake, it came to him that this was an odd thing to do, moving troops after midnight. But here they were, and he was not dreaming. The troops were surprisingly quiet considering their numbers and the swiftness of their travel. Though he was no military expert, he knew these men were on the move for a battle.

He was suddenly aware of himself: a fat sweating man lying on a log in the brush at midnight. Cowering, he feared he would be sighted. But no one had detected him. Maybe, he thought, they'll not see me, and I can just stay here, melting into the log.

After a long time, his curiosity overcame his fear. Slowly and carefully, he rolled to his stomach and pressed himself into the log, staring in the direction of the pathway. He had no idea what time it was, but it was not even early dawn.

He made out they were Redcoats, and they were marching four abreast. He waited for the line to break, but they kept coming. How long was this line? It seemed to be without end, there must be hundreds of them. He watched with growing alarm at the sheer number of soldiers.

He felt a sudden urge to sneeze but held it in. Holding still for so long made him sore, but there was nothing to be done about that. His muscles ached, and the mosquitoes were thick and biting. The humidity was a lead weight on his chest.

He waited in silent stillness as what seemed like the entire British army tramped by him in perfect formation. He wondered how such a small place as this, this little corner of Long Island could support thousands of troops.

Despite the heat, he shivered when a dark cloud of fear crowded his thoughts. He turned his mind towards his farm, his home, what he would give to be away from this scene, and back in Hempstead, at the side of his nagging wife. Would the Redcoats attack Hempstead and his farm? If they did, how would she fare? The Redcoats were coming, but more quietly now as early dawn was barely breaking.

CHAPTER 30

August 27, 1776

ONCE BACK AT THE INN, William and his son returned to their house where the rest of the family was, behind a stout door. From within the house, they listened as the troops marched on, by way of the Rockaway path. His wife asked how many soldiers there were and William estimated the troops numbered in the thousands. It was a wild guess because of the dark night.

"When do you think they'll get where they're going?" asked his wife.

William shrugged and yawned with exhaustion. Their son had been listening closely to the British. He interjected, saying they were off to Bedford.

"Why Bedford?" his wife wondered.

William tried to sound casual, "Probably to meet another detachment."

Exhaustion overtook him and he fell asleep in his sweat-drenched clothes. When he awoke his wife was sitting up in bed and a candle burned low at her bedside. She had not slept.

Groggy as he was, William made himself cheery, "You needn't be too worried, because the American regulars are in Brooklyn and George Washington is commanding them!"

"How many are there?" she asked.

"Don't know," he confessed. "I heard it was maybe 4000? Or was it 3000? I forget. They are mostly at the Heights of Gowan, and Brooklyn Heights."

His wife frowned, still anxious, "Is that all?"

"Most of the rest are in the Brooklyn forts, next to New York City."

She rolled her eyes. Fighting back his drowsiness, he set his mind to thinking about the strength of the British force. If he was right, Howe's line alone was more than double the 4000 of Washington's. Howe's line, the one that passed his inn, were not the only soldiers on the Island. He now saw reason for his wife's fear.

From the recesses of his memory, he pulled information passed around at the tavern this summer, this month, this week. Howe's command was but a portion of the British army. Who knew how large? He was certain the British army would be careful, and not haphazard, in engaging the Americans in battle—or battles. Where or when, he did not know, but probably not too far from his home.

Now alert, the full importance of how he had just helped the British came to him. Regret surged, and he hid his face in his hands out of shame.

"What's wrong?" his wife asked.

When he finally gathered himself, he whispered so low the children would not overhear. "Ma, I, at the point of a bayonet and under threat of death, done an awful thing this past night. I led them where they wanted to go."

He told her how the British had threatened their son. He confessed his fear at their flashing weapons and commanding presence. He could do nothing to change it now. It was done; he put his face in his hands and bawled.

"This will be crushing. The Americans will not look for an attack from the north. I am at fault because I showed the British Rockaway path. Those who marched by us is more than we have all together! The

Brits could put an army of troops to the south on Flatbush Road. If they do, then Americans will lose the battle!"

"Are you telling me they will make a 'hangman's noose' with their men?"

"Yes!" William was profoundly distressed.

"Let's not speak of this again," said his wife, taking his hands comfortingly.

Within an hour of their conversation, the troops William had helped through the pass were at Bedford village.

The Americans fought doggedly, it was of no use: they were outnumbered and they were cornered. The British had pinned the 3000 American troops in the forward positions at the Heights of Gowan, and on Brooklyn Heights, overlooking Flatbush, Flatlands, Flushing, and Jamaica Bay.

Before the day was over, British troops covered all of Kings County, except for the few American fortifications in Brooklyn. Stuffed into Brooklyn were thousands of American soldiers. They were trapped in a corner as British ships packed New York Harbor. Across the East River to their west was the much-depleted City of New York. Everything below them, and to their east on Long Island was secured by the British.

Much to his shame, William Howard always believed that he was partly responsible for the calamity the American forces were faced with that week in 1776.

* * *

The following day, Wednesday August 28, General Howe began to build regular siege works. But the British did not move on the Americans. The officers were of the opinion that the Americans (certainly an officer like Washington) would recognize that coming to peaceable terms with Britain was their only sensible avenue. But if not, British officers believed were on firm footing. Once fair weather returned, their military superiority would overcome the newly demoralized and vastly outnumbered Americans.

CHAPTER 31

New York City, August 1776

AT THE END OF AUGUST, Rachel's nurse and new friend, Mary Hawxhurst, received bad news. Her mother at Nine Partners had a sick spell and her needed attention. She had to leave. It was another boiling hot day when Mary stepped into Rachel's room with the news, clutching the note in her hand, her face a rumpled mess of tears. She and Edmund would depart immediately for Nine Partners. And Edmund was, at this moment, arranging Rachel's exit from the City.

"We had planned on leaving after next month!" she moaned to Rachel.

Until now Rachel had thought nothing of her hosts, but Mary's plight and her distress shocked her, casting light on her own selfishness. Rachel leapt to her side, taking Mary's hand in hers, giving her the most Friend-like affection. Without realizing it, Rachel had adopted many of the Friends' mannerisms. Rachel insisted Mary leave to tend to her own mother.

Later, Mary's husband Edmund shared a sliver of good news. Although Howe's troops were jamming New York Harbor, there were still ferries and boats across the East River to Long Island.

Edmund and Mary disliked breaking promises, and were unhappy that Edmund could not escort Rachel across East River to Long Island. But Rachel convinced the couple she would be happy with any new plan to get her home.

The following day everyone was up early to pack up the Hawxhurst household. Edmund exited early to take care of some business before departing the City. Rachel had very little to do to ready herself. Her only possessions were those Mary had given her.

Edmund returned from his predawn mission, shutting the door against the noise, dust, and heat of the streets. Mary and Rachel turned to him expectantly.

"I sent word ahead to Mother Dodge to expect Rachel," Edmund told them. Rachel marveled afresh at the networks the Friends maintained. Edmund turned to Rachel, "I asked my steward, James Thrush, to escort thee across the East River."

Rachel felt a surge of joy. Her life on Cow Neck had given her contentment and peace. Then for months she had been yanked out of that and had grappled with fear, hate, illness, and an aching loneliness for home. Now thoughts of home filled her heart with joy. Whatever happened next, she was now ready to face it.

CHAPTER 32

New York City and Kings County, New York, late August 1776

The grimy City air was both smelly and muggy and it made the Wanderer Big Jack long for the fresh air of Long Island all the more. Although the air in the City was always foul, he found it worse than it had ever been. When a New Yorker agreed, he blamed it on the extraordinary amount of people and animals moving in and out of the City, adding that a third of the city's population had already left. If the man was right, it explained why Big Jack could not find his friends.

The City felt tense, or was it a feeling of doom? He could not put his finger on it. He was sure it had to do with the British presence everywhere. Everyone expected British General Howe, or his brother Admiral "Black Dick" Howe, who commanded the great fleet of ships, to take the City at any moment.

The Americans had just been soundly crushed in Kings County on Long Island. They now had but a delicate toehold in Brooklyn Heights where they huddled defensively behind their forts and bastions. Admiral Howe had clogged New York Harbor with hundreds of British ships, barricading an American escape by sea. His brother,

General Howe with his tens of thousands of soldiers would certainly take the Americans in Brooklyn. After that, Howe and his forces had to but cross the East River from Brooklyn to take the City. All talk of independence for New York had ceased; the City would soon be overrun by the British invaders.

The agitated City unsettled him: it was empty of its normal life, its vitality drained by panic-filled civilians and unhappy soldiers. There was no one to drink with. Big Jack wanted to gamble, but he would have to play with strangers. People were on edge, all lives were upended, and there was no sense that it would be righted soon. Big Jack had no reason to prolong his visit. He cut it short and was fixed on returning home.

The sweltering heat had finally broken the day before, and the sky had opened up. Yet Big Jack did not sleep well. As he lay there in the dark, listening to the ceaseless pummeling rain, he ticked off reasons to leave right away. Howe's forces would be coming into the City. His army, like any other army, must eat. The army would take all the food they needed. New York was already bad off, and when the army swept through, there would be no food for the rest of the folk. He would leave right away.

But Big Jack would have to go east across the East River. Normally, crossing the river was simple but since the battle in Brooklyn everything was in chaos. Although the battle was over, the campaign to take New York City was ongoing. There would be spies from both armies and other soldiers eyeballing everyone who crossed the river. That thought sent shivers up his spine.

He got up right away and headed down to the wharf where he was surprised at the number of deserters from the American side. One man had deserted Washington's army before they even got to Brooklyn. He was looking to join a ship going north to Kingston. After Big Jack pointed out to him that he would be safer in civilian dress, the man was happy to trade his uniform for Big Jack's hat and clothes. During the transaction, the man going to Kingston complained about the deficiencies of the American army.

"We ain't gonna beat them Lobsterbacks," he moaned. He told of the tens of thousands of soldiers who had marched into Gravesend and Flatbush, and were to take Brooklyn.

"Betcha' after a quick break for grub, they'll be in this City. I ain't gonna be caught dead as a rebel American." He gave Big Jack the side eye, "You gotta be crazy to want this uniform. You'll be dead or captured as soon's it's on yer back." He removed his uniform jacket, and the two men exchanged clothes.

Big Jack did not care what the man thought of him. He would brave being an American soldier to get from the City to Long Island. He wondered if the size of the British army was but a rumor. He asked the man, "Did you say there are 30,000 of them?"

"Some say 20,000, some say 30,000. It don't matter much when it's that big. I seen enough of them. We're gonna lose the war and they're gonna crush us beneath their boot." He set Big Jack's hat on his head, and turned, setting off for the North River.

The morning had been hot with short periods of light drizzle, interrupted every now and then by a downpour. Big Jack donned the jacket, and he found it was too tight. But a burst of rain soon soaked the jacket through, turning the dirty jacket to a wet muddy one. This suited Big Jack, for a soaked and muddy jacket completed his disguise as an American regular.

He searched for a ferry to take him across the East River to Long Island. Luckily, he had coffee, which was better than cash and shortly he found a ferry boatman willing to make the trade. As they crossed, the oarsman complained about the wind, suggesting that he was underpaid. Big Jack ignored him and turned instead to view the harbor chockablock with ships and boats.

But what about the Americans? The Heights came into view. From what he could see the American defenses were a motley bunch of breastworks along with some hurriedly thrown up earthworks. When he caught sight of a fort, it was small and frail looking.

Once ashore, he found something about the air was different, strange, as if there were so many smoking fires alight all over Brooklyn. The smokiness hung heavy and gray in the air. The summer's humidity exacerbated the feeling of oppression. Every now and then he heard a booming sound certainly coming from the opposing armies on this small tract of land. But most disconcerting, the normal sounds of farming and boating were missing, either gone silent, or topped by the sounds of the encampments. At least he was across the East River. The only thing between him and being in the countryside of Long Island was getting around the army (or armies).

As he moved inland, he saw no large-scale movement of regulars. He believed that the Continental regulars were staying put, at least for the moment. He mulled over his next move. How would he get past Brooklyn and on his way unmolested? Should he try to go around the army? He was still in the American soldier's uniform. He needed to figure out a way around the encampments and then push east.

As he walked in the direction of a small fort, his answer came to him. He would use the American uniform he was wearing to his advantage. He noted a continual stream of men hauling water back and forth from the river and streams to the camps, the breastworks, and the forts. He turned towards the fort and, using the uniform to pose as a water hauler, he slipped easily into the fort.

Big Jack roamed the fort till he found the officer's dining area, then he strode into it confidently. He ported in the bucket. He immediately picked out the cook, easily identified by the filthy apron he wore. The cook was standing over a table strewn with scrawny vegetables, bowls, and cleavers. But the cook was not working. Instead, he was in a fierce argument with a man sprawled on a stool nearby.

After setting down the bucket, Big Jack faked his exit, withdrawing to the shadows near the doorway. There he remained in the officer's dining area unnoticed.

The argument stopped abruptly when the man on the bench fetched a nearby bucket and marched out the door. The cook returned to his work, vigorously chopping, and tossing stumps and inedible food into a nearby bucket. Once he had finished chopping vegetables, he dumped them into the cook pot, and he hauled it to the cookfire outside, bellowing to someone as he went. A moment later a young boy appeared, and Big Jack heard the clatter of bowls and utensils as the boy set the camp table. The table was barely laid when officers filtered into the kitchen, seating themselves at the camp table. The boy left but re-entered with a pot, from which he served food to the seated officers.

Big Jack overheard snatches of conversations. He learned why the atmosphere was tense: the Americans were losing badly. It was worse than he imagined. The Americans were desperate.

Nearly 1000 Americans had been killed, and about the same taken as prisoners. He could not believe his ears: that was a quarter of the entire American army. He practically gasped aloud.

The main topic amongst the officers was the size of the British force. He was puzzled that Washington did not know the size. Or, perhaps, he knew. It did not stop his subordinates from speculating. Their guesses ranged between 20,000 and 30,000 troops; only one believed there were as few as 10,000. There was disagreement about what to do next, but most believed they ought to flee. To do that, one man suggested they use the rain to cover them (which made sense to Big Jack) as pouring rain made soldiering nearly impossible. Someone else said that the General was looking for the wind to change direction. Another advocated slipping across to New Jersey. This idea roused strong opinions on both sides, and they argued loudly. Big Jack pitied the Americans.

They had thrown their lot together, and they were now fleeing the most powerful army in the world.

A young regular arrived to announce they had to make haste: General Washington had given orders for that night. The officers gulped down the remainder of the meal before rushing out the door. Only two men remained, one was the newly arrived messenger, and the other was an officer.

"What's the General having us do?"

The messenger hesitated, tongue-tied, and mumbled something incoherent.

"Come on, out with it," the officer pressed. The officer spoke like he had known the messenger for years.

"I'm not certain, sir," he stuttered slightly as he spoke. "Something about New York."

"Tonight!?" The officer was shocked. The seat tumbled over as he jumped up and rushed out, with the messenger following.

When the room was empty. Big Jack crept to the table to take several mouthfuls of stew. He snatched what bread he found, stuffed it into his pouch and slipped out before anyone returned to clear the table.

He slipped out the door. No one stopped him nor had anyone paid Big Jack the slightest mind; they were busy attending to the night's orders from Washington. The rain had nearly stopped. He easily found his way out of the fort and headed away from the setting sun, going east in the direction of Bushwick.

Soon as he found a thicket, he hid behind it to turn the jacket inside out before starting out again. Though the jacket looked peculiar, at least it would not be taken as a military uniform. He felt renewed, every step was taking him further from the battle front. His feet ached from his rapid pace, but he pushed on. He was delighted when he realized he was near his "gal's" home in Bushwick.

* * *

Betsy was his "gal" when it was convenient for them. There was no fixed word for their kind of friendship, just an understanding. Betsy had men all the time, so his timing today would have to be good. He hoped that she would not have a new man. He liked the fiction that she was his gal, and he would be heartsick if she was with another man. But today especially he hoped she was alone for all he needed was a nip of grog and sleep, and no questions.

He approached Betsy's cottage, a tiny, thatched roof stone house her old ma had given her. Outside her cottage was the usual gang. The wind had picked up and was drying out the day's rain. Responding to the change in the weather, the gang had moved from their huts to gather and to game. Only a few were gaming, the rest giving advice, and convivially swapping jokes. He recognized Jim, Betsy's brother, and called out his name. Jim was a man who acted like a boy.

"Big Jack!" Jim looked up excitedly, jumped up, and threw his arms around him. Jim always greeted him this way.

"You stink!" Jim reeled back, holding on to his nose but Big Jack chuckled. Jim always spoke his mind.

"Did you see them Redcoats!?" Jim asked.

"I just come over from New York. What do you think?"

"Are there an awful lot of soldiers?"

"Aye!" Big Jack affirmed.

Jim switched subjects, "Here to see my sister?"

Jim waved towards her cottage. "She's been asking about ye." Upon hearing a whoop of victory, Jim turned back to the dice game in progress.

Big Jack pushed open the cottage door, Betsy was inside lying on her pallet. The setting sun had broken through the clouds but there was still enough light for Betsy to see herself reflected in the piece of glass Big Jack had given her. Most women fretted about their appearance.

Not Betsy, she simply loved the wonder of seeing herself in the small glass. She kept admiring herself in the glass even after he entered.

Betsy was short, dumpy and bore pox scars on her rosy cheeks. Her teeth were in fair shape, but her brown hair was rapidly losing its youthful luster. But she was not bothered. She had an odd blindness to her shortcomings, and believed she was a true beauty. Oddly, her childish lack of self-consciousness added to her attractiveness. But importantly, she liked Big Jack.

"Big Jack!" She jumped up off the pallet, "I knew you'd come!" Her warmth lifted his spirits. He picked her up and gave her a kiss.

"Bets! You're a sight for sore eyes. It's been hard traveling. I need vittles and grog."

Before heading to the nearby brook to clean off, he added, "And I need clothes." he jerked his thumb towards her brother. "Jimmy won't mind?"

She was happy to hand over her brother's clothes. The clothes, baggy on Jimmy, were tight on Big Jack, and apart from being too short, they fit all right. He felt good in fresh clothing.

Before drifting off to sleep that night, Big Jack thought over his last 24 hours. Everything had changed this week, and his corner of Long Island would never be the same. That thought riled him up: how would he live? He relied on gifts from kind people, from petty thievery and then trading that which he had thieved. He knew he was good at it. He knew which goods people wanted most. But now the British had taken over, and he reckoned they would stay on Long Island for a long time. This would change everything. Other than food and munitions what, he asked himself, do warring armies want most? Farmers would hoard once food became scarce.

His recent stop at the American fort had told him that reliable information was in short supply for both sides. And if the war dragged on, then it seemed to him information would be prized. Perhaps he'd found a new form of currency to live on?

CHAPTER 33

New York's East River and Brooklyn, Kings County, NY, Thursday, August 29, 1776

IT WAS EVIDENT TO WASHINGTON the American regulars could not hold out much longer against the British, a truth impossible to hide from his army. The size of the British force they faced was staggering, and yet it was only one-third of the total British army in Brooklyn and other locations on Long Island.

The American regulars were poorly equipped, and though a few were seasoned, the seasoned few were mostly officers. The regulars had little or no training. Washington had nothing to fight with but green soldiers who were facing a force ten times its size.

Washington had only one choice: to move the entire army across the East River. Once the Americans were off Long Island, there was a chance of fending off the British in New York City. But if they were unsuccessful in New York, and were forced out of the City, they would at least be able to exit Manhattan Island, to resurface elsewhere in the American continent. Not being constrained to maneuvering on an island would give Washington more choices. The Americans desperately needed more options.

For the moment, the British army was no longer actively engaged. Their pause was lengthy. Washington knew they were waiting for his concession. When the odds are overwhelmingly against you, reaching an agreement with the enemy is the standard procedure. In other circumstances he might have done such a thing, but the Continental Congress would have no quarter with concessions.

Having cast his lot with the Continentals, Washington had to find a way to keep his army alive to fight another day. He viewed this brief pause in military action as a gift. Now was the ideal moment to move the regulars from Brooklyn, and out of Long Island.

But he could not count on an extended cessation in the conflict. He had to move the army without drawing attention to it, and he had to move it rapidly. Though the venture was risky (some argued it was more apt to failure than success), Washington had no choice but to attempt the impossible.

He canvassed his men, and the officers recommended the most skilled boatmen amongst them: those of the Marblehead Massachusetts Regiment. The Mariners were generally a tight-knit group. These northerners had been molded by northerly conditions and its sea. They were tough, rugged, dependable and proud of their work.

Washington immediately met with Glover, head of the Marblehead Regiment. Washington charged him with the task of doing the impossible: of ferrying all troops from Brooklyn to New York City. Not only that, but Glover and his men had to do it in complete silence.

Glover waited for favorable winds late on Thursday to start ferrying all 9,500 American soldiers. The anxious American officers had placed the entire army in the hands of one regiment, trusting entirely on the expertise of the Marblehead mariners.

As the mariners began the ferrying job, the waiting regulars grew restless, some grumbled, questioning the success of the silent escape. Then when they learned the mariners were working against the ebb tide in conjunction with a strong northeast wind, their fears heightened.

Ferrying their equipment, ordinance, horses, and field pieces worried some of the officers and they suggested these essentials be left behind. But Washington turned a deaf ear to their request to travel light. The seasoned officers knew why he would not consider the motion. This was the first real battle of the war, and if they relinquished their necessary war horses and hardware at the start, they would have no hope of winning the war.

When at last, Washington put away his field desk, his private belongings were readied. He went outside to ask an officer for news. The news was good: the officer said the wind had changed. Another officer added that a heavy fog had come in.

"It's a gift of God, sir." he said.

His mate added in agreement, "Aye, God is with us."

Washington watched the fishermen-soldiers (as he called them) struggling to get the men and their field equipment across the East River, the oars muffled against the splashing of the water to be as quiet as possible. He paced nervously. They had but a couple of hours before dawn now.

An officer asked him if he would like to make his passage to New York now.

"No, I'll be with the last crossing." he responded.

When Washington finally crossed the East River to New York, he was the last man in the final boat. It had taken nine hours, but the Marblehead mariners had done it. Dawn was breaking as the General moved from Brooklyn on Long Island to New York on Friday morning, August 30. As if by miracle, the task was in its final stage just as a heavy fog was lifting, this same fog had allowed the men and material to be shuttled in secrecy from Brooklyn to New York. When word got out, foot soldiers and civilians hailed the well-timed crossing as "providential." Whether or not it was, this wide-spread conviction spoke to the officers of the Americans' optimistic determination to beat the British.

CHAPTER 34

New York City, Final week of August 1776

WHEN THE LAST of their essential goods were packed in a wagon, Rachel's caretakers, Edmund and Mary Hawxhurst, were up before dawn to depart for Nine Partners. Edmund had charged his trusted steward James Thrush with the responsibility of getting Rachel ferried across the East River to Long Island. More than once, they had apologized to Rachel for leaving her in the hands of someone else. Mary gave her a tearful farewell as she crushed Rachel to her.

Midmorning of the same day the Hawxhursts departed, their steward Thrush found he had to change his plans. He had to go to New Jersey. At first he hesitated, remembering his promise to the Hawxhursts, but he had no choice. Thrush hurried straight to the Hawxhurst house to speak with Rachel, he had a new plan. When he arrived that afternoon, he was out of breath.

Rachel admitted him but Thrush refused a seat, he was in a hurry. He cleared his throat, "My plan to help you has to be changed." He blurted out, "But I did not know about it until this morning. There is an urgent matter in my family I must tend to and it will take me a few days. I am sorry!"

Rachel sat down suddenly in nearest chair. "You cannot take me to Long Island?" She could not hide her disappointment.

"Aye, 'tis true. I cannot take thee across the river this week." Thrush apologized several more times, awkwardly.

Seeing her downcast face, he quickly added, "But I shall keep my word. Thee has a choice: thee can wait and I will take thee in a few days. Or thee can go with someone else. If thee does not want to wait for me, I arranged a capable and willing boatman who can escort thee there."

Thrush knew Rachel had been convalescing and had been shielded from what was happening. He believed she ought to be aware of the recent events, and the conditions of the City, of Brooklyn, and of the rest of Long Island.

"Also, I have some news. Washington has suffered a terrible defeat in Kings County and the army is going to flee." He coughed, realizing his news would affect her decision, he added, "I reckon the City will no longer be safe."

"What should I do? What would you do if you lived on Long Island?" she asked.

Thrush was honest, "I do not know. But I would not remain in the City."

Hearing this, Rachel suddenly knew that she was ready to swim across the East River. "Tell me about the boatman."

Thrush looked uncomfortable, "Umm—yes, though he's very good at his job, he's no Friend. He's the best person to do the job. But, he is harmless."

Thrush knew no other men willing and able to do this job. When she looked at him questioningly, he added, "I've known him since I was wee. He is a seasoned boatman and knows all about the East River."

Thrush did not add that tall gangly Tom Warner was a bit of a risk because he was a drunk. But these were strange times. Normal life was disturbed. Even though Warner was not the preferred man, he was at least sufficient for this task. And importantly, he was also available.

Thrush again explained he had little choice but to engage Tom for his experience as a boatman and deliveryman. Rachel felt empathetic toward Thrush as he repeatedly apologized for handing her off to someone else.

"Is Friday too soon to leave?" Rachel wanted to leave as soon as possible. Having gained her approval, Thrush hurried off to send a message off to his childhood friend. He prayed that Tom Warner would deliver Rachel safely.

* * *

New York City, Friday, August 30, 1776

The late summer air hung heavy all week: Wednesday was oppressive, but on Thursday showers arrived. Tom Warner was surprised upon receiving Thrush's message right before heading to the public house. He returned late Thursday night to lay down his head, but he awoke in the early morning hours. As he lay prone, he recalled Thrush's engagement: Friday, he thought, was a good day to make a farthing.

Tom had been on the water since he was a child. His father had been a boatman, and he had worked alongside his father his entire life. He had an instinctive feel for the changeable weather of New York's harbor and its rivers. He could tell you what the next day would bring by assessing the sky and the humidity. When he awakened that Friday, he remembered Thursday's showers, and it came to him that fog would have rolled over the river, but it would clear off shortly.

As he lay there, he mulled over his timing. The best time to make some coin and then spend it would be right now. After all, a body never knew when Death would overtake. Once the fog cleared, the soldiers would be fighting again. And, he had a few items to deliver across the East River. He got up right then and made his way to the Hawxhurst house.

Rachel too had awakened long before dawn on Friday. The morning had a strange cast of light, blanketed as it was by fog. Since she could not go back to sleep, she got up and dressed, filled with eagerness (and some anxiety) over leaving for Cow Neck. Mary Hawxhurst had given her handkerchiefs. She had also given her two of her old dresses which Rachel had turned out for herself. Rachel eyed the second dress but decided to leave it behind. There was a loud, long knock on the front door. Rachel answered the door, hoping it was not a soldier.

The man in front of her spoke to her without preamble, "Me name's Warner."

Rachel looked him over sharply. Sometimes you had to abandon yourself to Providence, and trust.

Warner waited for the woman to say something, but she was silent. The house behind her was dead quiet.

He shoved a note at her, "Here."

Warner watched her, unsure if she knew how to read. In his world few could read. Women and negroes usually could not, and she was both.

She read the grubby note of introduction. When she looked up, Warner had already stepped a few feet back from the house, anxious to leave.

"I'll be here," he called. She could barely see his form for the fog that enveloped him only a few feet away.

Rachel ran back to the kitchen. There was food on the table, but no one was there. There was no sign of the cook nor of the lad who helped about. Was their absence an omen that she had to go now? She left everything behind, toting only some food.

Rachel walked along with Tom, glad he moved rapidly and said little. Now and then he wiped sweat from his flat forehead and wiped his sleeve across his long flat nose. He muttered that Long Island was about to be had by the Brits. He added that their crossing of the East River was like trying to "milk a pigeon."

When Rachel voiced her worry about crossing, Warner placated her. He told her it was good that it was not yet dawn and there was heavy fog, he would try to get her across (by which he meant he would succeed).

At the dock she was aware of bulky, shapeless forms: they were men moving inland, in the opposite direction. When Rachel turned back to ask Warner a question he deliberately looked away and shook his head, a signal to stay quiet. Something was happening here, but she would be better off if she were ignorant of it. Did it have to do with the news about Washington and his army? She decided to keep her own counsel.

Tom was awkward on the street. But at the wharf, he moved swiftly and his movements precise. He had readied his vessel and indicated that Rachel wedge herself between boxes of unknown items to be exchanged for farm goods.

Warner draped a heavy cloth over her back, ordering her to stay still. Rachel, a novice, remained low, motionless, and silent. She prayed Warner would not make the wrong move, and that they would not be suspected.

Tom took pride in his skills as a boatman and those skills were fully exercised that morning as he threaded the bark between the threatening and countless British ships.

Before long, the bark was scraping bottom, and Warner called for Rachel to show herself. She clambered out, Tom disappeared, and she found herself on what she hoped was the shore of Brooklyn Heights. The fog had just lifted, and in the distance Rachel could hear the exchange of muskets. Before she turned back to the river, Warner reappeared and was dragging the bark ashore. Rachel helped him hide it in the bushes.

Tom then quickly bound together a bunch of small items in one larger packet which was to be slung across his back. Then he dug out a canvas bag and began stuffing it with smaller items. By his figuring he had only a few hours to get the items traded and to return to the City with the farmers' goods. He had a feeling it would be a profitable trip.

Rachel watched him, engrossed in his business. Finally she asked, "Where are we?"

"Hey? We're at the Strand."

Rachel was perplexed. She rarely left Cow Neck but for a few side trips and knew little else. She had, in her naiveté, believed the man who helped her cross to Long Island would also lead her to Cow Neck, or at least close to it. "But I need to find the grist mill—"

It was hard to believe but Tom was working even faster than ever. He cut her off. "This be Brooklyn."

"Where's North Country Road?"

He shook his head, unsure, he did not know road names. "Don't know where that be. I know only the road to Jamaica," he offered. Before turning back to his labor, he showed her the road to start on, advised her to keep heading northeast she would eventually reach Jamaica. "But do not," he warned, "turn south as ye go."

Fortunately for her, by now the sun had burned off the fog. Using the sun as a guide, she made her way over rough terrain, through mud and swamps, by the fields, around the strangely quiet farms. Rachel did her best to travel to the north of the forts and redoubts. She noted she was walking away from the sound of musket shots. If the soldiers remained in their lines, she might make it home alive.

CHAPTER 35

Kings County, Friday, August 30, 1776

Betsy was sleeping soundly, Big Jack watched her as he lay next to her on the pallet. He was tired, too tired to sleep. He did not know why he could not sleep. Was it the continual sound of fire, or the weariness from travel? He was not as young as he used to be. He pictured the day ahead. This was the day to stretch his legs and to make his way back to the "Lords Meeting House" to Amos and Squirt. Besides, Jim was grating on his nerves. He suddenly remembered that if he stayed around Jim much longer, he might have a spell. It happened now and then. When he had to think on his feet, when there was action happening all about him, he thought clearly; but when life slowed down, and people like Jim got on his bad side, it sometimes brought on a spell.

That clinched his decision. He moved closer to Betsy and blew air on her face, causing her to stir and stretch. He leaned over to give her a farewell squeeze.

* * *

The sun was high in the sky. To Rachel's eyes Long Island was strange. The farm animals, cows, goats, horses, pigs, and sheep were hidden from view. Now and then she heard the bark of a dog. There were few people on the road, and the ones she saw had their heads down and scurried by her. She hurried, anxious to widen the distance between her and the City. Though her legs had started cramping, she did not pause, nor slow down.

She was on edge. Why she was fretting? She knew the answer: re-capture, re-enslavement. A black woman alone on the road made her feel like a vulnerable chicken, and above her was a circling hawk.

She rounded a bend. Before her was a tavern, and she made a snap decision to approach it. She was hungry. The food she had carried, she had shared with Warner before his hasty departure. She knocked on the back door, praying for pity from the tavern-keeper. But the tavern was shuttered and no one answered her knock. She sat down on a nearby log briefly, sapped of strength. A few minutes later she got up and again knocked on the door. There was still no answer, a frantic Rachel started pounding loudly on the door. When to her surprise the door suddenly flew open, Rachel almost fell on the Dutch woman who stood before her.

"Good day, madam," she spoke in her clearest voice, not knowing if this family was Dutch.

The woman quickly took in her appearance, "What are you doing out here when there's a battle!?"

Rachel scrambled to answer, trying to retell her long tale, but failed. When she spoke, her throat closed up and tears filled her eyes, then flowed down her cheeks. She was surprised by how much she had missed the familiar sights and sounds of home.

The woman looked her straight in the eyes and her face creased with sympathy. She leaned out the doorway, glanced around furtively, took Rachel by the wrist, and hauled her into the darkened tavern.

CHAPTER 36

Kings and Queens County, Saturday, August 31, 1776

BIG JACK CAME WHISTLING down the road, traveling east. He would start on Middle Country Road for a bit, then take North Country Road, and from that the path to home, the "Lords Meeting House." He idly wondered if there might be lost objects on Middle Country Road; a battle would be a good time for finding those things.

The British were stove up against the East River near Wallabout and to the south. On Long Island British encampments were all over, but concentrated mostly in Brooklyn. It would not be long, he thought, before the British would wake up to their surroundings and notice the delights Queens County held: it was a land rich in farm wealth and plenty of trees good for wood. The British would want the abundance Long Island offered. He hoped their stay would be brief and they would do no great harm here.

Big Jack was rounding the corner of the closed Wycoff tavern when he saw a negro woman leaving it. He had to step aside to avoid colliding with the stranger. But it was no stranger, it was Rachel. Big Jack quickly grabbed her arm.

Rachel turned and exclaimed "Oh! Big Jack!"

Rachel's face broke into a smile and she threw her arms about him. Although they lived in separate worlds, seeing each other brought home close. The familiarity of the other was made sweeter by what the two had been through separately: the turmoil of the City, the strain of skirting the military, and simple homesickness.

"Blow me down! Rachel. Why be ye here?"

Rachel was hardly recognizable: her clothes were dirty, and she was bone thin. With relief she told her story. As he listened to her tale, he was dumbstruck at her dreadful suffering. He felt something in his chest—what was it? Yes, he was angry for her, but he also felt protective.

She finished her story, "I just want to go home!"

He understood, for he had the same wish. When his first impulse was to help Rachel without a thought of reward, it came to him that he was somewhat changed. What had happened to him? Had the sights and sounds of the war done this to him? This was a new Big Jack, he was perplexed at the change in himself.

He stroked his chin thinking, "Ye'll have to do as I tell ye because we need to be like snakes—silent and sometimes still."

"Oh, I will! I just want to see Mother Dodge!" She promised.

Mother Dodge. The woman who had never let The Wanderers down. He smiled at the sound of her name, "Aye and ye shall."

Big Jack led her closer to the bushes edging the woods as he told her of his plan. They had to be cautious, traveling was perilous business since the battle and the British takeover of the Island. Because the two of them would be easily noticed, they should not travel in daylight. The fewer encounters they had, the safer they would be.

Rachel confessed she was ignorant of the size of the British military forces. Judging from hearsay, the Redcoats would be chasing Washington to New York. He believed from the size of their army, the British would be fanning out all over Long Island. Cow Neck, with its proximity to New York City and the rest of the colony, would be irresistible to the conquering army. In his instructions to Rachel, he included this knowledge.

They tarried in hiding, waiting to travel till dusk. Then Big Jack had Rachel trail closely behind him, warning her not to strike off on her own. They would skirt populated areas, including many places familiar to her.

They started out with the setting sun, creeping through the underbrush, staying away from open land, and avoiding clear trails and roads. When they caught sight of people, they melted into the brush and waited. Although Big Jack usually traveled alone, with all the danger around, it was thrilling to be Rachel's protective escort.

It seemed like they had been walking for hours. Big Jack, hearty and strong, felt no need to stop. And though Rachel was still weak from illness, each step brought her closer to home, a thought which energized her. They were past Jamaica on North Country Road when Big Jack melted in to the bushes and in the twilight he signaled for her to follow.

He spat, "Gonna piss. Here," and he handed her his old flask, "You go upstream there and draw both you and me some water."

"How far…?" she began, but Big Jack had already vanished.

For a while they rested in the cool of the brush near the small brook. Rachel spoke of her expectations of what it would be like to be home.

"The King's Army has expectations, too—they have to enforce the King's will." Big Jack cautioned her.

Rachel soberly, reflecting his tone, "I reckon that it is expectations that keeps everyone alive." Big Jack stepped cautiously out of the brush to continue their trek.

"When will we get home?" Rachel asked a few minutes later.

"Bout midnight, I reckon."

Certain they were further, Rachel voiced her dismay, "Oh! No! At dawn I was in Wallabout. I thought I would be home by now."

Big Jack encouraged her, "You dun alright."

Upon hearing something peculiar, Big Jack stopped suddenly, and signaled Rachel to get on the ground. They both flattened themselves, hiding their faces, barely breathing. A small detachment of Redcoats passed by.

Once it was safe, they set off again. It was not long before Big Jack began to recognize the landmarks of Cow Neck. They were more cautious around Onderdonk's mill. Big Jack reasoned because Onderdonk was a rebel American, he would be carefully watched. For all he knew, the British had already taken Onderdonk's mill.

Moving cautiously through the fields was slow, but they pushed steadily northeast up the Neck to Mother Dodge's homestead. Rachel made involuntary gasps of delight when she recognized where they were.

Finally, they crested a rise and Rachel saw Mother Dodge's house outlined against the dark sky. Big Jack put his hand on her sleeve to stay her as he crept forward. When he returned, he put his finger to his lips, as a warning.

"I don't see her; she must be abed. There's a lass sleeping in front of the fire." He whispered. Rachel guessed the woman would be Elizabeth, keeping watch with her mother. Excited, she squeezed his arm and whispered her thanks. He patted her shoulder, and she raced off to the Dodge house.

CHAPTER 37

*Queens County, New York,
Early September 1776*

It was September 1. It had not been a week since the battle at Brooklyn. Few residents of Queens County stirred from their plots. It was First Day, but the Friends did not open the Meeting Houses, meeting instead in homes. On Long Island the churches had scant attendance. It was not until the second Sunday of the month that congregational gatherings were close to normal.

But at least Mother Dodge and Rachel were happily reunited. Phebe spent long hours interviewing Rachel about her experience. She absorbed every word and mulled over the complexities of freeing slaves in these strange and strained circumstances.

Phebe was approached by the other members on the special Committee for Manumission. Jacob suggested they suspend their meeting for the month. Silas agreed with Jacob. The entire committee bemoaned their difficulties.

"My farm is in chaos." Mary pled, tears filling her eyes.

Jacob was adamant a meeting this month would be fruitless. Silas' very posture reflected his fatigue. Phebe submitted to their collective will. Their next meeting would not happen till October.

As it turned out most committees did not meet at all that fall, including the Committee for Clearance. Since Edmond Prior had first applied to be a Friend, the Committee for Clearance had already been reorganized more than once. Then the Battle of Brooklyn had occurred. The two events were unusual, and the latter had a shattering effect on the committee.

But the lives of Long Islanders were more seriously disrupted when, by the end of September, a month after the fall of Brooklyn, British soldiers were quartered in their houses. The Friends, though neutral, were not exempt from having their homes occupied by soldiers. The Islanders had only just come to terms with having soldiers outside their homes and using their roads. The British military formations and exercises frightened both young and old. Now everyone was shocked by the quartering of soldiers in homes.

Even Long Island Loyalists took the quartering of soldiers as a personal insult, as if their loyalty to England was in question. But most had a more prosaic reason for their anger: their resources were taken or shared. The soldiers in their houses were taking up space, using extra water, adding to the chores, eating their food, and taking farm instruments as they needed or wanted. Long Islanders feared that the British would be on their island for a long time.

Quartering soldiers turned households topsy-turvy. Families struggled to accommodate the British, and to keep up with regular domestic tasks. For the moment Phebe had been spared from quartering soldiers, but she assumed her reprieve would be short-lived.

Meanwhile Edmond Prior, afraid his request to be received as a Friend was forgotten, was agitated. He took action and called on two of the members of the Committee on Clearance. But they were both so busy with their own matters, they were of no help. Desperate, Edmond sought out the Clerk of Meeting, but he was not home.

Out of ideas, he hoped Samuel or Mary Willis might aid him, and he went directly to the Willis house. When he arrived, he asked Keziah to see her father, and was shown to Samuel's small unheated office, which held the gleaming belongings of an unseen British officer. Seeing the regimental uniform hanging from a peg on the wall, Edmond shook his head at the dispiriting reminder. Samuel entered the room, having just come from outdoors.

"Good father," Edmond began, "It's been a year now since I applied to be admitted to the Society of Friends."

Samuel was still making himself comfortable in his chair. But Edmond continued, "Nothing has happened—the reorganized committee has not yet met."

Sitting back in his chair Samuel shook his head in dismay, "Thee knows the problems we all have now. And to be frank, it's—it's a difficult time." His embarrassment was on his face.

Samuel believed his words sounded hollow and lacking in heart, but Edmond heard sympathy in Samuel's voice. Yet Edmond pushed, pleading with Samuel for his help. He was, he explained, anxious to be wed before the next planting.

Samuel leaned forward. "Edmond," his tone was somber, "I speak to thee as a son: have patience. Thee will be wed to thy wife for a life time. And thee knows, the delay is all because…" He trailed off as he waved his hand in the direction of the British regimentals on the peg.

Samuel continued, "This conflict has disturbed us so. Truth be told hardly any committee meets now."

Edmond's heart sank. He had suspected as much but he had held on to a shred of hope. And now that hope had vanished.

Edmond thanked Samuel and took his leave, shuffling out of the house, his head low. He and Feeb were no nearer to being husband and wife than they had been in the spring.

Unexpectedly, Samuel called out to Edmond from the doorway.

"Edmond, I believe thee shall be a good Friend, and good to Feeb. I shall do what I can."

Later when Samuel related this conversation to Mary, he recalled his own youth and eagerness to wed. "I was hard-pressed to say something hopeful. When the young lose hope, we are all lost."

CHAPTER 38

Queens County, Late October 1776

Fall's vibrantly colored trees on the Island were steadily but slowly losing their brilliance with each passing day. The flaming, brightly hued trees faded imperceptibly, and slid to brown. This year only children had hearts light enough to revel in the luminous brilliance of the trees. For adults, the turning of the leaves served to be a harbinger of winter and its coming deprivations. This year felt different: the very atmosphere weighed heavily on everyone. Daily routines were altered, then altered again as the British military flexed their authority over the residents, now fully under martial law.

Since the fall of Brooklyn and the taking of Long Island by the British, a visitor might think that life for the locals was back to normal, apart from the unusual number of horses and the men in British regimentals. Residents went about their chores, smithies smithed, carpenters worked, and farmers farmed. Unless you looked closely you might even believe that the colonists' lives would continue as they had before the occupation. But a closer examination would reveal that they had lost the calm assurance that used to surround them, much like the air they breathed. Every day brought new, unsettling events, and every week had new challenges.

Officially the soldiers were restricted to occupying only rooms with fireplaces and those which the family did not need. But they looked hungrily at every room, and it was not long before this regulation was broken regularly, covertly.

Nor was it long before the locals, even declared Loyalists, wearied of the continual rubbing of shoulders with the army. Residents struggled to find wood as the soldiers chopped trees for their own firewood and took what they wished to feed themselves. Householders engaged in a never-ending struggle to keep and protect livestock and poultry to feed their own family. When they were getting in the last of the harvest and readying for winter, the occupying army would interfere. As if out of nowhere, British soldiers would appear, and snatch away what they could of the stores ready to be put up.

By now Loyalist households knew their loyalty was of no importance to the occupying army. Henry and Leticia Smith, having no allegiance to either side, did not divulge the location of their guns. They did not live in the City, and they were not merchants and they reasoned both a gun and a plough were vital to their continued well-being. Besides, who knew how long the army would be on the Island? Leticia summarized everyone's feelings by flatly stating that the King would feed the army before he fed the Smith family. Henry sneaked off to secretly check on the condition of the plough's moldboard. He even took stock of his farm implements, something he had never done.

But for Becca Doughty, the invasion by the British was personal.

Her father had become a Friend after his marriage to Becca's mother. The British singled out Becca's parents as potential "rebels." They claimed that Friend Doughty supported the American rebels and therefore the Doughtys were to house a superior officer. But the real reason was obvious: his house was one of the largest, and the most centrally located in Queens County. Moreover, the land the homestead sat on was at a strategic and accessible crossroads for the military.

Placed in the Doughty house was an officer named Lymes. Since Lymes was charged with making sure all information was circulated in a timely fashion, the Doughty homestead was the best place for his quartering.

Before he was installed, Lymes outlined the requirements for his quarters: a bedroom, and a sitting room as well as a separate study for his private correspondence office. Several other British regulars on the Doughty farm were quartered in the kitchen or in the outer buildings. The Doughty house, while large, was no mansion. Yet they made accommodations for Lymes and his men.

At 15, Becca Doughty was old enough to consider marriage. Indeed, last spring and summer – how long ago that seemed now—a Friend had expressed interest in her. By July both families believed there would be a wedding within a year. But this fall all thoughts of starting a married life were put aside. Life was so very different under the occupation. They all felt the burden and stress of soldiers in the houses and on the farms. The strain of it all was crushing.

Becca had enjoyed the passive, benevolent vigilance that a tight-knit community affords. But now she, along with the other young women on Long Island, suffered regular encounters with leering strangers, and endured rude or obscene comments from both soldiers and officers. Unfortunately for the Doughtys, Officer Lymes was one of the worst in this respect: his ways and words were coarse and obscene. Protected as he was by his military rank, and his high-born status in society in England, he had no conscience and had no incentive to have one.

From the start, Becca had moved from her room in the Doughty house to accommodate the officer's room demands. Her new room was but a makeshift sleeping area. To get to her new "bedroom," she had to pass by Lymes' suite of rooms. Unfortunately for her, encountering Lymes was unavoidable. Lymes leered at her when she passed him or passed his door. She was so uncomfortable that (had it been unoccupied) she would have slept in the barn.

When Lymes' language toward her turned nasty she ignored him. But that seemed to encourage him for he grew bolder towards her, making profane comments when she was near, no matter who was nearby. Then it was not long before his profane comments turned to sexual advances.

Both afraid and repulsed, she told her parents of his behavior. Her father, a normally placid man, felt like tearing into Lymes. His wife, despite her distress and her anger, talked him out of it. Instead, they confronted him together. But when they challenged him, Lymes waved them away as if they were but gnats in the air.

Frustrated, Doughty reacted as he would have in his youth, before he was a Friend. He challenged Lymes to a fight. Lymes merely laughed in his face and spun on his heel, hiding behind his position as an officer in the occupying army.

The couple tried several more times to speak with Lymes, but without success. But the confrontation with the Doughtys made Lymes wonder if his standing as an officer would be affected. After making discreet inquiries, he discovered some fellow officers (including his superior officer) thought the Long Islanders were overly sensitive. Lymes and his superior officer schemed together, forming a pact to protect one another, they would lie for one another if needed, to safeguard their rank and reputation.

In desperation the Doughtys sought out Lymes' superior officer, requesting a replacement for Lymes. The officer heard them out, expressed false sympathy, and proceeded to make a show of writing up their complaint. He sent them away with an empty promise and raised hopes. Nothing came of his promise and their complaint was burned in his fire.

When the Doughtys left that meeting, they had already decided not to wait for help. They immediately moved Becca into their bedroom for her safety. But she could not stay in the bedroom, nor tail her parents all the time.

Her move only provided Lymes with a challenge. He continued to make himself a pest. Although Becca succeeded in keeping herself safe, she felt that her life was unraveling, her nerves were frayed, and she was continually scared.

The Doughtys brought their complaint before the Friends Meeting. They were not the only ones in the Meeting who had a similar problem. Their situation was one of several brought to the attention of the Meeting. The members were indignant, they drew up a formal complaint and had brought it before the British officer in charge. But despite their collective pressure, the formal complaint effected no change. The British officers were engaged in a larger battle. The mischief of a few officers on Long Island was minor and the Friends' complaint was buried at the bottom of their list.

By now Becca's parents were helpless and hopeless. They were at their wit's end: what could they do against the British army? Their helplessness was unbearable. Over time, Becca grew increasingly quiet and withdrawn, as if her silence would make her invisible. This had the opposite effect on the officer, and Lymes chased her even more as she withdrew.

Lymes' attitude and actions grew bolder by the week. Becca's siblings grew increasingly annoyed at him. One evening as Becca and her brother George were returning from the evening chores, her brother gave her unsolicited advice. "Don't take it."

Becca did not respond.

George looked around furtively, then told her, "I should not say this, but next time he touches thee, thee must strike him."

Becca stopped in her tracks. Friends were not to touch anyone in anger: it was not done.

George went on, his brow furrowed, "Thee must protect thyself by striking him, biting him, or pulling his hair, or—" He lowered his voice to a whisper, "Kick him between the legs." He scuttled away.

Becca was at a breaking point because she existed in a perpetual state of anxiety, sometimes rising to panic. She was exhausted every day: she had to hide from Lymes, and then scurry about, doing her chores when Lymes was gone or otherwise occupied.

Every night Becca would lie on her bolster thinking for hours before dropping into a troubled sleep. Later that day as she lay down, she thought of her brother's advice.

What could she do? How could she get away from Lymes? Maybe George was right. She lived with that thought for a while but then pushed it aside. She was a Friend, and fighting brought more problems than solutions. Although she despised Lymes with everything in her being, she also understood for the first time how hate can destroy a person.

* * *

In early October after Meeting, most people stayed on to discuss winter preparation. This was an annual job. They met to discuss whose house to meet in over the snowy winter months. Now that so many houses were occupied by British soldiers, the discussion took longer than normal.

Becca Doughty did not mind the longer wait because it meant she was away from Lymes. She was thrilled to be with her close friend, the 10-year-old Phebe "Anna" Mott. Phebe Anna and Becca were playing "Dream About," a game Anna had made up when they were younger.

"And what does thee Dream About?" Anna was lying squinting up at the tree colors. She knew what she dreamt about. She dreamt of sewing a quilt that looked like autumn leaves, but as if the person was seeing them from their underside. From this view, the bright leaves were a patchwork of muted vibrancy, their colors were like hearing a sound in the distance.

Becca replied, "Anna, I dream of one thing. I dream of all the British dying."

Anna sat bolt upright in shock. Sympathetic, she begged, "Oh, Becca! dear! How bad is it? Tell me."

For a long time, Becca said nothing, then she finally turned on her side towards her friend and whispered, "Anna, it is worse than thee can suppose."

After her first tear, the rest flowed freely. Finally, Becca was able to whisper a summary of Lymes' behavior and how crushing it felt. Her story chilled Anna to the bone. She wondered about the beastly people who would allow this behavior. What could she do for her best friend?

"Becca," her voice throaty with anger, "How could he treat a girl with such disrespect? How vain, how venal, how horrid!"

Back home Anna told her parents of Becca's problem, thinking it was news. Her parents had not told their daughter they already knew of the Meeting's complaint against Lymes. They confessed their knowledge of it to her, and the Meeting's efforts. They explained due to martial law they were powerless. But Anna had expected a different response from her parents.

"Where," she asked, "is thy sense of righteousness? Would the God of all creatures wish for us to allow harm to come to any? It's neither right nor proper to defend the British who allow this behavior from an officer!"

Anna marched out of the room, leaving her parents dumbstruck at the vehemence of her words.

CHAPTER 39

Hempstead, New York, 20 Oct 1776

In Hempstead, Gideon Seaman had just finished organizing the committee minutes of the Westbury Friends Meeting. He counted, summarized, placed them together in a neat bundle, and labeled them. He then placed them in the leather receptacle used to hold minutes.

He was finishing up when his wife rushed in the room, her face flushed, "Gideon!" she was breathless, "The British have taken over the Flushing Meeting House!"

Gideon stood bolt upright; the bottom of his stomach felt suddenly very empty.

The British had commandeered Flushing Meeting in September, but certain persuasive Friends kept showing up, and had refused to remove themselves. One of the Bownes was so angered by the British that he argued with them, insisting they had the sole title to use the Flushing Meeting House. He even hauled out a paper declaring such. He threatened to present it in court. But the British had ignored him. The Flushing Meeting House was necessary to the army.

"This is but the beginning of our privations." Gideon muttered. He added, "Thank God someone had foreseen something like this occurring." He was referring to Flushing's irreplaceable Minutes and not to the building.

The Flushing Meeting Minutes as well as the New York Yearly Minutes (which were stored together) had already been moved. Both sets were secure at the Westbury Meeting House. Although Redcoats had long since taken advantage of many of the outbuildings at the Meeting Houses, they had not taken over the Westbury Meeting House.

Gideon wasted no time; the Friends must push back on the British. He went straight to the home of his neighbor. The two of them immediately decided to call for a Special Business Meeting regarding Flushing Meeting House. The meeting would be on the Sixth Day.

For decades Flushing Meeting House was the traditional connecting point between the Long Island Friends and the New York City Friends. Due to its size and proximity, it was the favored site of the New York Yearly Meeting. But its value to the Friends went beyond mere custom: it was an essential link for Friends in the entire colony of New York.

* * *

Flushing Meeting House, Flushing, NY, Saturday 26 Oct 1776

The Flushing Meeting House was packed for the hastily called business meeting. The question today was how to fend off the British reach, and retain the Flushing Meeting House for the Friends. Stephen and Amy's family were amongst the last of the arrivals. Most Friends were already gathered inside for the meeting. In a private corner outside the Meeting House, a handful of weighty Friends conferred with a few British officers. Stephen headed directly inside, hoping the matter would be settled by the weighty Friends.

Outside the Meeting House, wandering around or lingering in tight groups, were a few low-ranking British officers, British regulars, and Hessians, who had no particular role today. These soldiers meandered the grounds, squatted in circles smoking and joking, a few snoozed in the brilliant sunlight.

Like a fever you cannot shake, since August there had been a low-lying sense of peril blanketing the island. But now there was no sense of peril, but a real terror because the British were seizing the Flushing Meeting House for use in the war.

No one uttered the unifying worry, possibly because it was too sudden and too sharp to even consider. The Meeting House was more than a structure of wood planks, it was a memorial, a symbol which reminded them of that which their grandparents had worked hard to obtain, the freedom to gather in Friendly worship.

The mothers of small children and their caretakers, aunts and cousins remained outdoors on the fall afternoon. Amy joined them. Amy's children ran to join their friends scattered abroad. When Anna glimpsed her friend Becca at a distance and asked her mother if she could play with her, instead of her agemates, Amy considered. What harm could befall her? She gave her consent.

The October sun hung warm in a cloudless sky. At first the women had chafed about leaving work undone at home. Now once gathered, homestead duties were were forgotten. They drew comfort in seeing familiar faces and their deep fears remained buried. Their conversations drifted from one topic to another. Everyone shared the same trouble but had neither the power nor authority to right it.

The grounds of the Meeting House that golden autumn afternoon were filled with the sound of humanity: the women's quiet murmurings were punctuated by the shouts and laughter of playing children. Suddenly, the harmonies of human interchange were shattered by a high-pitched shout, "No! No! No!"

Amy and the rest of the women, turned to look in the direction of the urgent cry. To Amy's relief, it was not Anna. A British officer whose back was to Amy's group looked to be struggling with someone at his side. From where she was, Amy could not tell what was going on nor who the other person was. Then out of the corner of her eye, she caught her nephew's expression. He was standing below her, on the far edge of the lawn, his eyes were bulging, and his mouth was wide in shock.

Then in a flash, when the officer turned around, she could see he was releasing the arm of Becca Doughty, Anna's friend. The vigor of her struggle and his release sent Becca toppling over on her back and sent her sprawled out on the ground.

He spat out curse words, but Amy could discern only the words "next time" amongst his stream of profanity. Then the officer turned and started up the lawn, away from the sobbing Becca. As he trudged up the rise, Amy saw her own daughter Anna beside the officer. Her face was unrecognizable because it was so twisted in anger.

The officer was oblivious to the girl coming behind him. Quick as lightning, Anna rushed him from behind, mounted the tall officer's back, and climbed up him with the speed and agility of a squirrel on an oak tree. Then in one motion she knocked off his hat, grabbed hold of a tuft of his hair, and yanked it with such violence, Amy was sure she had pulled it out by the roots. At her yank, his head jerked backwards and which set him off balance.

He staggered and swore. He batted at her, but Anna held onto his hair, and somehow remained on his back, her legs clamped around his belly, and her free hand gripping his uniform. She did not loosen her hold on his scalp but had got only a better grasp on it. He staggered, screamed, and continued to bat at her. When he saw she was not coming off, he dropped to his knees to roll on the ground.

But she had anticipated his move, and jumped catlike as he started down to the ground. Anna landed upright on her feet.

"Foul swine!" she screamed at the officer.

Amy had remained rooted in shock until that moment, when she took off like a bolt to snatch up her daughter.

Before she could reach the two, the officer lunged at Anna, seizing her slight form, and flinging her skyward. Amy watched in horror as Anna flew above them, sailing like a spear overhead.

Simultaneously Becca's scream of alarm punctured the air causing all humans to halt their speech. The horses shied and the dogs lifted their eyes. Both the Friends and the British turned in the direction of Becca's scream.

When Anna landed, her head came down with a resounding crack. She hit a partially sunken boulder whose sharp edge protruded from the ground. The cracking sound of her head hitting the rock reverberated in Amy's ears. She knew at once the ugly man had killed her sweet little daughter.

Unaware of anything else, Amy crumbled on Anna's form. Her pulse loud in her ears, clinging to a frail hope: perhaps she could somehow give her daughter life for a second time. Suddenly Stephen was there, wrapping them both in a hug, even as Amy's arms held her still, still child. Someone was wailing.

CHAPTER 40

Hempstead, New York, Late Autumn 1776

Later Amy had no recollection of how she stumbled through that fall. The days were darker. Everything seemed muted; vibrancy and light had vanished. It was not just her fancy, people spoke to her in low careful tones. The world felt at once too close and too far from her. Nearly everyone lost a child but there was something special about this child. Anna had been unique she brought a fragrance to life, but now the beautiful flower of her heart was pulverized, gone. That Anna had been interceding for her friend Becca made her death more poignant. And of course, the circumstances of her death were particularly ugly.

Amy no longer paid attention to much. She was vaguely aware that her husband and her friends were troubled. Stephen told her he believed the British were tempting the people of Queens County. It was claimed that if they swore loyalty to the Crown and if they enlisted with the British, they would receive 50 acres of land, at least that was Howe's promise.

Stephen was unable to absorb the loss of Phebe Anna. Her absence was palpable and his pain felt physical. Phebe Anna had been brave, clever, loving, and lovely. Everywhere he turned he recalled her joy. He was sure he would never again enjoy life. He had buried enjoyment with Phebe Anna. The presence of the occupying army exacerbated his bad mood for they served as a continual reminder of his daughter. And, why had the British needed the Flushing Meeting house? They used it for their war horses! Stephen was revolted at the thought.

The British were not completely insensible to the suffering their presence brought on Long Islanders. After the incident in Flushing, they had removed Lymes from Long Island, and a superior British officer made a formal call to apologize to Stephen and Amy Mott over Phebe Anna's death. Before he departed, he mentioned that they had earlier intended to quarter an officer in their house but now out of regard for their loss, they would be spared that.

Yet Stephen's anger and grief over losing Phebe Anna was not diminishing but growing. At dawn in early December, a British regular showed up at their door, but Amy barred him from entering the house. The soldier sought and found Stephen in the barn milking, a time of day he cherished. This, the earliest waking hour, was Stephen's time and place to shed his own sadness before facing his grief-stricken wife.

The regular walked up to Stephen from behind, startling him so that he nearly fell from the milking stool. "I am charged by the army." He announced without introduction or ceremony. He proceeded to ask Stephen about the number of livestock and horses, and of light and heavy wagons on his farm.

Stephen could barely collect his wits. Normally there was a numbness which allowed him to go about his chores, but now anger overtook him. Before he knew what he was doing, he was yelling at the man, dumping all his pent-up rage on him until he chased the soldier from his property.

Later that day, Stephen made a formal complaint at the British headquarters. A yawning commander tried to rebuff him, yet Stephen pressed his complaint. The officer shrugged indifferently and had a clerk take down his statement. A few days after his visit Stephen learned their exemption from soldiers was short-lived and there would be regulars to quarter on his property after all.

When he told Amy about his rage, his throat was tight even as he spoke.

"Amy," he choked out, "Phebe Anna gave everyone sweetness. She was the child we prayed would come into the world."

At this he broke down and sobbed, finally pouring out his sorrow and his despair. Amy comforted him as only the grief-stricken can, crying with him and rocking him in his woe.

When he was able to speak again, he told Amy of the true strength of the occupying army. Brooklyn and Queens County was now filled to overflowing. There were more than 30,000 troops on Long Island.

Stephen also revealed their son Daniel had been approached by the British. Had he not resisted them, they would have pressed Daniel into joining the roving gang of woodcutters who were continually chopping down the trees for the British army.

The couple's shared tears had drawn them together. Stephen had worried his grief would exacerbate his wife's mourning. But after Amy's sobbing tapered off, he sensed a renewal of his wife's spirit. They were not going to fall apart. This knowledge gave them heart.

But Stephen's own bitterness turned to hardened resentment. He would do what he could to discourage British victory. Aye, he could be a good Friend without fighting, but the injustice and the violence of the past few months was intolerable. He would do what he could to prevent the British success.

CHAPTER 41

Cow Neck, New York, November and December 1776

The fall of 1776 waned, then evaporated, leaving an open door to winter's chill. They all sensed by the end of the year, though no one breathed a word, that the new year of 1777 would be a year of endless darkness and hardship.

The Friends were surprised by the punishing effects of the war and how deeply it affected them. Friends were not unique in this: Long Islanders, no matter their loyalties, yearned for the old days. Now everything was unpredictable, and they had to continually adjust as their world was always changing.

Every day had become a struggle. The steady stream of soldiers and venturers created a strong demand for black market sales and trading. Theft was on the rise as food was always good for trade. Everyone carefully guarded their livestock and chickens.

Since the loss of Phebe Anna, Mother Dodge took stock: somehow, she felt time was shortened. Consequently, the freeing of slaves was her first waking and last thought each day. She summoned the one man she felt she could trust for news, the former Friend and kinsman, Willet Seaman. He had the temperance of spirit and wisdom to impart war news. He told her only what she needed to know, and nothing more nor less.

Willet settled into a chair. "Mother Dodge, I see there is much trouble here on Long Island."

"Willet, thee is sharp as a needle," Phebe joked and then turned somber. "What news has thee?"

"Thee knows of the great fire in the City in September?"

"Did thy house burn up!?"

"Nay, one shed burned down, and my house caught fire, but it was not bad." He switched topics, "Thee probably heard of the hanging of Nathan Hale in the City." She had heard the story, for he had been captured in Long Island, and marched to the City.

He cleared his throat, "In October things got worse for the Americans. Washington was chased from Harlem Heights and scuppered at White Plains. They had to flee. Valcour Island in Lake Champlain was also a humiliation for the Americans. In all, when October was over, New York was given over to the British.

"At the end of 1776, the British had greatly expanded their reach, and the Americans lost Fort Lee in New Jersey. Oh, also, the British took over Newport, Rhode Island."

"What of the American regulars?" Phebe wondered.

"Although he's much depleted, Washington pushes on. In fact, he took the British in Trenton, in New Jersey."

"How does Philadelphia fare?" Phebe asked. Philadelphia, the largest city, had always been the center of inspiration and fresh ideas for Friends in the colonies.

"Now Philadelphia is overrun by the British." He shook his head. "It's said that Washington's army is camped somewhere outside the city till after Christmas."

She turned her attention to the general interests of the American rebels, asking, "What of the Provincial—I mean, Continental Congress? Have they been keen-witted? Have they supported Washington?"

Willet shook his head. "I cannot work out their discussions. I heard they sent delegates to plead Europe for aid.

"Right now, the firm stance of the Continental Congress brought wrath from many people. Indeed, they were so unsafe in Philadelphia that they left the city altogether.

"But besides losing battles to the British and being chased hither and yon, the rebel army fares poorly. It lacks men because soldiers are deserting at a staggering speed."

"Why?"

"I don't know. I heard Congress does not supply enough money." He waved his hands. "But the spirit is still strong in the cities."

"And the colonies, what are our prospects, in reality?"

"Unless the British withdraw," Willet said, shaking his head, "which I doubt, or the rebels get help, America will feel the wrath of British vengeance for decades." He paused then added with heaviness. "Even if the British win, the Loyalists will never see their loyalty repaid."

He was silent for a long moment as if puzzling something out. "There is one thing I have observed in my travels: the American rebels, though losing badly, are a hopeful lot."

From his pocket Willet pulled out a broadsheet, the paper much folded, and spread it on the table.

"The Americans are encouraged by the circulating press. These pamphlets are popular and are read all over the colonies," He cleared his throat, "A familiar rabble-rouser Thomas Paine, wrote this." He glanced up, checking on her interest.

With her consent, he read aloud,

"These are the times that try men's souls: The summer soldier and the sunshine patriot will, in this crisis, shrink from the service of his country: but he that stands it now deserves the love and thanks of man and woman. Tyranny, like Hell, is not easily conquered. Yet we have this consolation with us, that the harder the conflict, the more glorious the triumph."

He stopped reading, "This is oft-quoted—and in all sorts of places—trading houses, corners, inns. Grandmother, this piece of writing is different. For some reason it hits people in the middle of the soul, and it remains there.

"At first, I could not understand why. Aye, it is a stirring bit of prose. But it's more than that and I understood why just yesterday."

"Share thy idea with me." Phebe had always appreciated Willet's perceptiveness.

"His words echo their sentiment, naturally. But more than that I think it also echoes the sentiment of their forebearers. Listen again," he looked down and read, "*Tyranny is not easily conquered.*"

"Here is my understanding of why it is captivating. It speaks to the non-conformists who found refuge here, decades ago. But its appeal is broader.

"It speaks not to them alone. But to people of all sorts: Irishmen, negroes, Scotsmen, Jews, and others told me these words have stirred them. Tyranny by one man, or even one group, is despised."

Phebe's curiosity was stirred, "Could the American rebel be led to see that negro slavery is not so different from being under the boot of the British army?"

"I don't know. Slavery has been established for so long! But if the Americans win, and if these manumissions continue while the memory of British oppression is fresh, it is possible."

"What about thee and thy family? What shall thee do?" Phebe had asked him this at the start, but he had never answered her.

He shrugged, "For now we are still in the City. The British burned and looted my farm here." He chose not to share the deep fear their family lived with, nor the close calls. "Soon we will move to Connecticut where my wife has family. The city is too violent and unstable for us now."

"For how long?"

"I don't know," He returned the broadsheet to his pocket, "I must take my leave. As the British have taken New York, Long Island and New Jersey, the New York Manumission Society is now suspended but only temporarily." He pivoted to Long Island, "Tell me how the Long Island Friends fare in manumitting."

"Since the battle in August we have moved at a snail's pace." Phebe's lofty ideas for freed slaves had been consequential and far-reaching. She was discouraged for it seemed like the eventual independence and self-sufficiency of the negro was at a near standstill.

Willet was somber, "Aye, it has been nothing hardship and privations since the battle on the island. Getting a situation for a freed slave will be nearly impossible until this war is passed."

As it was under martial law the power, authority, and presence of the most powerful army in the world now laid claim to Mother Dodge's allegiance, property, and movements. She was, in a way, enslaved to the military might and authority of the British overseers.

At the same time the British authority and its very presence worked against the Friends' manumission of slaves. The army was a danger to her plans. It was, in as sense an ironic twist that under martial law a *freed* slave could become a human tool in the British army.

"Since the battle at Brooklyn, a few were freed, but they chose to stay on with the family." There was nowhere to go.

It came to Willet this was most probably their final visit. Though the Manumission Society of New York was inactive, he hoped for its revival. He urged Phebe to continue her efforts, "Still, if Long Islanders carry on manumitting their slaves despite the war, it's possible that New York City will be stirred to life to do the same thing once the war is over. The Friends can keep this alive despite the war."

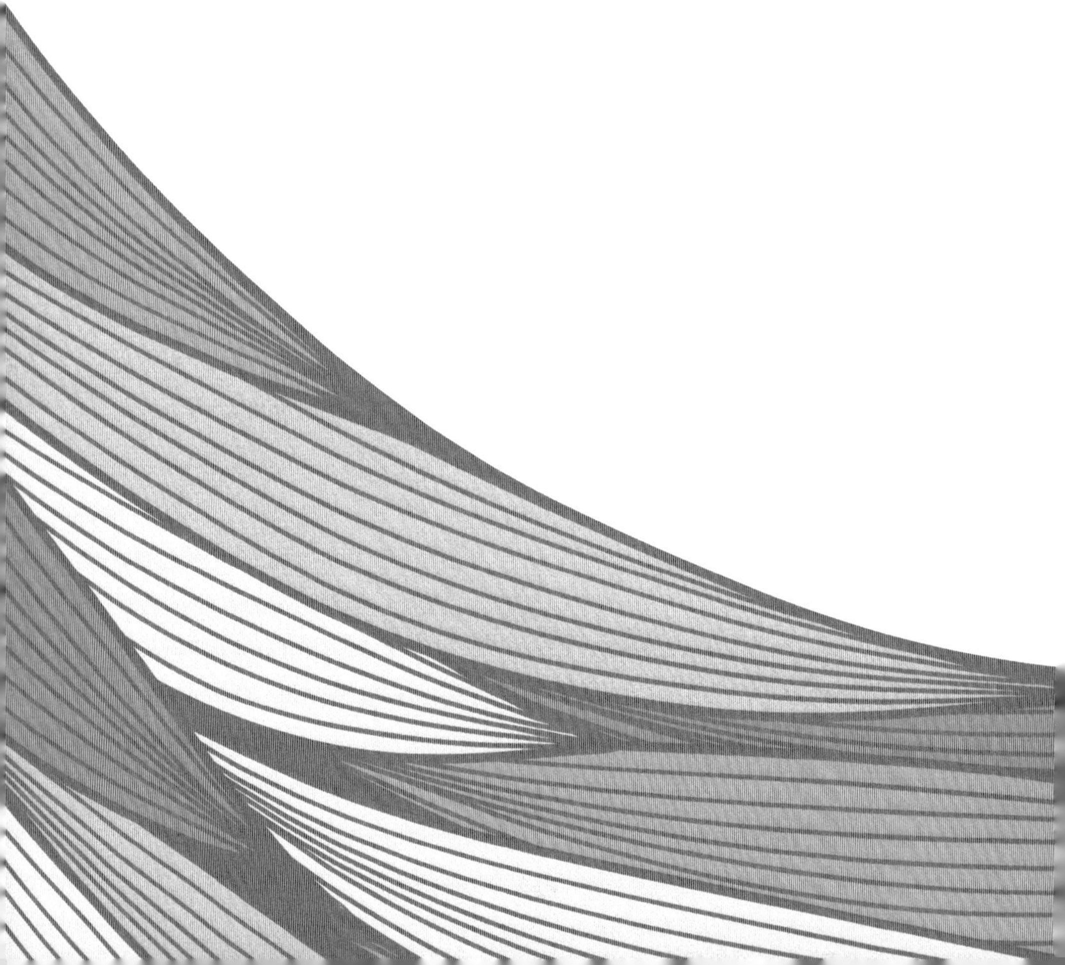

Part 3
UNKNOWN TERRITORY

CHAPTER 42

Long Island, New York, Winter and Spring 1777

The winter of 1777 was strange, long, and hard. The British army, believing they were prepared for a frigid winter, still were surprised by the severity of it. It was one of the snowiest winters in recent memory, and the locals were sparing in their sympathy towards the occupying army.

As the British settled in for a long war, they continually searched for goods to confiscate. But, apart from the most obvious such as land and livestock, families who reportedly were prosperous, had precious little to seize. This led the British to wonder if they had overestimated the prosperity of the colonists.

In the main the colonists were wary of the British. Soldiers were soldiers, after all. Once the locals understood the permanency of quartering the British army and what that would mean to them, most of them had taken actions to augment their resources and to secure their assets. In practice they had hidden their prized possessions (which included any spare weapons) from the occupying army by secreting goods or wealth would tempt the army. They found underground storage or built hidden storage areas. Some had even shipped away their goods to trusted family members in other colonies.

For Leticia Smith, who had been housebound all winter, the season had felt more isolating than usual. To make things worse, through the darkest months she was plagued by one worry: how would the Smiths survive, what with Henry still gambling, and the British seizing everything not nailed down?

Winter slowly withdrew but only in fits and starts as March and April, with their frequent showers, spread gloom. Finally, May brought warmth to the entire earth, and everything in it. The flowers and trees burst forth in buds, as if the war had never begun, as if the British had never attacked, or marched on, or planted themselves on the island.

But Leticia was so preoccupied by the crush of Henry's debt, she did not notice spring's glowing beauty. She would not admit it to herself but her financial woes were rooted in pride, she feared she would lose face. She would rather die than let her neighbors know she was watching her pennies.

One day as she was passing the mill, the miller came round the corner, weeping and babbling about the loss of his property to his wife. Out of the corner of her eye, she saw the officer responsible for the miller's woes riding away.

She realized then that the same thing could happen to the Smiths. She was dogged by the fact they were no longer wealthy. While she liked Henry well enough, and she felt he liked her more, she was troubled that she be much diminished in state soon. Then shortly they would be indistinguishable from the farmers around them.

It was then that a simple plan came to her—perhaps her days of desperation might be foreshortened? She started eyeing the British officers keenly, studying them closely. One day she crossed paths with Samuel Birch, a British officer of the 17th Regiment of Dragoons, the kind of high-ranking officer whose attention would benefit the Smiths.

Birch was bound to show up at their large farm, and she knew she could charm him. She made up her mind: he would become her benefactor. Aye, she felt a twinge of guilt about doing such a thing to Henry, but it hardly seemed to matter as he was away so much. And, besides maybe she could help them both by keeping their farm.

By coincidence, a few days after this decision Samuel Birch came by her house. It was a beautiful May morning and the sun was bright in the meadow as he drew up his horse. Leticia was overseeing the collecting of eggs.

"Goodwife," the colonel began.

Leticia was so used to being addressed by name by Quakers, she was brought up short hearing herself addressed as a free woman. She looked up at him, the bright sun was behind him, creating a kind of halo behind his head. He was brilliant, splendid in his spotless regimental uniform. Even his mount mimicked his upright and shining presence.

Could this officer be enticed into favoring me? If so, then perhaps I can find a way to free myself from the shackles of debt my idiot husband has bound me in! She wondered.

Now the opportunity to secure her prize was in front of her. She tipped her head respectfully and performed a half curtsey.

"Yes, honorable sir. Would the general," she intentionally overstated his rank, "give me the honor of being my guest for morning tea?" She gestured towards her house. She had no tea. Her invitation was about deference, not about tea.

Birch smiled briefly at her overstatement and eyed her speculatively. His look lingered so long she became uncomfortable.

"Aye, I accept the invitation. But you err, I am no general; I am but a Lieutenant Colonel," he touched his chest as if she could interpret the insignias.

Though there was no need, he introduced himself and when he did, something niggled in the back of her mind about Birch. She had shoved away vague rumors earlier, but they resurfaced. Rumor was that he had a violent temper, drank in excess and was a brute. But he had been selected and remained an officer in the respectable British army—how true could these rumors be? Besides, he presented himself honorably and looked magnificent! She brushed aside her doubts.

"Not yet a general, though I have been in the colonies for nigh on five years now." He seemed wearied by that.

Leticia chose to ignore his feelings about the colonies and instead she made a sound which she hoped sounded like he impressed her.

He continued, "You may know that last year the dragoons razed the home of Francis Lewis? The rebel and a signer of that absurd Declaration of Independence?"

She remembered it well. The story was memorable because it was so horrible: the dragoons ransacked and burned the Lewis home at Whitestone.

His voice lifted in pride, "I was the one who ordered that. But unfortunately, only his wife was home." He sounded disappointed at that. When they could not find Francis Lewis, they instead took his wife Elizabeth as prisoner.

His callousness sent a jolt of shock through her. She succeeded in hiding her feelings about what he had just told her, concealing it with a beaming smile.

Her feelings well masked, she said, "I feel sure our King and your superiors are gratified." She beamed at him hoping to dazzle him, as her mind raced.

She brushed a lock of hair off her forehead; she knew she could still look young. She gave him a coy look and led him inside. Why wouldn't an officer feel happier in the presence of a pretty lady in a comfortable home? It would be a cinch to be his kept-lady; Henry was always at the gaming board or tavern.

They took a bitter concoction that was now called "tea." She bit her tongue when he took three teaspoons of her precious sugar. She listened with feigned interest to Birch's complaints, making appropriate noises of sympathy and awe.

Before he departed Leticia made it clear to him her husband was away most of the time, and that should he ever, ever need to visit their home he was more than welcome.

"Any time," she stressed and without a shred of guilt held his gaze, believing that he understood what she would not say aloud.

Birch stood up to leave. "I see you need to be schooled! As a Lieutenant Colonel, I do not require an invitation. At present, I am in Jericho. The owner has," he cleared his throat. "Umm—moved out, and I must quarter there." He added, "For now."

CHAPTER 43

Hempstead, New York, Summer 1777

The British army was sprawled across the island. Officially they ran the entirety of Long Island, with the rebel areas receiving extra attention. The island was entirely under British control, and they had eyes and ears everywhere so they feared no reprisals in the rest of Hempstead.

The British officials who oversaw the occupation had no particular interest in this colony's civil and legal affairs. They believed that they were doing a satisfactory job of allowing fair and lawful commerce to continue. For the most part they kept themselves out of non-military affairs. They retained the appearance of the time before the occupation by levying justice through local intermediaries, so the towns were still overseen by locals. They hoped the military occupation of the Island would be tolerable if locals remained in charge of local issues—it was still a British colony.

Henry Smith was at the tavern. As much as he hated what was going on all about him, his home was now strangely placid. Leticia seemed happier and she no longer complained when he went out to game nor when he came in late. Things were going well for him, and he was finally winning more games.

Joseph Kemble entered the tavern, "Did you hear what happened to Jones?" he asked his friend. "Colonel Birch gave him a visit the other day at Tyron Hall."

At Birch's name, Henry's ears pricked up. Birch spent at least as much time at his own home as Henry did. If Birch kept Leticia occupied, if she stayed out of his hair and did not nag him, then he was willing to turn a blind eye towards Birch's interest in Leticia. At least that is how he felt at the moment.

"Aye," Kemble continued, "Birch had his men ransack the house. They carried off every stick of furniture."

"Is that right?"

"Every stick," he downed another mouthful of his draught, "even down to the windows!"

"No!"

Kemble had Henry's attention: he was astounded by Birch's audaciousness.

"But Jones! Why bother him? He's a Tory!"

"Aye, he is." Kemble shrugged then continued, "Jones even entered a written plea to get his belongings returned, as they should be, him being a Tory and all."

"And?"

Kemble shook his head, "Birch didn't reply. He did not allow Jones to come to his presence when he asked."

"What did Jones do then?"

Kemble shrugged, "Nothing, I suppose. He's madder than I ever seen, he says this is not martial law— this is no law."

Henry had stopped his game, so shocked was he by Birch's disregard for even Loyalists.

From nearby Jimmy Naylor added his own story about Birch. "Birch regards no one. Reverend Cutting of the English church needs to find a place for the flock now because of Birch."

They turned their attention to Naylor. Naylor explained, "My wife tells me Reverend Cutting says Birch and his regiment are worse than useless. They take what they want, and are now taking the church, and the land it's on."

This created a stir, but someone scoffed at Naylor's story. How could this be, when the English church was used by the occupying English soldiers and officers?

Naylor insisted on the veracity of the story, "It's right from the horse's mouth. Cutting's, I mean."

Henry Smith was sick to his stomach. He got up suddenly and stumbled out of the tavern and into the woods nearby, walking aimlessly. The thought of Birch in his home made him ill. But he could not do anything. When it was fully night he made his way home. As long as Birch felt their home was open to him, Henry believed they were entertaining the very devil himself.

* * *

After this Henry spent almost no time in his home, he did not have the stomach for it. Birch remained on Long Island and spent many late afternoons and evenings in the company of Leticia as she was so very welcoming and pliable. Late one afternoon, after several weeks of this, Leticia's brother-in-law stopped in to return some equipment. As he arrived, he passed Birch as he was turning out of their gate.

He mentioned seeing Birch to Leticia, "That bastard," he spat, "Took the South Meeting House! He ripped out the pulpit and the pews and cut them all apart."

His vehemence surprised her, for he was not an overly religious man, nor was he an American rebel. He made it clear that he believed Birch had gone too far and added a brotherly warning, "Leticia, he's a dangerous man, given over to violence and to drink."

Leticia was disbelieving and insulted. She denied it, "No if he were, I'd not be keeping his company."

He shook his head, disappointed and dismayed by her willful blindness.

CHAPTER 44

Hempstead, New York, Early October 1777

Elizabeth Willis was putting out the wash. It was a beautiful day to be outdoors, at least this part of the wash day was pure pleasure. She had forgotten to tuck her hair back into her cap and the wind gusts, coming this way, then that, whipped her loosened hair wildly. An entire year had passed since her niece, Phebe Anna, had died. Elizabeth wondered if Amy would recover from her daughter's death: she often talked about her loss, weeping.

Elizabeth puzzled over her brother. Stephen used to laugh frequently; he loved a joke. But now he brooded and hardly laughed. At first Elizabeth fancied his brooding meant his wound was still tender, still open.

But now the sharp edge of his mourning was dulled. His attention was on the British. She was certain his rebel sympathies had sprouted and grown since Lymes had killed Anna. He was always inquiring about the comings and goings of strangers across the Sound. The more she thought of it, the more certain she was that he had full-grown rebel sympathies. Although she had no evidence, she suspected he had actively helped the rebels.

If he did see the British as the enemy, it was an unhealthy and un-Friendlike attitude. She stretched out the final garment over a large bush in the furthest corner. Before returning to the house, she paused to soak in the rays of the autumnal sun.

When Elizabeth turned back to the house, she paused to tuck in place her unruly hair. While doing so, she spied Birch in the doorway of the Smith's house. Something in her chest roiled.

Elizabeth had never had a problem with Henry Smith until his second marriage. Then after Leticia wed Henry, things went downhill between the neighbors. At first, Leticia viewed Elizabeth and John with suspicion. But she had slowly warmed up to them (though remaining a gossip and a busybody).

Leticia was tiring and irksome. One day when Leticia was especially wearisome, she complained to John and asked for his advice. He admitted that he too was bothered by her. John reminded her that patience was not patience until it was tried. After this, though Leticia was unchanged, Elizabeth was calmer. Time had a way of ironing things out.

* * *

Leticia heard the door shut as Birch left for the day. It was a sunny morning, and she lay abed waiting for breakfast, knowing Bess would shortly call her to it. Her mind wandered and she smiled at her own ingenuity. All about her, the occupying British had taken land and farms, wood and animals and all kinds of moveable objects from every resident. But, thanks to her foresight, they wouldn't take hers. No, she had provided for herself and had no reason to fear.

With a sense of satisfaction, she reviewed her success: since Birch had given in to her charms, she had not lacked anything. Indeed, Lieutenant Colonel Samuel Birch secured everything she asked for. Sometimes he was peevish, but it was understandable for he surely was under a strain.

Leticia blocked her ears to gossip about Birch and especially the rumors about his temper. She felt secure and a bit smug, because he had never shown her anything but his fair side.

To be sure, he was prickly now and then; he was but human. When she grew impatient with him, she would remind herself why she was with him. Although her conscience gnawed at her now and then, she blocked it out by justifying what she now had attained: a comfortable station in life. When she thought of that, she felt proud of herself.

Birch was with her most evenings and a few days in a week, but he slept in the seized quarters in Jericho (which were, according to all reports, luxurious). All he demanded from her was to be available to him.

Now that it was a year into the occupation, she was finding it difficult to dress to her satisfaction (for she wished to be seen at her best). They were not completely cut off from New York, but it was work to look as she wished. First, she had to decide what she required from the City, then she would give Birch her list of fabrics, buttons, ribbons, lace, trim and the like. Eventually, through Birch's superior military networks, he not only paid for but cleared the way for her items.

Luxuriating in bed awaiting breakfast, her mind roamed and questions bubbled to the surface: What would happen when Birch moved on, or when the British won? Birch and every other British officer seemed confident the British would win. How could they not? Why, everything about them was superior, including their experience, their training, their discipline and their vigor. Maybe, she mused, Birch will take me to England after the war. How fine I would be then!

That thought made her feel like dancing. She swung her legs over the bed and placed her feet on the floor. It had been daylight for some time now. She moved to her table to wash her face. But when she went to pour water from the pitcher, it was empty.

"Bessie! Bess!" she called for the slave. She called again but there was no answer.

"Lazy lass," she grumbled to herself and marched downstairs with the empty pitcher in hand.

All was quiet downstairs. Leticia looked about and saw Bess was just coming through the doorway from the yard. In her hands she carried a bucket full of water. Had she slept in again? Leticia's face reddened with anger; she was about to chastise her when Bess broke in.

"I'm sorry, ma'am," Bess began, looking over her shoulder.

Leticia asked for her tray in her room before sweeping out, leaving Bess behind. She returned to her room and waited impatiently. Finally, Bess entered with the breakfast tray, put it down, pivoted, and returned downstairs. After breakfast, Leticia managed to dress herself. Something was not quite right downstairs.

When Leticia descended the stairs to take up her letter-writing, Bess was sweeping the floor. Something was amiss. Leticia's breakfast had not only been late, but it had been meager. She tried to read Bess's face but failed. Except for the mooing of the cows, the farm was strangely silent.

"Bessie, where is everyone?" Bess kept sweeping. Leticia came close to Bess and stayed her arm, "Tell me what is going on!"

Bess stopped. "You asked, but you aren't going to like it." She paused, "They ran away."

"What do you mean ran away? Who ran away—why?" Leticia began to panic; she and Henry had more slaves than anyone in Hempstead. But they needed them. "Where did they go? You get them!"

Bess had stopped sweeping, and looked calmly in Leticia's face, "Some ran away to be British soldiers, and a few went to the Americans, I guess. You better ask Birch why," she sniffed. "He knows, not me."

"This cannot be!" Leticia flew into a rage. "What could they gain from that? Have they gone out of their minds?" Bess shook her head and continued her work.

Leticia knew her slaves were not happy, but they had a place on the farm, and they were never treated with cruelty. Henry would never harm a flea. Now and then she had to be strict with them, but never cruel. Of the slaves, Bess and her near-grown son Jacob were hers, her late husband had given them her in his will.

Leticia went directly to her writing table to write a note for Samuel Birch at his headquarters. She told him to come in haste. She had Bess' son to deliver it to Birch, promising him a small reward. Henry was away on a gaming trip. This situation needed a man to sort it out, and Birch could do it.

The day dragged on and Leticia fretted about the chores that were not getting done on the farm. She had to prepare her own dinner because Bessie and her son were tending to the livestock, poultry, and horses.

When Birch finally arrived, it was well after she had eaten. Birch said little to her. His silence unnerved her, he was brooding about something. Leticia tamped down her own swelling anger. His moodiness gave her pause and she wondered if she should still ask for his help. She had no choice.

"What have we to eat?" he asked, curtly, putting his feet up on a chair.

She made sure he had dinner first, then massaged his feet. When she believed he was relaxed, she told him her problem and pleaded for his help.

He looked up, "Nay. They should not be here."

Leticia froze and stared at him in unbelief. What he had said was foolish. Such a foolish statement was unlike him.

Birch settled back in his chair and exhaled, breathing out smoke from his pipe.

She smiled thinly, "Why is that?"

"When I was leaving last, I heard them complaining. To put an end to that, I took a whip after them all and sent them away."

Leticia's mouth hung open in shock and disbelief.

He pulled on his pipe. "Aye, I was sick of hearing them bellyache."

She stared at him and said through her gritted teeth, "Thanks to you my farm has no slaves. Without slaves, I have no help! We shall have to do all the work ourselves!"

Birch stared at her as if this were a new thought. He shifted in his chair, "Nonsense! You have her…" He wagged a hand in Bess' direction. "Never mind, my men can hunt down other negro slaves to replace them."

Leticia was incredulous at his recklessness. He had driven away all her slaves because their grumbling bothered him. And now he meant for her to acquire new slaves? Even though she had never thought about slaves except as an aid to her comfort, she was revolted to hear him speak of hunting them down, as if they were game for the table.

"But…" she started to object. She stopped when she realized the game she was playing was treacherous. Birch, she now saw, was a callous man and he despised opposition of any sort.

She had kept his attention only by pretending to favor him. She had been malleable to his opinions, whims, and wishes. But now her situation had grown tricky. She had to remain in his favor. She chose to stop talking before she ruined the standing she had gained with him.

"Oh dear, what a bother," she said faking mildness she did not feel. Then she stayed silent, feigning resigned introspection. But Birch did not notice, withdrawing instead to his own thoughts. Leticia could be patient when necessary, and she remained silent. Eventually he took note of her prolonged silence and asked her what her problem was.

Her tone was heavy with drama, "Without slaves around, we won't have food here. It will be just me and Bessie. And even if I had the money, there's no food to buy." She wrung her hands. There was truth in her sense of helplessness.

As she had hoped, Birch grew livid. "Are you telling me that I won't get a decent meal here?" he stormed.

For the first time Leticia noted his misplaced, but genuine anger. It was not his house nor his farm, yet he was as wrathful as if they were. This was a man who took what he wished.

"Aye, I suppose, you are right," she said, shrugging helplessly, and looked down at her hands folded in her lap.

Birch shot to his feet and marched to the stool, pulling on his boots.

"Are you going out?" she asked stupidly.

"I'm going to find your slaves and return them."

"But how will you be able to find them? You cannot know which are mine! Besides, by now they might be gone!"

"It won't make any difference; you'll have all you need." Leticia cocked her head in question. Birch's hand was on the latch, "Now that they're freed, I can take my pick of any of them."

"Who? What do you mean by "them'?"

"Any negro I find! It doesn't matter," he said, slamming the door behind him.

When Bess entered the room to pick up the dishes and to put things away for the night, she found Leticia sitting alone, dazed, and staring into the distance.

Bess asked, "How're we going to run the farm?"

"Birch is getting slaves now."

Bess was confused. Leticia explained, "It's the oddest thing. Aye, he drove all but you away. Now that he sees that the farm needs hands and he is going to fix it by grabbing anyone he can find."

Bess shook her head, disgusted.

"Birch came from comfort. Now that he lives on Long Island, he won't live in a much-degraded state—without slaves he will leave here!" Leticia explained feebly.

As she said this, she looked away, wondering whether outsiders could run her farm. Distracted by her thoughts, she was blind to the wrath that took hold of Bess.

Bess's anger had reached a tipping point. She was a musket, full and tamped down with gunpowder, and now she was ready to fire. Her entire life had been spent in service, giving someone else comfort. Now she had reached her limit. Bess untied her apron and tossed it in Leticia's face. "I, nay, we, are leaving too."

"No! You cannot!" Leticia stood up and threw her arms about her neck. "I don't understand what's going on, but Bess, at least for now, we, you and me, we need each other. Please stay!" Leticia's desperation turned liquid, and she cried great heaving sobs.

In truth Bess had nowhere to go, and her son Jacob had no trade. But they now were well tired of being ill-treated, and suddenly she saw a toehold in Leticia's desperation. *Hold firm. Press for what you must have.* Bess told herself. This was the moment to barter craftily and fearlessly.

She stepped back eyeing Leticia and waited a long minute, lowered her voice, and replied, "I—no, Jacob and I, will do chores in exchange for a place to stay and for food. But I'm not going to be walked on." She held up a finger as she spoke to indicate the seriousness of her intention.

Leticia looked at her as if she had never seen her before. She now beheld a stranger. Bess caught sight of Leticia's disorientation, but she did not care. Leticia's feelings no longer mattered to Bess.

CHAPTER 45

Hempstead, New York, October 1777

LATE IN THE MORNING Henry Smith was returning home. To his astonishment, one of his carts passed him going in the opposite direction from his farm with one of his slaves at the reins.

"Jacob," he stopped him in the road. "Where are you taking these?" Smith indicated the cart, which was full of rails.

Jacob looked scared. "I was ordered to do this; I didn't want to."

"Who ordered you? Leticia? Did she tell you to do this?"

"No, sir, it was Colonel Birch who told me."

A sudden breeze came up, so strong that it almost blew Henry's hat off. He grabbed it, indicating with his other hand that Jacob should remain.

Jacob said Birch had ordered him to remove the cart to where he was quartered. His mother had told him not to go. But by then the cart was loaded and ready. When Jacob said he could not go, Birch brought out a whip. He did not want a lashing.

Henry was perplexed by his story. He was still thinking about the odd scene when he heard a wagon coming round the bend. Both men turned towards the sound. When it came into view Smith saw Birch, mounted on a horse. Behind him, a stranger drove a wagon piled high with household belongings. Henry's belongings.

Incredulously, Birch was carting away Henry's possessions. Without thinking Henry stepped into the way of the wagon and rider to block progress. The wagon creaked to a stop.

"Stop!" yelled Smith, "These are mine! What are you doing with them?" he demanded.

Birch turned his mount to face Henry. Henry's heart pounded and he hoped his indignation would overwhelm Birch's sense of superiority.

Birch said nothing. Eerily silent, he looked down his nose at the man in the road, then dismounted. Smith froze at Birch's movement. Once dismounted, Birch's nostrils flared, and his lip was curled in cruel pleasure.

Then without warning, in a smooth flowing movement, Birch unsheathed his long sword and ran at Smith, a sword in one hand, flailing his riding crop in the other. A frightened Jacob took off with the cart.

Smith was unarmed and desperate, he grabbed what was at hand, a stick from the ground. He immediately realized the futility of this: a stick was no match for a sword. An energized Birch charged towards him. Smith needed to move—he was out of time. He tossed the stick aside, and took a flying leap into his own pasture.

Henry's sudden jump to the pasture took Birch by surprise. Birch had believed Henry would fight, not flee. Birch's hesitation gave Henry a slight advantage.

Birch dismounted to give chase. But he was unfamiliar with the terrain, and when he came to the pasture, he leapt the ditch clumsily. Coming down, he stepped into a hole, and his knee crumbled into the wet earth. Cursing with rage, he scrambled up to pursue Henry.

Henry's dash for his pasture was intentional, deliberate. He was betting on his private knowledge of his fields against Birch's ignorance. The pasture had a pocket in it, a kind of den, small enough not to be seen, but large enough to hide in. The den was his only hope in fleeing Birch's rage.

Henry zig-zagged across the field, hiding behind the largest of trees. Birch chased him in a mad fury, yelling at the top of his lungs. Henry's crazed run made Birch angrier.

Henry was strangely calm. Although he ran as if crazed, he was not. He knew he would benefit if he stoked Birch's rage. He already had in mind the final tree; it would be the one nearest the den where he would hide.

Birch's knee was burning in pain from his fall in the ditch, slowing him down. But he was undeterred, spurred on by anger. The embarrassment and the knee pain fueled his rage. He refused to give up, chasing Henry in his crazy ramble across the pasture, shouting and cursing loudly as he went.

But then suddenly Henry disappeared. Birch scanned the pasture in search of his quarry. Hiding out below him in his den, Henry could hear Birch's ragged breathing.

When Birch realized he was thwarted, he raged out loud, incensed. Then he dropped to his knees in the field and yelled out, shouting, "As God is my witness, I will cut ye to pieces, ye and anyone who opposes me!"

Hearing him, Henry believed every word. Trembling in fear, he stayed hidden till well after sunset. When total darkness had fallen, he cautiously emerged. Hungry and stiff, he wished he could safely go home. He could not—he might find Birch there, still vivid with anger. He was overly careful, creeping low to the ground, watching for any sign of Birch. He breathed a sigh of relief when he reached the neighboring Willis farm. They were a safe family. He knocked on their door.

The lad Samuel opened the door. Upon seeing Henry's condition, he looked perplexed and sympathetic.

"Good evening," he stepped back for Smith to enter the room.

John Willis came forward, putting out his hands to clasp Henry's,

"Thee looks starved," he said. His eyes roamed across Henry, but he said nothing about his dirty and rumpled appearance.

"I am—a horrible thing has happened."

He stopped abruptly, catching sight of Elizabeth. She was sitting by the fire gently wrapping the head of a man who was wounded. "What happened to him?"

"That's Big Jack," John explained. Moving closer to Henry, he lowered his voice, "It was Birch who did that."

Smith's heart pounded as John explained in hushed tones, "He was dragged before Birch for questioning. Before he could answer any charges, Birch knocked him down with something heavy. Before he was done with Jack, he beat him 29 times.

"This, for no reason. Then the soldiers left him half dead outside on Kings Road." He shook his head mournfully, "I was on my way home when I found him."

Henry's lips were loosened, "Birch told my slave to haul away my split rails and half of my household goods. I confronted him. And without warning, he attacked me with his broadsword, and then he chased me. I've been hiding half a day from him—he's out of his mind!"

The boy Samuel added his story to Smith's. "I just finished telling Father that the other day two families came to Birch with a dispute."

His father clucked his tongue, shaking his head, "But their fix was worsened."

"What happened to them?" asked Henry.

The lad continued, "Something sent him into a rage, Birch raged so much that he cut James Morrell with his sword—almost killing him. Joseph Kemble was waiting his turn to speak. When Kemble tried to help Morrell, Birch struck Kemble. Then Birch set alight a bundle of sticks and thrust it into his face.

"Kemble escaped, but not before Birch chased him around the room like a madman with a gun in one hand and a sword in the other."

Henry was dumbstruck by Birch's mad conduct.

"Come," John invited him. "Thee cannot return home till thee has taken something."

Samuel left with a bucket to fetch water. Henry could feel his wounds and scratches and his fatigue. He could only guess what a mess he must be: he must be filthy. He thanked God silently that Elizabeth and John Willis were his neighbors, he counted on their care and kindness more than he had realized.

CHAPTER 46

Hempstead, New York, November 1777

Leticia had seen neither Henry nor Birch since October. She was lonely and now she feared the farm was rapidly going to ruin. Although Birch had kept his promise and had delivered negroes to her farm, the farm was not running well. It could not, for they were strangers, forcibly dumped on her plot.

Where he had found the help, she had no idea. They did not hide their resentment at being here, and yet they remained on the farm. She assumed they had nowhere else to go. Maybe they feared retribution from Birch?

It did not matter anyway. Things were in such a state. The farm animals were constantly getting loose, and they were not tended as they should be. Leticia was not sure, but she had a feeling there was not sufficient wood for the coming winter. Nothing seemed to work properly, and the remaining harvest had not got put in for the winter. Desperate, Leticia hired some hands to put in the last of the harvest.

Leticia had a habit of blaming others for her own problems. Henry was to blame for their money problems, which was why she had enticed Birch. Birch was to blame for her not having slaves. But now she had a real problem. She had a failing farm and no solution.

In her heart of hearts, Leticia sympathized with the new negroes' anger at being forced onto the Smith farm. Even negroes were human. Leticia had begged Birch for the return of her slaves. But he ignored her. Instead, he spewed out vile comments, saying, "a negro is a negro, and that equals a slave."

The group of negroes on the farm were generally bitter and indignant. At first Leticia had been too scared to speak to them, she was afraid they would lash out at her. But she soon learned her timidity was interpreted as indifference, making their interactions worse. Now their relations had improved. Understandably some refused to speak to her, many would not work, and the handful that did anything did so because they were bored. Only a few had left.

If only Birch had not driven away her slaves! And now, alas, faithful Bess showed up to work only two days a week, and then for pay. Bess had other places to work, and Jacob was working too. Bess had determined to never move back to the Smith farm.

Birch had not sent word nor stepped foot on her land since the day he left in October. At first, she had been angry at herself, and for a time she had wandered around her house in a daze. How could she have misjudged Birch? The first few days she was shocked and angered, which turned to disbelief and hurt. But by the second week, she imagined Birch was not that bad and should at least get a chance to redeem himself. Then by the third week, she had determined if Birch would only see her, then he would be filled with remorse, and mend his ways. His heart would soften, then he would return as a better man.

Winter was coming soon, and she was desperate. She determined to find Birch. She called in Bess's replacement to ask for her help in getting dressed. The woman did not hide her grievance at having been forced into the role of a slave. She grudgingly assisted Leticia, leaving right after, ignoring Leticia's pleas to help with her hair. Leticia managed her hair as best she could, then set out to find Birch.

She had to drive herself in a simple pony cart (at least that was still in good repair).

Since she was not sure where to go first, she started off on Middle Country Road, the central route across the island and heavily traveled. It was the right choice. In less than an hour she rounded a bend and spied a familiar figure stopped on the side of the road.

She halted and greeted Birch warmly. His greeting was decidedly cool. She interpreted his coolness as being occupied with tightening his saddle.

Leticia tamped down the bitterness within and put on her best face. "Samuel," she cooed, "Wouldn't you like to come for dinner today?" She smiled so her dimple would show.

Birch turned an icy blue eye towards her.

"Leticia," he lowered his tone, but not the volume, "it's time you took up knitting like the old hen that you are."

Leticia was speechless. She climbed down and approached him. His back was turned towards her as he continued to adjust his saddle.

"How dare you insult me, sir!"

He turned towards her. "Move along, hen. I'm off to York City." He grinned a sly grin, "To take pleasure in new company."

"What do you mean new company?" she stalled him. He could not abandon her!

"You can indulge in savoring the delights of the rest of the officers of His Majesty." He chuckled. Then wagged a teasing finger under her chin.

"How dare you!" She moved close to him and dug her fingers into the fabric of his regimental jacket. "You wouldn't do that to me! You cannot do that!" she shrieked.

Birch pulled back in revulsion. But she did not release him, nor did she cease harping at him. Instead, she kept at it, pleading and scolding, till Birch snapped. He gave her a backhanded slap on her cheek, knocking her to the ground. Mounting his steed, he looked at her sprawled on the ground. He spat on the road not far from her head, wheeled around and cantered off.

Leticia was too shocked to think. She had never been treated so shabbily. She was too dazed to stand up for fear of falling and remained where she was on the ground.

She soon heard the approach of a wagon from the opposite direction. It pulled to a stop. Soon John Willis and Elizabeth were gently helping her into the wagon.

Leticia was more humiliated than hurt. She braced herself for reproaches or questions from them, but none came.

Once at the Willis home, the family treated her kindly, as they always had. As Elizabeth gently cleaned the soil off Leticia, she hummed softly. Where Birch's blow had landed was bruised. Elizabeth applied a poultice to it. Leticia allowed her to inspect her for further harm. In addition to the bruising on her face and arm, Leticia had a small cut on her face.

Elizabeth finished with one final inspection, "There's a bit of dried blood." She wiped the corner of Leticia's mouth carefully.

Leticia's mouth throbbed. Then she realized Birch's blow had knocked a tooth out of her head. Elizabeth gently suggested she lie down. Leticia complied, still shook by Birch's rage and violence. She lay on the pallet as her hostess covered her with a light quilt. Till now she had been holding herself together, while shaking within. Now everything spilled out. As she cried with abandon, Elizabeth sat nearby, soothing her brow. Her gentle touch was a calming balm. After a spell, after Leticia's tears wound down to a soft whimpering, she dozed off.

When she awoke Elizabeth was finishing up mending her torn dress. Samuel brought her a mug of cider and mentioned he had already got the pony cart to her home. Leticia lay there, trying not to think about Birch's cruelty, but failing.

Helping Elizabeth in the house was a young girl Leticia did not recognize. The girl was heavily pregnant, close to giving birth. Leticia asked about the girl, and Elizabeth told her quietly that she was one of many girls who, since the British had taken Long Island last year, had found themselves pregnant. This girl's parents had sent her away from home in disgrace. The callousness of her parents shocked Leticia. She made sounds of disapproval.

Elizabeth quickly added, "Perhaps it shall be well, her parents have agreed for her return home. But not until after she has delivered the baby."

"What about the baby?" Leticia whispered.

She shook her head. "The grandparents do not want to accept her. But at least the child will be taken in by the Friends."

CHAPTER 47

Hempstead, New York, November 1777

Henry and Leticia's problems were now a Willis family burden. They had tended first to Henry and then they had tended Leticia, each of them a victim of Birch. Elizabeth believed they should help the Smiths. She asked why should Birch be the cause of their misery. Before the occupation, the Smiths had at least lived together, if not in perfect harmony, with some friendship and care. That evening, after Leticia's safe delivery to the Smith farm, Elizabeth suggested they persuade Henry to return. Though his wife's reasoning was sensible, John had his doubts.

"Can we not try it?" she pleaded.

John resisted but Elizabeth argued that the survival and fitness of the whole Island hinged on unity, even for folks who were not Friends.

"Mayhap now that Birch has shown his true colors, Leticia's eyes are opened and she'll be kinder towards Henry."

Doubtful but willing to try, John set out to seek Henry. Henry would have to be in the frame of mind to hear him out.

John soon found him, Henry was sitting outside his usual spot, his favorite tavern, broodily smoking a pipe.

"Henry, Leticia needs and she wants thee to return to the farm." John was direct.

Henry shook his head, squeezing his eyes shut. "You do not know." He was mournful, "John you're a good man but ye cannot know what's going on inside of me." Henry's shoulders slumped. John detected tears in the corners of his eyes. Henry's naked reaction caught him by surprise.

"Henry, Leticia is somewhat changed, at least to me."

Henry looked up at his neighbor, a flash of hope crossed his face.

"And this be true?" He doubted.

"Aye, she seems so to me. Since thee has been away Birch has treated her cruelly. Thee knows the sort of beast he can be. But now he has left for good." He paused, "Thee and she could at least talk. Thee would be welcomed, because she badly needs thy help with the farm—and what with the British here it makes nowhere safe."

John emphasized the danger because he doubted Henry would go otherwise. If he could get Henry back to the farm, then maybe Leticia would see the use and the practicality of having him back to stay.

Henry surprised John when he shot off the bench. "Can you take me there, Quaker-Man?"

On the way to the Smith farm, Henry asked where Birch was now. John was happy to tell him Birch had been ordered out of Long Island.

"Birch's own violence finished him here. Without cause, he attacked several men. The King's army found his conduct unbecoming for the countryside, and he was packed off to New York."

Once reunited, Leticia and Henry found common ground as they rehearsed their separate woes, adding their mutual wish for peace.

"Dear wife," Henry began, "Would to God none of this had happened. What has driven us to this point?"

Leticia confessed, "Husband, I have always been afraid of starvation. Nay, of more, of loss. But starvation as well."

"Call me the fool and unschooled in your fears. I thought you hated me, but I reckon it was not hatred, but fear that drove you. I have not been a good husband." He flushed in shame thinking of the days and nights he had left her alone while gambling and drinking. "Now," he hesitated, "we are at a crossroads."

"Come back. I need you here."

Henry had married her because he felt an attraction to her. He knew she married him for money. And yet this was the first time she had said anything that sounded faintly affectionate. He blinked hard but it did not stop tears from coming down his cheeks. He reached his arms around her, and Leticia gave in to him. Leticia had never loved him, but if he could make her happy enough, that was enough.

CHAPTER 48

Cow Neck, New York, Mid-December 1777

Rachel found Quipinoq outside her door again this morning. She did not know how long he had been there. Quipinoq was a man who lived by his hands, he tinkered and traveled about. Often, she called him here when Stephen or Adam could not fix something, or for a job requiring a certain skill she did not have. Oddly, Quipinoq had shown up every morning for a week now. He always asked if she needed help, and every morning, she had to turn him away.

Quipinoq was of uncertain origin. She used to think he was an Indian of the Matinecocks, which would explain why he could come and go as he pleased. But then she learned Phebe had known his parents, and one of them had been a negro slave. When she learned this, she had to push away the stark truth: no matter how much slave blood, Indians were always Indian. And though one of his parents had been a negro slave, he was a free man.

Quipinoq said nothing until she spoke to him. "Good morning." He nodded to her.

"Did Mother Dodge call you?" he shook his head. "Did Stephen call you?" He shook his head. He stood there. Rachel felt suddenly awkward.

"Please break bread with us. We have but little today, yet we have enough to share." He turned down her offer, and then, like the other days, turned and left.

Once in the house, she filled a kettle to make hasty pudding. She was late today. Their meals were now shared with the young Hessian quartered there, Jacob. While she worked, she told Mother Dodge about Quipinoq's daily appearances.

"Did you or did Stephen ask for him?" Rachel asked. Mother Dodge shook her head.

Rachel wondered if he was there for her. Today she had been aware that he had been looking at her as a woman. She told Mother Dodge her thoughts.

Mother Dodge smiled. "Suprises have no end; maybe he finds thee fair." She added, her tone sober, "Or maybe he comes here because thee has always been here, and what with all this happening—" she nodded in the direction of Jacob who was polishing something, "Perhaps it is comforting to see thee is unchanged. And the house, me, the plot, we are unchanged." She was alluding to the continuing war and the hardships of the occupation.

Rachel considered that possibility. "Aye. I never think about the Indians—they have always been here and so I think no one will bother them. I confess to my strange belief that they never have fear."

The Indians were permanent; they were part of the landscape, much like a meadow, a hill, a rivulet.

Mother Dodge was silent and when she finally spoke, she was troubled, "I doubt he is afraid. But these changes cause a body to think, to wonder. I reckon he is curious about the changes."

A small smile creased her face. She teased, "But, then again, I could be wrong and mayhap Quipinoq wants thee as his woman."

* * *

The evenings were dark early now. Even the afternoon was dark in early winter. Someone was pounding on Elizabeth's door. She opened it to Henry Smith. He dashed inside her house before she had a chance to speak.

"You have to help me!" Smith was bedraggled, his hair askew, his face blotchy.

"Is it Leticia? Is she hurt?" Elizabeth pictured Leticia burned badly or hurt in a fall.

"Yes! No! Oh, dear Lord! What am I to do!?" Henry paced like a mad man. "It's all because of me! What am I going to do?"

The door was open, unlatched. A sudden gust of bitter wind blew it wide open. She turned to latch it when John saved her the trouble when he entered the house.

Upon seeing John, Henry yelled, "Thank God you are here!" What am I to do?" He grabbed the front of John's cloak, his hands shaking as he clutched it.

When he let go of John, Henry rambled and tore at his hair as he spoke. The ranting man was incoherent but John finally coaxed Henry outside and into the barn to unburden himself. The barn had a measure of privacy not found in the house.

The night drew in and the two men were still in the barn. Elizabeth placed vittles on the table for the quartered soldier. She threw a cloak about her and set out for the barn. She had gone only a few paces when she met John returning.

"Henry is headed home." John sounding weary. Elizabeth matched his steps as they went back to the house, John recounting Henry's situation.

The Smiths' happy reunion had been brief. They had had foot soldiers but no officers since Birch's departure. That is, until last month when another officer was placed in their home. He was a Scottish Highlander who made much of his heritage. Elizabeth remembered meeting the newly quartered officer but once.

A few days ago, when Henry had returned from his errands, the officer and his belongings were gone. Henry's wife and her belongings were also gone, and neither the quartered soldiers nor the negroes knew where they had gone. But the two had indeed left together.

After a frenzied search, Henry visited the officer's commanding officer. It took several days before they could confirm the Scottish officer had abandoned his post, and in doing so, the British army. They believed that the Scotsman was destined for Canada and Henry's wife was with him.

"Henry blames himself. He says he overlooked her."

Elizabeth expressed her pity for Henry, "Aye, that may be true. But she gave him little chance. Henry could not give her what she most wanted: high standing."

John agreed, "Henry shall heal. Thee is right. Leticia will quickly find life in Canada worse than life with Henry Smith." As a gust of December wind went down his collar, he wondered how she would fare in Canada's winter.

Elizabeth thought of her neighbor. "Henry has to be bereft."

CHAPTER 49

Hempstead, New York, December 1777

THE EARLY MORNING SNOWFALL had melted when Edmond Prior set out for the Willis home. Feeb and Edmond were by their mutual agreement to be married, that was not a question. He now believed he had passed the scrutiny of the Willis family. Yesterday a message arrived asking him to come to Samuel and Mary Willis' house, an invitation which perplexed him. Even at this late date he had still not heard from the committee as to whether he was accepted to Meeting as a Friend.

His "clearing" or formal application to the Society of Friends had first stalled when the British had taken over Long Island. The chaos of the British occupation, and the seizure of the Flushing Meeting House especially (Feeb had said), had shaken everyone and had broken up the established routines in the community.

In frustration, Edmund had gone to Feeb's brothers-in-law, the Mott brothers, about the matter. He voiced his concern to the two sympathetic men. Edmund caught a certain look that passed between them, but all they would tell him was that he was close to being cleared. Edmond left confused but somewhat comforted.

As he drew near the Willis home his nervousness intensified. Why had he been summoned here? Had Father Willis changed his mind and withdrawn his consent? What could he say to Samuel in that case?

What would change his mind? And how would he bear up if he were denied Feeb's hand? He shuddered at the thought.

Upon entering the house, Keziah showed him to the back of the house where the kitchen was. At the back of the house and off to the side was a combined sitting and work area. The space was cluttered: small projects were scattered here and there, as if put down in haste, to be taken up later. It told him the family was too busy to put away the projects, only to take them up again. Somehow this workspace spoke to him, perhaps because it contrasted with Meeting Houses which were tidy, plain, and orderly. And the Friends kept their persons similarly: their hair always in place, their clothes though plain, were neat and clean. He had wrongly believed in the Friend's home nothing was out of place, and nothing was messy, yet here was evidence contradicting his assumption. This was daily life inside the Friends' household. He was pleased by its ordinariness, it was no different from everyone else's.

Samuel Willis was not in the room. Instead, seated at a large worktable was Feeb's mother Mary and her kin Mother Dodge. Keziah took his hat and cloak. Mary greeted him and gestured for him to be seated near her. Keziah set a cider down in front of him and smiled reassuringly. Edmond anticipated Samuel's entrance at any moment but Samuel did not appear.

After he was settled and after the preliminary greetings subsided there was no small talk. Mary laid her needlework in her lap and cleared her throat.

First Edmond's curiosity overcame him, he blurted out, "Is Samuel to join us?"

Phebe chuckled and Mary laughed, "No, I summoned thee, not him!"

"Oh!" Edmond was confused. What could Mary say to him?

Phebe spoke first, "Mary asked me to speak with thee as I have more experience with young couples in thy situation." Phebe continued without pausing, "Thee has much work. In truth, thee has got a double load of learning before thee: becoming a Friend and, at the same time, a husband.

"Thee ought know thy spousal duties will bear some differences from those of thy parents.' And because of that, Mary has asked me to school thee a bit about Friends' marriages."

Edmond scratched his head and shifted nervously in his chair. He was not sure how to respond. He was not yet a Friend, yet the family was already speaking about their marriage practices. Though perplexed, his hopes rose.

"To begin with," Mary started, "the wedding itself will not be fancy. We go by plainness and simplicity, so as not to tempt anyone to pride or to jealousy."

Edmond did not care about the wedding.

"The closest thing thee will hear to a wedding vow will be thy solemn promise, by Divine assistance, to be a loving and faithful husband till death."

"That's not so very different," Edmond said. He relaxed for the first time since arriving, squaring his shoulders.

Phebe eyed him closely, "Thee has not asked about the woman's part."

He was lost and groped for a response, "I assume she shall honor and obey her husband."

Phebe smiled but contradicted him, "Nay. Thy wife is thy equal in marriage."

"She will be loving and faithful?"

"Aye, she will, as will thee."

"But she is not to obey?" He guessed correctly.

"Nay. For Friends, the promise to one another is mutual. Neither of thee obeys the other, because neither can replace God in a marriage."

Edmond had never heard of such a situation and was speechless.

"We hope, nay, we pray thee to be worthy of her love and respect. For Friends, men and women are equal in God's sight, and that does not end when they are wed." said Mary. Edmond knew of this equality, but he never thought about it functioning within marriage.

"This frame of mind is a precious thing: that husbands and wives have the same grace. Equality of wife and husband is the right and proper expression of Divine love," explained Phebe. She added, "I see these are new thoughts, new ways of thinking for thee. Thee shall need time to take them in."

Edmond was frank, "This certainly is a new way of viewing wives. I never thought that being a Quaker would be so…" he did not know what word to use for fear of offending Mary and Phebe.

"Hard?" asked Phebe. Edmond flushed.

"Aye," Mary added, "It will be hard to learn, but learn thee will. Thee will have to view thy wife as a creature made in the image of God first."

Mary turned practical, "Thee shall never deal her a blow nor withhold from her her independence. Thee shall not control thy wife, she is not thy possession. And thee and Feeb shall speak frankly and openly on everything."

"Everything?" Edmond asked, astonished.

"Aye," Mary said, "With time, thy talking shall necessarily lessen."

As Mary continued explaining something about the "warp and weave" of marital accord, Edmond, still in shock, barely heard her. After a half hour, she had talked herself out.

When Samuel Willis finally entered the room, Edmond was standing ready to leave for home. But Samuel blocked his way, and smiling, shook his hand. Mary suddenly stood up. She smiled warmly then shocked Edmond by giving him a maternal kiss on the cheek.

Phebe laughed at his surprise. Then she added happily, "Edmond Prior, at long last, thee is now a Friend!"

Edmond stuttered, "What? Why?" All words had left his head.

Samuel grinned, "Thee has waited too long, and then the Committee was re-organized many times. It takes only three people to approve of thy clearance, and two of us here are Weighty Friends."

That evening, Edmond was up late thinking of his new status as a Friend. Even his role as a husband would be different. Until a year ago, everything had been set and ordered. There were lords, kings, and classes; the bound, the free and the slave; the owner and the owned. But that was changing. Something revolutionary was going on that had nothing to do with the King of England, or the powers in Europe. Would mercy and fairness finally become a characteristic feature of society? Were they rounding a corner in history? It was past midnight before he went to bed.

* * *

When Edmond later recalled the gathering at the Willis house, he would remember the warmth and friendliness. When he had first told his mother and sisters of his intention to wed Feeb, he was greeted with skepticism and contempt. His sister told him bluntly that he was too vain to be a plain Quaker, and that the "exotic" feeling of being with the Plain People would shortly feel dull.

His mother sniffed and voiced her doubts. His mother had been born, raised, and married in the same church. She refused to believe he found her church service stultifying. Although several relatives were Quakers, she said it was beneath her son to become a Quaker.

At dawn the next day, Edmond awoke to the happy thought that he was accepted as a Friend. He was eager to tell his family his good news. His happiness pushed out all other thoughts for he had forgotten his mother's displeasure at joining the Friends. When he happily told the family his news, his mother's disapproval took him by surprise. She flew into a rage. She screamed at him, accusing him of abandoning her, and even of destroying her greatest hope: to go to church someday with her grandchildren.

When she finally paused for a breath, Edmond scrambled to show her his sincerity. He explained he had journeyed to the place where he no longer cared about the rites of the church, structures that were pleasing to the eyes, but were unimportant. But his words made his situation worse, for she interrupted him, exploding in renewed indignation. When he tried reasoning with her, she grew teary and self-pity oozed from her.

In desperation he pointed out she could take solace that he was not marrying a Catholic girl. However, she found a way to twist his words to make it seem as if he was uncommitted to the Society of Friends.

A week passed, a week of either verbal combat or enduring an enfeebling cold silence. By the end of the week, on a chilly December night he crawled into his bed, emotionally bedraggled. He had never felt so poorly. How strange to think the toll levied on him had come from his own family.

After his family's alarm, protests and ploys, there followed a period of coolness and distancing, as if to shame him to change his mind. But Edmond was unmoved.

CHAPTER 50

Cow Neck, New York,
Late Afternoon, December 1777

Stephen was searching for Thomas Dodge, a neighbor and kin to his stepbrother Joseph Dodge. He was not at home but his wife directed Stephen to look for him at the Sound, down at the beach. After a search on the bitter, windy day, he found him at Sand's Point, down the cliff at the shore. Thomas was unloading small crates, helped by another man.

"What's that thee is unloading?" Stephen asked naively.

"To save your skin, Stephen, I'll not say." Thomas was peeved. Thomas did not introduce Stephen to the other man.

The two men worked quickly, finished, then exchanged words and a few notes. Within moments the stranger was in the bark, pushing out into the water, bound for Mamaroneck or maybe New Rochelle.

Thomas moved to a small fire in the narrow stony alcove. He tossed some wood on it and fanned it high. Thomas and Stephen sat before it, warming themselves. Stephen explained he was there on behalf of his father-in-law who wished to buy a plot from Thomas.

Thomas needed no time to deliberate, "I'll sell it to him—tell him I shall see him shortly." He lit his pipe. After a few draws on it, he offered a puff to Stephen, who accepted.

As Stephen warmed himself at the fire, he gazed across the Sound to where the rest of New York lay.

After a short silence he indicated the small crates. "Are those from smuggling?"

Thomas did not answer him at first. Finally, with undisguised displeasure he said, "What we make, we should be able to sell! The Brits get enough from us!" Once started, his speech poured on, "They cry about paying back their debts for their wars in Europe. So, whose money do they take? Ours.

"But it is not the taxes alone. The acts that pushed taxes on us are only a few of the burdens they forced on us. They have a hundred ways to rob us of what little money we have.

"Stephen, does your wife want fabric? We sell them cotton, but we buy it back through England's stores and only after they put the price up!

"Why are we barred from selling what we grow to other nations? We got no choice: what we grow, must be sent to England. Then they make a good profit selling it to nations like France or Spain. Yet the King always wants more money from us. His demands do not stop.

"Remember the fabric I got for ye last month? I got it cheap. But only because someone in Connecticut boarded a British ship coming into Boston harbor."

"It was stolen?"

Thomas glared at him, "It came on a ship with white pine masts—where do ye think they get those masts from? I know ye don't like it was taken off a bark like that, me neither! But how long can we go on this way? The King could end this war."

After a long silence, Stephen asked the question no one had been able to answer, "What is the plan if the colonies win the war?"

The look on Thomas' face was hard to read: was he confounded, surprised, or insulted? Stepen could not guess. But from Thomas' answer he surmissed he had never given it much thought, "I suppose a new nation of colonies."

Stephen would favor a fairer government, but he had no concept of it. He knew only the monarchial style of England, France, and Spain. It was not important because the Americans were not going to win this war. Few, if any, believed the Americans would triumph over the British army. Most wished England's meddling to stop.

Thomas placed more wood on the fire, as if to ward off the darkening creep of the lengthening shadows. Stephen mulled over the past year: this was the last month of 1777 and well over a year since the British had taken Long Island. He wondered how they would all hold up under the British occupation: their life was frayed at the edges, their property was seized, families were divided. Lives were adrift. Long Islanders lived in a constant state of panic and exhaustion. Ahead was the New Year. But his apprehension caused him to dread it already.

The rattle of Thomas emptying his pipe bowl awakened Stephen from his reverie. Thomas stood, stuffed the pipe in a pocket, bid Stephen good night and vanished, dragging the crates behind him.

* * *

Stephen was not alone for long. He heard someone approaching, and within minutes Squirt sat down in Thomas's place.

Squirt too had been deeply affected by recent events. Squirt believed the recent years had so marked everyone he knew that 1775 and 1777 could be two definitive eras: "the before and the after."

"Evening, Squirt. Has thee found Big Jack?"

"Nay, he's nowhere."

Big Jack had disappeared again. Squirt knew why. It was because of what happened to Amos. Amos had drowned to death.

Amos had heard a distant cousin was being held a prisoner on a

British prison ship in the harbor. Amos was outraged. After he got roaring drunk, he set out for the harbor, rum in hand, to rescue him. Amos' body washed up on shore the following day. When Big Jack heard of Amos' drowning, he had gone off in a rage of despair. Squirt was waiting for him to return.

For a spell, the two men sat in silence under the stars near the sea. When they heard a noise, they looked around for the source: someone was there, beyond the glow of firelight. But whoever it was remained out of view. Just as Stephen was about to get up the man stepped forward to show himself. It was Quinipog.

Quinipog did not speak but instead handed a sack to Stephen. When Stephen asked about it, Quinipog told him to accept it because he was going to marry Rachel.

Stephen was startled and speechless. Squirt had the presence of mind to ask Quipinoq, "Shouldn't you give that to Adam and not Stephen? Adam is the eldest."

Quipinoq shrugged. "But he is here," indicating Stephen with a nod of his head. Then Quipinoq moved away, vanishing into the night.

Stephen was dumbfounded, "What's in the sack may be for me. But I hope and pray Rachel and Quipinoq have already spoken."

Squirt opined, "Rachel's tough. Her husband was killed by a falling tree, now her son joined the British army. She braved the blackbirders and the slave ship. After all that, I reckon she is fit enough to know if she ought to wed Quipinoq!"

They sat in silence once again.

"You're here late." Squirt framed it as a question. Squirt was worried about Stephen Mott for he had not recovered from his hurt. Now Stephen wanted justice. Justice was a fool's errand: when approached, justice slips through your fingers. And even if you have it, there is no such thing as having it. It was like holding an ocean wave, it could not be done.

"I'm here to think." Stephen's tone had a sullen edge.

"You hate the Redcoats." Squirt prompted.

"No. Yes." Stephen's second response was truthful. "We are prisoners in our own land," he groaned.

"I grant you." Squirt added, "But we are still free: God has made us all free, no matter what hinders our movements."

Stephen considered, "Would that be why Rachel argued to stay with my mother? Because she, at heart, felt she had liberty?"

"Perhaps. She had love. She also had respect and trust. Maybe she felt she had all a person needs."

Squirt was still worried about Stephen, "Thinking 'bout your daughter?"

"No. Yes." Stephen confessed. Anna's death was on his mind all the time. He could not stop rehearsing her death. And although he wished to stop, he also saw no reason to.

"It's been over a year. But you still want to right this." Squirt had read his mind. "You want revenge." It was true but Stephen did not answer.

"You are bitter."

Stephen looked at him and growled a warning, "Squirt!"

Squirt compliantly stopped his questions about Phebe Anna. The silence that followed was long.

Squirt ventured to say, "What's past is past and cannot be changed." He spoke slowly and softly, "But what is to come can be molded."

Stephen looked out over the darkened Sound. He could not accept the future.

"Should I stop thinking about my daughter!? What can thee know about it? There was but one Phebe Anna and they *killed* her!"

"Aye, your daughter was a sweet blossom of goodness! A lovely flower. Her bloom was bright and sweet. But too short. Like the flower, the Dutchman's Breeches which pops up for a time, but vanishes like smoke. Today you still have a good wife and a family."

Stephen's cheeks were suddenly wet. He stuttered, "But they're, they're… in pieces." Stephen's objection was untrue, he was speaking of his inner state.

Squirt was not put off, "Life is delicate, but it is not gentle. And when it is harsh, must it tail us to the present? Nay. We lost the past, and we are always losing it. What you have, what remains, your family, your friends, these are the broken pieces. And they are the stuff to make something new."

Squirt stood, pacing back and forth behind the log he had been on. His movements punctuated his words, "Move on, Stephen. You cannot move backwards, only forward. If you remain in the past, you will shrink." Had Squirt seen a bit of fire in Stephen's eyes at these words?

Squirt pushed on. He trusted the truth, "Do not deny it. Since her death everything changed for you. But time passes. In a way, like making new clothes, you cannot use old measurements. When your body changes form, you take new measurements. Today is not yesterday.

"Now here is the test: Do you *want* to amend your thinking? It is in your hands." As soon as he had issued his challenge, Squirt knew his words had hurt Stephen.

"I cannot do that: It's too hard! I am in a corner; I am hopeless and helpless. You *cannot* understand!" Stephen cried.

Stephen's words stirred Squirt. When he sat again, he sat nearer Stephen. "You are wrong. I do know how you feel. Look at me. I have nothing, I have no family, I have no home. I am a nobody. I am an outcast. And yet I am happy." Squirt said, "Yes, even in my condition. God is now at work even within your suffering."

Squirt's tone changed, it grew personal and close, as if it was inside Stephen's head. "If you want to honor your daughter, then you must love well all those she loved."

At that Stephen was finally broken open. He held his face in his hands as he wept, heaving. "Phebe Anna, my golden child, had so much! So much life, so much heart, so much generosity!" When Stephen's sobs settled, he choked out, "Why? Why did she die?"

"That is a question without an answer. But any answer as to "why" would never satisfy. But you do not need the answer to *why*, nay, you need her to come back again."

Stephen blinked, "But what of *my* desolation? I am—" he groped for the words, "I am dislodged!"

Squirt had felt homeless. "Your sorrow will fade but will never vanish. It's in the living that makes its own balm, soothing it."

"This pain, the sadness, will it never leave?"

"Nay. But it will be used."

It took a minute before Stephen knew how to respond. "I can but hope thee is right; but for now—" his throat contracted, strangling the rest of his sentence.

"You are hurting. The world is no longer kind and beautiful. Your world is empty."

Stephen nodded, sadly.

Squirt kept speaking the truth, "But people need you. I, no, we, look to you."

"What for?" Stephen was baffled.

"To mend wounds, and to attend to the hurt. You and your kind are an earthly hope. Somehow you level our mountains. I live with fear, suspicion, and dread but if I'm near you, I'm calmer, peaceful-like."

Stephen was struck. He never thought about his life beyond his own circle. He had grown up in, swum in, and always lived in the waters of love. And so, he had never had cause to think about his life, or the touch of the Friends' on others.

Squirt continued, "As long as you sit in your grief, life will never be better for me, but worse. Guilt over losing Phebe Anna drained you, and now it has moved beyond you. Now it is hurting me." At this Stephen sat upright.

"You still have gifts for the world. Do not allow Phebe Anna's death to transmute you for the worse, but for the better. We need you, nay, I need you."

Stephen had to give in to accept his reality: that is, his daughter's shocking death had eaten away at him, transforming him. But now he was tired of it all, he felt greatly aged. He wanted to laugh again. But first he had to release Phebe Anna. He put his face in his hands and exhaled. His shell cracked and within moments, he was sobbing, deep and heavy.

When his sobbing ceased, he lifted his head and asked, "Thee is right. I ought to live the days ahead lovingly." Then he added, "What can I do for thee?"

"Maybe someday, but now," Squirt shook his head, "nothing can be done. Quakers have always been our friends, but it is not our time. Apply thy hand to helping who you can."

"Thee speaks of the negro slaves?"

"Aye. A man can feel like a king; but only if he has the blessing of choice."

"Well said. Squirt, thee is always watching, never seen; forever listening, never speaking. But tonight, I learned something of the pain thee lives with."

The fire had died down to embers. In the dark shadows of the coming night, darker in the alcove, it was not possible to say who was the freeman Friend, who was the Wanderer. In the darkest time of the year at the darkest hour of the day, the two regarded the other, seeing not two men, but one, as in a reflection.

With surprising clarity of mind, Stephen broke the stillness, "Anna's death is a puzzle with no answer. Yet I serve her no justice by living a much-diminished life, or by making too much of my own sadness."

Silence swaddled them again until Squirt spoke, "Some people are here to bring harmony to the world. Yet others have a knack for bringing joy. You, Stephen, are one of those people."

"Huh?" Stephen was puzzled.

"You are a clever man and much schooled, and yet you are a child at heart. You are playful. I saw this when you laughed at ditch water, because there were pollywogs in it.

"Your lightness, your good-natured heart warms me. I don't know why. Maybe because laughter is so level and everyone, highborn or low, laughs.

"The heart is fed on laughter. And when we share a laugh, tightly held secrets, fall apart. We all need relief. You come along and you make our hearts lighter. We leave you refreshed.

"You lighten our hearts, and we can sing again. When you help us forget ourselves, you will forget your troubles. Laughter writes in a bold hand that you are, nay, that *we* are all, children of God. That is your gift." Squirt stopped. It had been years since he had spoken for so long and he had surprised himself.

Stephen's heart swelled, he had forgotten the pleasure of laughter.

The waves pushed and dragged at the pebbles at the beach. In the silence they could hear them roll. The waves gave a slight hiss, as if inhaling and then exhaling. Stephen tuned his ears to the breathing of the Sound, it always put him in mind of the Breath of God.

To Stephen's surprise Squirt pulled a flute from his jacket. Stephen instantly recognized his flute, the one he had flung aside the week his daughter died. When one of the Wanderers had found it, Squirt held on to it to return to Stephen.

"There is power in your flute." Squirt placed the flute in his companion's hand, "When I hear you play, it's like a miracle. Because, I reckon, your heart and your faith are in step. Then what I hear is the joy pouring from your heart."

Stephen's heart stirred when he wrapped his hand around his flute. He had not sung nor had he played since his daughter's death. The memories which tumbled over him were followed by a wave, and then a flood of joy and gladness. His heart filled. He smiled and lifted the flute to his lips.

EPILOGUE

The problems on Long Island put us all in a much-reduced state, but the state of affairs did not stop the Quakers. They were able to free over 100 slaves by the year 1778.

Mother Dodge slowed down but till her final days she was an advisor for the manumission committee. She died in 1782. The next year in November, the British finally left from New York City. General Washington came back to New York City to see them off.

We had a joyful wedding when "Feeb" married Edmond Prior in 1779. Stephen and Amy lived together in joy, even without Phebe Anna. And they added two more children to the family.

As for my business, it only grew. And Quipinoq and I were married during the war, but only briefly. He took ill after a couple years and died. He was a good man.

Close to the war's end, Azuba got no more money from Solomon. After the war, she learned he was in Canada. By then I was alone and when Azuba asked me to stay with her, I did. Then a few years later, a friend invited me to move to Philadelphia. She knew I was interested in the African Free Society here.

APPENDIX 1 - HISTORICAL FACTS

1. The original slave manumissions on Long Island. Voluntary manumissions by the Quakers. See "A Record of the Discharges of the Negroes set at Liberty by Friends of Westbury Monthly Meeting, March 15, 1776-May 11, 1798." View the records at the Friends Historical Library Archives, Swarthmore College, Swarthmore, PA.

2. In 1774 the New York Annual Friends Meeting passed a resolution to free all their slaves.

3. Rachel was a slave of Tristam (or Tristram) Dodge. Upon Tristam's death, she was willed to Phebe (Mott) Dodge, his 2nd wife. Manumission records indicate Rachel was manumitted by Phebe Dodge in March 1776.

4. Phebe Dodge was born Phebe Willets. She married, 1st, Adam Mott the Younger. They had three children. She married, 2nd, widower Tristam Dodge. All her children married the offspring of Samuel and Mary Willis. Phebe was a Traveling Preacher and Weighty Friend.

5. In September 1776 North Hempstead separated from Hempstead when the neutral Quakers in Hempstead refused to swear allegiance to the Americans.

6. The Flushing Meeting House was commandeered by the British occupational force on Long Island in the fall of 1776. Not used for regular worship since.

7. A daughter of Stephen Mott and Amy (Willis), Phebe Mott died in October 1776, of unspecified causes.

8. The Mott and Willis family trees included are accurate but are presented here only till 1777.

9. After Elias Hicks' mother died, he lived with relatives in Rockaway, LI until his father remarried. Elias Hicks was made a Public Friend in 1778. He and his wife Jemima (Seaman) lived in Jericho, NY.

10. Events surrounding the Battle of Brooklyn are accurate, but not comprehensive. The owner of Howard's Tavern (Halfway House), William Howard, was forced to lead the British to Rockaway Path.

11. Regarding the British Occupation: Most names are fictional. Nearly all events are derived from documented contemporary accounts, or ones published after the war, such as Onderdonk's book: *Onderdonk, Henry. Documents and Letters Intended to Illustrate the Revolutionary Incidents of Queens County: With Connecting Narratives, Explantory Notes, and Additions.*

BIBLIOGRAPHY

Books and Articles

1895 Biennial Quaker Records, Flushing NY. PDF online, (Internet Resource).

Bacon, Margaret Hope. *Mothers of Feminism: The Story of Quaker Women in America.* 1st Ed., Harper & Row, San Francisco, 1986.

Barbour, Hugh. *Quaker Crosscurrents: Three Hundred Years of Friends in the New York Yearly Meetings.* 1st ed, Syracuse University Press, 1995.

Bergen, Teunis. *Register in alphabetical order, of the early settlers of Kings County, Long Island, N.Y.*, 1881. (Internet Resource: Archive.org)

Bowden, James. *The History of the Society of Friends in America, Vol 1.* London, 1850. (Internet Resource: Archive.org)

Brekus, Catherine A. *Strangers and Pilgrims: Female Preaching in America, 1740-1845.* University of North Carolina Press, 1998.

Brinton, Howard H. *Friends for 300 Years: The History and Beliefs of the Society of Friends Since George Fox Started the Quaker Movement.* Wallingford, PA: Pendle Hill Publications, 1997.

Bunker, Mary Powell. *Long Island Genealogies....descendants of Thomas Powell of Bethpage, L.I., 1688*, Munsell's Historical Series, No. 24, Joel Munsell's Sons, Pub, Albany, NY 1895. (Internet Resource: Google Books)

Cock, George William. *History & Genealogy of the Cock Family, 2nd Edition*, Private printing, New York, 1914. (PDF, Internet Resource: Archive.org)

Cornell, Thomas Clapp. *Adam and Anne Mott: their ancestors and their descendants*, Poughkeepsie, NY, 1890. (Internet Resource: Archive.org)

Cox, John. *Quakerism in the City of New York, 1657-1930.* New York: 1930. (Internet Resource: Google Books) Permanent Link: https://hdl.handle.net/2027/uiug.30112003375406

Densmore, Christopher. "From The Hicksites To The Progressive Friends: The Rural Roots Of Perfectionism And Social Reform Among North American Friends." (2006) *Quaker Studies.* Volume 10, Issue 2. 243-255. PDF / https://works.swarthmore.edu/sta-libraries/29

Crotty, Joseph John. "'Times of Peril': Quakers in British-Occupied New York During the American Revolution, 1775-1783." Quaker History, vol. 106, no. 2, Friends Historical Association, 2017, pp. 45–71, http://www.jstor.org/stable/45180030.

Day, Lynda R. "Friends in the Spirit: African Americans and the Challenge to Quaker Liberalism, 1776-1915." *The Long Island Historical Journal*, Vol 10, No 1, 1997, Dept. of History; State University of New York at Stony Brook. NYS Library, Madison Av, Albany, NY.

Eardeley, William, Applebie Daniel. *Friends, Society of Flushing Monthly Meeting, later called New York Yearly Meeting, Intentions of Marriage 1704-1774, Queens County, Long Island, New York.* Typewritten, Brooklyn, NY, 1913. (Internet Resource: Archive.org)

Dodge, Robert. *Tristam Dodge and his descendants in America: with historical and descriptive accounts of Block Island and Cow Neck, L. I., their original settlements,* JJ Little & Co, New York, 1886. (Internet Resource: Archive.org)

Emory, Esther Hicks. Personal correspondence with great-niece and genealogist Margaret Tilton Walmer (Collection: A Charity Johnson)

Field, Thomas W. *The Battle of Long Island: With Connected Preceeding Events, and the Subsequent American Retreat.* Brooklyn: Long Island Historical Society, 1869.

Forbush, Bliss. *Elias Hicks: Quaker Liberal, Etc. [with Plates, Including Portraits.].* New York, Columbia Univ Press, 1956.

Friends' Book and Tract Committee; Robert S Haviland, Chair. *Bi-Centennial Anniversary of New York Yearly Meeting of The Religious Society of Friends at Flushing, Long Island 1695-1895.* New York, 1895. PDF (Internet Resource: Archive.org)

Gaines, Edith. *The Charity Society, 1794-1994: An Institution for the Use and Benefit of the Poor among the Black People.* History of the Charity Society of Jericho and Westbury Friends Monthly Meetings. [Hospitality

Valuation Services], 1994. New York Public Library, Stephen A. Schwarzman Building, Milstein Division, NY, NY, 10018.

Garman, Mary. *Hidden in Plain Sight: Quaker Women's Writings, 1650-1700*. Wallingford, Pa: Pendle Hill Publications, 1996.

Hallowell, Anna D. *James and Lucretia Mott: Life and Letters*. Boston: Houghton, Mifflin, 1896. (Internet Resource: Archive.org)

Harris, Edward Doubleday. *The Descendants of Adam Mott of Hempstead, Long Island, N.Y.: A Genealogical Study*. Lancaster, Pa: New Era Printing Co., 1906. (Internet Resource: Archive.org)

Hewitt, Nancy A. *Radical Friend: Amy Kirby Post and Her Activist Worlds*. University of North Carolina, 2018.

Hicks, Elias. *Letters of Elias Hicks, Including Also the Observations on the Slavery of the Africans and their Descendants and on the Use of the Produce of their Labor.* 1811; reprint, Philadelphia: T. Ellwood Chapman, 1861. (Internet Resource: Archive.org)

Hicks, Elias, *Journal of the life and religious labours of Elias Hicks*, New York, 1832. (Internet Resource: Archive.org)

Hicks, Rachel S. *Memoir of Rachel Hicks Late of Westbury, Long Island, a Minister of the Society of Friends: Together with Some Letters and a Memorial of Westbury Monthly Meeting*. New York: G.P. Putnam's Sons, 1880. NYS Library, Madison Av, Albany, NY.

Hinshaw, William Wade; *Encyclopedia of American Quaker Genealogy, Vol I–VI, 1607-1943*; Volume 2: New Jersey and Pennsylvania Meetings/Volume 3: New York Meetings; Original collection held by Swarthmore College Friends Historical Library, Swarthmore, PA. (Internet Resource: Ancestry.com Quaker Collection)

Jones, Rufus M, Isaac Sharpless, and Amelia M. Gummere. *The Quakers in the American Colonies*. London: Macmillan and Co, 1911. (Internet Resource: Archive.org).

Kruger, Vivienne L. *Born to Run: The Slave Family in Early New York, 1626 to 1827*. Dissertation, New York, 1985.

Larson, Rebecca. *Daughters of Light: Quaker Women Preaching and Prophesying in the Colonies and Abroad, 1700-1775*. University of North Carolina Press, 1999.

Luke, M. H. and Venables, Robert W. *Long Island in the American Revolution*. NYS American Revolution Bicentennial Commission, Albany, NY.

1976 (Official publications of the State of New York, v. 31, no. 7, reel 1, item 1) NYS Library, Madison Av, Albany, NY.

Morris, Susanna, et al. *Wilt Thou Go on My Errand? : Journals of Three 18th Century Quaker Women Ministers.* Wallingford, Pa: Pendle Hill Publications, 1994.

Naylor, Natalie A. *Women in Long Island's Past: A History of Famous Eminent and Everyday Lives,* History Press, 2012.

New York Genealogical and Biographical Record. Volume XLV, pp 263-269, New York Genealogical and Biographical Society, 1914. (Internet Resource: Google Books).

Mass, Sister Mary Martin, R.S.M., St. John's University Ph. D. dissertation, 1976. NYS Library, Madison Av, Albany, NY.

Mather, Frederic G. *The Refugees of 1776 from Long Island to Connecticut Declaration Signed by Sundry Inhabitants of Queens County, New York, January 19, 1776,* J. B. Lyon Company, Printers; Albany, NY 1913. (American Archives, 4th Series. 4.858) (Internet Resource: https://sites.rootsweb.com/~nynassa2/History/refugees2.htm)

Moore, Charles Benjamin. *The early history of Hempstead (Long Island).* Trow's Printing and Bookbinding Company, New York, 1879. (Internet Resource: Archive.org)

Nuxoll, Elizabeth M., Ed. "John Jay, Anti-Slavery, and the New-York Manumission Society: Editorial Note," *Founders Online,* National Archives, https://founders.archives.gov/documents/Jay/01-04-02-0013. [*The Selected Papers of John Jay*, vol. 4, *1785–1788*, ed. Elizabeth M. Nuxoll. University of Virginia Press, 2015]. Permanent Link: https://founders.archives.gov/documents/Jay/01-04-02-0013

Onderdonk, Henry. *Documents and Letters Intended to Illustrate the Revolutionary Incidents of Queens County: With Connecting Narratives, Explanatory Notes, and Additions.* New York: Leavitt, Trow, 1846. (Internet Resource: Archive.org)

Onderdonk, Jr, Henry & Frost, Josephine C. *Baptisms from Reformed Dutch church at Success (now Manhasset, N.Y.) 1742-1793 Reformed Dutch church.* [from old catalog]; typewritten & bound, copied by Onderdonk, Typed by Frost, original book held by Long Island Historical Society of Brooklyn, NY, 1913. (Internet Resource: Archive.org)

Paine, Thomas. *Common Sense* (Appeared in *Pennsylvania Journal*, 1776) Philadelphia. (Internet Resource: Google Books)

"New York City directory" 1786. Rare Book Division, The New York Public Library. "New York City directory." *The New York Public Library Digital Collections*. 1786. (New York Public Library; Digital Collection) https://digitalcollections.nypl.org/items/70bcc910-d5c9-0134-fbe5-00505686d14e

Scudiere, Paul J. *New York's Signers of the Declaration of Independence*, New York State American Revolution Bicentennial Commission, 1975. Albany, NY. NYS Library, Madison Av, Albany, NY.

Soderlund, Jean R. *Quakers and Slavery: A Divided Spirit*. Princeton University Press, 1985. (Internet resource: Archive.org)

Stoneburner, John, and Carol Stoneburner. *The Influence of Quaker Women on American History: Biographical Studies*. Lewiston, NY: E. Mellen Press, 1986.

Unknown Author, *History of Queens County, New York, with Illustrations, Portraits, & Sketches of Prominent Families and Individuals*. W.W. Munsell & Co., 1882. (Internet Resource: Archive.org)

Velsor, Kathleen G. *The Underground Railroad on Long Island: Friends in Freedom*. Charleston, SC: The History Press, 2013.

Wheatley, Phillis. *The Poems of Phillis Wheatley, As They Were Originally Published in London, 1773*. Philadelphia, Pa: Republished by R.R. and C.C. Wright, 1909 (Internet Resource: Archive.org).

Whitman, Walt. *Prose Works. V. November Boughs, 21. Notes (Such as They Are) Founded on Elias Hicks.* Philadelphia: David McKay, 1892. Bartleby.com, 2000 https://www.bartleby.com/229/5021.html

Willett, Albert J. *The Willett Families of North America: Being a Comprehensive Guide Encompassing Willett, Willet, Willette, Willit, Willot, Willets, Willetts, Willits, and Other Variations and Early Spellings of the Willett Surname*. Easley, S.C: Southern Historical Press, 1985. (Internet Resource: Archive.org)

Wood, William H.S., *Friends of the City of New York: in the nineteenth century*. Privately printed, 1904. (Internet Resource: Archive.org)

Archives

Digital Records Westbury Historical Collection, Hicks Family Papers, Friends Historical Records, Swarthmore College, Swarthmore, PA.

Digital Records of Westbury Monthly Meeting Archival Manuscripts, Friends Historical Library, (Society of Friends: Hicksite: 1828-1955 : Westbury, NY), Westbury Monthly Meeting (Society of Friends: ca.1682-1828:Westbury, NY), Swarthmore College, Special Collections, Swarthmore, PA, USA) Permalink: https://tripod.brynmawr.edu/permalink/01TRI_INST/1ob2id0/alma991012753519704921

Archives. Also, Manuscripts and Special Collections, New York State Library, 222 Madison Av, Albany, NY 12230.

Libraries, Historical Societies and Internet Sites

Ancestry.com *Special Collections: Quaker Records.*

New York Manumission Society Membership book.

Long Island Surnames website https://longislandsurnames.com/

Longwood Genealogy Group.

Cow Neck Peninsula Historical Society https://www.cowneck.org

Historical Society of the Westburys, 445 Jefferson St, Westbury, NY 11590.

LIBRARIES

Friends Historical Library, 500 College Ave, Swarthmore, PA 19081. (For manumissions: U.S., Quaker Meeting Records, 1681-1935, Minutes, 1775-1798.)

Hempstead Public Library, 115 James A. Garner Way, Hempstead, NY 11550.

Jericho Public Library, 1 Merry Ln, Jericho, NY 11753.

Port Washington Library, One Library Drive, Port Washington, NY 11050.

New York City Public Library, 476 5th Ave, NY, NY 10018.

New York State Library, 222 Madison Av, Albany, NY 12230.

Personal Collections

Correspondence of Willets/Mott/Willis descendants: Edwin Tyson, Esther Hicks Emory, Margaret Tilton Walmer, Corrine Tyson Lambert. Held by Edythe Walmer Sarnoff.

Family genealogies of the Willis family, Hawxhurst and Hicks family and extensive genealogies of related families of Long Island. Collected by Edwin Tyson, William E Hawxhurst and Margaret Tilton Walmer. Held by Edythe Walmer Sarnoff.

Margaret B Tilton Walmer's misc. correspondence and digitalized papers. Held by A. Charity Higgins Johnson.

Original letters, genealogies and ephemera of the Hawxhurst and Hicks and collateral families. Held by A. Charity Higgins Johnson.